RED SNOW

Books by Oliver Lange

VANDENBERG

INCIDENT AT LA JUNTA

RED SNOW

RED SNOW

OLIVER LANGE

Seaview Books

For Gaye,
with love

Library of Congress Cataloging in Publication Data

Lange, Oliver.
    Red snow.
    I. Title.
PZ4.L2764Re   [PS3562.A485]   813'.5'4   77-25310
ISBN 0-87223-481-9

33

PROLOGUE

―――――――――――――――――

―――――――――――――――――

. . . in the nineteenth century the puma, or mountain lion, ranged freely throughout the Rockies from Canada to Mexico, and was ranked among sportsmen as being among the noblest of game. In recent years, however, stockmen and bounty hunters have drastically reduced the population of wild lions, arguing that they are a menace to livestock, especially lambs and young calves. Nowadays they are best hunted with a trained pack of dogs, as they have become increasingly shy and solitary, yet the difficulty of tracking them merely adds to the pleasure of the hunt. The sportsman does not exist who is not thrilled at the sound of a pack baying beneath the tree in which a snarling, cornered lion crouches.

. . . they are largely nocturnal in their habits but range about a great deal, regardless of the time of day. And though they prefer to avoid man, it should not be forgotten that they are a relation to the common household cat. At times, they exhibit a natural curiosity that knows no bounds. They have been known to track a person for miles, undetected, and can often be fetched with a scent fashioned of beaver musk-gland, or even ordinary catnip. This perverse, almost playful, curiosity has caused the demise of more than one lion.

—R. M. WILLIAMS,
Hunting Big Game in North America (c. 1913)

ONE

THE CAT LIES in the sunlight on a flat outcropping of rock in a clearing halfway up a sparsely wooded slope. *Felis concolor*.

A large tom, now long past maturity, almost elderly, with a heavy sprinkling of gray shading its elongated flanks. Lacking somehow that sleek tidiness natural to healthy animals in their prime. Its coat scurfy. Here and there particles of dirt, dead grass, and twigs cling to the dry hair, along with a leaf or two. The long serpentine tail that twitches constantly as the cat stares about has gray in it too.

Close up there is a powerful smell of cat urine, as if in voiding its bladder the animal has splattered its hindquarters. The head itself is small, almost out of proportion to the rest of the body, and is set on a sinuous neck. Like all mountain lions, it carries its weight and strength in its legs and paws . . . big, furry feet, clublike, with the rear legs long and massively developed, oversized really, so that when the cat walks it has a swaybacked gait. The front paws are big too, large-boned, heavily cartilaged and muscled, and though they look clumsy they are in fact marvelous weapons, powerful enough to crush the spine of a deer or a calf, and capable of striking out in a darting movement too fast for the human eye to follow let alone anticipate, a flicker actually, yet carrying enough strength in its impact to break bone . . . and at that the curved claws are still sheathed. When bared, and when that strength

and swiftness are triggered, the claws can rip through anything, including bear—they can disembowel a fully grown elk
or cow.

The cat lies on its left flank, head erect, and again age is
apparent in the gray-white fur of its underbelly, with its
loose and sagging folds of skin. But, old or not, one fact is
obvious. It is huge. It would weigh in at over two hundred,
and from nose to tip of tail it must be near to ten feet. A big
granddaddy tom. An old rogue male, maybe ten or twelve
years by now, maybe even older than that, no telling for sure.
Its muzzle grizzled white.

It sits up now, stretches indolently in the mild heat of the
wintry sun, and yawns, the great feline jaws gaping incredibly.
Its upper left incisor has been snapped off clean at the base,
perhaps in some long-ago hunt or fight, or maybe recently, but
the remaining three, curved, tartar-brown and worn with
age, are still dangerous.

The cat rises at last, long-bodied, the flat belly slung beneath the heavily swayed back. Stares around in the pale
sunlight, regarding everything in sight with expressionless,
unblinking amber eyes, and then moves out.

Jumps from the rocky outcropping to the ground below
in a short, silent leap, landing with a faint crunch and breaking through the crust of a drift of snow at the base of the
rock, and ambles off into the pines silently, moving with a
splendid n .tural ease and gracefulness, such a leisurely flow
of motion, the loose rolls of fur at its belly swaying back and
forth with that walk that seems so unhurried but that a grown
man would be hard put to keep up with unless he broke into
a trot.

THE HUNT BEGAN in this way:

Down in the village that morning a child had been sent out
to play alone in the back yard of her parents' home. The
child's name was Teresa Apodaca, and she was seven, and

actually it was her mother's home, since the father and husband, a local man, had dropped out of sight four years ago, leaving the mother to get along as best she could. There were two other children in the family, but they were in school. Teresa had a slight cold and so was kept home, but later in the morning her mother gave in to her restlessness and dressed her in a warm parka and mittens and sent her out to play. The parka had a hood on it that came up over the child's head, with a drawstring that tied under the chin. She was put out the back door, and the mother went into the kitchen, where she had set up an ironing board beside a basket of clothing. The house itself was shabby and run-down, but Mrs. Apodaca had a thing about seeing to it that her children went to school wearing halfway-decent-looking clothing. She was four months pregnant and was drawing welfare, and in the town of Pecos, New Mexico, neither of these conditions, taken separately or together, was considered out of the ordinary for a pretty young woman whose man had taken off on her.

THE LION, OR whatever it was—"some kinda big goddamned critter" was the description that soon went through the village—came in over a chain-link fence five feet high.

The single shriek carried easily over the sound of the TV quiz show Mrs. Apodaca was watching as she ironed. She looked out the kitchen window and saw that the back yard was empty, and this frightened her, and then she was running to the door, knocking over the cup of coffee she had just poured for herself.

Outside, she saw the child, or more correctly saw the bright red parka coat her daughter was wearing, some fifty yards off, up on a slope behind the house, near a midden of refuse, rusting cans, and fifty-five-gallon drums. Beyond this litter of trash lay the forest itself.

The child was alive when Mrs. Apodaca got to her, and in fact was to live, contrary to rumors that she had been killed instantly. Even so, she had been badly mauled and bitten.

A friend of the family, Peter Griego, who was also the area's one state policeman, was called. He drove the injured child and the hysterical mother down to Santa Fe in his prowl car, and the Emergency Room at St. Vincent's did what it could until she could be gotten to X-ray and surgery: plasma, sedation, wound cleansing, and examination.

Her jaw was broken, and four or five baby teeth had been knocked out. Most of her forehead had been torn or clawed loose in a dangling flap that covered her eyes and nose. There were also claw marks on her shoulders and back, but the worst wound was a terrific laceration at the nape of her neck, a bite that had gone clear through the parka hood.

Looking at this wound, the emergency-room physician guessed intuitively that irreparable damage had been done to the spine, and if that was so then there was not much chance she would pull through, but here he was wrong, as the rumors about her death were wrong: She lived, and was to recover with a stunning lack even of scar tissue, such is the resiliency and self-rejuvenating powers of the young.

In fact, she never even remembered what had happened. It was obliterated from her child's mind, so that afterward, when asked about it, all she could describe was that she had been playing by herself in the yard that morning and had then wakened, seemingly in the very next moment, in the hospital, with her weeping, swollen-eyed mother beside her.

Still, the prowl car that Peter Griego drove back to Pecos later that morning was testimony enough. Men and women came to stare into the rear windows at the back seat. The nylon covers were a welter of blood. Towels, applied as compresses, lay on the floor, lumped wetly and stained a thin, clear red. So on this day it was easy enough to think that the child was dead or at least dying. A glance at the back of that state police car was enough to make a person marvel that so much blood could come from a fully grown person, let alone a child.

NOR WAS IT true that positive identification had come from the faint traces the animal had left up on the slope. The ground was December frozen. There had not been much snow, and what thin scattering there was of it had been trampled by the shoes and boots of neighbors who had responded to the mother's screams.

Even so. One fair-to-middling print was discovered—some ten yards above the midden heap, where the first stands of ponderosa began—at the base of a tall pine, where a drift of snow, crusted now, had not been touched by the sun. A print leading away from the prey this animal had attacked and then abandoned for no known reason. By now George Dalton, the local game warden, was there. The injured child, her mother, and Peter Griego were halfway to Santa Fe, twenty miles west.

Dalton was a large, gray-haired, slow-moving man, with hound-dog jowls and sad eyes. The first thing he did was run everybody off—at least fifteen or twenty people must have been wandering around. "All of you just get out of here now," he told them. "Goddamn it, go on. How in hell we going to get anything done with all you people messing around?"

He cordoned off the back yard and the entire slope and midden heap, then picked some men to help him search. These men who lived in the mountains were all hunters, or mostly all, and they understood what Dalton was telling them.

So now a slow exploration began. All of them squatted down, some even on their hands and knees, with their faces close to the ground, almost ludicrous in their slow and methodical quest. They were looking for something that wasn't easy to find. Then somebody spotted the print under the ponderosa. Dalton and the others came over to look at it.

Dalton with a ballpoint pen, down on his knees, outlining the blurred impressions left by the footpads. "I would judge it was running, all right," he says. "Its claws was probably

out, only you can't see 'em. I would say it was running, sure
enough."

"Bear, George?" a man beside him asked.

"Nope."

"Dog?"

Dalton took his right hand and placed it over the snowprint,
an inch or so above the crust. It was a big hand. Yet with the
fingers and thumb outstretched it did not quite cover the print
in the snow. "You ever see a dog has a paw that big? Dog with
a paw like that'd be bigger than a pony."

"Lion?"

"More'n likely."

"Big one?"

"Pretty big," George Dalton said, staring down at the print,
and then he amended himself. "Yessir, if this critter is a lion, I
would say he was one hell of a big cat." Continued staring at
the print. Then judged again: "Sure looks like lion to me."

DALTON CALLED IN a man who knew about such things. Lester
Johnson took one look at the print and confirmed the game
warden's hunch.

Johnson was with Game and Fish, and in fact was field
supervisor of a federally funded three-year study on mountain
lions in New Mexico. He knew as much about cats as any
man, and then some. Or so it was claimed by his superiors
down at the department's executive offices in Santa Fe. These
men were professionals, top-echelon conservation experts who
had graduate degrees in game management and were at ease in
the bureaucratic world, but who still had the habit of keeping
waxed-paper cups beside their desks or at the conference table
to contain the overflow generated by the chewing tobacco
most of them had taken a liking to as field men, years ago.

They said of Les Johnson that by natural inclination he
would rather bed down with a bobcat than a movie starlet,

because it was obvious to him that the bobcat would provide more interesting company.

As for lions, Johnson himself admitted that his feelings were based on a conviction that these animals had superior qualities compared to most human beings. Speaking of them, he had once declared, on a live talk-show broadcast over the Albuquerque educational channel: "Well, now, they are real neat and clean and nice to have around, and they know how to get by and take care of themselves. Except to take meat they don't bother anyone, and when a big tom is onto a female in estrus the two of them can make some very interesting sounds, some of which can be heard as far as a couple of miles off on a calm night. By God, some of those old fellers get so musical it's downright deafening."

Understandably, the sheep and cattle lobbies were not fond of Les Johnson. They called him a senile old reactionary who was "out of pace with the problems of the present day," but then, they said the same of the Sierra Club crowd. He had one champion, though. This was Monty Cartier, the director of G&F. At a recent meeting of his board of directors one member had proposed to Cartier that they slot Johnson over to a more useful job, specifically, supervising the fish hatchery up at Red River.

The board member—a fellow named Bud Hunnicut—had a point. "Hell, Monty, there isn't really that much for the old fart to do, keeping statistics on lion and bobcat. He's due for retirement soon anyway. You could put a younger man in that job at a third the salary."

Cartier said this: "We have the best lion man in the Southwest in Les Johnson, and I'm not going to lose him. He goes back with Game and Fish a long way, and he was a professional hunter when I, and some of you, were still in grade school."

Cartier was a tall, leathery man who spoke like a country boy . . . he looked a lot like a movie cowboy, but he also wielded a lot of clout with the state legislature, and he had a reputation for running his own show. Bud Hunnicut decided that if Cartier wanted to keep a grizzled old has-been like Lester Johnson around, then let him.

So Johnson stayed on. Working out of an office on the third floor of the Game and Fish Department that was not much bigger than a broom closet. In it there were a small work table, a couple of filing cabinets, an electric coffeemaker, a map of the state thumbtacked to one wall, and, tacked to another, the tanned hide of the largest mountain lion ever shot in New Mexico—ten feet three inches, killed by Johnson himself in 1938—a packboard, to which was strapped the old man's .32 Winchester, a bedroll, and an ashtray. There was no spittoon or waxed cup, because Johnson smoked a pipe. The camping gear was for field trips. The filing cabinets and the plywood bookshelves above them were in effect a repository of statistics, correspondence, and analytical data on how well the mountain lion was doing in this still wild and unpopulated part of the United States.

By eleven that morning Johnson was on his way to Pecos. Out of habit, he listened to the KOB-News Rocky Mountain regional weather forecast. The announcer said, ". . . a massive cold front now in Central Utah, bringing heavy snow and near-blizzard conditions, is expected to move east, missing New Mexico. The weekend forecast is continued clear and cold. The Utah front, however, is worth keeping an eye on."

Johnson's assistant would be following later, with the dogs. On the passenger side of the front seat of the four-wheel-drive pickup assigned to him were his packboard and rifle. There was also a large plastic box, and this contained a heavy-duty air rifle that operated on CO_2 cylinders and fired hypodermic darts filled with Sernolin, a tranquilizing drug. The local warden, Dalton, had said over the telephone that he couldn't be sure it was a lion but he thought it probably was. If it did turn out to be a cat, Johnson was willing to try to take it alive.

SPRAWLED ON ONE flank in a dense thicket of willows near a stream, the cat blinks and stares off down the heavily wooded slope. It is resting now, and the stream is perhaps three miles from the village, but its movements have ranged erratically, so that it has traveled closer to five miles.

What has attracted its attention is a faint sound, hundreds of yards downslope. Something out of sight but moving in the forest below, perhaps a deer or some other fair game. Though old, the cat has hearing beyond the capability of men. The round, furry ears, bearlike in their soft-furred texture, drop back flat against the skull—a nasty warning that the lion has been alerted. Then they cock up and forward like two listening devices as the snaky head moves this way and that, the big, gold-brown eyes alert. Presently the cat rises and slides silently through the willows and heavy underbrush to investigate whatever is moving down there.

It is a man, a hunter, and a marvelously oblivious one at that. And now the mentality of the big lion gives in to an ancient game. Cat-and-mouse. The stalker stalked. The hunter as prey. For no apparent reason, the cat begins tracking the hunter. At times mere yards behind the human with its intolerable scent, at times ranging some distance ahead on the trail, to lie in wait, thick tail barely twitching as the hunter passes by. It is a kind of game. Old or sick or crippled or starving, the cat will still play the game.

The hunter carefully works his way up the trail that meanders through the woods. He believes he is an experienced tracker, an expert at this kind of hunting, and he is entirely right. Yet he is unaware of the cat, behind him, ahead of him, on either side of the trail. He is armed with a heavy hunting bow of laminated fiberglass and Osage orange—a rather beautiful weapon—and nocked on the bowstring is a big-game arrow. He moves very quietly, but that is nothing. The lion, in this curious game, is absolutely soundless.

TWO

. . . unprovoked attacks upon human beings by the mountain lion are rare, as it is an exceedingly shy animal, and under normal conditions will go to great lengths to avoid the proximity of man, its only natural enemy.

—Field Bulletin #28,
New Mexico Department of Game and Fish

. . . from the very start, because of its highly abnormal behavior, we could not dismiss the possibility that the animal might be rabid.

—News release,
New Mexico Department of Game and Fish

EVEN BEFORE IT began, the hunt seemed wrong. Pecos is an isolated mountain village, ten miles up a spur road north of Highway 85, and its people are isolated too, as well as independent. Beyond the village lies Pecos Valley and then, climbing higher, Pecos Canyon . . . these are on the edge of the vast Pecos Wilderness Area, and so represent a kind of last steppingstone between civilization and a stretch of mountainous forest that reaches north almost to Colorado. In the summer, tourists and heat-weary Texans come to camp and fish along the Pecos River, but during the winter months the town closes in upon itself. The people are mostly Spanish, with a sprinkling of Anglos. There are no blacks at all. Dude ranches, cattle, small-time farming, and lumbering bring in money for those who can work—the rest get by on welfare and food stamps. Along the main street, which is also the highway—and the only decently paved street in the village—there are a few run-down stores and filling stations, and in these places a kind of local Spanish patois is spoken more often than English. Except for the summer tourists, who are coldly ignored, outsiders are regarded with distrust, and even hostility. So when Lester Johnson, who wasn't Spanish, and who wasn't even from around there, showed up and started running things, there were mixed feelings.

After inspecting the slope where the child had been abandoned, the lion expert held a briefing. George Dalton and eight or nine men who had helped search for prints gathered in the recreation room of Father Cornelius's church. It was here that an argument got started that later almost turned into a bad fight. Except for Les Johnson, a local resident named John Sedgewick, and Cornelius, the old Franciscan priest, the men at the meeting were Spanish . . . stolid, taciturn men, watchful by nature, not easily given to demonstrativeness unless drunk or driven to anger.

By now word had spread about the attack. The villagers, especially the women, were alarmed, but there was not the kind of fear that would come later in the day, when the lion struck again.

Now, Johnson was answering questions about the hunt the men wanted to organize. Cornelius had set up a large coffeemaker on a folding bingo table, and had passed around a sack of doughnuts.

One thing was pretty obvious. Les Johnson didn't care for the men sitting here any more than they cared for him. He talked to them in a language they could understand, yet seemed oddly reluctant—at times almost evasive—to reveal all he knew. From his expression and flat tone of voice, he was holding this meeting against his better judgment. Without exactly saying so, Johnson did not seem to favor having a lot of hunters up in the mountains at this time of year, when the weather was tricky. His mood seemed to say that if he could have had his way he would have gone after the cat with just his assistant and his dogs, instead of trying to ride herd on a crowd of deer and elk hunters, most of whom had never even seen a lion. In response to a question about how best to get the lion, Johnson said soberly, "How to hunt this cat? Track it, and finally get to it? Why, there ain't nothing to it at all." He paused and stared down at the cup of coffee he was holding. "If you do things right, you get the cat." He paused again, as if thinking this over. "It always works that way. If a feller just stays calm and works things right, nine times out of ten he will get that animal where he wants it."

"And it definitely was a lion?" Father Cornelius asked.

"Maybe."

"But you saw the print."

"Yes. Dalton and I looked it over," Johnson said.

"Well?"

"More'n likely a cat did it," Johnson admitted. "Yes, a cat could have made that print. No way to tell for sure, though. Wasn't much of a print."

"Bear couldn't have made it?"

"It wasn't a bear track."

Daniel Jaramillo, a teacher at the high school, said, "You don't seem sure it was a lion."

"Well, I ain't," Johnson replied. "All I'm saying is, it seems likely a cat did it." He took a long drink of coffee, and went on. "What makes me think it was a lion was the method of attack. A hunting lion will naturally go for the neck if it can, and usually from the rear. After it springs, it'll hang on with its claws, ride its prey if need be—like if it was a big elk or a steer—and all the time it will be going for the spine, trying to bite through, to bust the critter's neck." He paused again, choosing his words. "Also, that little kid was carried some distance away from the house. Bear wouldn't do that. Bear might worry its kill, tear it up, drag it around maybe, but it wouldn't jump no five-foot fence with it."

"But a lion might?" Jaramillo asked.

"Oh, why, surely," Les Johnson said. "Wouldn't be any problem at all. That little girl, she probably doesn't weigh more than fifty, sixty pounds dripping wet. I've watched a full-grown cat bring down a calf—weighs maybe a hundred and fifty, maybe more, maybe closer to two hundred—and sling it across its own back with a flip of its head and walk off with it with no more effort than a woman lifting a ten-pound sack of flour. One time I saw one jump a four-foot split-log drift fence carrying a deer like that. So clearing a chain-link fence with a small child wouldn't be any trouble at all for a cat. If it was a cat."

"Well, what else could it have been?" Cornelius asked.

"Beats me," Johnson said. "If it wasn't a cat did it, I don't know what it was." He stared down at the coffee cup he was holding in both hands. "There is just one thing don't fit. Lion ordinarily won't go after a human, leastways not without provocation. I got statistics back in Santa Fe, and newspaper clippings and accounts in old diaries, that tell stories of lion attacks. None of 'em amount to much." He drank some more of his coffee. "It's like those stories of eagles that used to carry off infant children. That is just nonsense. Mostly, a lion will go out of his way so as not to smell man. Most times they'd just about starve to death than come close to humans. Ordinarily the meanest cat alive will stick its tail between its legs and make fast tracks if you so much as pitch a rock at it. They kind of like to stay off by themselves. Like a story I investigated one time down in the Mogollons. This fellow, he claimed a lion just jumped him. He sure had the claw marks all up and down him to prove it. But when I talked to him I found out he'd been out in the high country, maybe doing a little poaching, with his rifle, and had shot this old lioness. She only had one kitten with her, just a little cub, and this fool went over and picked it up, only the lioness wasn't dead yet. So she came over and grabbed hold of him and chewed on his ass for a couple of minutes before she cashed in. This feller, you see, was the sort who liked to brag around. I guess he didn't want it told how he was ignorant enough to grab a nursing kitten without making sure first that its momma was good and dead."

Johnson finished his coffee and went over to the electric pot and refilled his cup. "Even with provocation I've only had about five or six cases." He dumped sugar into the cup, one spoonful after the other, absent-mindedly. "This cat, if it was a cat—well, that it would come right down here into the village and go after a kid. That beats me. Mighta been starving. George, you said the kid had a bright red jacket. That could have been like a bait, maybe. The way you fish for bullfrogs on lily pads, with a pole and a string and a piece of bright flannel. Still. That's sure a new one on me. I never heard of anything like that before."

He shook his head, tasted his coffee, and then looked up to regard the men before him. "And now, of course, nothing else'll do but that you fellers get this critter. Well, it ain't no picnic up there at this time of year. Just remember that."

IT WAS AS if Johnson, who in his time had shot enough game to populate a forest, simply could not understand why men were drawn to hunting. There just wasn't anything to it at all, once you learned how. He had long ago lost his taste for this so-called sport, and with other men besides these he bad-mouthed the outdoors. In the presence of some affable out-of-state U.S. senator he was coordinating a big-game hunt for, his behavior was sulky and his conversation truculent. It grew downright gloomy with a prospective G&F employee, some crazy long-haired young kid who imagined he liked the outdoor life: "Hell of a lousy career, going up high in the dead of winter, freeze your balls off, trying to dynamite some goddamned beaver dam, trap them nasty fuckers, they'll bite your hand off quick as look at you, gotta truck 'em around to new locations, you'd be better off going to school, finish up your education, get into some kind of decent line of work, living up high like that makes a man old before his time, a rotten life, and if you get a woman, why, what female wants her man up in the mountains most of the time counting bighorn sheep, women get antsy, they want company, not living like a widow, not for months at a shot anyway."

Johnson himself was living proof. It wasn't that he was a widower who lived alone except for his dogs. It was the look and style of the man.

He seemed worn down somehow, distilled, metamorphosed in some fashion by close to forty years in the mountains. He was different. These men in the church's rec room could sense it. There was a certain resignation in the faded blue eyes, but there were glimpses too of a bitterness and an unhappy loneliness that set the wrinkled, bony face—he was sixty-four—in an expression of sour hostility. As if he—all on his own—had long ago figured out some things other people didn't know. There was a lot about Les Johnson that gave lie to the myth that solitude imparts a tranquil peacefulness. He was civil when the occasion demanded it, but his natural disposition leaned toward crankiness, and, if badgered or harried, he could get nasty.

In a way his hands were the most expressive thing about him—they told the truth about the life he had lived. He always seemed a trifle embarrassed by them. As if, somehow, he wished that they belonged to someone else. Yet they were always in view, as they were this morning. Encircling a cup of coffee, or holding a pipe—as if they needed to take warmth from such items.

And gradually, anyone who listened to his talk took notice of them. They had been so ruined by work and weather—were beyond repair, beyond the soothing help of any lotion or unguent. They were small hands, callused, dry, chafed. Unbelievably scarred. Burned by the sun. Frozen by subzero weather. Cracked by freezing water. Scratched, abraded, cut by latigos, tree bark, stones. The backs of the knuckles and fingers literally split apart with large, inflamed, half healed or unhealed—or even infected—cuts. Yes, the hands, deeply mottled in purplish grays and reds, crushed, swollen lumpily, encrusted with brown scabs, enfolding a coffee cup, were a visual shock to most townspeople. Johnson never looked at them, but went on talking, as he was doing now, in a thin, laconic tenor. A skinny, wizened little old fellow who weighed his words.

Even in the neat departmental uniform with the insignia on his left shoulder, he seemed an anachronism, someone lifted clean out of the last century. The men gathered here might not like him, but some of them had heard of his reputation. He had hunted in the Rockies since the early thirties, before settling in New Mexico. His fame as a lion and bobcat man had spread to Arizona, Colorado, and even as far as Idaho. He talked on, laboring, a gringo outsider, yet he was in charge.

It was then that Guillermo Apodaca, an uncle of the mother of the child that had been attacked, suddenly rose to his feet and said, "Well, I don't see why in hell we just don't go shoot this cat and bring it in. I don't see what kind of problem there is to this, that we got to sit here all day talking about it."

Guillermo was a round-faced, blue-jowled man in faded jeans, bowlegged and potbellied. The tone of his words made it clear that his feelings toward Les Johnson, and even some of the others here, were openly unfriendly. He had a thick neck and mildly bulging thyroid eyes and was nicknamed— behind his back—*el rano*, the frog. He wore an old gray Stetson, so floppy and sweat-stained, so disreputably crudded with dirt and ancient mold, that it obviously had to be an object of deep pride to its owner. As if to emphasize this, Guillermo had mounted at the base of the crown a tooled rim of turquoise and solid silver, and not cheap stuff at that. He worked as a maintenance man for the Benedictine mona- stery up the road from the village. He had sad brown eyes, set below brows so thick and furry that they met in a solid, frowning line, so that with the eyes and the beetling brows and the big fishy mouth he was by any measure a remarkably ugly man. Guillermo was bad with his drink and handy with his fists. He said now to Les Johnson, "I already got my rifle out in the truck."

Johnson said, "We have to wait for the dogs. The feller who works with me is on his way up with them right now."

Guillermo said, "We mess around here all weekend, those dogs of yours will be chasing chickens." Lester Johnson nodded at this, and Guillermo went on, "They lion dogs or bear dogs or what kinda dogs, mister?"

"Lion dogs," Johnson said. He got out his pipe and a sack of tobacco.

Guillermo said, "All I want to know is can they do the job? I got two good hounds of my own. I trained 'em for bear, but they'd do fine on lion."

"Mine are lion dogs," Johnson said. "I don't mean to put your dogs down, but my pack has done this all their lives. They know lion scent. They know what to do to get one treed. They know how to work a cat. I sure wouldn't want to see you lose some good dogs if this here cat gets to them."

"That's bullshit," Guillermo said obstinately.

Father Cornelius raised a hand to get Johnson's attention. "Is there a possibility it could be an old cat?"

"Could be," Johnson said. "It would have to be a pretty

decrepit animal for it to come messing around a town, though. Could be it's wounded—or one that got trapped and escaped but was hurt pretty bad." He stared at the men. "Any of you fellers heard anything about a cat getting trapped or shot?"

They stared back. The question was wasted. They were local people. They all knew, and in many cases were related to, one another, and they would not be giving information to Johnson or anyone else from Santa Fe, because they sensed that one thing had a habit of leading to another.

If somebody up in the mountains was trapping lion illegally, then that person might be doing something else. Or some friend of his might. He might be into a little rustling, that person. Or big-game poaching. In this country, certain kinds of activities were handled differently.

Careless talk had a way of making trouble. These men might gossip or even make an occasional disparaging remark, usually over beers at the Crippled Horse Saloon. Daniel Jaramillo's beautiful wife, Karen, a gringa outsider from the Midwest, had been mentioned more than once in that troublemakers' hangout. But they weren't much for talking to outsiders, and even among themselves they were usually careful. A man with a loose mouth could find himself in a lot of real trouble.

It was known, for example, that Father Cornelius, the stocky Franciscan originally from Cincinnati, always had deer or elk meat in his big parish freezer. Sometimes hundreds of pounds of it. For a priest he spent a lot of time up in the mountains, dressed in Levi's, boots, and a mackinaw, packing his .243 Winchester. He loved hunting. He gave the meat away, as he did most of the produce he grew in the garden plot behind his run-down church. That was considered his business. Many families in the village were poor—what used to be called "dirt poor"—and Cornelius, with a Teutonic bluntness not without charm to his Spanish parishioners, was fond of saying that man did not live by bread alone, or zucchini—or tortillas, either—and that good red meat was a useful adjunct in the diet of growing children. Everyone knew he was an obsessive poacher—even George Dalton—but no one spoke of it.

Johnson said now, "We have some other possibilities. If an animal don't act natural, I'd want to know why. I'm wondering if maybe this cat might be rabid. Though this ain't really the time of year for it. That might explain plumb-loco behavior like this. And if it is rabid, then we have to get it fast, before it maybe infects some other animals. Or it might come down here again, before it gets too sick to move on. For that matter, if it's real sick, it might be holed up not far off."

Guillermo Apodaca was growing angrier. He stood there with his hands on his hips, scowling. "Well, by God, talking ain't going to do no good!"

Most of the men seemed to be in agreement about this, including Father Cornelius. Daniel Jaramillo and his friend, Sedgewick, did not comment.

Peter Griego, the state trooper, had something to say, though. He had let himself in the back door some moments earlier, and had been standing at the rear of the recreation room, listening, arms folded across his chest. Now he stepped forward and interrupted: "Guillermo, just for once in your life why don't you shut that big mouth of yours."

GRIEGO WAS LAW here, a fair-sized but by no means unusually tall man, now in his late thirties, with more than sixteen years' service on the state police roster. Powerful in the arms and shoulders but with a layer of fat growing round his waist, no real paunch yet but just that thickening. It showed in his face, too. His features were still good, almost handsome, but a touch heavy around the jowls. In his twenties he had been slender, but now he needed a size eighteen shirt, which later was custom-tailored. Griego lived in a mobile home at the south end of the village with his wife and three children.

Peter was respected here, and not because of the charcoal-gray uniform. Pecos men were not easily impressed by any kind of uniform, or what went with it: the polished Sam Browne belt, notebook and pen, the encased wrist-twisters or the blackjack, or the big .357 Magnum, with its oversize checkered African cocoa-wood target grips, buckled into a tooled fast-draw holster.

What counted about Peter Griego were the stories that went around concerning his toughness and how he took no backtalk from anyone. He was a *rojo* . . . among the locals this meant a man with Anglo blood, that is, a Spanish person of intermixed lineage, which was either a distinction or a taint, depending on how one felt about such things. His complexion was fair and freckled, and his hair was a sandy red, curly and short-clipped. The eyes were slate blue, and they regarded everyone (even Father Cornelius) with a cold suspiciousness, as if in his many contacts with the human condition Peter had proved to himself over and over that people were not worthy of trust, love, or Christian mercy. Peter was, for a fact, a very tough young man.

Like the time, last summer, when he closed the Crippled Horse on a noisy Saturday evening. The Brown Berets, a militant ethnic group, a sort of Spanish-American version of the Black Panthers, were in to whoop it up, and the jukebox was going, and there was dancing and local girls and Fascination Pool. As the evening progressed there had been— so claimed the owner, Johnny Larragoite—overt displays of weapons, including hunting knives, a .25 Beretta, and a .410 double-barreled shotgun that had been drastically cut down to pistol size and which some honcho was wearing stuck in the top of his boot. So Peter walked in and closed the place at a quarter after ten. Stood there in the middle of the barroom. Looked at the crowd with that stolid expression on his beefy, flat, freckled face. He said simply, "I'm calling it a night, so all of you get on home now."

But in a town like Pecos this was draconian treatment, especially on a Saturday night, because the nearest other bars were in Santa Fe, thirty miles off. There were some unfriendly comments among the patrons who, minutes later, were stumbling around in the parking lot behind the Crippled Horse, to the effect that something ought to be done about Griego. It was dark out there, except for the dim red blinking neon sign on the roof. Ten or twelve old pickups and busted-down sedans were in the lot along with Peter's prowl car.

Peter got into his own vehicle and started off with the idea of making a swing around, so that he could have all of them in his headlights, but before he had gone very far there was the heavy thump of a .30-30 going off. The slug went through the rear window, expanded as it passed Peter's right ear, and blew away most of the front windshield.

The prowl car skidded to a halt. Lights went out, ignition too. Slam of door on the driver's side. Then silence. It was pitch-black out there at the far end of the parking lot, where the prowl car sat, half in a ditch. After about a minute the silence got pretty heavy to take, because the drinkers standing around by their pickups and sedans were sure of one thing: Peter was sprawled in the dirt somewhere near the prowl car—who could tell where?—belly-flopped in the dirt and weeds, up on his elbows in the prone combat position, both hands gripping that big, long-barreled .357. They knew that he wouldn't take another rifle shot of that sort, and that Peter, being the sort of fellow he was, would probably shoot to kill.

So everybody left that parking lot in a hurry. As Johnny Larragoite later put it: "For a while there, why, it was kind of like one of those demolition derbies. I never saw such a scramble for first, second, and third places, trucks and cars backing up, transmissions just ripped all to shreds, cars banging into one another, gravel spraying everywhere."

Whether Peter actually unlimbered the big Magnum that night was never proven, because he never talked about it. And of course no one was about to ask. But, knowing Peter, it seemed likely. The refusal to talk about it was like him too—

in spite of his aloofness he didn't seem to mind adding to the myth and mystery of his toughness. In this area he was all-powerful, was almost an abstract symbol, carrying out the concepts of law enforcement with a machinelike impartiality. He had no friends, and he took no sides. And despite the dull, almost phlegmatic—in fact, stupid—set to his countenance, he was bright: He had graduated from the state police academy with the sixth-highest score of any trainee in that institution's history.

Stepping forward to the bingo table, Peter said now: "There is something I want to tell all of you. If you're set on organizing a hunt, that's okay with me, but as far as I'm concerned this game-and-fish fellow here is in charge. You might just as well understand that, Guillermo. I'll be cooperating with him, and you damned well will too. I'm not about to have a crowd of you men running around these mountains taking potshots at everything in sight, including each other!"

DANIEL JARAMILLO BROKE in: "Peter, is the child alive?"

"The hospital's listed her in grave condition," Griego said.

"All I'm saying is that we're wasting time," Guillermo Apodaca broke in. He was still scowling, as if he wanted to make it clear that he accepted—but not by much—Peter's bossiness.

"Well, there isn't anything we can do about that, because this man has the dogs, and they aren't here, and you can't hunt a lion without a pack," Peter Griego said. He turned to Johnson. "Is that right?"

The old hunter nodded. "All that interests me is that we get the right animal," Johnson explained. "There are a number of lions living in the mountains between here and the Colorado border, but not anything like what there used to be. They're barely holding their own, with timbering and all that. They shoulda been on the endangered list years ago."

"How many would you guess?" Guillermo demanded.

"Couldn't say," Johnson told him. "Down in the Gila Wilderness, we been sedating them and putting collars with radio transmitters on 'em, so we can keep track of what they're up to, so we have a rough idea of what the census might be, but up here there's no telling." He motioned toward George Dalton, who was sitting nearby. "George and I, and the young feller who works for me, keep an eye out for their droppings and tracks, and their kills. The females only produce two kittens a year. Sometimes we know about them too." He paused. "Mind, I'm not arguing about this particular lion. We'll get him, surely, one way or another. But all the same I don't want to kill off some others that aren't bothering anyone. There ain't that many of 'em left. There wouldn't be any sense in that."

"How far into the mountains will we have to go?" Father Cornelius asked. "Weather's been good, but it won't stay that way forever."

Once again Johnson's reply was guarded—almost truculent —as if he hated telling them any more than he had to. He said, "Not far."

It was as if he was aware that at a later date someone— maybe someone sitting right here in this very room—might, out of boredom, or vanity, or maybe just for the hell of it, feel the urge to go out and collect a couple of lion pelts. There was no bounty on them any more, but still, hunters were hunters. It didn't make any difference that there was no sport in lion hunting, nor any danger either, that Johnson could see. Once you learned how to do it, it was easy. All a man needed was a good rifle. The supposedly finer aspects of the hunt— the long-range shot, the particularly difficult stalk—were nonsense.

"How far?" Guillermo Apodaca asked.

Johnson said, "George and I know of three dens, less'n a day's ride from here."

Father Cornelius stared at him with a look of surprise. "That many?"

"Yes."

"That close?"

"Yes." Johnson was on shaky ground with them now. They were alerted. He wanted to take this cat alive, but he knew that there would be no chance at all of his using a tranquilizing dart, even if he could, as he hoped to, position himself for the first shot.

As for the dens' being within a day's ride—well, that was true enough. Though a horse, and for that matter its rider, would be hard put to reach the farthest in a day, although Johnson supposed it could be done.

The priest, Cornelius, was staring at him in disbelief. In his role as priest-poacher, he probably had walked over most of these mountains on foot. He ought to have been the logical man to know about three lion dens.

But old man Johnson was right. Three dens there were. Two were being used by pregnant females that would birth early in the spring. It didn't make any difference if Cornelius or any of the others who hunted high had never caught a glimpse of these big cats. A hunter could track one for a month and never catch sight of it. That was why dogs and horses were needed.

Lions were funny animals, for a fact. They weren't cowardly, although the old man had more than once shooed one off with a rock. You could even make them abandon a fresh kill like that. Still, it paid to have a weapon handy, just in case one hadn't heard that it was supposed to skedaddle every time a human bluffed it.

It was also true that most times a lion would tree when cornered by a pack. In which case it was as good as dead, a perfect target twenty feet up on a branch, glaring and spitting and snarling—snaky tail whipping back and forth—while it waited for the hunter's bullet to knock it out of the tree and send it thudding to the ground in a frenzied death-throe.

But it also sometimes happened that one would come out of a tree without waiting to be invited. As if almost sensing that it was as good as dead already . . . and in the knowing of this had elected to go out with a flurry. That was when a hunter had to be quick. Because when a fighting lion dropped off a branch, into, or onto—or all over—a pack of howling dogs below, it was the dogs who took the punishment. In the end they'd get the cat, would literally tear it to shreds, but before that happened some of them—maybe most—would be dead or crippled for life.

Johnson had lost dogs this way. Big, tough hounds that could have held their own against any bear but that had gone down, disemboweled, broken-backed, clawed and bitten, their bodies laid wide open so that their paws caught and tangled in their own guts. All because a cat had decided to come out of a tree. It wasn't just the big old toms that could do this. A little seventy-five-pound female could tear up a pack just as nicely, looking not much different from an overgrown Siamese, but prettier, often white-bellied to set off the honey-yellow coat, and with that small, round, snaky head, yes, they were nearly as bad as some big rogue males Johnson had taken.

And now this one, that had come right into the village and attacked a kid. As Johnson admitted, that was a new one on him. He said, "Matter of fact, speaking of these dens, I sorta have a hunch which one I want to look over first."

"You think you know which animal did it?" Jaramillo asked.

"Just a hunch," Lester Johnson said. He struck a match to his pipe. "There is one big tom lives by himself up in a little canyon north of the sawmill a few miles," he said. "Cat like that, it wouldn't think anything of ranging twenty miles when it was hunting, though usually he'd head north, deeper into the mountains, where there's no people. But if something had happened, like if he was hurt or sick, and if maybe he'd gone a week without food, why, he might come south toward town." Johnson puffed at the pipe and went on. "Mind, I'm only conjecturing. I'm kinda trying to reconstruct what might've made this happen. Like if he was starving and had come down this way, maybe figuring to pick off a calf or a sheep in pasture, well, he might've been up on that slope by the kid's house, might've been looking things over, you know, a cat will do that, and if he saw the little girl, saw her movements, well, that coulda been enough to set him off. I don't know, but that just might've been enough to set him off."

"How big is this cat?" Guillermo Apodaca asked.

Again, that faint tone of regret: ". . . Oh, he's big enough, all right."

"Well, damn it, *how* big?"

"Pretty big, I'd say."

"Record size?"

"Couldn't say," Johnson replied. "Probably not." It was here, for the first time, that he lied outright.

HE AND GEORGE DALTON had watched this lion through binoculars late last summer. Had finally set down the pair of glasses, which they had been sharing, and stared at each other.

Dalton had said it: "Les . . . that has got to be the biggest goddamned cat in this state . . . and maybe Arizona, Colorado, and Nevada, too, while we're at it. Why, Jesus Christ Almighty, that critter down there's liable to be the biggest lion in all these Rockies for all we know."

The notion of a cat that size was in Johnson's mind now, and with it the knowledge that some of these men here in the church would go to a lot of trouble to have a pelt that big mounted above the fireplace in their living room. He said, "It's sizable enough. But I want to tell you that that ain't reason enough to go killing off half the cat population in this area."

When there was no response he went further: "I happen to have a pretty good game balance in this range right now, of predators to herbivores. Ranchers haven't been complaining about livestock loss. That means that lion, bobcat, coyote are all living off'n wild game. That's as it should be."

"Johnson, you're describing normal behavior," Daniel Jaramillo said. "This animal attacked a child. And you just admitted that it could be diseased."

"We can't shoot every lion in this range because one has turned bad," Johnson insisted.

"If it's rabid, you'll have to kill it anyway," Jaramillo argued. "I know that much. They do that with dogs. The vets take off the head and run a culture on the brain matter. That's where the disease focuses."

"They only do that if it's really sick, like foaming at the mouth or running crazy," Johnson said. "They analyze the stomach contents too. A rabid carnivore gets what they call a perverted appetite. It'll leave off its regular feed and start eating things like sticks and small rocks."

"Well, I would judge that this critter was off its regular feed, as you call it," Apodaca said sourly.

"Yes," Johnson said. "If it was a lion, which I'm fairly sure it was." He paused. "I think it might be this big old tom. I'd sure like to try to capture him."

"You mean take him alive?" Jaramillo said.

"Yes, if I can."

"That's crazy," Apodaca said.

"Nope," Johnson said. "I got a rifle in my truck that can tranquilize anything up to a thousand-pound grizzly. If I could get this cat alive and put it under observation, we'd know if it was sick. We might even learn why it attacked that poor child. You have to understand that the child is alive, and if she pulls through they'll start anti-rabies treatment—that's a painful series of injections. They don't take chances with that kind of thing, because by the time the symptoms show it's already way too late. The mortality rate is a flat one hundred per cent. So we have to get the cat. But we don't know that it's sick, and we can't decimate the entire cat population either."

Guillermo Apodaca spoke again, glancing from Peter Griego to Johnson. "I don't care about this fancy talk, because I don't have much education, but I do know that my little grandniece is down at St. Vincent's. I couldn't care less about no lion population. I'm coming along with you on this hunt, and, Griego, there ain't no way you're going to stop me, not unless you want to arrest me right now. I don't care about no fancy tranquilizing guns either, Mr. Big-shot Game Warden. I just hope you're pretty good with it, and fast *también*. Because I got my old .30-06, and I'm pretty good with that. Mister, I'm going to make it my business to get that cat you been telling us about, and every other one in these mountains too, before I'm done with it."

THREE

"Oh, I guess I'm content to stay on, Les. Hell, I'm probably better off here than I'd be pumping gas in some fucking Exxon station for two bucks an hour, where the only thing you have to brighten your day is looking up some cunt's skirt while you're doing her windshield."

—LEWIS BOWMAN, *in camp, 11,400 feet*

". . . We didn't want this turning into a massacre, in which half the lion population in that area of the wilderness might be shot up, all because of one beast. The townspeople were frightened and angry, but it wasn't just that. An incident of this nature has a way of getting out of control. In fact, I know of quite a few wealthy sportsmen around the country who, if they'd heard a hunt was on for a record-sized lion, would have dropped what they were doing and booked a flight on the quickest jet into Albuquerque for a chance at a trophy pelt."

—MONTY CARTIER, *in conversation*

Les Johnson's dogs were being driven up in another pickup by a young man named Lewis Bowman.

Bowman had an enormous regard for old man Johnson, and thought of himself as one of the luckiest men in the department to have been picked by the lion man for an assistant. The job took them from one end of the state to the other, and while Lewis did not care for a great deal of what he had to do, such as helping compile endless statistics on predator activity, there were other aspects of it that he liked very much and that were considered therapeutic for a young man who had served nine years of an armed-bank-robbery conviction at the state pen south of Santa Fe. Hard, tough outdoor work, often in weather that was heartbreakingly cold or wet and unappealing. Or that should have been unappealing to an ex-con who had lived most of his adult life in a cell that was maintained year-round at a steady, zoolike seventy-two degrees.

The simple fact was that Lewis loved the outdoors. He had gone to prison at twenty-one, a big, rangy, black-haired kid with a glowering expression and a Zapata moustache. The hostile scowl said something about his inner nature, as the first bull homosexual to make advances discovered. Lewis, without even seeming to think about it, picked up a length of two-by-four on the floor of the maintenance shed where they and a group of other cons were working and almost killed the bull with it, which earned Lewis thirty days' solitary. After that he had been more or less left alone.

He had seemed to like it that way, and stayed friendless for the rest of his stretch, devoting his leisure time to weight lifting and karate in the gymnasium, along with the other iron freaks, and reading books on outdoor life.

When he finally came up for review by the parole board, Lewis spoke his piece, standing before them in a sullen stance, hunch-shouldered, tight-lipped, scowling down at the floor: "I think the best chance I got for rehab is to work out in the country some place, because this psychiatrist, he says I got all kinds of antisocial problems I can't hack yet."

The parole board went for this, as did the Division of Vocational Rehab, which slotted him with Game and Fish. Monty Cartier and Les Johnson were the only ones who knew he had done time and that he would be on parole until 2020.

Lewis stood six foot four and had a twenty-eight-inch waist. During his sentence he had put on fifty-nine pounds of solid muscle from working out with the weights, and he could clean and jerk a three-hundred-pound barbell without even straining.

Once outside, he remained friendless except for old Johnson. With him something vaguely akin to hero-worship evolved in Lewis. What else could a young man who neither drank nor smoked feel for a worn-out-looking old crank who outwalked and outclimbed him steadily, day after day, with each of them carrying rifles and twenty-pound packboards? A shriveled old gray-haired character with false teeth, who scarcely came up to Lewis's armpit? Who smoked a pipe round the clock, and who put away most of a pint of bourbon every night beside the campfire?

And oddly enough, Les Johnson, who liked no one, in turn developed a kind of low-keyed flair for the teaching role. He had a tolerant and good-humored affection for his hulking assistant, who could have broken his back with his bare hands, and who engendered a sensation of outright fear in most people he came in contact with. (By then, Lewis's nose had been broken twice in prison brawls and was spread over most of his face—he had a bad habit of not backing down, even against odds of four or five to one—and this, along with the Zapata handlebar, give him a true *bandito* appearance.)

In the year he had spent with Les Johnson, Lewis had learned more about wildlife and the wilderness than most country men put together in a lifetime. Not bad for a young hood out of Albuquerque's southside slums.

The old man liked Lewis for three reasons. He was strong.
He never complained. And he had a marvelous way with dogs.

THERE WERE FOUR of them. Johnson had raised them from
pups. He considered them the finest lion dogs in the Southwest, though none looked much like the sort that would be
at home in a lion pack except old Cacique, an oversized Lab,
jet-black, huge in the shoulders, and with a massive head.
Cacique had a cocked hip that gave him a gimpy gait. The hip
had gotten that way when a lion had sent him tumbling over a
thirty-foot cliff to land among a spread of boulders. But even
with the bad gait he could travel well enough, though not as
fast as the others. It didn't make much difference, because as
the dominant male of the pack he set the pace anyway. What
Johnson loved about Cacique was his voice when he struck
a trail, such a deep and sonorous baying that was resonated
and amplified through that great skull—so sad, almost lugubri-
ous, yet full of joy at the same time—that relentless, slow-
timed baying that marked the way for Johnson and Lewis to
follow, through underbrush and scrub oak and across slopes
of deadfall pine, old Cacique, full of combat and ready to go,
bugling steadily for his master, a sound, Johnson knew, that
in the quiet, clear air of a mountain dawn could easily carry
a mile or more.

Windy, a decrepit Australian-shepherd male, was next, with
a matted coat and the clear, icy-pale blue eyes of the Australian
strain. A born troublemaker, purchased by Johnson at the
Santa Fe Animal Shelter for five bucks because, so Johnson
said, "it was a pup with a real mean look to it." It turned out
Windy was that way, and cunning too, with a kind of nasty
bravery. It was he who would go in after a cat that had
dropped from a tree, from behind if possible, trying for the
soft underbelly.

The third was Oona, a black-and-white Malamute bitch,

four years old, with a face that was a pure witch's mask, almost the face of a weasel or a skunk, out of which shone eyes
as blue as Windy's, but slanted in a wolfish cast.

The last was Alf, and he was big, and there was not much
more that could be said about him than this, except that he
was flatulent. There was nothing distinctive about his lineage.
It was a mess, that was obvious. Maybe some Dane or a dash of
mastiff, some shepherd, and maybe some wolfhound too. His
mangy, wiry coat would have looked more at home on a
fox terrier. Alf stood thirty-two inches at the shoulder and
weighed one hundred and forty pounds. He had about him,
along with a powerful doggy smell, an air of affectionate
gentleness that was so unassuming and timorous that he seemed
perpetually embarrassed, as though, somewhere along the line,
he had once gotten a chance to take a good look at himself in
a full-length mirror, and had been so appalled by what he
had seen reflected that he had been doubtful ever after that
anyone, humans especially, could or would want to have anything to do with him, and in the realization of this had
decided that his Sunday-best manners were the least that could
be expected of him. Except for the flatulence, and there was
really not much Alf could do about that. He was a big, sweet
old dog. If spoken to sharply by Lewis, Alf would collapse
in a limp heap of nondescript fur, long legs, and rolling eyes.
But he would also, with the assistance of Windy and Oona,
who knew how to keep a lion busy, go in after the jugular.
And, given half a chance, those big jaws could close on a cat's
throat and put it out of action in a few seconds.

IN A SENSE the fifth member of the pack was Lewis himself,
the huge, misanthropic ex-con, who cursed and loved those
dogs, and who would bed down right among them in a high
alpine camp. They would curl around or even on top of his
sleeping bag for warmth and companionship, and Lewis didn't

seem to mind . . . would lie there, contentedly staring up at the constellations wheeling overhead, fingers interlocked behind his head.

His pleasures did not seem much more complicated than theirs. In his off-duty hours he liked to roar down highways in a secondhand limited-edition Mustang done in cherry red. The Mustang could hit fifty in first and sixty-five in second. It fitted the other, supposedly "social," side of his prison-polished personality, for with it Lewis allowed that he could be like other young men as much as it was possible for him to be. Specifically, with such an automotive bomb he could move about, and get beaver.

With women, his style and demeanor—at times, anyway—seemed to have a certain well-nigh-irresistible charm. The virtually inarticulate reticence. The scowling, combative expression. His sullen watchfulness in the presence of other males—and that splendid hostility that mostly stayed latent but that was always ready to erupt.

Trucking or trashing with Lewis was, as one young lady put it, "Sorta like hanging out with a bomb that has a short fuse, only big Lew's fuse ain't so short."

Perhaps not surprisingly, he found that a number of Santa Fe women were gravely interested in him. Older women, some with class and sophistication, and money too. Anyway, their sophistication seemed a cut above Lewis's notions of courtly wooing, which usually ran along the lines of buying four or five bourbons for his date, a dinner for two at Maria's Mexican Kitchen, and a room for the night at the Ramada Inn out on Cerrillos Road, which he claimed had the best showers in town. It was not at all a bad life for a tough stud. And with Les Johnson vouching for him to his parole officer, he was content enough. On duty he and Les were out in the field most of the time. When in Santa Fe he counseled once weekly with a psychiatrist, whose fees were paid by the state. The psychiatrist, a Dr. Myron Roth, told Lewis that he was happy with his progress, and recommended in writing that Bowman be continued on the Game and Fish Department's payroll.

In private, though, Dr. Roth made the following notations in Lewis's case-folder: ". . . the behavior of this type socio-psychopathic personality is clearly predictable—coexistence in a peer group is marked by suspiciousness, an inability to relate, and a general feeling of uneasiness in the patient. Eye movements are rapid, and watchful. Anything resembling an overt attempt at dominance is likely to be met by an outburst of verbal or even physical aggression. The therapist, needless to say, must exercise prudence in treating or working with this sort of patient. Considering all the factors, it is just as well this young man is where he is—up in the mountains most of the time—since he is obviously far too emotionally crippled a specimen to ever really integrate with normal society."

Lewis's own assessment of his situation was not much different. One night, as they lay in their sleeping bags beside a campfire, Johnson said, "Lew, tell me, what would you have done if it turned out you didn't like this line of work?"

Lewis thought about this for a bit, and then glanced over at the old man: "Why, I guess I woulda just gone out and gotten a pistol somewhere and hit a bank—one of them branch-office tin cans—and then cleared out real fast."

LEWIS GOT TO the parking lot of St. Francis Church just as the meeting inside broke up. Men were standing in small groups near their cars, smoking and talking. They glanced at the G&F truck as Lewis parked it, got out, walked around to the rear, and let the dogs out of the cages one by one, snapping chain leashes to their collars.

He saw his boss talking to, or rather being bawled out by, a man—Guillermo Apodaca—who was gesturing angrily.

Lewis and the dogs came over to them as Les Johnson said, "Mister, I'm not allowing potassium cyanide. It's too dangerous."

"Good a way as any to get that cat," Apodaca insisted. He

was talking about coyote "getters"—spring-loaded devices that, when triggered, released a mouthful of poison dust in the face of an unsuspecting animal.

"And a good way to get any carnivore that stumbles across that bait," Johnson said. "No, I won't have it."

The arguments for and against poison bait were age-old. In its favor as a predator control was the fact that it was cheap and effective, especially with the ubiquitous coyote. Against it was the unarguable tendency it had to make a clean sweep of everything in the area in which baits were put out, including weasel, otter, skunk, bear, and coon. Johnson had time and again come upon the bodies of lesser creatures whose life-styles could not be construed as capable of impeding the cattle and sheep industries: kestrel, chicken, and sparrow hawks, and an occasional bald eagle whose stomach contents, when analyzed, revealed a dose lethal enough to knock out an elephant.

Guillermo was not a tractable man. He didn't like outsiders telling him what to do, especially gringo outsiders. In his younger days he had considered himself a fair bar fighter. He was older now but still powerful, and he liked the reputation of himself that he imagined he had . . . that of a middle-aged family man but still a tough hombre if anyone pushed at him. Actually, Guillermo was a lousy family man and a drunk, and in the next few minutes he was to learn something about his toughness.

Disgusted by Johnson's refusal to use cyanide, he stepped up to the old man and poked him in the chest with a rigid forefinger. He was about six inches taller and fifty pounds heavier than Johnson. He said, "I'll use bait and a gun and anything else I need to. I don't know who you think you are, telling *me* how I'll do this an' how I'll do that!"

The other men, including Peter Griego, looked on with interest as Lewis Bowman dropped the leashes, commanded the dogs to sit, and moved closer to the two men. He stared at Guillermo and then said, "Hey, man . . . what's bugging you?"

Apodaca glared at Lewis and then turned back to Les Johnson. He was about to say something more, but Lewis sort of shoved at him with one hand, the fingers extended stiffly. Just a shove, but a pretty stiff one, so that there was no mistaking that he wanted Guillermo's attention. With that, Guillermo wheeled on Lewis, a mean look on his face, starting to get really sore now over this unwelcome touching of his person by a stranger he'd never even set eyes on before —but not that much of a stranger, because Lewis had on the same departmental uniform as Les Johnson.

Guillermo half in a crouch. Old Les Johnson forgotten, abandoned now. With his age and runtiness, he was no fit opponent. But Lewis. Well, yes! This was something different.

Whether Guillermo might have started something then and there, whether he might have, gauging the moment, fired off a right hook at Lewis's jaw in the irrefutable knowledge that in a confrontation of this sort he who moves first and demonstrates clearly that he is the aggressor has a hell of a lot more than mere luck on his side, was never known— because Lewis bristled.

Even when Lewis was more or less at peace with himself he looked scary enough to make most people turn and walk away from him. Now, starting to feel a little pissed off, he took a deep breath, almost a snort, and bristled. He towered over Guillermo the same way Guillermo towered over Les Johnson.

Guillermo held the punch. Just as well. Lewis stared hard at him for a moment and then said, in a stentorian growl loud enough for everyone to hear, "Motherfucker, you mess with me, I'll kick the living shit outa you!"

As warnings go, it was not much. Sterner threats are uttered every day on any school playground. Nor had Lewis made any physical movement to lend emphasis to his statement.

The difference, though, was that Lewis so clearly meant what he said that there was no doubt, even in Guillermo's slow mind—especially in Guillermo's mind—that he could and would do precisely that thing . . . literally kick his bowels loose from the rest of him. It was an unpleasant image, made even more so by the obvious implication that Lewis meant to accomplish this atrocity not sometime in the future but now, in the next two or three seconds. Right in front of everybody.

Guillermo backtracked—without grace or dignity.

Later, over a beer in the Crippled Horse, he claimed he had done it out of sheer intelligence. After all, the big thing was to get that cat before it hurt anybody else, *que no?*

But this sensible approach fooled no one, because, first of all, Guillermo was no prize winner in the deductive-logic department, and, second, everybody in the church's parking lot saw that Les Johnson's giant sidekick had flat scared hell out of Guillermo. The patrons of the Crippled Horse got some quiet amusement out of this. They didn't like outsiders any more than Guillermo did, but then, they didn't like Guillermo either. In fact, most of the local people of the valley didn't like anybody. It was this lack of social amiability that led folks in a city, like nearby Santa Fe, to remark that the fistfights and knifings that took place in Pecos were normal to the villagers, many of whom were so ignorant and culturally deprived that they had not acquired the mental equipment necessary to process even a Saturday-night television movie.

FOUR

"... *there is no such thing as prejudice in this valley, and I speak as one who oughta know. 'Cause I'm just an old redneck east-Texas farm boy, straight out of Beaumont. Nothing fancy. They said of my paw that he could grow okra on a cinder block, and that has been my style too. I come here sixteen years ago, and made a go of it. Put my kids through school here, with Mexican kids. I got no kind of complaint about dark-complexioned people. My own daughter, Lucinda, goes with one, is engaged. After I got to know him a little, why, I saw right off he wasn't no different than anyone else in spite of his color.*"

—VIRGIL McCORMICK, *in conversation*

... *the partially digested stomach contents of this 184-pound male disclosed heavily matted lumps of what was later analyzed as human hair and scalp tissue, other flesh and masticated bone, fabric identified as cotton denim of the sort used in overalls, two human teeth, and a brass .38-caliber cartridge casing.*

—*Arizona Department of Game and Fish, Yuma, Arizona, 1911*

A FLOO-FLOO is a blunt-headed hunting arrow. Instead of the three conventionally fletched feathers at its nock end there is a cluster of fluffed, or splayed-out, plumes, so that when the arrow is shot it will not travel more than twenty-five yards or so before air resistance slows it and drops it to the ground.

It is used for hunting small game such as rabbits, where a standard arrow, glancing off a rock or hard ground, might easily ricochet for a hundred yards and so be lost. The blunted head of the *floo-floo* will effectively stun a small animal, and it can even cause it to die of shock.

Raymond Maestas was carrying three of these special hunting arrows in his hip quiver. He also had four heavy-duty broadheads suitable for big game. The cutting edges of these had been filed by him and then honed to a fine sharpness.

The *floo-floos* were an alibi in case George Dalton caught him. Raymond had the idea that if this happened he would ditch the big broadheads, which were illegal at this time of year (so was any hunting on state land, for that matter), and claim to old man Dalton that he was out practicing archery on rabbits, exhibiting the *floo-floos* to prove it.

Actually he was after deer. Several had been visiting a block of salt he had set out in a small clearing in the woods. The salt lick was also illegal, because deer, like most hoofed animals, lose whatever little good sense they possess around this ingredient.

Ray worked as a checkout clerk in a Santa Fe supermarket. He was a slim, athletic young man, and he was very good with the big bow he was carrying. He was dressed in a full-length camouflage suit patterned in dead-green and brown. Earlier, he had smudged his face and hands with pigments of the same colors. About the only time he was visible in the thick underbrush was when he moved. Standing still, he faded into the natural background and was invisible ten yards off. This was no exaggeration. He had, more than once, managed to get within ten or fifteen feet of grazing deer, moving with infinite

caution, an inch or two at a time, freezing when they looked
up, then beginning his advance again when they lowered their
heads to feed.

Maestas was out to get his third deer of the year, using the
same technique that had gotten him the first two—the silent
bow. The one he carried had a sixty-five-pound pull, and was
powerful enough to send one of the heavy broadheads clean
through a five-gallon can. It was accurate out to thirty-five or
forty yards—accurate enough, anyway, to place three out of
four arrows in a mark that could be covered by one hand.

Ray considered this the purest kind of hunting possible.
One that gave the animal a fair chance and required real
stalking skill and year-round practice on the part of the
hunter. Getting within sure bowshot range of a deer was a
real accomplishment compared to using a scope-sighted high-
powered rifle, which in the hands of an expert could knock
down an elk a quarter of a mile off.

The fact that Raymond could not brag much about his
kills, except to his family and girlfriend, did not trouble him
much. The truth is that he did get a lot of fun and excitement
out of the ritual and ceremony of the stalk—and of the image
of himself that he conceived, a near-invisible, camouflaged
wraith, ghosting silently along meandering game trails.

This pleasant picture was in his mind as he rounded a corner
of the trail he was following, ducked silently under the limb
of a young conifer, and came face up against what seemed to
be the biggest mountain lion in the world. Raymond froze,
blinked, and said, "Oh, God!"

THE LION WAS down in a crouching position, less than twenty
feet away. From the look of it Raymond got the idea that, as
quiet as he had been, the lion had heard him from some distance and had decided to hang around.

The animal's tail was twitching nervously. Young Maestas
stood very still. This cat—which was at least twice the

damned size of anything he had ever heard described—was staring at him with huge, wide, unblinking eyes, the irises dilated blackly.

Raymond, still not daring to move, reviewed very quickly in his mind the small fund of information he had: how they were shy, how they might track a man. He remembered something else he had heard once . . . something about how lions detest the sound of a human voice.

And so, still staring at the cat, he cleared his throat—it took a couple of tries—and said the first thing that came to mind, in froggy tones: "Hey, Mr. Cat . . . why don't you shag your ass out of here? You go your way and I'll go mine, okay?"

The lion regarded him.

Maestas began to think about getting out of there—that is, if the cat was agreeable. Without looking around, he began inching his way back along the narrow trail. At the same time, he began to draw the nocked broadhead—the hunter in him thinking ahead to the possibility of a clear, dead-on shot that might put the arrow feather-deep in the lion's chest.

He never got the chance to try this, because the lion jumped. Raymond was never to forget that momentary image . . . as though a shutter in a camera somewhere inside his head had suddenly snapped. The lion in midair. Seemingly all claws and fangs. Big paws extended. And those great, glaring, insane eyes. Staring into his.

And then he was knocked off his feet by the animal's weight crashing onto him. Was down on the ground with the animal atop. The bow went flying off somewhere, with a loud twang; the arrow, too.

Beneath the camouflage suit he was wearing two wool sweaters against the December cold—their material was noiseless compared to the nylon-down jackets most hunters wore in the field. Now he felt their thick weaves rend—disintegrate —under the big claws, felt the camouflage suit go too . . . and then there was pain in his upper left arm and shoulder as he fought to get away from the animal.

What he feared most were the hind claws. He had never

seen them in action, but he knew what would happen if the
cat got to his stomach. A kick from those massive hind legs
and his entire front would be laid open, coiled intestines
spilling out over shredded jeans. Terrified, he kept twisting
so as to present his side and shoulder to the cat.

Thereafter his movements were automatic rather than deliberate. Strapped at the rear of one hip was an expensive
sheath knife, but he knew that he would never get a chance to
use it, that the cat would not allow this. And then, still pinned
with his right arm under him, he saw, with a faint astonishment, that the bow quiver, slung by a leather strap, was up
under his chin, and that his left arm and hand were entirely
free. And so, twisting still farther, he plucked loose a shaft,
freeing it from the rubber clips inside the quiver, sensing without even looking that the stiff, cocked turkey feathers belonged to a broadhead and not a *floo-floo* . . . and reached up,
more by accident than by design, just as the cat darted its
head at him, impaling itself—the triangular broadhead entering the right eye. The lion let out a squall. Reared back.
Clawed at the shaft. And then squalled again. Not a snarl, but
a deafening scream—a simply terrific pitch of sound and volume that impacted on Raymond's ears. Made all the more
horrifying because no distance was involved . . . the cat
screamed practically right in his face. All bared fangs and
gigantic yawning mouth. The breath horribly fetid.

Then, it half bounded, half fell off him, in a somersault of
pain, to grasp at the arrow shaft with both front paws. A curiously humanlike gesture, the heavy paws cupped. Hissing and
snarling frightfully, somehow it got rid of the arrow. Plucked
it clear. And, with another wild and dismal shriek that again
was somehow human in its fury, the cat took off. Maestas lay
there alone, bleeding slowly in a welter of torn fabric.

Too paralyzed with fear to even move, he was—oddly
enough—aware of one thing. In that atavistic gesture of striking out at the glaring eye so close to his own . . . in the thrust
and stroke of his defense . . . he had felt, along the length of the
shaft and up through the bones of his hand and wrist, the

dagger point of the broadhead scrape and deflect off bone. The angle of attack was wrong. It had not penetrated deeper than the socket itself.

"I ACTUALLY SAW it with my own eyes," Virgil McCormick was telling Griego, the state cop. This was after lunch. Griego, McCormick, and Les Johnson were standing in the front yard of Griego's housetrailer. Elsewhere, the hunt was being organized.

Sitting at McCormick's feet was a large white Alsatian shepherd bitch on a chain leash. Most of her head was wrapped in surgical gauze, through which here and there a weep of blood showed.

McCormick was a tall, thin man in his early fifties, sandy-haired, with a narrow, serious face and an undershot chin. He spoke in a dead-flat drawl. He had a farm farther up the valley, and on it he raised beans and alfalfa. Not big-money crops, but safe ones.

He and his family had settled here permanently—or "come in," as the local people would say—and while Virgil was not exactly accepted, he was at least tolerated. He was a good farmer, a hard worker, and he paid his bills, and people respected these qualities. One of his few faults was that he had never been able to break himself of the habit of calling anyone who spoke Spanish a Mexican. There was nothing wrong with this down in east Texas, where he'd come from, but in these parts it tended to rub people the wrong way. To Pecos folks, a Mexican was a low-down, shiftless, ignorant son of a bitch, and a whorer as well as lazy and dirty. Up here people called themselves Spanish-Americans, or simply New Mexicans, although every single one of them, or their ancestors anyway, had followed Coronado's route, the way of the conquistadors, up from Mexico City, sticking close to the meandering muddy thread of the Rio Grande. Actually, Pecos men were as shiftless, ignorant, and lazy as anyone else, and they had nothing against whoring, whenever the chance came their way, only they didn't care to have this pointed out to them in a Texas drawl. The villagers had a reputation for being noticeably touchy about things like that.

Virgil, like all men, was prejudiced, but with him it was more interesting because he was so beautifully unaware of his hard-nosed interpretation of life. He was honest and straight-forward, and more intelligent than might be supposed at first glance, and if his speech lacked polish it was also to the point, without frills, and this was the kind of talk valley people understood and appreciated.

For him, everything in God's creation had its proper place, and he was the first to admit that his own niche was pretty far down in the lowermost echelons of our divine hierarchy: ". . . just an ol' farm boy, no schooling or education to speak of, but I got my pride, and I'm thankful for that," he would say. Which was an oblique way of pointing out that he was also thankful that there were niggers and Mexicans and Orientals and Jews, who, to his way of thinking, were somehow less sophisticated, less civilized. Most likely, it never occurred to him that this viewpoint might be open to argument. If such a suspicion had ever come to him, he kept it flawlessly concealed behind pale-blue, sun-reddened eyes. Virgil wore his prejudice the way an Arthurian knight wore armor—there might be a few openings in it, but they weren't easy to get at. What's more, McCormick thought of himself as the most fair and open-minded man around. When that kind of opinion combines with prejudice the two make for a practically un-beatable combination.

Like the time he telephoned one of the radio stations down in Santa Fe to tell them what he thought of television. This station had a morning talk-show called *Open Line*, whereby people could phone in and air their gripes and peevish phi-losophies to the listening public . . . high taxes, hippies who got food stamps illegally, and the like, but what finally spurred

Virgil to call in was a subject he had been brooding over for some time.

What he said over the telephone that was patched into the station's transmitter was this: "I am not what they call a complaining man, but I would just like to point out that I don't think it's necessary to have so many nigrahs on all these here television advertising commercials. Now, I don't mind the colored race . . . it has produced some fine people. But it seems to me that a man is entitled to a little privacy in his own home, wouldn't you say?"

"Sir—" the announcer began; but Virgil doggedly continued: "I just don't see any reason why we got to have so many nigrahs on the TV, leaping outa the screen at you every time you blink. Where I grew up we didn't truck with them, and they didn't bother us."

The announcer at the station broke in again: "Sir, what point are you trying to make?"

Virgil McCormick said, "I don't especially like to look at 'em, that's all."

"Look at who?"

"Television niggers."

The announcer flipped the console jack on Virgil's call, cutting him off, and said something about the views expressed by callers not necessarily being those of the station.

Later, when his outraged wife found out about the call and asked him what ever had possessed him to make it, Virgil said, "As a matter of fact, I don't respect all these cranks who telephone in to that station, but I was sitting here with a cup of coffee this morning, and all of a sudden it just dawned on me that nobody had ever said anything about all these flashy nigrahs, so I just up and dialed, that's all." He paused. "And now that I think about it, I'm glad I did."

He paused again and then added reflectively, "By God, I was in the right, too! I'm old enough to tie my own shoelaces, and I don't need any uppity black man who's all teeth and big ol' rolling eyeballs yapping away at me about how I oughta spray my armpits, leastways not when I'm trying to relax in my own durned living room."

Whatever, Virge McCormick had settled in. And, to be fair, a lot of the old-time families admitted privately that if outsiders had to be tolerated then they might as well be people who had some feeling for the land. Better that than some of the crazies who had moved in . . . hippies and back-to-nature types, religious freaks, and artists. Such as John Sedgewick, for example, who lived alone in a high cabin and who wrote elegant music, and who was rumored to have a big thing going with Karen Jaramillo, the teacher's wife. Which was why local people considered most outsiders *estúpido* . . . a man living alone like that could be forgiven for looking twice at a woman, but not his best friend's wife—nobody with any brains would come within two uphill miles of Karen Jaramillo, who although she had to be the best-looking woman between Pecos and Wagonmound was also shooting trouble, pure and simple. And Sedgewick almost old enough to be her father at that!

Virge McCormick had another thing besides his farm and his Texas ways. He raised white Alsatians in a kennel he had built behind his barn. He had more than twenty animals, from pups to stud males, and the kennel had individualized chain-link compounds and a concrete run. That may sound like an idle hobby for a working dirt farmer except for one thing: Virgil's dogs were AKC-registered, and his starting price for an eight-week-old pup began at three hundred and fifty. In a good year the litters brought him and his family an extra five or six thousand.

So now Virgil was telling Peter Griego and Johnson what happened:

"I was out taking a walk with Lulu here, and Sam, my big feller, up by that old logging road that cuts over to Fitch Canyon below my place. I had them off the leashes because they're trained to heel, and I like 'em to have a run every day or so. Well, you know, the underbrush and scrub oak is real thick in along there, and the dogs were running up and down, letting off steam, when all of a sudden old Sammy, he lets out a howl and tears off into the underbrush, with Lulu hot after him, both barking up a storm. So I thought they'd jumped a coon or a porkypine or maybe a skunk, and I yelled at 'em to come back, because I didn't want them messing with any skunk, nor porkypine either. I've lost good dogs to porkypines. Only last spring I had to shoot a nice young male who'd gotten to one. Or rather it'd got to him. He must've had fifteen quills stuck clean through both jaws. Some went right through the nasal passage and the bridge of the nose bone, and they were in his tongue and lips, it was a mess. You can save a quilled dog if they ain't in too deep, by clipping 'em short and letting 'em infect so's the flesh gets pussy around the quill, then you can pry 'em out easy, but with this dog there was no hope, so I put him away—there must be something about the smell of a porkypine that drives a dog pure loco, the way they grab hold and bite down like that.

"So when Sam and Lulu took off, I called 'em fast. I couldn't see what they was at. The underbrush was real thick, like I was saying.

"All of a sudden, they both sort of bounced back out of that underbrush onto the road, still making that crazy fuss. Never paid me any mind.

"Then I about jumped outa my skin, Peter, because what they'd been after jumped out into the road with them. It was this mountain lion . . . biggest damned cat I ever saw. It just made Sam look like a pup, and he was no small dog, weighed ninety-seven pounds.

"They wasn't any more than thirty yards or so up the road from where I was standing. I could see that this critter was bleeding, that it had blood all over one side of its head. If only I'd had my pistol.

"Well, the big critter slithered down in the road there, all flattened out, like a pancake. It's amazing how they can flatten themselves down like that. And my dogs were tearing around in front of it, outa range, barking and raising all kinds of hell. Then this cat kind of just jumped forward a bit, so fast you couldn't believe it, and it reached out and slapped at my dogs, like a house cat will do sometimes if you tease it. Didn't even have its claws out that I could see.

"It didn't make any sound. Just slapped out like that. Sam went down. And then there was another, and Lu let off a yip and went flying across the road.

"Then that goddamned thing turned around and looked at me, and I could see its eye was hurt. I stood stock-still. I wasn't about to make a move. After a bit it turned and went back into the underbrush and was gone.

"It's amazing how something that big can move so fast. One second it was there, then it was just gone.

"I went up to my dogs. I saw that old Sam wasn't knocked down. He was dead. His neck was broke, and his jaw too. Damned near knocked clean off. No claw marks or anything like that. I never knew they had that kind of strength, that they could just kill a big dog like that with one swipe.

"Lulu here was trying to pull herself together and get her senses back. I think if that lion had caught her a fair swipe it would have caved her whole head in. As it was, she came off lucky. The ear was knocked off, but that was all. I stitched her up and gave her some penicillin, and then drove down here. She'll be okay for breeding, but I'll never be able to show her again."

Virgil paused and then went on. "I think we ought to get together and hunt that cat down before something worse happens than what happened to my dogs."

"It already has," Les Johnson said. He told McCormick about the Apodaca child, and of how some of the men in the village were already getting horses and gear together for the hunt. "I'm going to have to impound your dog, Mr. Mc-Cormick," Johnson said. "For observation. There may be a chance this cat is rabid."

"No need to do that," Virgil said. "I can isolate her in a pen at the back of my kennel. For as long as need be. Nobody'll go near her. Neither dogs nor people. How long will we have to watch her? Two, three weeks?"

"At least," Johnson said. "That is, providing we haven't caught the lion first."

THE LAST, AND deadliest, attack by the lion happened soon after, at a small farm a mile north of the village. The farm lay between the Pecos River and the road that led to Cowles, and was owned by a *viejo*—an old-timer—named Agapito Benavidez. Agapito—a name that can be translated loosely as "to-make-a-whistle"—had six merino sheep in a corral behind his house. He was fixing himself a bowl of beans and meat for lunch when he heard the commotion they were making.

Unarmed, he went out the front door and around the side of the house. By the time he got to the corral only two of the merinos were alive, huddled at one end of the enclosure, bleating piteously. The others were dead or dying, flung about in a welter of blood.

Agapito approached closer and saw what had caused this disaster . . . a cat, *un tigre*, of immense proportions. It was eating one of his prize ewes, tearing out bloody mouthfuls, and the awful thing was that she was still alive. The ewe struggled, at times lifting her head and crying out, but was held down by the weight of one of the cat's forepaws.

Shocked, Agapito stood still. At that moment the cat noticed him, looked up out of its one good eye, and then abandoned the ewe. Sensing his danger, the old man backed away a step or two, then turned and began running for the house, and with that the cat came out of the corral after him.

BY EARLY AFTERNOON a reporter from Santa Fe's *The New Mexican* had interviewed enough people, including Les Johnson, to write a feature story.

The little girl was still alive, but Agapito Benavidez was not. At the old man's farm, Les Johnson, the reporter, and Officer Griego more or less pieced together what must have happened. "More'n likely this animal's starving," Johnson said, looking over the mangled carcasses of the merinos. "The old feller must've surprised it, and it jumped him."

Benavidez had been found up by the road. A gash—probably from a kick from a hind leg—had opened a major artery on the inner side of his left thigh. Two ranchers in a pickup truck had spotted him. He was still breathing, but died minutes after they stopped.

A little earlier, Raymond Maestas had been found wandering along a logging road in a dazed, hysterical state, bleeding, his clothing in shreds. Under Peter Griego's questioning, he admitted wounding the lion with an arrow. His version was a little different, though. He claimed he had shot the animal with his bow, in self-defense.

The newspaperman, whose name was Charles Day, was staring into Benavidez's bloody corral, his arms propped atop a split-log gate. He said, "Four attacks in one morning. Three against humans. One dead. No telling about the child. It doesn't look good, does it?"

"You can say that again," Johnson agreed. "We got us a cat that's hurt bad. I don't like that at all." He looked at Peter Griego. "How far was it from where that feller's dogs were attacked to where they picked up this bow hunter?"

"Mile and a half, maybe," Griego said. "No more than two."

"Cat's sticking close," Johnson said. "Wounded lion hanging around a town . . . I surely don't care for that." He glanced at a partially devoured merino carcass. "One good thing, though. It's fed. Ordinarily, after a cat feeds it'll hole up somewhere to rest up. No telling what this one'll do, though."

"You think it's still around?" the reporter asked.

"Hard to say," the old hunter replied; then he corrected himself: "Yes. My guess is that he won't travel far."

The reporter said, "A man I interviewed said you described

a really big specimen that you'd observed last year. Could this be the same cat?"

"Yes. I think so," Johnson said. He took a map of that area of the wilderness out of his hip pocket, and indicated to Griego where he intended setting up his base camp, tracing with one forefinger the canyons and alpine meadows that would have to be checked for signs of cat.

"How soon will you be moving out?" Griego asked.

"Sooner the better. Couple of hours," Johnson said. "Be late afternoon by the time we get up there. Too late to do much. We could be out first thing in the morning, though. I sure hope this weather holds."

FIVE

"... well, I don't care, no woman ought go around like that, wearing those tight-assed jeans, with nothing under her shirt for anyone to see, and fancy hippie boots, stepping out in a man's walk, with that blond hair flying, like she owns the whole damned town and every soul in it."

"That is one woman sure puts herself above others. Anybody with two eyes can see that. She sure is something, que no?"

—Conversations in the Crippled Horse

THE BUSINESS WITH Karen Jaramillo and Sedgewick had been going on since last summer, or maybe even before that.

She could be honest enough about it, at least with Sedgewick. Could regard him with those clear gray eyes that seemed unfathomable, yet sad in a way, and say of herself: "I guess the only thing that's worse than a woman who can't be satisfied with what she's already got is one who gets to wanting something she knows isn't going to do her any good in the long run."

This was in May, when she had been going to the cabin for a while. At first she went there pretending to borrow albums from his record collection. But she could say now, with that wry honesty that in a way was almost good-humored, as though the joke was on her: "I don't understand any of it. It must have been building in me for such a long time. Years. It's like I was coming apart, piece by piece, sort of cracking up, really, you know? An outsider can't fight these people. The women in this valley don't like me, and neither do the men. There's no defying them. You lose every time. I thought I could be happy here and make a life with Daniel, but in this valley there's no way you can be yourself. So I put those feelings away and buried them, but all the time it was growing inside me. I didn't know it could be that strong. I didn't know any kind of feeling between two people could ever get so strong. That's the part I hate, not being in control of yourself that way."

Sedgewick picked at the bowl of his pipe with a reamer. "But you must have known what this life would be like."

"Not really," she said. "I never thought anything about Daniel being Spanish—I swear, the idea of prejudice never occurred to me—but up here people feel differently. You'd be surprised."

"No, I wouldn't," he said. "I've had my own problems with them. You know that."

Almost stubbornly, as if determined to make a point, she said, "I came here with good feelings. Down at the university, Daniel and I were fine. But he was born and raised in this valley, and when he came back it was almost like he'd never been away, except that he'd brought me with him. I really did try hard the first year, but there wasn't that much for me. There are church socials, and athletic events at the high school, and things like that, but a woman isn't supposed to have a lot of outside interests. She's supposed to have her house and her man and her children. Maybe if we'd had children it would have been different. I don't think so, but maybe it would have."

"You felt empty?" Sedgewick suggested.

"How many books can a person read?" she said. "How much time can she spend gardening? Or cooking a fancy dinner? I've lived here for six years now."

"And now there's music?"

"Yes," she said. "You taught me that."

That was how it began. He would talk to her about music. The two of them sitting quietly under the portal of the cabin, with cups of coffee, and a breeze coming across the flower-strewn mountain meadow, so beautiful and cool and clean in the morning, while from inside there was the sound of whatever he had put on the stereo, maybe the Mozart horn concerti, or the *Goldberg Variations*. Regal melodies, so calm and precise. A stately and elegant procession of notes. The interior of the entire cabin filled with a paced and musical beauty. So that later she was able to say, "There was such a curious mixture in me. One part half crazy. But the other part—all the rest of me—felt such a peacefulness, a completeness, you know? Just to be alive and to be with you felt so good. As if I had been waiting my entire life to feel that. And that wildness, yes. During those first mornings when we just sat and talked, we were so careful not to touch each other."

And so then on that day when they finally did. When he simply looked at her. With such a quiet regard. They stood, and went into the cabin, and there, with the music playing, he finally did that, put his hand to her shoulders, in a way that was curiously crude—coarse, really—as though he was angry with her and with himself. Neither of them speaking, but her breathing was heavy, as though she had run some distance. She got dizzy—swayed, as if she might faint—braced herself against the rough hands, such a stern fondling, unbuttoning her shirt and then going to the front of her jeans, a hard tug at the belt, so that now she couldn't seem to breathe at all any more . . . swayed again, so that he had to support her as he led her into the bedroom. In there she said aloud, "I want everything . . . I have to—" and sank to her knees as if in worship, and in fact did, taking a prayerlike stance, in gentle abandon, a cer-

tain gracefulness to her every movement, and yet her expression had a faint, sly mischievousness. He said, "You like that?"

She paused, sat back on her haunches there on the floor, so
naked and beautiful, to stare up at him. That sly, shy smile.
Eyes wild, yet sleepy and sloe-eyed. Dreamy. "Yes," she said.
Then tossed her head to fling the long blond hair free of her
face. Psst, psst. Smile again. Muttered, more to herself, "Hair!"

"I like it in braids."

A lazy glissando of slow-spaced kisses. "Not now . . . I
want it loose now."

"It hides your face."

"You like to watch?"

"Yes."

Tongue like a cat's . . . leisurely washing its paw. Endless
application. A punctuation—a passacaglia—of wet kisses, and
then again that shy, appraising glance: "Why?"

"Because you like me to watch you."

"Yes."

"Am I right?"

"Yes . . . I like you to be watching me."

"Let's not talk."

At that she smiled, murmured something unintelligible . . .
tacit agreement. Blew an imaginary smoke ring, a gentle vor-
tex, a billowing, voluptuous O into which he was drawn and
lost forever.

And later, on the bed, sprawled beneath his strength, forcing herself to be passive so that he could use her the better,
she heard sounds coming from her—a venting of pathetic cries
that were not uttered so much as wrenched loose from her—
and then he went out of control too, forcing her brutally, and
her mind stopped. Her brain empty . . . floating above an
abyss. From far off she heard someone sobbing. Later, they
were lying there, and he looked at her in that slow and easy
way of his . . . smiled, and she smiled back. Took his finger
and wiped her cheek where it was still wet with tears, and
then he said, "Thanks."

It was half a tease, true, but she knew it then that she was the one who was the lover, and he the beloved. She hated that. Even then. There was nothing left of her, just the pleasure, but a part of her hated him for having her like that.

Later she was to tell herself, That's how I knew he owned me. And he knew it too . . .

What he did that day, and on the other days, made me different. He did something that changed me. I could never be the same person again after that.

I don't know how he did it, but he did.

He has that power over me. And he knows it.

And all he said was "Thanks."

SHE STAYED AWAY for two weeks. Fought against it. So did he.

But Sedgewick could be honest too. He knew this much: that one time would not be enough to make it stop. He knew that if it happened once, they would go on.

One of them would seek the other out. He would go to her or she would come to him. It didn't make any difference really. One of them would succumb. They would be fighting it, but really it was just a matter of waiting. In that knowledge lay defeat.

In the cabin, alone, he tried to concentrate. He would say, aloud, "Well, today, I am going to sit down and work," but it was no good. She was all he could think about.

Later, he could say this to her: "I swore to myself that I wouldn't go to you. And I didn't. I did stay away. But if you hadn't come, I would have gone to you. I knew this. You must have known it too. So it makes no difference who gave in first."

And then she did return. A bright, sunny Thursday morning. He knew Daniel would be at school—knew that she had thought of this too.

He stood there by the living-room window of the cabin and

watched her walking along the narrow dirt road. She had a marvelous walk for a woman. Straight-backed. Stepping out in a long-legged stride. Swing of hips. So tall and slender.

At the door she didn't speak. She stepped inside, and they looked at each other. She was breathing a little fast from the walking. They stood there like that for a minute, regarding each other. Then, almost brusquely, he turned his back on her and went into the bedroom. He heard her footsteps behind him. In the bedroom he shut the door, and they looked at each other again. Her eyes were troubled, almost alarmed, and then he stepped up to her, and she closed them and leaned back against the wall, waiting. He put his hand on her shoulder. His touch gentle now. As though violence was no longer a pressing need. Under the cotton shirt he could feel her collar-bone—a curiously fragile bone structure for so tall a girl, almost birdlike. And then she was shaking her head back and forth . . . slowly, her eyes shut, as though obliged to refute herself, or him, or both of them—finally, to surrender . . . helping him with her clothing, and then his too, and on the bed he tasted her slickness—there was no part of her he did not taste.

Afterward, on the portal, where he had brought a de-canter of wine and two glasses, she sat back, relaxed, calmly regarding the mountain view. She said finally, "You know, two weeks ago you should have told me, 'Well, so you walked all the way up here . . . but, listen, I don't believe you should be here. You ought to go now. You better go back down there to your own house.' But that would have taken strength, wouldn't it?"

"Yes," he said.

"So you have your weaknesses too."

"Yes."

"You couldn't just say 'Go away' and shut the door in my face."

"No."

"What do you like best about me?"

"Everything."

"No, really."

"Everything," he said again. "Your eyes . . . they're expressive. Very intelligent, telling nothing, and yet telling everything . . . such a slow and heavy discontent. I like how we are. Do you?"

"Yes."

"Everything?"

"Yes."

"We'll end up in love, you know."

"Don't talk about it," she said, frowning. "I just don't understand why. I mean, I don't understand *how*. Why does it have to happen this way? That's something I just can't figure out."

He tasted his wine, and then, after a while, said, "Is there a lack in Daniel?"

"No."

"But there must be. In him—or in you. Maybe in both of you. Any marriage gets dull."

"Perhaps," she said. "But this is too scary—it really is."

He looked at her. "Why me?"

"What?"

"Why did you pick me?"

"I didn't," she said. "It just happened."

"Did you see in me a way out of this life?"

"No."

"I settled here two years ago to make a life of my own," he pointed out. "I'm not interested in leaving. I like it here. I'm too old to start again. If you were looking for a way out, you picked the wrong man."

"It wasn't a matter of choice," she said.

"If that's true, then you're flirting with self-destruction. And that's worse," he said. "If you'd picked me out, cold-bloodedly, as someone who could help you and take care of your needs . . . well, that's the normal, healthy predator instinct. But to let something like this happen when there's no way out—that can be dangerous." He paused and sipped at his wine. "What was your life like before? I mean, before Daniel?"

She regarded him. "I was free."

"That must have been good. For a long time?"

"Long enough."

"Family?"

"My father was a lawyer. He had a pretty successful practice, in Illinois. After college I worked at whatever interested me."

"What brought you to the Southwest?"

She shrugged. "I wanted to see the country."

"Trying your wings?"

"I lived my own life," she said.

He nodded. "That's the best time. To be young and free. Or at least to believe you're free."

"It doesn't last."

"Nothing does," he said.

She glanced at him. "When you were young—were you like that?"

"I enjoyed life," he said.

"I think women have always liked you," she said, still looking at him.

"Yes," he said. "And you? There were other men?"

Her expression was grave. "Men have always paid attention to me."

"Many?"

"Not so many."

"You loved them?"

"Yes," she said. "Sometimes."

"Was there perhaps something of defiance in your marrying Daniel?" he asked. "An urge to do something different?"

"I don't know," she said. "Maybe."

"And when it didn't pan out—here, in Pecos—was there more defiance on your part? Or resentment? The way you dress. Your manner. You know it rubs these people the wrong way, yet you do it." He looked at her. "Touch of the maverick?"

"I really tried to make it here," she insisted. "But even Daniel's own family cut me dead, right at the start." She drank her wine, and then suddenly turned to him with a wry grin. "This is a great village for talk," she said. "Never to your face, of course—that would be bad form. But behind your back—ah! The men are as bad as the women. Maybe worse." She laughed aloud. "You know what they'd say? Not to Daniel's face, of course, but, still, they'd be saying it, in a thousand little ways . . ." Still smiling, she fell into the local dialect, mimicking it almost perfectly: "They'd say, 'Daniel, we told you so, don't say we didn't warn you, years ago.' They'd say, 'She won't stay put, not that one, you just watch. In time she will stand up and walk out the door, drift back to her own kind.' They would say, 'Yessir, there ain't nothing in the world wrong with taking one of these here gringas to bed, that's for sure. These blonde gringas, they are something else, all right, lotsa fun, kinda different, *que no?* You just can't blame a feller for wanting something a little different once in a while, but that don't mean he's got to go off and marry one. That is just asking for trouble, Daniel, and sooner or later it's bound to come to you, and just 'cause you wear a suit and a tie and a white shirt and have some college degrees it doesn't mean you're not liable to get yourself some real trouble you can't handle, because it will come, Daniel, yessir, you mess around with one of these pretty blonde gringas and get *sereee-ous,* why, you've planted trouble in your life the same as corn is planted in spring. Woman is trouble, but with someone like her, there just ain't no end to it.' That's what they would say."

"When did you know? I mean, about us?"

"I just knew," she said. "Maybe right from the start. When you first began coming by the house. When you and Daniel first started becoming friendly. Then, one time, I had a dream, in bed. No, I was awake, but it was so scary it was like a dream. Daniel was asleep beside me. We were in bed like that, and there was a lot of moonlight that night, shining in through the window. I lay there watching the moonlight move down across the far wall, and his hand was on my breast. He always liked my breasts. His hands are small and beautifully shaped. So I began to get that way. I lay there so still and hardly breathing, looking down in the moonlight at Daniel's hand on my breast, just watching, moving slowly up and down with my breathing . . . lying on my back, my legs straight and together, almost as if I was arranged in a coffin. Then his hand was gone. I mean, it wasn't his hand any more, it was yours. There was no mistake, it was yours, so big and rough, the fingers thick and square-tipped, and it seemed to weigh a hundred pounds. That was a crazy thing. I had to touch myself then, and I was very gentle and careful, so that if Daniel did wake all I would have to do was shut my eyes and make believe I was asleep, and he would never know, it would just be the two of us lying there in the moonlight. But it was your hand. So I did that . . . moving carefully so as not to waken him . . . moving it down under the covers to touch myself. He must know something."

"He's an intelligent man."

"And the two of you are friends," she said, looking at him. "Yes."

"And when did you know?"

He shrugged. "I tried to put it out of my mind. I said to myself, 'Listen, if you are going to have some friends here in the valley, these two are all right. They are secure about each other, and they'll make good friends. You've certainly had enough of the other kind. They won't bring their troubles to you and bore you with their problems. You can't live like a hermit up here at the cabin—you'll go crazy.' "

"Daniel admires you," she said.

"I know. I feel the same about him."

"But this—"

"It's not your fault," he said. "I couldn't help myself. I gave in. And that's my responsibility."

"Guilt?"

He poured more wine for both of them. "I don't believe in guilt. But you're responsible for every act or deed you commit." Now it was he who was smiling. "I thought I'd given all that up—letting a woman do that to me. Here at the cabin I've been happy enough. So it seemed. I'd learned that trick finally of living alone. Or thought I had."

"You were dying of loneliness," she said bluntly.

"Maybe I was. That's not the worst thing you can die of."

She gave him an irritated look. "And you talk to me of self-destructiveness!"

BUT PERHAPS DANIEL too had his own variety of self-destructiveness. Some basic inability to act in his own behalf. In the Crippled Horse they said of him, "Jaramillo is the most decent and even-tempered man in this valley . . . a real credit to this here community."

This was true. He had never been known to lose his temper or raise his voice in anger.

But then why, that autumn—when the aspens were turning to gold—was he seen, on more than one occasion, entering the side door of the church, where Father Cornelius had his private office? Like many villagers, Daniel took religion casually. Baptized Catholic, but indifferent about Sunday mass. As for confession, he hadn't participated in that for years.

The two men seated in the office, their heads bent close in conversation. Daniel's expression serious. The old Franciscan's brow set in an angry scowl as he listens to what the younger man has to say. "Father, what exactly should you be doing about a woman like her? I mean, if she was cheap or common that would be one thing. Or if she was selfish. Or shallow. That would be something else. But she isn't any of these things. That's the problem."

"You mean, it's her problem," Cornelius interjects. With a

ticklish situation of this sort, the priest falls back on a kind of religious pragmatism of his own devising. (There is a story about Cornelius, which may even be true, concerning a private interview he once had with Archbishop Montcroissier, in Santa Fe, who at the conclusion of their talk blessed the priest and added the remark "God will forgive us for all our sins." To which Cornelius was said to have replied, "Well, why shouldn't He, Your Excellence. That's His job, ain't it?")

Daniel labors on: "What hurts is that she is still trying not to let me know. She's fighting letting me know. As if she doesn't want to hurt me."

"Funny way of showing it, if you ask me."

"She's really a fine woman. I can't deny that. Sometimes I see her looking at me. There's such sadness in her eyes. She's so unhappy."

"Well, if she's unhappy, it's her doing." The priest paused, as if to consider this. "Lord, I don't know what gets into people."

"It's like she wants to say 'I'm just so miserable I'm dying of it.' But she can't get the words out."

"Doesn't have much to say for herself, eh?"

"We don't talk much."

"But you love her, I suppose?"

"Yes."

Cornelius sighs. "People just don't act sensible any more."

"She's a good woman, Father. I couldn't argue that."

"So, then, what do you want to do about this?"

"I don't know."

"Nothing *I* can do, you know," Cornelius says.

"I know."

"Damage's been done," Cornelius remarks. "Case of locking the barn door. This Sedgewick feller. My God, Daniel, how in the name of common sense could you have picked him for a friend? That beats me!"

Daniel most uncomfortable now. He stares down at his hands, lying in his lap. "Well, Father, the choosing of a friend is a curious business, I suppose. First, you're acquaintances. And then you find out that you have some mutual interests. So then maybe later you learn that you share some common attitudes and beliefs . . . and then maybe still later you might ask this friend to do something for you that needs doing, and if he does it then you begin to know that you can depend on him, and then sometimes still later he may ask you to do something for him, so then he knows the same thing too, and then you are friends. So, that's a good thing . . . to have someone you enjoy being with, and who likes you, and who is dependable, and who'll stand back of you when something needs doing. But now—I don't know."

"Stand back of you! He was in back of you, all right. Clean around behind you. Next I suppose you'll be telling me *he's* a paragon of Christian virtue too."

"He's a good man."

"Man with a friend like that doesn't need enemies."

Daniel more miserable than ever. "Perhaps you're right."

The priest sits back in his easy chair. Shoots a hard look at his companion. "How long have you known?"

"From the first."

Now, IN THE early afternoon, the two men are laying out their plans for the hunt. They are in the living room of Daniel's house, talking quietly. Cups of coffee are on the low cocktail table before them.

She is across the room, in an upholstered chair, a book spread open in her lap—something to do with Indian pottery of the Southwest. From time to time she looks up at them. Her expression then is pensive—her eyes serious. And yet she does not seem really interested in them or the plans they are making, as if her occasional glances are merely a way of confirming that these two men are still here with her in the warmth of the room.

Her mood appears calm. Now and then she will turn a page of the book, and then, presently, look up at them again with that imperturbable expression. There is no one in the house save these three.

The house is several miles up the valley from the village— located, really, where the valley narrows into the high, rocky cliffs of Pecos Canyon, so that the climate is almost alpine. The northern end of the long, winding canyon reaches into a spur of the Rockies, and the house itself might almost be a fulcrum or balance point, because at night you can look out the living-room windows that face south and see the hard-pointed lights of the village below, a scattered incandescence of habitation. But the framed picture window that faces north is dark and empty.

This is the window that looks out on the forest and the mountains that go all the way to Colorado, so that in the daytime it is like seeing a series of monstrous, frozen waves advancing on the eye, the nearest foothills high and ever-green-covered, and, beyond, and higher still, great sloping snowcapped masses—a jagged and broken land, but frozen somehow in a sedate relentlessness.

She turns another page and then glances at them, thinking: I believe he knows—or is beginning to know. I just don't see how he couldn't know, and that is what frightens me. It isn't right for a man to keep an injustice inside him like that. If he really knows, I don't know what will happen. He might do something. He wouldn't lose his temper, but Daniel would think out a way.

She stares down at an illustration—a color plate of an elegant turn-of-the-century Acoma pot, a museum specimen —scarcely seeing it, her mind a brown study: These two have no business on this hunt. They aren't hunters, but now they are borrowing rifles and camping gear to go up into the mountains. They aren't stupid men.

It isn't just the sex. That's what they'd say down in the village. Loving is giving and taking. My God, what is a woman for if it isn't to breathe life into a man? How can he be so loving and yet so untouchable, so dead inside? But that other thing happened—with all that emptiness, it was he who brought me to life. So he gave me that like a gift. How can you hate someone who does that for you? All the years of my life I thought I'd been alive. Damn him! I guess that's the worst luck that can happen to a woman. After all these years, to learn something new. That there is some part of a woman that isn't ever going to be satisfied. Like if she had the whole world wrapped up in the palm of her hand, pretty soon she'd start feeling that something wasn't right with her life. I think most women never get a chance to sit down and feel themselves out in their needing. Somehow, they never get the time.

I think most women even in these times would still say something like "Well, if I had a decent man in my life who I loved and who loved me—someone who would let me have my privacy and not do putdowns—well, I wouldn't ask for much more than that, that wouldn't really be so bad."

But I had all that, and it did me no good.

I think there must be a natural perversity in a woman, that she should turn from everything that is good in her life, turn and go toward something that she knows will ruin everything, will make no end of trouble.

There is such a sadness in that kind of woman then. As if she wanted to weep for the whole world. If that is the way all women are, then there is no end to the business of trying to make them happy and forever failing.

Daniel gave me everything any man could. He loves me. I'd never question that in him. And now, it has come to this. What rotten luck.

SIX

The Mora people have never personally given me any kind of trouble. I take a hard stand with them. They understand that kind of approach.

—*Statement*, PETER M. GRIEGO,
New Mexico State Police

". . . . if you have them arrested, they'll get you. They don't really understand what law and order means. Why, old Feliciano and Ruperto, they hardly speak Spanish let alone English! Half the time they talk in grunts. People hereabouts stay out of their way. My thinking is that you had better make a choice. Either learn to get along with them, or give up your cabin. Everybody else around here would say the same."

"Dan, there's got to be something I can do about them."

"You're wrong. You're intelligent, and that's a disadvantage. They're ignorant, and that gives them the winning hand every time. You can rebuild the cabin a dozen times, and they'll wreck it on you. That is, as long as they find it amusing. But if they get bored, they're liable to set it afire some night, maybe with you in it."

—JARAMILLO *and* SEDGEWICK, *in conversation*

FELICIANO AND TOMAS Mora learned about the hunt by accident from Sedgewick.

There is a rich Spanish heritage in the Pecos Valley. Some of its residents are direct descendants of the original fifty-two colonizing families who trekked northward out of Mexico City hundreds of years ago. Names like Ortega and Garcia and Rivera.

Many of these people—particularly the older folks—exhibit an inimitable graciousness, an unsophisticated courtliness, that is nearly patrician. Such as Juan C deBaca, who, at seventy-seven, represents an unbroken line to the old-time Castilian aristocracy. Juan is tall, gaunt, and his posture is ramrod-erect. He dresses in worn, almost threadbare, but nonetheless immaculately laundered and ironed jeans and work shirt, and a flat-brimmed, round-crowned Stetson of pale gray felt. He has a face straight out of Isabella's court—long and narrow, high-cheekboned, thin-lipped, the weathered skin parchment-thin. A face, really, so handsome that it is nearly beautiful in its sculpted emaciation. The name C deBaca is ancient too. An abbreviation of Cabesa de Baca, or Vaca, meaning "head-of-a-cow." Old John Head-of-a-Cow, who, though he cannot read or write and must sign his Army pension checks with an X (he was gassed in World War I) still merits enormous respect and honor in the valley, simply because of the way he is: tall and regal.

There are other local people who are less distinguished in looks or style. And then there are quite a few who are totally undistinguished.

Then, finally, there are the Moras.

The Moras, in a way, are a legend among the local people.

Daniel Jaramillo, who was a cousin many times removed, put it nicely enough. "They are sort of a class unto themselves," said Daniel.

He happened to be speaking to John Sedgewick. There was a reason why these two were discussing the Moras.

Daniel went on, "Anthropologically speaking, if you don't mind stretching the primate definition of 'Hominidae' and actually classify the Moras as members of the human race"—and considerable stretching, he conceded, was in order—"they might rank with the Neanderthal. Maybe a touch lower. Those Neanderthals, you know, showed lots of talent with their cave drawings in southern France."

None of the Moras had any artistic talent. Feliciano Mora held on to a pencil as though it were a prybar.

Daniel's friend, Sedgewick, smiled at this observation, but his smile was perfunctory.

Daniel tried again, in a more serious vein. "I guess they represent a vanishing breed. Old-time mountain people. People would say of them, 'They know how to get by.' They farm that little patch of garden back of where they live. They steal a little. Poach deer, when they're sober enough to. The old man and his son are first-rate hunters. Things like that are, well—admired, in a way. Seventy, eighty years ago, most people in this valley lived like that. The Moras are hard, and nobody fools with them. In a negative way, they're almost famous. Oh, they're respected, all right." He paused. " 'Feared' might be a better way of putting it."

Daniel didn't add that they were also unwashed, ignorant, mentally retarded, inbred, and shiftless. Sedgewick had pretty much learned all this already. In fact, the Moras couldn't really be said to be functioning members of society, except in a peripheral fashion—their existence justified the salaries earned by some other people, like welfare and child-care workers, the public-health nurse, correction officers at the state pen, and the like.

The Moras were known around Pecos for their mean ways. Someone like Guillermo Apodaca—*el rano*—who thought of himself as a brawler, at least until that fellow Lewis Bowman arrived, would in comparison rank as a model of propriety.

Guillermo, after all, would not calmly and with premeditation shoot a man in the back. Old Feliciano Mora had, and had proudly served time for it.

Feliciano, the cacique, or headman, of the Mora bunch, had also served time for committing rape and incest with Alma, his fourteen-year-old daughter. In addition to getting the retarded child pregnant, he had infected her with the syphilis he had carried in him for most of his adult life.

The pregnancy was aborted. At the same time Alma got a tubal ligation, which was probably a smart move, since she had told the child-welfare worker that she sort of liked what her father did to her.

Feliciano served ten months for the incest business, and thereafter was set free to stalk the streets of Pecos, or hang out in the Crippled Horse Saloon, where he would hold forth, after he had gotten enough muscatel into him, on the fallibility of our judicial system: ". . . all this here focken' lawyers and courts, he ain't nothin' but sheet!"

And offered himself as living proof. Beating a clenched fist against his scrawny chest, his lips drawn back in a hideous grin: "There ain't no ways you ever gonna keep a smart hombre in jail ver' long!"

THERE WERE SIX Moras, counting Feliciano. All of them lived in two *jacales*, or split-log cabins, up on the ridge past John Sedgewick's place.

The interstices between the logs of the jacales were chinked with mud plaster. Actually, they weren't even true *jacales*, since almost two thirds of the interior of each was recessed directly into the side of a slope on the Mora property, dugout fashion.

The *jacales* were roofed over with crude planking, a layer of tar paper, and a heavier layer of dirt. The earthen roof was held in place and kept from being washed away by an occasional seeding of grama grass, so that during the summer months the Mora goats could often be seen browsing, or simply standing like sentinels, atop the roofs.

The interior of these dwellings, both of which were reluctantly but regularly visited by the county nurse, was so dark and foul and generally loathsome—so ridden by a thick buzzing of flies in summer, and so pervaded by an overwhelming and near-palpable stench at any season of the year—that, as Dan Jaramillo remarked, it pretty near defied description.

Ammonia-rich, pungent, ancient urine. Excrement, both human and that deposited in the corners by any of the various mongrels that lived with the Moras. And the funky, sweetish odor, richly reminiscent of a slowly decaying compost heap, of rank sweat and crud, layered in secret folds of the body and feet and toes. This last was not the smell of bodies that experienced clean soap and hot water maybe once or twice a year, but of those that never felt water at all.

Worse, in winter they all used galvanized tin buckets to collect slops. The outhouse was too far away to trudge to in heavy snow. This accumulation was flung daily out the front door of the *jacales*. A veritable Comstock Lode of manure and urine, frozen rock-solid, to await spring thaw.

It was no exaggeration for a visitor to the Moras', say, around April, when the first new green grass was shooting up in the alpine meadows, to get wind of the place about ten minutes before he actually set eyes on it.

BESIDES FELICIANO, THERE was Tomas, an imbecilic thirty-four-year-old son, who lived with his wife, Josefita, in the second *jacal*.

There was Feliciano's wife, Eduvigen, also retarded, but with the gentle soul of a child, with very nearly a full growth of whiskers sprouting from her chin and upper lip. Eduvigen had internal disorders and terrible glands, and was so grossly obese that she had never been accurately weighed by any doctor who treated her via welfare medical benefits. No office scale had the range. A guess was that she went somewhere between three hundred seventy five and an even four hundred. For that matter, entire areas of her health history were as blank as an unexplored desert on a geographical map, because of the difficulty—impossibility—of putting her through a complete examination. It was known that she had a bad heart. But how bad was anybody's guess. There was no way a stethoscope could fathom valve action through the immense layers of fat that encompassed her rib cage, and even an EKG gave a confused reading. She had phenomenally high blood pressure. Impetigo. Fallen arches, mild diabetes, as well as rheumatism, but here the story ends. As one physician wrote in his case history, after she had made an office visit: "I did not attempt a vaginal, since it seemed impractical, if not hopeless." Eduvigen lived on beans, tortillas, and Kool-Aid.

There was also a grandmother Mora, and the less said about her the better, and an old uncle named Ruperto, so far gone in senility and terminal alcoholism that hours of planning and concentration on his part were needed to get out of his chair and become ambulatory.

The sexually abused daughter, Alma, had been committed to the state mental hospital at Las Vegas, where she died at the age of nineteen from the effects of a habit she had picked up somewhere, that of obsessively plucking at her anus, until she finally tore loose the sphincter muscles and hemorrhaged. She was found in bed in a great pool of blood, with a transcendentally beatific smile on her lips.

THE MORA PROPERTY directly adjoined Sedgewick's place. Which in a way explains how Sedgewick got the cabin and the five acres it stood on so cheaply.

The views from the windows of the cabin were stunning, fully equal to the mountain wildness of Bavaria's Schwarzwald. Happily, the Mora spread was hidden on the far side of the ridge that separated the properties. Still, no local person with any sense would have taken the acreage as a gift, know-ing it meant having a common fence line with the Moras.

It wasn't until late in the summer of the first year that Sedgewick lived in the valley that he caught the impact of what his neighbors were like, and what they stood for in these parts.

By then it was too late. He had already put thousands into the cabin, insulating it, installing modern plumbing, rewiring, and the like. He had some money set aside in savings, but he was not a wealthy man. His first mistake was getting in-terested in this style of life. The second came when he estab-lished an up-to-date survey on the property, and a clear and merchantable title. What he forgot to do was check out the neighboring properties. If he had, it would have explained why acreage and cabin were listed so cheaply.

By the time the first confrontation came, he had become friendly with Daniel Jaramillo. What happened with the Moras was this:

Sedgewick had risen one morning and was making break-fast when he heard the dry, steady sound of a bucksaw on the slope of the ridge above the cabin. He walked up there to see what was going on, and found Feliciano, Ruperto, and Tomas. They were midway through a thick and lovely old ponderosa. There were dozens of weathered stumps along this section of the ridge to show that this was not the first tree they had cut.

The three did not even speak to him. Tomas did give him a grin, though. Tomas had an imperfectly repaired harelip, and when he smiled the clumsy suture scars made him look like a rabbit.

Sedgewick was positive they were on his property. But, wanting to be sure he was in the right, he left them and walked on up the slope to where his fence line ran. He had put in a new fence earlier that summer, hiring some local men to do the job. The new barbed wire—five-strand stuff—had been cut.

Sedgewick returned to the three men and introduced himself. He pointed out that they were on his property, and that his fence had been cut.

"The fence, he were that way," Feliciano said.

"You didn't cut it?" Sedgewick asked.

"No, he were that way, Señor," Feliciano said again.

"Well, you can't cut trees on my property," Sedgewick said.

"Long as I remember we get our firewood here," Feliciano said.

"Not any more," Sedgewick insisted.

The Mora men looked at one another and then picked up the bucksaw and, without a word, walked up the ridge and disappeared into the trees.

Later that day Sedgewick drove down to the post office in his jeep. He returned around two, parked the jeep, and saw immediately that every window in the cabin had been smashed with rocks. He went inside. Nothing had been taken or disturbed. The Steinway was all right. But he was out almost five hundred in labor and materials. The windows had been double-sheeted Thermopane, expensive stuff.

Then, from up the slope, he heard the steady sound of the bucksaw. He walked up there again and found the Moras at work. He asked if they had heard anyone drive up to the cabin while he was gone. Feliciano shook his head and said, "We don' know about that, Señor . . . we jus' cutting a little wood *aquí*, like we always do."

Sedgewick went back down and got his jeep and rode into Pecos, intending to see Peter Griego but stopping instead at Jaramillo's place. Daniel knew the valley. He told Sedgewick about the Moras, and concluded, "Either learn to get along with them or give up the cabin."

Sedgewick went back to the ridge and told the Moras that it was all right for them to cut wood on his property once in a while.

"Well, that make sense, 'cause this is where we always

coming to cut wood when we need her," old Feliciano said. He didn't thank Sedgewick, but merely nodded his head, as if the whole affair had been perfectly clear to him from the start.

The second incident came the following April, when the little stream that ran through the Mora property dried up. They began coming down to his place with buckets, three and four times a day. The stream wouldn't flow again until the dry season was over. Sedgewick finally asked around town about the price of putting in a shallow well and a hand pump beside their *jacales*, and this was accomplished.

Something good came out of this, though. For the Moras, he became a kind of hero . . . a *rico*, or rich man, *muy hombre* . . . that is, a kind of unofficial Anglo *patrón*. Their *patrón*. The Moras had never had a *patrón*. And, after all, wasn't it a civilized and Christian thing for the rich to share their wealth with the poor? To be fair, there was no one in the entire Pecos Valley, and maybe all the rest of New Mexico, poorer than the Moras.

They still came to visit every now and again. Ostensibly for social reasons, but actually to put the bite on Sedgewick for small sums, like fifty cents or a dollar, "till the welfare come, on the end of the month." They also cadged his pipe tobacco for their hand-rolled cigarettes.

Sedgewick found a use for the Moras. From time to time he left the valley, for a week or so . . . to get away from the grinding peacefulness and terrific silence he had imagined he needed so sorely. The high alpine meadows were lovely to the eye, but, like any steady diet, they had a tendency to go flat after a while. So he would go off to Santa Fe, or Albuquerque, or even to Denver, to book a motel room, drink too much, go to movies or the theater, or perhaps a liaison with a woman.

Before leaving, he would stop in at the Moras' and leave five dollars or so with Feliciano and ask him to keep an eye on his cabin. This was the kind of job the old man could take to heart. He and Tomas, sharing one rifle between them—an old Savage Model 99 lever-action—watched Sedgewick's place with such dedication and overt hostility that no one dared go near it. Not even the town's wild teen-agers, who were not above ripping off an unoccupied house for the hell of it. The Moras simply shot first and, with their crippled command of English, asked questions afterward.

So in a way it might be said that Sedgewick and the Moras were friends, although it was something of a symbiotic relationship.

THAT AFTERNOON SEDGEWICK walked up to the Moras' place to tell them that he was joining some other men to hunt a dangerous mountain lion and would they please watch his cabin for a day or so.

But before he could get around to telling them, he had to first watch Feliciano and old Ruperto go at each other in a drunken fistfight that had got started for some confused and wine-soaked reason.

They were outside. Feliciano was screeching curses in Spanish. He picked up Ruperto's guitar and smashed it into kindling against the side of the ancient pickup truck parked in the yard.

Ruperto gave a croaking *"Cabrón-cacado!"* and lunged. Both men squared away, and between occasional roundhouse swings made vague boxing motions.

Both were drunk. Despite the below-freezing weather and the snow on the ground, they had on only undershirts and unbelievably filthy striped cotton pajama trousers.

Both also wore brand-new Schmidt-Helstedt ski boots, which Feliciano had stolen a few days earlier down in the village, from an out-of-state Volkswagen whose doors had been left unlocked. Feliciano's were sky blue, and Ruperto's cherry red. They were constructed of heavy, insulated plastic, with oversize quick-buckling straps, the most expensive kind of boots imaginable, the end product of years of design . . . ideal for lightning-fast slaloming down steep slopes, but perhaps not the best gear for prizefighting in the snow. The two old men boxed with Frankenstein footwork, staggering around stiff-leggedly.

Eventually both fell down, without ever really connecting. Then they discovered that they couldn't get up. Rabbit-faced Tomas, standing in the open doorway of his *jacal*, laughing insanely, urged them on in Spanish argot. This went on for another minute, and finally they gave in to exhaustion, the cold weather, and the perversity of these *estúpidos Anglo-zapatos* that refused to bend at the ankle.

Sedgewick helped them up and told Feliciano about the hunt for *el tigre*.

Feliciano thought this over, and then told Sedgewick that old Ruperto could guard both his and the Mora properties, because that kind of a hunt didn't come along too often, and he and Tomas wanted to get in on it too.

SEVEN

"... you're wrong when you tell me I act used up or dead inside. I was. Yes, I wouldn't deny that. But not now."

—JOHN SEDGEWICK, *in conversation*

OF COURSE THE Moras thought Sedgewick quite mad, as well as an enigma. So did the rest of the valley. They considered him a mystery in the Crippled Horse, too, where he sometimes did some drinking.

Dan Jaramillo knew a little of his past. Very probably because Daniel was the only one in the village—except for Karen, who was to come later—who could comprehend what Sedgewick had to tell about himself.

Except for the career in music, it was a common enough story these days. At the age of fifty, Sedgewick had burned out. In doing so, he exhibited a lot of irrational behavior, which his wife ascribed, incorrectly, to male menopause. Why else would a man abruptly turn his back on everything he had spent a lifetime building?

"In Academialand did Kubla Khan a stately pleasure dome

decree," he had once written. At the height of his powers—or career. The two were more or less synonymous.

"It depends on what you want out of life," he had once told a wife of his. This wife was the last one he had. There had been two others. All of them had been fine wives, and each in her own way was beautiful and intelligent and spirited, and in time he had left the first, and then the second, and finally the third. The years he spent with each varied, but the three of them added up to twenty-one years of marriage. Some of these years had been very good indeed, and it had been pleasant to share them with one wife or another. He had two daughters, but they were grown now and off on their own.

The last wife he had said this to had replied by asking, "But do you know what *you* want out of life?"

"No, I don't," he said.

"Then I'd say you had a problem," she told him, and of course she was right. That was a quality of hers, being right more often than not. She was a decent woman and she loved him, and she'd greatly enjoyed the years they'd had, and now he was getting ready to leave her too, and she didn't like that at all.

"What more do you want than what you already have?" she asked.

He said he didn't know.

At this time they were living in an expensive town house they owned near the campus of a large university in the East. He had taught there for fourteen years, and he made a good salary. During the summers, they took vacations to New Mexico, the Maritime Provinces, and Yugoslavia. It was on one of the trips to New Mexico that he had discovered Pecos.

She said, "You've got tenure, and recognition. You can get two thousand for a recital."

"In Pocatello, Idaho," he said.

"So what if you can't command the fees that Gould or Browning or Van Cliburn get," she argued. "You never had that kind of egotistical competitiveness anyway. You'll end up dean of the school of music by doing nothing more than hanging in tight. You're still young, and you're healthy. You've got four honorary doctorates. If you don't mind my saying so, I don't know what in hell you're so miserable about."

"I don't know either," he said.

"If only you didn't drink so much," she said bitterly. "That's really the worst habit you have."

And he thought: The only one . . . now.

It had taken him a long time to get the woman problem under control. In that respect Academialand was also the land of the lotus-eater. That was where so many young women came to find themselves. With a little help. To him, as to most men, they all seemed lovely and on the gad.

Music is an expressive art. Young women devoted to it frequently have an emotional temperament not unlike a Mills grenade, which is an explosive device that is perfectly safe to handle and that will lie dormant for years until the detonating pin is triggered. Such young women also frequently come equipped with a sexual psyche designed to respond to a sensitive, understanding, older man. So it had been the most natural thing in the world, and that was how he had lost the first two wives. He had been astonished to learn how possessive they were about him. He was also surprised to learn the degree of unforgivingness of which they were capable. This of course was naiveté on his part. He was intelligent and he had an impressive musical talent, and he had known a lot of women, but he was still naive, and by the time he got things figured out he had gone through a couple of expensive divorces.

With the last wife he had behaved properly. But even this wasn't enough, and after twelve years he—and she too, though she couldn't admit it—sensed that they had no real future together.

That was when he turned his back on Academialand. Actually, he turned his back on everything.

THE FRENCH WORD *cafard* fitted Sedgewick in those last months back East. Meaning a cynical disenchantment and weariness with the world. A deadly ennui.

All the Everests he would ever conquer had already been attained. They were not mediocre summits by any ordinary measure—but neither were they Olympian. As pecking orders went, he was a long way from the lowest echelons. Still, he would never walk with the mighty. As a pianist and organist, he was very good. Perhaps fantastically good. But being fantastically good is a long step from being great. Sedgewick knew this. He embraced the knowledge with as much dignity and grace as any top-notch second-rater could be expected to muster.

As an academician he ranked better. Had written a book on J. S. Bach, and one on that Lambaréné crank, Schweitzer. Had gotten his Fulbright. Was elected a Fellow of the Suisse Académie des Arts. Taught his students well—far better than most of them deserved. Chaired Tanglewood seminars, wore expensive tweeds and London-made shoes. And drank more.

In those last days he thought a great deal about vanity and ego, and believed that he had too much of each. How else to explain this gnawing discontent?

Musically, he was a romantic traditionalist. His tastes began with Palestrina, plainsong, and Gregorian chant, and went as far as the expressionism of Orff, to embrace partially, but not completely, Stravinsky. It was also true—and he knew this—that on a good day, when his hands and his head and emotions were all working together, he could execute a Liszt sonata with a tender command that only a few other pianists in the country could equal. This didn't happen often, but when it did he knew it. So did the critics.

There is another word that fitted Sedgewick, a Malaysian one—*amok*. The common meaning that has passed into contemporary language denotes a ferocious attack. But the older sense of the word is richer. In nineteenth-century Asia it used to signify a kind of pointless madness . . . a self-destructive and violent departure from normal existence. Back then, the rainy season, or monsoon, was blamed. Months of humidity and heat were said to affect the mind in a mysterious way—which may also explain why the American Pacific Northwest has such a high suicide rate. In practice, an *amok*er could go for years without detection, carrying out the small celebrations and agonies of his life: work, marriage, children, famine, feast. Until on a particular day, or night, a sudden inundation of disenchantment and disgust over living swept him away. In which case he sometimes strode through the lanes of his village, working methodically with machete or serpentine kris, leaving a bloody swath behind, until such time as his neighbors and friends banded together to put him out of his misery, with gun, spear, or knife.

So, then—Sedgewick. To have it all. Too civilized, though, to take in hand a weapon he might turn against others . . . or himself.

He simply dropped out of sight. Abandoned it all. Packed his bags and walked away.

By then he was living alone in a rented apartment. Before he left he had a brief fling with a student. There was no reason not to since in his mind he was no longer married and hence was free of the exigencies of monogamy. Also, as he admitted to himself, he wanted to see if that sort of thing still held the same interest it once did.

She was a girl of French-Lebanese descent. Barely nineteen, and almost five foot eleven. A dark Levantine beauty, with a body and a face out of *Playboy*, and a musical talent that wouldn't have filled a thimble. Her right hand was marvelous—it had a bravura velocity, and in the upper registers she could make the notes sound like sharply snapped shards of crystal—but the noises her left hand made were like dumplings being dropped into boiling water.

She was earnest and sweet and not very bright, and was

capable of antic sexual excesses. She played Chopin like Lawrence Welk, but in bed was prestidigitationally adroit. A dark, silky peach fuzz went from the small of her back downward, to disappear into Browning's peach left. Her thighs and arms were just as downy. She had a twenty-three-inch waist, and her loins smelled of a clean and salty ocean. At the motel where they spent a week, other men practically passed out when she ambled out to the pool in a bikini.

As his student she had been demure. This was not an act. She had made a recent vow to herself to abandon earthly pleasures and work at developing her musical abilities. Sedgewick learned that from the age of fifteen to eighteen, at the various European schools she had attended, she had had eighty-six (her count) LSD trips, as well as some sexual adventures that made his own history look ridiculous.

In bed her body was hot and sweaty. She seemed to be constantly running a high fever. To him, at fifty, she seemed not capable of multiple orgasms, but of one ongoing, endless, dizzy climax. She said she loved him, and went out of her way to prove it. At their bedside table were rum, Coke, ice, limes, and marijuana. In the morning he woke with puffed eyelids and a taste in his mouth of bitter artichoke.

He saw very clearly that she—or someone more or less like her—would always be in his life if he kept on. The next would look different, have a different name, and might even play the piano better, but she would be the same. In Academialand, her type was ubiquitous.

Lying in his arms, she spoke of the life they would have together. She promised that she would make a point of always giving him credit for all that he was going to do for her —his teaching, his mastery of technique. Together they would gain fame.

That Saturday he drove her back to the campus. A week later he was in Pecos.

IF SEDGEWICK WAS a mystery to the people of the village, perhaps Karen Jaramillo was too.

Certain things were known, or surmised, about her beside the fact that she was the wife of the high-school science teacher—a local fellow, at that—who was liked by almost everyone.

It was felt, somehow, that she did not fit. This was not just because she was a stunningly pretty young woman with a thick mane of hair the color of honey. Nor was it because she stood half a foot taller than most of the Spanish housewives in the village, or wore immoderately—in fact, alarmingly—snug jeans, faded a pale blue in the seat, along with suede Wellingtons and cheap cotton shirts . . . in some way such junky clothing looked fine on her, fitted right, and in them she seemed so easygoing and free, stepping out with that long-legged pace on the few concrete sidewalks the town had, not a man's stride, but not a woman's either.

There was nothing anyone could put a finger on, yet she didn't seem to belong. Seemed self-contained, too independent, somehow, and entirely at ease with her femininity. No wonder half the women in town loathed her. As well they should.

Some of the men in Pecos hated her too, for different reasons. She was, quite simply, a woman most men coveted—and could not get.

When feelings like that exist, those who are observers—men and women both—can only watch and wait. Knowing full well that in the long run patience invariably wins. In a small town, privacy is a premium commodity.

Still, not everybody was interested when she began going to the cabin. Peter Griego, the state cop, for example. In fact, he may not have known anything at all. Peter's freckled, hostile expression somehow did not make him the man an avid gossip would spill rumors to. Peter, in his glacial way, was out for crime and real malfeasance. The trivial moral wrong-

doings of his neighbors he would have deemed beneath his
attention.

And rightly so. Because if this had been his natural bent—
rooting out adulterers, whores, cheats, and hypocrites—he
would have been able to find enough in the township of
Pecos to keep him occupied till Armageddon Day.

Nothing outright was ever said about her trips to the
cabin. Though of course people wondered. There were oblique inferences and a sly joke or two, but that was all. No
definite proof existed.

But as it turned out, it was that old villain, Feliciano Mora—
paid by Sedgewick himself to act as guardian watchdog—
who tumbled.

It was Feliciano, with his retarded and spirochete-riddled
brain, who was the one to tell.

THAT STAND OF timber up on the slope. The one that rose behind Sedgewick's cabin. It was a pretty enough place.

Dark and shadowed for the most part, but lit here and
there by the sun that struck through the tall, densely packed
pines, spaced sometimes no more than yards apart. Mostly it
was hidden and shadowed except for little clearings . . . these
were the places that got the sun, and here the grass grew in
a bright wild green, packed with buttercups and sweet clover
and lupine that gave off a heady, clean smell.

In the shadowy places there was a smell of dampness and a
slow decay from growths of dull green and brown lichen that
festered along the thick-barked pines. Here, in the dark gloom,
the ground was mossy and springy to the foot and always
damp, and in the darkest places of all fruitings of mushroom
and toadstool blossomed through all the summer.

It was here that she and Sedgewick came to walk on
several occasions. Not often—surely no more than two or
three times that entire lost summer—and not necessarily for

any illicit purpose, for they had the cabin below for that. Perhaps, in a way, they even walked together along the wooded slopes for the purpose of escaping or avoiding—or maybe delaying—the cabin and the purpose to which they put it. As if choosing of their own volition to hold off that moment in time when they would at last abandon their casual pretense of a stroll. Perhaps to regard each other silently before turning at last to retrace their route back down the meandering trail to the cabin.

Whatever. On these walks they talked little. As if sensitive to the fact that their merely being together was statement enough.

Sometimes strolling hand in hand but just as often some small, short distance apart. Keeping a mutual pace, yet alone. Very likely their minds were full of thoughts. Idle contemplations. There are places in the mind no outsider knows. What better time for private introspection than in the company of a beloved friend?

Perhaps, too, they each experienced the rise and swell of other profound feelings. Not unlikely, since they were that way together.

In these moments there might have been more working than simple lust. They were together, yet were isolated and doomed and lost forever to each other.

To be fair, it was they who came to old Feliciano. Not he to them.

He did not seek them out.

On THIS SUNNY, late-summer midday he was hidden alone up on the slopes, among the trees.

He sat on the ground with his back propped against a large pine. His mind was blank . . . or rather filled with the pleasant emptiness that comes to a man when he has set out with sullen determination to get stone-assed drunk.

This much Feliciano had already accomplished. Afterward he would get drunker still, to the point where he could not walk and would lie there, slumped against the pine, to sleep noisily until the coolness of dusk finally roused him.

Sitting there against the tree, he looked like a Rip Van Winkle. Was dressed in ragged and filthy jeans, a work jacket, an old blue wool sweater—even though it was summer—and a decrepit and moldering Stetson. His gaunt face stubbled by a three-week-old growth of gray bristle. Dirt and soot imbedded—almost grown—into the deep folds of flesh that ran down his cheeks on either side of his mouth. An emaciated, stinking scarecrow. Scarcely breathing.

His expression and slumped posture were somehow reminiscent of an orang-Utan. Those massive, dour, brooding Sumatran anthropoids . . . that, in a kind of self-despair at never having made it any distance up the evolutionary ladder, had turned back and retreated deeper into their tropical forests. Where they were sometimes found, in exactly the same pose, by old-time hunters, defeated and pitiable in their lack of comprehension or reason—seated with their backs to a great mahogany or teak—simply waiting for the hunter's bullet that would put an end to their fearfully stultified existence. French colonists named the big apes the "old men of the woods," because they seemed so ancient and lost and prepared for death, even at birth, that there was something depressing and frightening about them. Old Mora had something of these same qualities as he sat there, working steadily at the gallon of red wine he had gotten down at the Crippled Horse earlier that day.

He had climbed over Sedgewick's fence and gone into the stand of timber to be alone because he wanted the wine to himself, without sharing it with his son, Tomas, or his brother, Ruperto.

He sat there now, alone, already too drunk to stand, talking to himself without speaking aloud, his lips moving, sometimes in an angry or bitter smile, or even pressed together in an impotent and unreasoning fury. His lips had an odd color against the pale gray of his face. They were a curious bluish-red as if somehow engorged with blood. Often he would unconsciously push them out in a sulky pout, or lick at them, as though he had some need to keep them wet.

Sitting now, he heard a sound.

Some moments passed before he realized that it was a woman's low and pleasant laugh.

PRESENTLY HE SAW them—a man and a woman.

Less than fifty feet away, as they stepped out of a shadowed place in the woods. They approached closer, to a patch of sunlit glade. An illuminated field, or miniature arena of bright green and yellow. No more than a dozen feet across.

The woman in faded Levi's and half-boots. Bits of chaff and thistle clinging to her calves. A light blue checkered shirt. Open at the throat, and around that throat a red kerchief, knotted. The long hair fastened with rubber bands, in twin ponytails, one to each side of her skull, behind each ear.

She stopped there, smiled. Stood and stared for a moment up into the eyes of the companion with her, and Feliciano knew them both.

He was, in a sense, trapped. Though it would be fair to add that he was not unwillingly trapped. Since there was nothing else to do, the old man slumped comfortably back against the trunk of the big pine and watched.

He had fine vision. His teeth were gone, a mess of rotted and septic, broken snags. The bone and marrow of the very skeleton that supported his skinny frame had long since been honeycombed by the organisms that had made of him a home. His breathing was wheezy, and a chronic catarrhal discharge further inflamed a nose congested by decades of wine. But he could see!

Feliciano's eyes were yellowed and bloodshot, the lids rimmed by a dried crust of rheumy mucus which in his leisure moments he would pick at with filthy fingernails. But he could see with those eyes, could spot a deer standing quietly in scrub oak hundreds of yards off—could identify a hawk from an eagle or vulture as it soared a good quarter of a mile above him.

In the bright sunlight of the glade they could not see him. Although he was less than ten paces off, hidden in the pines.

Above the glade, a flight of tiny midges hung. A thin, translucent, humming cloud. Off in the dark woods, jays called angrily back and forth to each other. But beyond this there was silence.

Nor did the man and woman in the clearing speak. Except by look and gesture. Her serious smile and expression. Eyelids crinkling as she squinted in the brilliance. His own expression friendly too. They did not touch.

And so old Mora watched and saw their moment come. The cabin forgotten now. The stroll abandoned in favor of an unvoiced but mutually agreeable awareness that this—here and now—was as good a place as any. Who knows, perhaps a better place . . . perhaps a truly perfect place. Such a pleasant recognition! Although now there was a certain shyness to their mood. Their movements—even their very postures—a shade studied, a touch abashedly alert. As if each had been startled, or even shocked—but not unpleasantly so—by the extemporaneous quality of this sudden need to couple in a sunlit glade.

Such moments may have come again to them that summer. If they did, they did not happen here. Not in this glade or part of the forest anyway. At least not to the old man's knowledge. Feliciano could testify to that. He was to spend a lot of time thereafter in this wild and overgrown area, hoping to see again what he was to see now. He practically haunted these piny slopes in future weeks. A veritable arboreal habitué. A woodsy spook. Without success.

THE MAN STEPPED up to her. Stood straight and tall. They embraced and kissed then, tenderly, still with that sober friendliness—with no great heat or passion but with a studied gentleness, like two old friends bent on giving comfort.

Her face and mouth raised to his. Eyes shut now, against the sun, the band-bound ponytails falling back over her shoulders. Her hand reached to touch his thighs. The gesture deliberate, almost sedate. She rested quietly against him. Then both were busy, calmly, rather lazily, as though they had all the time in the world and more, with zippers, buttons, clasps, assisting each other in this intimate shucking off of all that separated them. Then each going momentarily to his or her own purpose . . . standing one-legged to step-and-hop out of jeans, nylon briefs, socks, boots, all of it. For a second she half turned from him to strip her shirt sleeves free of her wrists, her breasts swinging free now as she turned back to him, rounded and white in the sunlight, the stiffened nipples betraying her easy smile and calm movements. Then finally clear of the last of their clothing they stepped a pace or two away from each other, still in the sunshine, the thick grass nearly halfway to their knees. Then joined again. Hand in hand. Kissed once more, so tenderly and reachingly. His hand moved to grasp and cup a breast. Then lower, both hands now, to touch the slender waist—mere tips of fingers—gliding down over flank and hip and buttock, thence to explore the cool-shadowed inside of a thigh, one finger probing and sinking into secret wet. She did not withdraw. Quite the contrary. Stood with legs slightly parted, the strong muscles at the small of her back tensed as she arched herself to this exploration, and then with both hands she herself reached to hold his member, as though one hand alone was insufficient to grasp and support its size and weight—she sank to her knees and still holding him thus began a lazy homage, her head flung back. Eyes still closed against the blinding light. Such a slow and indolent exploration with lips and tongue, but with a certain need now, and a quickening too, at last . . . her breathing deeper, almost labored, so that her ribs showed in curved white slatted ridges that appeared and then disappeared, and then reappeared, with each deep breath . . . and so, lost to her own needs as well as his, she finally tolerated and accepted him in her mouth, still holding him, her head moving slowly above her doubled grasp. And now—still— there was that certain splendid, sleepy indolence to her as she finally disengaged herself to rise. She led—or was led—another pace away from their heaped clothing, to where the grass rose higher still, there to lie, finally, in the bright heat, sinking back to face him, propped on elbows, legs casually flung apart. She smiled up at him, and he at her. He stood above her. Massive-shouldered, with a broad, heavy chest that was matted with hair. A slight paunch. Thick pelt of hair spreading downward. His legs and buttocks heavily muscled. He knelt to worship her as she had him, and for all his bull-like strength and size he too was oddly graceful—almost feline —in his attentiveness. In time he stretched himself atop her, balanced on knees and elbow, while with his free hand he held himself to probe and find entry . . . and finally did, with a single thrust that brought a cry from her, a muted bleat. Her knees went high to give him angle, and so they took and gave in searching rhythm.

Except for their low murmurs, the glade, it seemed, grew unnaturally still. Even the jays in the woods seemed to fall silent now. The faint humming of the cloud of midges above them died away . . . as if all the woods and everything alive in them were listening to the sound of her voice, so sweet and breathless and husky now, urging him on—such a loving entreaty—as she abased and opened herself to this splendrous moment—a continuous and low-pitched monologue flowing from her, broken now and again by fearsome gasps and obscenities—a tumultuous issuance of lewdness, uninvited, unasked-for . . . but there it was. The words rising steadily in the hot and quiet summer air.

When they were done with it they rested in silence, lying back in the grass. Presently, the man sat up, reached for his shirt, got out his pipe, filled it, and struck a match. She sat up too and looked around, as though conscious, really for the first time in a long time, of where she was and what they had been up to.

They smiled again at each other. Were relaxed and free with their bodies. The woman's long supple back was flecked with bits of grass and clover, marked red in places where it had pressed against twigs and rubble. She brushed at her shoulders, then stood . . . gave a lazy stretch . . . stroked her hair back from her shoulders. Then twisted sharply at the waist to pick loose fragments of chaff from her flank—twisted still more, to wipe idly at more green adhering damply to hip and buttock. Briskly brushed her bottom. Then reached to scratch casually at some tickle or itch along the inside of one thigh where a shiny slick ran almost to her knee.

Presently, they began dressing. And now perhaps there was more shyness to their activity. They turned half from each other as they tended to the business of clothing. As if each understood that while there may be endless anticipation in watching your beloved shed garments there is virtually none at all in seeing someone get back into them . . . to watch her labor, as it were, her way back into nylon briefs—and what a pretty pastel green they were (it was a Wednesday)—hauling them up over knee and thigh. Tugging at the elastic waistband—with an awkward, rotary hip-flip—setting them to where they ought to be.

And, finally dressed, but still without words, they kissed again, then regarded each other with affectionate knowingness. Both party to the private knowledge that they—although now poised and collected—could full well be a different way, and left.

At the edge of the glade she waited a moment while he struck another match to his pipe. When the pipe was going they walked off into the forest and down the winding trail, descending the slope, and were soon lost to sight. Back down

to the cabin and the rest of the world. Still hand in hand, like
two children. Talking quietly now. Leaving the glade, and the
jays, now calling back and forth again.

Without ever knowing that all they had done and felt together had been watched with rapt attention by Feliciano
Mora.

Who now, still slumped against the tree trunk, utterly paralyzed by muscatel and the rending vision of what he had
seen . . . this *tableau à deux*, so naturalistically choreographed
and divinely executed—well, it was simply too much! Without
knowing it, he had experienced, once and for all, the quintes-
sence of what every voyeur *manqué* is after. There is nothing,
really, in the actual presentation of such a spectacle. But there
is a great deal in vicariously participating in love and intimacy
with the amused and ironic detachment of an undetected god.
That is when the voyeur can snicker, smirk, or gulp with
envy, to his heart's content!

How to measure what he saw? Were these star-crossed two
better paired than others? In technique, or style, or the simple
burning up—expenditure—of energy and calorific body fuel,
was this amorous duo livelier than other men and women?

None of this was important. What counts is the measure—or
degree—of salacious esteem to be found in the eye of the be-
holder.

Feliciano Mora had never in all his years seen a woman as
lovely as Karen Jaramillo.

He had never seen a beautiful woman naked and free in the
sunshine.

In fact, he had never seen any woman naked.

And most certainly he had never experienced for himself
how a woman in the fullness of her emotions will play at love,
may indulge in all the variations of the game, with a wanton
freeness, yet with that reserved shyness, too, that is almost
good-humored . . . as if she privately knows but tacitly re-

frains from admitting that the joke is half on her companion, that she is in fact, by addressing herself to the game with perseverance, getting as much as she gives, or even—who knows—more.

Old Mora sat under the pine for the rest of that afternoon, working at his gallon of wine. Dozing a bit. Waking, to hand-roll a cigarette, drinking some more, dozing again. And all the while, perhaps even in his dreams—and dream he did that afternoon!—he considered what he had witnessed.

Toward evening, when he finally staggered up the slope toward the *jacales* he called home, still fearfully drunk, he was a different man.

His entire conception of life had been changed by that afternoon.

Feliciano was simplistic. Within the limited confines of his consciousness, sex—the sexual act—was an obscenity, a filthy abomination. For him, there was nothing at all below the waist except ways to defecate, urinate, and have intercourse. That was why all *that* had to be kept hidden. The act of love, for him, ranked on a par with voiding one's bowels.

And yet his mind was obsessed with it. Even now, in his late fifties. Dying already of the disease that has eaten away a hollow in the top of his cranium. He had only one term for sexual intimacy. He called it *cópula*.

As a young man the *cópula* part was always with him. Yet his history was unbelievably stultified. The younger Feliciano had, in the rural way of things, mounted sheep, not bad, and once a cow in estrus, and once too, if the fact must be known, a dog, a big and gentle water spaniel bitch. He had masturbated a lot when the mood took him, which was often, sometimes in places like the back of a grocery store or in the men's room of a bar, or in his truck. As a younger man he was vacuous and stupid, dull-eyed and nearly mute, with sullen wet lips that either pouted or broke into a lopsided grin that was half obsequious, half moronic. In 1940 he had met in Taos the girl from Pagosa Springs who infected him. She was stupid too, a fat, heavy-breasted slut. They spent a weekend drinking wine and bourbon in a motel and never saw each other again. He had the bad luck to catch her in the primary stage, when the walls of her vagina were spotted with contagious lesions, so that in effect he was plunging his penis into a petri dish of mortal infection. But, of course, this never occurred to him, then or later. The holes that developed around his glans corona—a quarter inch in diameter and equally deep—he cured by himself with mercurochrome. He believed they were *las ronchas*—hives.

The closest he had ever come to normal sex was with Alma, the daughter who died in the mental hospital. She was as simple-minded as he, and ultimately as syphilitic, but some kind of closeness must have existed between them. In the dark of the night he would go to her pallet, there in the *jacal*, with Eduvigen, his whiskery, four-hundred-pound spouse, snoring away on the far side of the single room, filling up most of the nuptial bed he was supposed to be sharing. He did it to Alma as he had done it to Eduvigen, her mother, as a form of excretion, a voiding of obnoxious matter. In a way that was too bad, because if it had to be done at all Feliciano ought to have enjoyed it more. At fourteen, Alma had the facial expression of an imbecile and the body of a Miss Universe . . . had a shape, in fact (if one could have scraped or exfoliated the layers of dirt away) that was as good as, or better, than Karen Jaramillo's. Not that Feliciano ever saw her beauty, if it could be called that. One night when drunk he simply went to her and took her, and the child did not object.

What he loved best about his wife was her bulk. It made a pillow and a source of warmth that his unwashed, skinny frame cherished. In over thirty-five years of married life they had never kissed. Too, with Eduvigen, the excretory-sex thing was magnified. She really stank fearfully. Once, wildly smashed on Tokay and with a hysterical need to make some sort of contact with another body, he had attempted to take her anally, but had failed . . . and become lost in an arena of flesh, and, in the mere seeking of an orifice buried between mountains and walls of suety avoirdupois, had utterly lost

track of what he was after, and so had eventually found his
fisted pleasure somewhere in the vicinity of Eduvigen's left
kidney.

In a way, then, Feliciano, with all his ghastly taboos, was
a hideous prude. There was a lot about life that he could not
even begin to imagine. And much of what he was able to
fantasy he shut away, putting on blinders, so to speak. In this
light it is worth noting again that he had never in his life
seen a naked woman, let alone a beautiful one.

He had, when shopping in town at places like Sandoval's
Groceries, stopped once or twice at the newsstand, there to
flip through certain publications. Had withdrawn with something akin to dismay at what he saw. Was really quite shocked!
Young women in full-page glossy photographs, leaning back
to present their horrible private parts to the camera lens.
Crenelated, hirsute lips, folds and petals of wet flesh, plump,
hairy mounds. Right there, in front of him. A little fuzzy in
detail—thank God!—but still, Feliciano had never seen that
part of a woman, even in a photograph. The vague and inter-
mittent entries he had made into Eduvigen had been done
with his eyes squinched tightly shut, as if to blot out where
he was and what he was engaged in. Eduvigen was in no
small manner of speaking vastly unlike the sleek creatures in
these pictures. After glancing at them for a minute Feliciano
would roughly set the magazine back on the rack with a
simple "*Cacada*," which means "feces," and a particularly
offensive and liquid variety at that. Again, an excretory comparison.

And excretory it would have stayed, except for that afternoon in the glade. Despite his slavering condemnation of the
events viewed, the act consummated.

A classic ambivalence took shape in his mind. The old rip
was hypnotically attracted by what had taken place, and at the
same time categorically repelled. Better men than Feliciano—
sound, decent, intelligent men—have gone mad trying to work
themselves out of ambivalences, or double-binds.

What counts is what happened not in the glade but in

Feliciano's addled brain, wracked now by small cerebral detonations.

What more can be said of Karen Jaramillo beyond that she is beautiful? Many women are that. What is notable about her? Her back in that dappled sunlight was heavily freckled across the upper parts of her shoulders, and blemished with flecks of grass and chaff—but the skin itself was smooth and clear. When she sat up in the grass before Feliciano's boggled gaze she very likely was a vision of femininity, the back and shoulders set straight, the skin flushed pink between the wings of her shoulder blades . . . and then the rib cage, the ribs ridged through the clear white skin, down to a marvelously slender waist, really nothing at all, so delicate that it was remarkable that it could hold up the rest of her . . . down to a rounded and full flow of hip and haunch—such a wealth of femininity—as she knelt or sat upon folded legs. Such a flow of woman's cool, white flesh Feliciano had never seen. And when she stood and turned, there was that much more to please—or paralyze—the eye. Her damp and hairy hidden sex.

Had Feliciano been able to rustle up a little appropriate background music that sunlit glade would have echoed to glissandoing harps and sonorous viols: nothing less than the best of Schubert or Liszt.

Feliciano had not only never seen female beauty, he had never actually been in the presence of anything that could be called lovely. He had managed to eke out more than half a century's existence immersed in the ambience of all that was ugly and intrinsically ignorant.

So Karen Jaramillo had been more than merely a vision. For old Mora she represented some kind of abstract symbol. It was as if a goat had been led into the Vatican to view a high mass in which the final benediction was a wild and wet act of love. Feliciano had the insight of a mussel. Yet in terms of emotion he belonged to a higher order. That afternoon left him in a terrific lather.

Brain cells are destroyed regularly. They are not replaceable, but there are so many that it usually doesn't matter. Cocaine, coffee, heroin, and tea destroy certain amounts, as do cigarettes and liquor, but on this particular afternoon Feliciano lost quite a few visually . . . could, in fact, almost hear them exploding inside his skull like small .22 bullets going off as he watched and listened. There was nothing really so unusual in seeing her, in a moment of friendly affection, stoop for a brief moment to lick her companion's still-turgid member clear of a drop of moisture . . . nothing at all, except that Feliciano was there to watch. Just as there was nothing out of the ordinary when, earlier, this tall and full-breasted girl knelt doggily in the deep grass to present her upraised, defenseless bottom to Sedgewick's oral address . . . except perhaps for a series of low contralto moos and heavy sighs that welled from her.

What a fearsome wonder all this was for Feliciano. Such a singular event! All in this glade. Perhaps Prokofiev or Shostakovich would have been more appropriate than Liszt.

Some thoughts wandered—perhaps careened, or sang, or roared—through that wine-soaked brain. It occurred to Feliciano that he himself would like to experience something like what transpired that afternoon. Despite his cretinous taboos. He would, or die in the doing.

That one particular vision remained to haunt him. Of her standing in the bright light, so tall and slender and unabashedly nude, twisting to pick at a speck of grass on her buttock, that slick of love glazing the inner flesh of one thigh. The ridges of her ribs showing on the white, delicate skin. This, and that sharper outline of shoulder blade and jutted hipbone.

She was a goddess defiled. And, in turn, she defiled.

It was only natural to Feliciano that anything so lovely had to be commensurately evil. Just as he wouldn't have questioned that Satan, before his fall, was counted as the most beautiful of angels.

There was something awesome to all this. And with the awesome and the sublime, there is always a taint of real fear.

To him Karen Jaramillo was a *bruja*. A true witch.

EIGHT

The act of exorcism involves a highly ritualized ceremony designed to drive away, or drive out, a daemon, succubus, or other evil spirit.

—W. Buennel,
Magic, Sorcery, and Black Art

Feliciano kept this knowledge to himself for more than a month, until one long and lazy Saturday afternoon at the Crippled Horse.

He was drunk again on this day, having cashed his monthly welfare check earlier at Sandoval's.

He sat alone on one of the wood benches that ran along the back wall of the barroom. Beside him was a water tumbler of Tokay, a sack of Prince Albert, and a packet of Zig-Zag papers.

Eight or ten men stood at the bar. Vicente Apodaca and some of his Brown Beret buddies were at the Fascination table. Vicente was the son of Guillermo—the one they called *el rano*—and in looks he was a younger version of his father.

No one bothered Feliciano. No one cared to. It wasn't just that he looked bad and smelled awful. The men here considered him to be *un poco loco*, which was a vague but handy definition they had for any mental deviation, from feeble-mindedness to schizophrenia.

Feliciano was also known to be reliably treacherous. More so than his son, Tomas, who with his round face and ineptly sewn lip was merely repugnant.

The fact that old man Mora had shot and killed a man from behind was considered bad form by local men—but they liked even less the fact that the man had been unarmed. Had been, for that matter, dozing in an armchair set out on the portal of his house when Feliciano got him with a single shot from the ancient Savage lever-action. What started the feud was by now obscure. What counted was that Feliciano blew the man clean out of the armchair and into the front yard. The bullet sent pieces of cotton batting through the man. A tuft of it was found sticking out of the place where his breastbone had been. This was viewed as a pretty untrustworthy way of settling a dispute with a neighbor. So people usually left Feliciano alone. And now, in the Crippled Horse, with him drunk, they wanted even less to do with him. That he was loco and mean was bad enough. But to be loco and mean and drunk all at the same time, well, nothing good was likely to come of a combination like that.

The men at the bar drank with their backs to the old man. This suited him fine. He slumped on the bench, leaning against the wall, in much the same pose as he had that afternoon by the sunlit glade. Muttered and mumbled to himself, grimacing and nodding his head. Carrying on a one-sided conversation, the topic of which was incomprehensible even to himself.

Presently Vince Apodaca and his friends finished their game of Fascination, put away the cues, and joined the other men at the bar.

In some fashion the conversation got turned to the Jara-millos. Someone made a remark about Sedgewick, the loco musician who lived alone, not far from the Jaramillos'. Nothing really derogatory. It was just Saturday-afternoon bar talk.

Vince Apodaca was a lot like his father. He had a tendency toward violence, and he wasn't very bright. He worshipped Daniel Jaramillo. He also had a fearful crush on Karen Jaramillo, though he would have died rather than admit it. Vince admired Daniel because, in addition to teaching math, biology, and physics, he was the school's wrestling coach. Under his training, Vince had, as a student not many years earlier, made it to the Southwest Regional Finals. Back then he had been a middleweight. Now, in his twenties, he was a heavyweight from too much beer and starchy food, but he was still tough . . . and he still thought the world of his coach, Jaramillo. In his mind, Jaramillo could do no wrong, and, by association, anyone involved with him was above reproach.

So, hearing the innuendo, or slur, and noting the exchange of glances it triggered among some of the patrons, Vicente took a long drink of his beer, and threw out his feelings for them to hear, like a challenge, glowering at the men along the bar: "Well, for my money, Dan Jaramillo's the finest man in this county. And Mrs. Jaramillo, she's okay too. She's one fine lady."

The other men stared at their drinks. One or two even nodded in agreement. No one wanted an argument to get started this early in the weekend. Besides, Vicente was not a good fellow to argue with.

There was a low sound of laughter in the bar then. It grew not so much in volume as in intensity. A near-silent, gasping, hysterical stutter, a delighted wheezing and snuffling. The men turned.

It was old man Mora. Back in the shadows of the long room, seated on the wall bench, one hand on each knee, as if to keep himself from doubling over, his hunched, skinny shoulders shaking with mirth.

He sat there laughing in that curious way, staring across

the expanse of planked floor at all of them, and at young
Vicente most of all, gasping, almost gagging as one burst of
wild giggles followed another—the tears streaming down his
stubbled cheeks, saliva working at the corners of his rubbery
lips, laughing as though he would die of it—a mad chortling
that exposed his rotting teeth in an apish grin, so vacuous
and silly that some of those present actually averted their eyes.

And then, still staring at Vicente, Feliciano nodded slyly,
his head bobbing up and down, and raised his right hand,
clenched into a fist. Raised it to the level of his face and then
extended the thumb rigidly . . . leaned forward and took the
stiffened thumb into his mouth to the base of the second joint,
lips funneled, and then slowly withdrew it with a sucking pop,
and the mumbled comment, "Fin' ladee!"

From behind the bar Johnny Larragoite said in Spanish,
"Old man, you better shut up, you know what's good for
you."

But this had the effect of sending Feliciano off into another
spasm. The men at the bar looked at one another. They were
troubled and embarrassed. They didn't know how to take
the old man's pantomimed gesture of condemnation. Of course,
it could have been some fantasy in his head. A kind of de-
mented putdown invented by Mora's wine-soaked brain.

But some of them understood too that the old man regarded
Sedgewick as his *patrón*. Mora did chores around the musician's place. Why would he put a slur on the man who paid
him occasional wages?

On the other hand, being around that cabin, he might know,
better than others, what was going on. The Jaramillo woman
was known to visit the place. This they knew.

The silence continued. The bar drinkers did not even look
at one another much. Nor did Vicente Apodaca challenge the
old man. He and the others turned their backs on him. Stared
down at their beers or wine or bourbon, thinking . . . and
listening to the low chortles that rose behind them, died
away, and then rose afresh.

MOST OF THE men who had volunteered for the hunt were already on their way to the rendezvous point Les Johnson had chosen—up near the headwaters of Willow Creek. From there he would break them into small groups and have them work the watershed canyons southward, back toward Pecos, moving all game ahead of them.

In the Crippled Horse Bar the last recruits for the hunt were getting ready to go out.

The Crippled Horse is owned and operated by Johnny Larragoite, which is a Basque name, not Spanish. Behind the bar, Johnny keeps a regulation-size Louisville Slugger bat. This is sometimes brought out to arbitrate lesser arguments or disturbances. On a shelf down by the beer taps there is also a U.S. Army M-1 rifle, loaded and with the safety off, and on occasion this is unlimbered too.

Johnny Larragoite inherited the bar, the bat, and the M-1 from his older brother, Willie, who in reality was as tough as Guillermo Apodaca imagined he was. Willie had killed a Sanchez from behind the bar one night, putting two rounds from the M-1 into the man, who, to tell it fairly, had come at Willie with a snakeskin-covered blackjack, some two feet long and as limber as a whip, which this Sanchez usually wore tucked into one cowboy boot. Something about not paying an overdue bar bill. So Willie had shot this man, and that meant trouble, because there were a lot of Sanchezes in the valley. They weren't especially mean, not anywhere near as mean as, say, the Moras, but, even so, the man was dead.

The Sanchezes avoided the Crippled Horse for three years thereafter except for a nephew of the slain man, young Eddie Sanchez, a skinny little kid, who seemed no threat to a man like big Willie Larragoite. Willie nonetheless kept an eye on the boy. Eddie behaved himself. Drank only beer and wine. Never got drunk or rowdy. Left the other patrons' girls alone, and bided his time. Which finally came one evening when

Willie made the mistake of turning his back on Eddie to make change at the register. Eddie Sanchez leaned across the bar and without a word sank a butcher knife into the flat space between Willie's shoulders.

Not done with it, he proceeded to pull Larragoite over the top of the bar, to the astonishment of the other customers, who had figured Eddie was a real nothing, and further harassed the dying bar-owner. Willie Larragoite scuttled crabwise across the planked floor toward the door, followed by Eddie. He made it out to the front steps before he collapsed, and by then he had thirty-three wounds in the head, neck, and torso. The coroner who examined the body later at St. Vincent's pointed out with respect and some admiration that every vital organ in Larragoite's body had been punctured at least once, and in some cases five and six times, and that it was, in his opinion, "just about the thoroughest killing" he'd ever come across.

That was how Johnny got the Crippled Horse, and a lot of people in the valley were glad to see him have it, because he had an easier disposition than Willie, and was a churchgoing man to boot. Eddie Sanchez went to the state pen, and Johnny ran the bar sensibly, abiding by the two-A.M. closing time and keeping the front door locked on Sundays, though it was legally permissible for bars in the state to open on that day.

He was a taciturn, rather somber young man with brown eyes and a powerful pair of shoulders and arms, and he made of the Crippled Horse something of a social club. It lacked fancy decor—there were two booths, the benches along one wall, a jukebox, the Fascination table—but then, the people who gathered here were pretty informal too. They drank their wine from water glasses, and took their beer straight from the can. "Escorted ladies" were welcome. The men who came here were ranchers or farmers, laborers from the sawmill, or road crews from the Forest Service. Except for the *la Raza* crowd, everybody dressed in work clothes.

Usually it was a quiet enough place, badly lit, none too

clean, musty-smelling, and with a limited selection of booze racked up on the shelves behind the bar, along with wire frames of stale cigarettes, even staler Fritos, Bar Nutz, and dusty cellophane packages of cashews. Yet, though easy, the Crippled Horse had a certain insularity and standoffish autonomy. The place had a way of somehow putting summer tourists in search of a cold beer off their mettle. The mood and ambience of its shadowy interior did not invite outside patronage, and as often as not when a couple of summer people wandered in and took a look at the row of drinkers who turned to regard their entrance, they turned and marched right out again. Those brown and grizzled faces wore expressions that ranged from unfriendly to—if old Feliciano Mora was there—almost bestial.

The *la Raza* crowd was something else.

All younger fellows, eight of them, led by the ex-wrestling champ, Vicente Apodaca. They wore, in addition to berets, black shirts and jeans, heavy black boots, and black leather jackets, often ornamented with metal stars and studs in the fashion that motorcyclists admire. They wore their hair long, and had black beards or goatees, and moustaches of a style variously attributed to Pancho Villa and Fu Manchu. They were a black crowd and were dedicated to broadcasting the fact that there is something especially fine in being of Spanish descent. They looked Chicano and sounded Chicano, and gave the impression of being prepared to kick the living balls off anyone who did not agree with them. Their credo, as Vince put it, was simple: "We ain't asking much, we just want our rights an' to do our thing. Nobody's gonna push us around, the way they been doing for years, no sir, we are done with *all* that!"

This attitude, overtly militant and magnificently paranoid, did in fact lead them into confrontations of a violent nature— so that the group usually numbered fewer than eight, because one or more members had to be temporarily discounted due to hospitalization, jail, or extended at-home bedrest. Johnny

Larragoite's one rule with them was that they could use the Crippled Horse as a meeting place so long as they came unarmed. But this was a token regulation, since he didn't have time to frisk a Beret every time he walked in, and besides, whatever gear they carried in the way of Saturday-night specials, switchblades, and brass knucks could be stashed as easily outside in the old cars and pickups they drove.

When word about the lion attack got around, Vicente sent word to his Berets to meet at the Crippled Horse. *La Raza* had to participate in this hunt. After all, the child who had been attacked was Spanish. And Anglos were known to be running the show.

Only two other Berets showed, though. One was up in the wilderness, cutting firewood. Another was in the hospital. Still another sat at home on a rubber ring, nursing a colonic fistula. He would not be in a saddle for some time. Three more were under arrest in Santa Fe for felonious assault. So Vicente and the remaining two would have to represent *la Raza*.

Counting these three, there would be almost fifteen men wandering around the mountains. The weather reports were still predicting clear and cold conditions through Monday, but now they mentioned a ten per cent chance of snow showers.

The massive cold front still in Utah had moved south a little, but was not expected to continue in this direction. You never could tell with weather, though . . . not even old Les Johnson, who knew these mountains better than anyone, took it for granted.

NINE

. . . a little after ten that Saturday I received a telephone call that reported fights breaking out in the camp. A man had been brought down in the back of a pickup by several friends. One of them told me he had been crippled for life. This same informant reported that in his opinion there was a lot of bad feeling among some of the people up there. Mrs. Jaramillo telephoned me around noon, to say that she'd heard too that there'd been trouble. I told her I would go up there and assess the situation later that day. She was pretty insistent about accompanying me. I told her I didn't think a camp of that sort was a fit place for a woman. She seemed upset. I finally agreed to let her accompany me because I didn't plan to be at the camp more than a few minutes, just long enough to get statements, and, if required, make an arrest.

—*Statement,* PETER M. GRIEGO, *New Mexico State Police*

THIS WAS HOW she knew he knew:

Later that afternoon they made love. They had not done this—come together in the daytime—in a long time. In a few hours he would join Sedgewick, and they would go up to the camp in Singer Canyon. They had drawn the heavy drapes and lain down together in their bedroom to rest awhile, and he had looked at her in that way he had. She smiled at him and said, "There really isn't much time."

"There is enough time," he said.

He always liked her naked. She stood and undressed quickly, stripping her shirt over her head, getting her hair in a tangle. Stood before him in the darkened room; then sat by him. He pulled her down and embraced her, riding between legs that were bent almost to her shoulders. Her mouth was slack, and she sighed and murmured encouragements to his rising need—nuzzled the curve of his neck and licked the faint salt of his skin. Pressed open, outstretched hands on his tensed buttocks, to guide and time his measured pleasure . . . remote and tranquil in her mind as he rode her to his final pitch and thrust. It took her with him. She tensed and strained, then thrashed and held him tight as the spasm tore at her.

A while later, she woke from a light sleep, feeling such an awful fear—an unnameable terror—as she had never known. Her body rigid with horror. She opened her eyes to the shadowy room. Turned her head toward his pillow. Then saw it. The glow of a cigarette from his side of the bed. He didn't smoke two cigarettes a year. She said, "Dan, what's wrong?"

"Nothing," he said finally. "I was thinking."

"About what?"

The tip of the cigarette glowed as he took a puff. He sighed, exhaling, then said, "I was thinking about Sedgewick."

She was silent for a moment. Finally she said, "What about him?"

There was another silence, as if he was considering this. Then, in the half light, she heard his voice: "I was thinking that he knows some things about life that I don't. And that it mightn't hurt me to try and learn about some of these things he knows about. Would you agree with that?"

She didn't speak. Was trying to control the fear. Then moved in bed, as if to settle herself more comfortably. Said, in a drowsy voice, "I don't know what you mean. Unless you're thinking of studying the piano."

The cigarette glowed again, once, and then the mattress creaked as he turned to stub it out in the ashtray on the table beside him. He must have gotten up when she was dozing to find that ashtray. The bed creaked again as he shifted on his side, facing away from her. He said presently, "No, I wasn't thinking of the piano."

THE CAMP ITSELF wasn't much.

It was set up in an open clearing off a dirt logging road that was in poor shape most of the year, spotted along its snaky length with stretches of washouts and axle-busting ruts, a four-wheel-drive road really.

Parked about the clearing were pickup trucks and jeeps and the horse trailers the men had used to get their animals up from Pecos. There was one tent for everyone, an enormous old Army wall tent, its sloping canvas sides patched and repaired. The tent belonged to the church. Father Cornelius had brought it along.

An outdoor hearth and cooking grill had been put together at one side of the clearing. The grill was made out of salvaged reinforcing bar, a welded grid sturdy enough to hold all the cooking gear they were likely to need, and there was a large pile of deadwood that some of the men had cut and dragged in earlier. It was a camp that could be set up or taken down in an hour, no fuss or fanciness to it, but adequate enough to keep all of them pretty comfortable for a week or more if need be. A small feeder stream cut past one side of the clearing, frozen now except for some deep pools. The men broke the surface of the pools with axes and dipped out whatever was needed for cooking and cleanup.

The good thing about this camp in Singer Canyon was that it was near the point of a watershed convergence. All the country generally south of it was lower, and cut into smaller canyons. There were feeder streams in all these canyons, and they joined the Pecos River. Some of these streams had names like Cow Creek, and Bull Creek, and there were Lower Colonias Creek and Upper Colonias Creek. Almost all of it was U.S. National Forest. In the summer, small-time ranchers grazed their stock in these alpine pastures, on leases they'd gotten from the government, but now it was cold and empty and desolate all through this high country, except for wild game, and the men who were here.

Les Johnson knew what he was doing. From here he could send groups of men along the ridges of the canyons that lay south. If any lion, wounded or otherwise, was around, there was a chance it might be flushed out of one of these canyons.

Most of the men had come up by Friday afternoon, with Johnson, Lewis Bowman, and the dog pack. After the camp had been set up, Johnson put them to work, sending them out in mounted groups to look for signs.

The horses the men had brought along were all right so far. There was very little snow. Actually, they would be useful up to a point, beyond which they would be no good at all. They could be ridden on the game trails that had been traveled and packed down by deer and elk, or along the high, rocky ridges bordering the canyons, where the wind kept the snow from catching hold, but down in the deep pockets and ravines where the snow had drifted they got into trouble. Then they had to be led as often as they were ridden, and either way their hooves balled with snow.

They all had thick, shaggy coats that made them look like fat ponies, and the men who rode or walked them looked bulky and somehow toylike too in their quilted goose-down parkas, gloves, and billed woolen caps. The men wore one and sometimes two pairs of long johns under their jeans. They had shoepacs of green or black rubber, double-insulated, and these were practical, although they were clumsy in the stirrups. This was the only way to dress. Even with the extra clothing the men found that they couldn't tolerate places where the wind could get at them, especially along the high razorbacks. Along these crests they turned the reins loose, letting the horses pick their own way. They buried gloved or mittened hands deep in their parka pockets. They rode this way with hunched shoulders, trying to keep their chapped, red faces turned from the wind. It was not really that cold. The temperature at the camp was in the lower twenties, but higher up the steady wind put the chill factor below zero. In their saddlebags or jacket pockets they carried pints or quarts of wine and bourbon.

Being in the sunlight helped. There was a wonderful amount of warmth to the sunlight, even with the wind. At this altitude the sunshine was different from at sea level, where the sun in winter has a thin, washed-out quality. Up here it was clear and strong and curiously intense. In the shade the men felt the cold instantly and suffered it, but when they were in the open, especially in a place where the wind couldn't harass them, the strength of the sun in the thin air was really strong, and it went through the layers of sweaters and shirt and quilted garments, so that, perspiring now, they would have to unzip the parkas to cool off.

The sky was blue in patches except to the north, where the storm front was moving through Colorado. Along the twisting dirt road leading to the camp the puddles of water that had collected in low places unthawed and got muddy if they were in the sun, but among the trees, where it was shady, the road itself was frozen hard as flint.

THEY HAD ALL COME back to camp by late afternoon. Some of the men had come in earlier than that. They were too cold and worn and bitten by the wind to do more, and by four the sun was already down in the west and the temperature was dropping.

So they returned, in twos or threes, or singly, and un-saddled their mounts, rubbing them down and walking them dry before tying them out on stake lines. There was no kind of grazing up here for the horses. Deer had already been through, and had stripped everything in sight, even the bark from the trees, standing on their hind legs to reach browse. The horses were given fresh oats and barley that had been brought up in the backs of pickups, and slabs of still-green alfalfa.

After this had been tended to and the rifles unstrapped from the heavy work saddles and stored in the big tent, the men went to the fire burning in the hearth—drifted to it with drinks of bourbon or vodka or wine in hand, there to stand or hunker down before its warmth.

It was a big fire, made with logs, not branches or chunked wood. They wanted all the warmth it could give. Someone had dragged the welded-mesh grill out of the way and thrown on massive billets, and the flames crackled and soared shoulder-high, throwing out a perimeter of hotness that reddened the weather-chapped faces of the men even more.

By then it was sunset. At this time of year there was not much dusk or twilight. Actually, the sun was already far down behind the mountains, and the sky was fast losing its light. The temperature was still in the twenties, but suddenly it seemed colder. They gathered round the fire, holding their drinks in enameled metal cups, smoking cigarettes, and talking of what they would be cooking for dinner. Each man had his own food and drink, and was expected to fend for himself.

THE NEXT MORNING—Saturday—with the sky over to the east already bright, they were no more cheerful as they waited for Les Johnson's instructions that would send them to the stations he had assigned.

Their faces showed hard and dour in the brightening light,

unshaven and dark-jowled. Most of them were taciturn, the way men are when they have slept poorly or not at all in freezing temperatures. Their expressions were brooding, melancholy, so that they had a solemn, almost dangerous air about them, a kind of sullen purposefulness to the task ahead.

Only Les Johnson and his assistant, Lewis Bowman, seemed easy in these high and lonely reaches. They and the dogs, who had been let out of their pen in the back of Bowman's truck but were still on chains, waiting. They had been watered but not fed by Lewis, so that they would be light and eager for what was ahead of them. They seemed to sense this. Were restless, uneasy, and whined from time to time as they paced back and forth until brought up short by the chains. Presently, Lewis Bowman went among them, speaking softly, "You just calm down, you hear? Goddamn. Just hold off. Just sit a bit, can't you. We'll be going out, by and by . . ." The massive Labrador, Cacique, went into paroxyms of delight, woofing noisily, almost as though the two of them—Lewis and Cacique —were carrying on a private conversation.

Like the others, Johnson and Bowman were unshaven, with the older man showing a thick stubble of white. Yet they had that difference. Seemed at home up on these freezing slopes. Could yawn and fart and pick at their noses as they went about preparing for this—their—hunt. As though too practiced or habituated about what might come to even feel excitement or curiosity about any of it.

The other men—those from in or around the village—were, in some intractable way, out of their element. Were unhappy and ill at ease here. Or perhaps their minds were merely not equipped to face this high and silent wintry loneliness.

From time to time they looked about them, as if searching for a clue to their discontent. It was dawn. It was cold. Steep, angled slopes of alpine spruce. The clear, blinding, electric blue of the brightening sky. High in the west, an eagle, silently aloft. The horses saddled nearby. Dumbly waiting, heads bowed in the frigid air . . . twin jets of steam blowing from their nostrils. Tethered to grazing ropes, hides thick with peltry winter coat. Scabbarded rifles lashed to saddles, mostly .30-30s, the polished walnut butts angled pommel-high. Canteens, their contents frozen, slung on saddles. Small carryall sacks with Campbell's soup, pork and beans, canned tamales, Vienna sausage, diced green chili, Ritz crackers, a frozen six-pack of beer. Harder liquor, extra toilet paper, Chapstick, maybe a pair of binoculars and an Instamatic camera or two to record the fabulous kills that would, or might be, made this day. Spare cartridges. There was enough ammunition at hand among these men to account for every lion in New Mexico, and probably Arizona as well. Along with sidearms—.38s mostly, or, in the case of Vicente Apodaca, the *la Raza* honcho, a massive, long-barreled .44 Magnum.

There were fourteen men so far. Les Johnson planned on putting most of them atop the ridges of one canyon where he figured the cat he was after was denned. The opening of this canyon fanned out into a little valley. If he could keep all the others busy up high, he and Lewis and the pack could come up this valley and maybe get to the lion first.

TEN

"*. . . you force a cat out of its den at this time of year without getting things set right, it's liable to make up its mind to do some real traveling.*"

—LES JOHNSON, *in conversation*

JOHNSON'S PLAN WAS easy. He had explained it earlier while they were finishing their cups of coffee and cigarettes, and now he was going over it again with them, at the edge of the canyon rimrock, speaking in a soft voice, though there was no need to, because the lion—if there was one denned in this canyon—would have been a thousand yards off:

"Old man Dalton, we were watching this feller last summer. You can't see his hideaway but it's there, way over there, just under the rim of that broken line of rock that's kinda yellowish. Just a little old cubby, but big enough for him. As I said, he's fair-sized. So he may be laid up in there. Now, if you men stay up here on the rimrock and shoo him off, he'll stay boxed. And with the dogs he'll tree. The dogs will bust him loose out of that den, and then he'll run a bit, and then he'll tree. I'll bet on that. If it was just us down in the canyon, we'd have some real tracking. But this way, if we do it right, he'll come out on the run, and he'll smell or spot those of you up here, and these dogs will be hot after his ass, and inside of five hundred yards we'll tree him good. You all understand that? I don't want any shooting unless we have to. You understand?"

Some of those he spoke to scarcely seemed to hear. Guillermo Apodaca and his burly wrestler-son, Vicente, did not even nod.

As for Feliciano and Tomas Mora, they probably did not understand half of what the lion hunter was explaining. To them, an animal—or animals—had to be killed. This was something they understood. Not because some child had been hurt, or for retribution, or any of that nonsense. For them this was a good weekend to be up high. They had some liquor and one rifle between them. Given half a chance, they might even nail a deer or two—Johnson be damned—or even an elk, and that would mean meat through the rest of the winter.

As Johnson talked, Feliciano turned and glanced at his son with a conniving and introspective look. He and Tomas were hunters. Real hunters, not *personas sin experiencia*—greenhorn *turistas*. The Moras hunted in secret and did not talk about their successes.

Tomas returned the glance and then grinned, the whiskery cleft of his upper lip parting. Without speaking, these two seemed to share a common thought, or memory. Of a hunting season two years ago—a season that was successful beyond description. In fact, it had been so good that Feliciano might even have gone out and bought a hunting license, if he had known where to go. But the old rogue had never in his entire life bought such a permit, or for that matter any other kind of license, including one to operate or own any of the broken-down pickup trucks he had driven through the mountains year after year. Feliciano was something of a free spirit.

Actually, he and Tomas had begun that particular hunt a little before opening day. Four days earlier, to be exact. When the mountains were still deserted, and before the deer had gotten gun-shy. So that by the time the official sunrise of the first, or opening, day of the season dawned, they had bagged their limit . . . and somewhat more. Fourteen all told, bucks and does. Who cared about regulations when deer were autumn-fat, and as easy to pick off as beer cans on a log? He and Tomas took turns with the old Savage 99, and between they they got all fourteen in a six-square-mile area between Windsor Canyon and the headwaters of Bull Creek. They gutted them and hung the carcasses among cool and shaded pines, where there were no blowflies that could get into the meat and lay eggs.

The does—eight of them—Feliciano and Tomas kept for their own use, but before nightfall of that first day they had sold the bucks, from a little double-spiker up to a superb twelve-pointer mulie, to one hunter or another. Feliciano might be illiterate, but he had an intuitive grasp of what it was that sent men hunting. A sportsman had to have a prize to show off to those back home. No matter if he was already too stumbling drunk or hungover on opening day to even raise his weapon, let alone sight it. That's what old man Mora was for. The twelve-pointer he sold to an Albuquerque insurance executive for three hundred cool. The smaller racks went from a hundred to a hundred and fifty. By the end of that day he and rabbit-lipped Tomas were nine hundred and fifty dollars richer. Pretty near a thousand for four days' easy work, all in folding cash, no *cheques*—not a penny of which would be reported by Feliciano or those who had paid him to the goddamned income-tax. Or *la Seguredad Social*—or that no-good welfare.

Tomas and Feliciano had stayed drunk for a good part of that winter on the money. They felt that this was their business, and that they had earned the right to a drink or two. With food stamps, the family really lived pretty high that winter. Right or wrong, the Mora men—and the same could be said of some others in the valley—had their own way of dealing with this business of life. When it came to interpreting law and order and how the game should be played, they had rules unique to them.

So did Father Cornelius, present on this cold and clear

morning, dressed in a heavy plaid jacket, Levi's, and a bright red wool cap that had the earflaps turned down. Slung from one shoulder was his .243.

Cornelius had a sensible rationale for his own poaching. He liked to point out that "God looks out for them that's got the guts to put their own shoulders to the wheel." It was a good excuse but it didn't fool anyone. His rifle might keep a score of hard-up families in the valley in venison for most of the year, but the truth was that the stocky old Franciscan was obsessed with hunting and fishing. He lived for the outdoors, and his parishioners kept him supplied with current information on the movements of elk or deer, and when trout were active. Once, when he was about to officiate at the funeral of an old-time resident, word came to him that record-size German browns were rising to a hatch all up and down the river. To the astonishment of those present, Cornelius was heard to say bitterly, "Why do they keep dying on me? Why are they always dying, or getting born, or married, or confirmed, when I got better things to do, darn it!"

So NOW THEY moved out, following Lester Johnson's scheme, and it would have worked fine, except for one thing: It was never meant to be.

He and Lewis Bowman were by now down at the lower end of the little valley with their dogs. Spaced out along the rimrock heights were the others, who would be listening for the baying of the pack, and then watching for the animal itself, when and if it moved out. If it attempted to escape via the cliffs, they were to fire their rifles in the air.

It seemed easy, and the first part of it went well. Johnson and Bowman moved up the valley. The dogs were still on chains.

Then, when they were still several hundred yards from where the den was supposed to be, and from where, for all they knew, they were already being watched by the cat, Les

Johnson stopped to catch his breath and said, "All right, Lew.
Let 'em go."

And Bowman did, unhooking the quick-release snaps so
deftly that it seemed all four of them were off and running
at once, bounding across the rocky debris of a shallow landslide at the base of a cliff, sending a spray and clatter of small
stuff flying, and the lion had obviously used this route to its
den because they had the scent at once.

Cacique threw back his big head and bugled once. A long,
resonant, anguish-filled howl that sounded across the valley—
a mournful hound's bellow that rose in the cold, unmoving,
heavy morning air and seemed to hang like a palpable, living
sound that lasted for seconds before the diminished echoes
began reverberating from the canyon's farthest walls. He
labored on, favoring his bad hip. Followed by the others. The
four of them beelining over the broken detritus of the shale-
slide toward the den.

Bowman and Johnson trotting now. Watching their footing
and at the same time trying to keep an eye on the den, or
where they thought the den must be.

Then Bowman said, "There!"

They both saw it.

No more than a flicker of movement really. A sort of in-
stantaneous impression of buff or tan—as though a camera
shutter had clicked—there, among the rocks and boulders.
Then it was gone, but they both knew it was the lion, and
that now he, or she, was out and running, and that, really,
for all practical purposes they'd gotten the animal. The dogs
knew too. Cacique's baying went hysterical.

By now the pack was out of sight, off in a high-angled mess
of spruce and aspen deadfalls, broken and rotting stuff, just
below the lip of the canyon. A bad place for dogs, and an
impossible place for men afoot let alone on horseback. It was
in here, among the impossible tangle of broken and smashed
tree trunks and limbs, overgrown with moss and lichen, that
the cat could have lost them if it'd had a mind to, or the sense.
The dogs crashed and bounded through the tangle, or some-

times one of them would leap high in the air to peer around, as if hoping to spy a quick and easy way through the mess.

And then, oddly enough, for no reason at all—as Johnson had predicted—the lion treed, choosing a tall, thin, long-dead aspen with bone-white, naked branches.

The two men, still far down the slope, saw it go snaking up the trunk for twenty-five or thirty feet, where it finally stopped, on a thick branch, to take stock of the situation.

Les Johnson stopped. He said, "She's treed." It was in fact a lioness, a small one. He said, "That big feller must have moved out."

He and Bowman started off again, at a slower pace. They had her now.

She'd stay.

She'd roost up there in that aspen all day or all week, until she dropped out of it from starvation or thirst. Or until they took the dogs away. Or until they shot her out of it.

So they took their time getting up there, making a long detour around the deadfall timber. From far above they heard yells from the men spaced along the cliffs. They were calling back and forth to announce the success of the plan. Johnson said, "We better get to her before those fellers do."

They got to the tree finally. Were directly under it, among the leaping, barking dogs. Lewis kicked them back a ways, and he and Johnson stood at the foot of the tree, staring up at the lioness. She was a fair-sized animal, about a hundred pounds. Maybe five or six years old, and well along with a stomachful of kittens. Johnson remarked on this as being un-usual. Ordinarily, a female wouldn't be admitting a male until about now, December, and with a three-months-plus gestation, most females wouldn't be littering until around April.

"She must be off in her cycle," he said, and looked up at her again. Then he squatted down and opened the plastic case that held the air rifle. He put the gun together leisurely, as if he had all the time in the world. And he did. The lioness didn't look like she was going anyplace. He locked the barrel into the receiver and then inserted a CO_2 cartridge into the chamber. "Good chance those kittens would die," he said. "Looks like she'll be dumping 'em around January."

"You think maybe that's why she didn't run far?" Bowman asked.

Johnson shook his head. "Ain't nothing'll slow a cat down if it's in a running mood—not when dogs are around."

Stretched out on the dead limb some thirty feet above, the cat glared down at them and the dogs. Foreclaws unsheathed and dug into the frozen wood, the long, thick tail twitching and lashing erratically. The heavy, tawny body and hindquarters all humped and tensed for a leap that would never come.

Once she snarled at those beneath her. Ears laid wickedly back against the skull, mouth gaped open, lips wrinkled back over the fangs. She snarled again and then half hissed, half spat, in a dangerous but impotent rage, for all the world like a common alley cat.

Johnson primed a hypodermic dart now, and loaded it into the chamber. He stepped a few paces away from the tree, just in case the cat decided to take off when it felt the dart, aimed, and fired. The air gun gave out a metallic, muted *chug*. Lewis Bowman stood ready too, a little distance away, his .30-30 cocked.

The dart hit the fleshy upper part of the right hind leg, and at that the cat let out a squall—as if a large sheet of tin had suddenly been ripped in two—turned, reached back, and got the dart, pulling it loose and chewing at it a second before letting it drop. Too late, though. The fluid contents were already in her, helped along by an explosive charge inside the miniature projectile.

Johnson lowered the air rifle and walked over to where Bowman was standing. The two of them watched the cat. "Won't be long now," Les Johnson said, and took out his pipe and filled it with tobacco.

Bowman sat down on a frozen deadfall, and presently the older man said, "You cover me, Lew, while I go down and try to move that rock out of the way. She lands on that, she might hurt herself."

Keeping an eye on the cat, he returned to the base of the tree. The lioness's head was starting to swing back and forth, as though the animal was confused or bewildered by what was happening. Johnson began kicking at the rock with his boot, but it was frozen to the ground and he could not break it loose. He kicked at it again, and was drawing his foot back for still another try when there was an earsplitting report that seemed to come from nowhere and everywhere at once. He jumped back in alarm, looking up at the tree overhead, to see what the cat was doing—drugged or not, he didn't want that critter landing on his head and shoulders—and even as he was moving he saw a fish-sized slab of wood explode from the weathered trunk, a foot or two from the lion's head.

Still scrabbling wildly toward safety, he yelled, "Lewis!" Glancing now toward his assistant, thinking Bowman was the one who had fired, but it wasn't him. Lewis was on his feet, rifle held ready, but he was staring around too, trying to pinpoint where the shot had come from.

And then there was a second report, a loud, jarring crack that filled the cold air and left their ears ringing, and this one took the cat squarely in the chest, the impact of the heavy slug carrying enough punch to rip loose the foreclaws imbedded in the limb and knock her out of the tree.

She came down with a screech, tumbling through the lower branches to bounce heavily on the ground, not quite dead now, but almost, with Les Johnson scuttling off to one side on all fours, wanting as much distance between him and the cat as possible, knowing that if there was any life left in her at all she would be deadly. The pack closed with the flailing body. Alf, in his eagerness, got too close to a convulsively kicking hind leg and was sent rolling twenty feet down the slope with half his back laid open. But by now Cacique had the cat behind the ears, by scruff of the neck, the way one might grasp and lift a kitten, except that the Lab's big jaws were locked in bone and muscle. So he had her good. Held thus, the cat, by now almost dead, went rigid, and the other dogs went in fast at the underbelly, slashing and tearing— "wooling" the carcass, as old-time lion hunters say. By then it was over. The cat was beyond feeling or fighting any more. After a while Les Johnson and Bowman came down among the dogs, cursing and kicking at them to break them loose, Lewis working with the snap-fasteners on the chains, getting the dogs away from the body and tying them to a thick branch on a nearby deadfall. In their frenzy they leaped again and again to the length of their chains.

Johnson stood for a moment, looking down at the torn body of the lioness. Patches and clumps of tawny fur taken from the hide were scattered about. The abdomen was laid open, and among the bloody mess were the savaged bodies of the half-formed kittens.

Johnson glanced over at his partner and then up the slope where the shots had come from. He said, "I'll be a son of a bitch."

And at that Vicente Apodaca and one of his *la Raza* pals, Billy Escudero, came out of the underbrush farther up the slope, and walked down to where the two men were standing. They looked at the dead lioness. Vicente grinned, and said, "Must have been eighty yards, easy." The big .44 Magnum was strapped to his waist.

Young Vince. Pecos High's wrestling hopeful, not many years earlier. A younger version of his dad, Guillermo. Not as heavy yet, but he soon would be. Round-faced and dark-jowled, with heavily muscled arms and thick, sloping shoulders. Already going to fat, but still in shape. Long-armed, and this had been an asset when he'd wrestled on the team, yes, his reach and strength made him, perhaps, the only one among all of them who was any kind of a match against Lewis Bowman, who had set down his .30-30. Vicente couldn't box, although he had once broken a fellow's jaw in a bar brawl. He had confidence in himself. The confidence gave him an air of aggressive insolence. It was obvious why he had become the natural leader of the *la Raza* gang.

He obviously didn't think much of Les Johnson or Bowman. Had heard, one way or another, the story of his father's confrontation in the church parking lot yesterday. And now he did not seem disturbed or unhappy by half that these two had something to be furious about with him, too.

Vicente seemed satisfied, perhaps even pleasured, at the prospect of what was about to take place—as if it was somehow long overdue. After less than a day of these two being in Pecos. He disliked outsiders. Had learned one thing from the militant *la Raza* approach: If you didn't step on people first, they were liable to step on you. There was no end to it.

Lewis Bowman had come a little closer, was perhaps five feet away, arms dangling at his sides. Vicente noted this and smiled pleasantly at Lewis, and said, "You better take it easy, *cabrón*." Still smiling he went on, "Pretty good shooting, *que no?*"

Lewis was beginning to breathe a little hard, and without looking away from Vicente he said to Johnson, "Les, you say the word . . ."

Johnson stepped forward and said, "Cut it out, Lew." And then to Vicente and young Escudero, who was close by, "What in the hell did you go and do a thing like that for? We *had* her!"

Vicente's smile grew blander. He shrugged. "Well, I guess I just wanted to see if I could hit her at that range."

"Well, you did," Johnson said sourly. "You also got two kittens with that shot. Also, she ain't the cat we're looking for. She didn't look or act sick, though we won't know now till she's autopsied. Also, sonny, she wasn't exactly any kind of dangerous critter, because I'd sedated her and she'd have come out of that tree by herself in another little bit. So what d'you think of that!"

"Offhand, I reckon it was just tough luck for that cat," Vicente said.

"Is that so."

"Any other cat comes around us this weekend is liable to have tough luck too," Vicente added. And with that Lewis Bowman moved closer.

In a way it was hard to figure later whose fault it was, or who started it. Lewis moved first. But it was Vicente who swung, either automatically or in what he imagined was self-defense. There was no way of knowing. He was fast enough—seemed hardly to have finished speaking his piece before he let loose with a right cross that certainly would have taken out half of Lewis's teeth.

But Lewis, with all those lost, empty years of working out in the gymnasium at the pen, was faster by far. He looked bulky and slow in the quilted down parka he wore, but he was already moving. Jerked his head to one side so quickly that Vicente's balled fist seemed to float past in slow motion, and by the time Vicente had recovered and was beginning to crouch down in a wrestling stance Lewis himself was on guard. He took a karate pose. Legs well apart and bent, arms cocked . . . left flank sharply presented to Vicente. Right arm up and back. Left hand and arm extended protectively, fingers joined but unclenched, palm facing his opponent.

Lewis had his own notions about karate. Most men who practiced the martial art regarded it as an elegantly stylized ritual. They worked out in gymnastic routines, and rarely, if ever, used their skills in an actual confrontation. The moves were really too dangerous. The trouble with someone like Lewis Bowman was that a fight seemed to be the only sensible place to use such skills.

He grunted—a kind of big, bearlike sound, from somewhere far down in his chest—hopped forward half a step, and struck Vicente in the mouth with his right fist, straight-arming the blow from the shoulder and leaning all his weight into it, his head held erect, almost cocked back. Vicente went down, not merely collapsing but literally flung onto his back by the impact.

Les Johnson . . . about to speak, to call a halt to it . . . one hand raised in protest.

Then, more.

Escudero, Vicente's *la Raza* buddy, made a small movement. Nothing much. Maybe he was just trying to get out of the way. But the movement was noted by Lewis. Now not even thinking, he spun. Lashed out with a Vibram-soled hiking boot that caught the other man flush on the kneecap. The entire leg collapsed, bent backward upon itself in an unnatural articulation. The rifle Escudero had been holding went clattering among the rocks, and Escudero too, with a frightful gasp, went down.

Johnson said, "Lewis! Jesus!"

To which Bowman replied, turning to regard the older man, "Les, one thing I learned down in the joint was that all these fucking Spanish dudes don't like nobody at all—and I guess I don't like 'em much either. Might as well be honest about it."

It was Escudero's loud cries, minutes later, that the men on the rimrock heard. They left their horses and clambered down the face of the canyon to the valley. They thought someone had been injured, or even accidentally shot.

They arrived, finally, at the base of the dead aspen in which the lioness had treed. There to find the dead cat, the chained pack, the old lion hunter, a glowering Bowman, young Escudero with what was apparently a horribly broken leg, and his friend, Vicente, conscious now and sitting up groggily, his entire mouth a pulp of smashed teeth and bloody flesh.

Another fight almost got started when Guillermo Apodaca learned what happened. He went straight at Lewis. Father Cornelius and Daniel Jaramillo grabbed him. Lewis was standing there again, waiting calmly.

When things finally cooled a little, Sedgewick turned to his friend Daniel and whispered, "For God's sake, what kind of a hunt is this!"

ELEVEN

―――――――――――――

". . . a weather alert is now in effect for southern Colorado and northern New Mexico, with expected snowfalls of four to six inches . . ."

—KOB-Accuweather

Around noon a second lioness had been killed, by Tomas Mora, in another canyon several miles east of the base camp. This was a small animal too, and the men brought it back to the camp and strung it, hind paws uppermost, from a tree. The first cat hung beside it. In this temperature the carcasses would keep until Johnson got back to Santa Fe and was able to send specimens to the health department facility in Albuquerque.

The lioness killed by Tomas had been taken without dogs, with a single hundred-yard shot from the old Savage. Tomas was as good with the rifle as his father was, and had gotten the cat in the side of the head. It had been basking in the winter sun, washing a paw.

This time Les Johnson didn't even ask why the animal had been taken without his permission. One look at Tomas's idiotic, split grin discouraged an authoritative or even a reasonable approach.

Johnson was getting the idea that bringing the tranquilizing rifle had been a waste of time. His wizened face turned grimmer when he saw the second lion carcass. As if he, too, had decided that this hunt was wrong to begin with, and that every goddamned thing that could go wrong had, and would continue that way. By now, some of the hunters were working the canyons to suit themselves, in pairs or trios, not even bothering to check with Johnson. The Moras were hunting this way, and so were Vicente and Guillermo Apodaca—the former still in pain from the punch he had taken. Three of his front teeth were gone, but the jaw itself didn't seem to be broken.

Some hunts are enjoyable, but this one wasn't. Tempers were up. Sedgewick put his finger on it in a remark to Daniel: "There are too many guns around, and I think there is a lot more liquor than we know about. Some of these men look like they've been drinking since dawn. Guns, and liquor, and hard feelings. I don't mind taking orders and helping out, but I don't like being drawn into something that's none of my affair and having to take sides in a feud. I don't know about you, but I think it might be smart for us to clear out of here tomorrow."

He was thinking of the expressions on the faces of the men when Escudero had been loaded into the back of George Dalton's truck. Escudero had screamed when they went to move him. They had slit his jeans to inspect the leg. Even with the swelling they could see that the kneecap was clean around to the side of the leg.

"Johnson wants to get that big cat he described," Daniel said. "He seems pretty sure it was the one that attacked the child."

"I still have a feeling you and I ought to have skipped this little weekend jaunt," Sedgewick said.

The two men were stationed along a ridge a mile or so south

of where the first cat had been taken. Johnson and Bowman and the pack, accompanied by Father Cornelius, were scouting the slopes below for possible dens. The area looked good for lion, but there had been no noise from the dogs, and that meant they were having no luck.

Up in the northwest, clouds were building, long, low, flat banks of dark-gray cumulus. Sedgewick pointed them out to Daniel and said, "Looks like a storm might be moving in."

"Clouds always come up at this time of day," Daniel said.

Presently Sedgewick rose and said, "I'm going over to that point there, to see if I can spot Johnson and the others." He slung his rifle from one shoulder, put his pipe in his mouth, and began picking his way along the lip of the ridge to a small crest, about eighty yards off, there to stand, rifle still slung, staring down the rocky slopes.

Both he and Daniel saw the bear at almost the same time. A fat black, that should have been holed up long ago to sleep through the cold months, but must have been roused by the men and dogs working somewhere below. It was almost three hundred yards from the two men on the ridge, and it was moving at a slow trot. Even at that distance they could see the thick rolls of loose fat undulating beneath the dark pelt. Once it stopped, looked over one shoulder, toward the timber below, where the men and dogs probably were. Then it started off again, in no great hurry, but not wasting time either, covering the open, rocky ground at a good clip, making toward another stand of timber—once in there, among the trees and underbrush, it would be lost.

Both men unslung their rifles and raised them. It was instinctive—that small spurt of adrenaline that always occurs at the sight of game—that reflective spasm that even a city dweller will feel. It was a long, difficult down-slope shot, but a clear one. More than likely they might have gotten the black, with three or four shots, but they held their fire. There was no need to shoot. They were not after bear but lion, and a particular one at that.

Daniel had by then gone automatically into a sitting position, heels wide apart and jammed into the frozen ground, cheek snugged against the comb of the stock as he settled down and sighted through the scope, the cross hairs dancing until he took a breath and held it; and then they steadied, centering on the small, far-off, lumbering black shape. A good shot.

He held this sight for a moment and then relaxed. Began breathing again. Looked up and over to Sedgewick on the point.

His friend too, almost ready to aim, staring down at the bear. Then, like Daniel, he let it go. Turned and glanced back at his companion. Pointed toward the bear, then waved his hand back and forth in negation, his message implicit: "Look at him down there, they really put him on the run, but let's not shoot him, not today, not this time, we'll let him go."

Daniel waved back to show that he understood, and Sedgewick turned again to watch the bear. It would soon be into the timber. Sedgewick stared down at the wild thing running below, a faint smile on his lips, experiencing the moment for itself—that satisfaction a hunter feels when he knows he has his prey where he wants it but can let it go free—his expression thoughtful. Daniel moved around a little to bring his own rifle to bear on the standing figure of his friend, the cross hairs dancing again, and then settling with implacable calmness on the space between those broad and heavy shoulders, eighty yards off, again a good shot, no, a dead-on ringer . . . providing that Daniel's forefinger, already curled around the trigger, tensed a shade more, releasing the firing pin. Such a shot would have blown Sedgewick's heart clean out.

But this too, like the bear, was not proper game. Or, perhaps, again like the bear, it was not the right time or place.

Or maybe Daniel merely wanted the feel of it. The risk . . . the knowing . . . of what it was like to have an animal, or someone, in that doomed position for just a moment. The risk was small enough. Some fool hunter was always being killed in a freak accident. It happened every season. It was a chance one took in the mountains, where men went armed. It was why a professional like Les Johnson could remark, in his cheerless style, "You know why I never wear a red jacket when I'm up in the mountains during hunting season? It gives these goddamned so-called hunters too good a target to aim at, that's why!"

Moments later the black disappeared into the far stand of trees. Sedgewick looked back again at his friend. Saw, even at that distance, that Daniel had changed his shooting position, while he, Sedgewick, had been watching the bear.

He could see that.

Could see the .257 Roberts, angled skyward now, held by the fore-end. And his friend's other hand, relaxed and propped atop one bent knee. Saw too that Daniel was regarding him from this position, across that open, rocky crest. The bear ignored. Almost as if Daniel was daydreaming. That kind of mental vagary or absent-mindedness was common enough. A trick of the mind. Standing there, Sedgewick did a little wondering of his own.

He would never know. But, then, it is easiest to feel guilt when one is in fact guilty. He raised a hand, finally, and waved. After a moment, Daniel brought up his free hand, the one not holding the rifle, and returned the salute.

Several forces were converging on the alpine camp. One of them wasn't even human, although it was argued later that another, in the form of George LaPorte, didn't have much in the way of human assets working in his favor either.

The first force was the storm whose advancing cloud banks had been observed by Sedgewick. Those banks of dark cumulus forewarned of a change of path by the cold front that was supposed to be passing to the north. They indicated that this front had bellied along its southern flank, spilling true arctic conditions into southern Colorado and northern New Mexico. Blizzard conditions, in fact, which would be further enhanced in the coming hours by wandering vortexes of sub-zero winds that would advance erratically from Gallup eastward, and that would close down highways and leave families and herds of cattle stranded from Arizona to east Texas. This kind of storm was not uncommon in the Southwest. Pecos regularly knew temperatures of twenty to thirty below. When it got that cold, life came to a standstill. Deer and elk, if they had their weather wits, moved to the lowermost valleys, sometimes coming right to the edge of the village in search of forage.

George LaPorte arrived with a flourish of a different sort, in a twenty-eight-foot-long Winnebago motor home, to which was hitched, via a tow bar, a Willys jeep. In the wake of this Goliath was a Dodge four-wheel-drive truck pulling a two-horse trailer. The back of the Dodge was piled with extra gear and bales of alfalfa.

LaPorte himself drove the Winnebago. His manager, Clyde Fox, was driving the Dodge truck. In the passenger seat of the Winnebago was Monty Cartier, the director of the Game and Fish Department.

LaPorte was an old-time Arizona Goldwater Republican who liked hunting. A self-made man. Had started with nothing, building up and then failing with one small business or another, at times filing bankruptcy, starting again, looking for the combination that would lead to magical success, until, finally, in middle age, he had hit it. Or if he hadn't hit it, he had at least come as close to it as he or most other men would ever get. Had begun, in the forties and fifties, buying up every irrigable acre around Tucson, Arizona, mostly in the southern and western sides of the city.

Such land was all right for alfalfa or corn, but these were not money crops. George LaPorte figured out that the sandy, often clayey, reddish-brown soil was good for something else. You could grow pecans in that soil like they were going out of style. That's what LaPorte did. Around Tucson he got to be known as Mr. Pecan. There was another fellow down around Las Cruces who had figured out the same thing, that the climate and the soil were just about perfect for pecans, but aside from him LaPorte pretty much ran the show. Pecans, it might seem, are a tasty snack. A handful over cocktails is enough for most people. But you are liable to have a different feeling about them if you own four hundred and twenty thousand pecan-producing trees, which, though they are slow to mature, will produce for years afterward. That's a lot of nuts. Or enough, anyway, for LaPorte. When his manager heard that a man-killing lion was terrorizing northern New Mexico, LaPorte set business aside, made a few long-distance calls, and then headed for his twin-engine Beechcraft. Two hours, Tucson International to Albuquerque's Sunport, counting pattern time. That was this morning. The motor caravan, including the Winnebago, had left last night, driven by a couple of ranch hands. When LaPorte and Fox landed, the rolling stock was waiting for them in the Sunport's parking lot.

Actually, LaPorte wasn't that anxious to get in on the hunt. Clyde Fox had talked him into it. But once he made up his mind to go, LaPorte organized the expedition with the same concentration he brought to a business deal. Now he parked the Winnebago in an unoccupied area at one side of the clearing, shut off the engine, looked at his watch, and said to Monty Cartier, "A shade over twenty-one hours. Since we got word about the lion. Less than twenty-four hours to move something like thirty thousand pounds of gear, horses, feed, guns, and supplies almost six hundred miles. That isn't bad, Mr. Cartier."

As Cartier was to explain to Les Johnson, a little while later, "This fellow likes to hunt, see? Also, he is a good buddy of the lieutenant-governor, and he knows a couple of U.S. senators besides. So he decided to come along this weekend."

Lester Johnson thought this over and then glanced at the

monstrous Winnebago. "Christ, as if I ain't got enough on my hands."

"Listen, old man," Cartier said. "When the lieutenant-governor puts in a personal telephone call to me and tells me how much he'd personally appreciate it if I'd make sure his personal pal LaPorte has a high old time hunting this raging man-killer, I have to pay heed. Can't you see that? So quit giving me a lot of static."

"It ain't a raging man-killer," Les Johnson said stubbornly.

"I don't give a goddamn if it's your Aunt Matilda's pet Siamese," Monty Cartier said. "All we're doing is greasing a pig for visiting royalty. Hell, why do you think I took off today and shagged all the way down to Albuquerque to be personally on hand when Mr. LaPorte flew in? Does that sink in on you a little?"

"Monty, this is one hell of a lousy hunt," Les Johnson insisted. "Nothing's gone right, and it's just gonna get worse."

Cartier ignored this. "All we can try for this weekend is to get this cat you talked to me on the phone about, and hope that we can give our Arizona friend something to brag about when he gets back home."

"It ain't gonna work," Johnson said glumly.

"Don't take on that way, Les," Cartier said. "This fellow's no amateur. I mean, if a man takes the trouble to fly all the way up here for the weekend, maybe drops a couple of thousand doing it, well, then we have a responsibility."

"Monty, I got half the goddamned town up here now, loaded down with cartridges and cases of beer and whiskey, like this hunt was some kinda picnic," Johnson said. "Besides which, the weather don't look so hot. And now this millionaire asshole has decided to come up and get in on the fun. How in hell you expect me to get anything done? Damn it all, Monty, whyn't you just run this hunt yourself?"

"I just might do that," Cartier said. Then he took a more reasonable line. "Listen, this LaPorte's a lifelong sportsman."

"Oh, shit," Johnson said.

"Les, you don't have to set him up," Cartier said. "I wouldn't ask that of you. But if it comes down to a proper shot at a record animal, well, then, let's do it right. That's all."

Lewis Bowman had walked over and joined them. He overheard the last part of this. He said, in his blunt way, "Sounds to me like that is exactly what you're asking us to do, Mr. Cartier. Set this rich old fucker up for an easy shot."

Cartier shook his head. "No. He's rich, but he knows hunting. In fact, he's one of the last big-time hunters. Been all over the world, from what I hear. He's taken everything that walks, flies, or crawls on its belly like a reptile."

"Sounds like a real pain in the ass," Bowman said.

"His breed of man is about gone," Monty Cartier said. "Sportsmen like him have ramrodded plenty of fine legislation."

"Sure," Les Johnson agreed.

Cartier didn't like the old lion hunter's tone. He said, "You will see to it that he has a decent hunt."

"Yessir," Johnson said dryly. "I will do my best."

"If need be, you'll do better than that," Cartier said.

"Well, goddamn it, I ain't God, y'know," Les Johnson said.

"I know this—you can give him a good hunt if you want to," Cartier insisted.

"Monty, I can't just conjure a critter up outa thin air to please this guy," Johnson said. "George Dalton and I, we knew where this big cat was back last summer. But the den he was using was taken over by a female that got killed this morning. So we been working one canyon after another, ever since. The dogs ain't raised scent once. That cat may have lit out for parts unknown. Or if that eye wound it got is bad enough, it may have gone off some place to die, I don't know. I'll do my best. That's all I can promise you."

CARTIER WENT BACK to the fancy Winnebago and reported Johnson's doubts to LaPorte, concluding, "It could be one of those drawn-out affairs, you know."

LaPorte thought this over and then nodded to Clyde Fox, who set out a third cup and saucer for the game-department chief. Coffee was poured. LaPorte said, "Of course, there's never a guarantee, is there? Not unless you're on a private preserve, where, say, a pheasant can be released thirty yards from the shotgun. That's not what I call hunting."

LaPorte was a round-faced, white-haired man. He wore gold-rimmed spectacles, and for a man of sixty he was amazingly trim and fit. He had an odd habit, or mannerism— that of staring intensely, almost hypnotically, at the person he was speaking with—but except for this he could have passed for the branch manager of a savings-and-loan company who was out roughing it for the weekend in a Pendleton shirt and custom-made slacks. He was not much of a talker unless he was drinking, and he was not a mingler at all.

So far he had not come out of the Winnebago. The rest of the men in the camp saw him through the large picture window that flanked one side of the big motor home. Visible through the window was a kitchenette and dining area. La-Porte sat at the dinette table by the window, drinking coffee and from time to time looking out at the camp. Clyde Fox was visible too, at the kitchen counter, making coffee in a large, old-fashioned percolator. To most men in the camp the Winnebago seemed incredibly luxurious.

LaPorte said now, "Mr. Cartier, let me tell you something. A long time ago I went up to the Aleutians. Three years running, looking for the right specimen of kodiak bear. I must have glassed fifty of them during those three seasons. I wasn't in any hurry. Figured I might have to go back up there three more seasons, or ten. I didn't care. Guide thought I was crazy. I guess old Clyde here did too. Turned down one animal after another. Two days before the end of the third season I found the one I'd been looking for, and I took him on a running shot at three hundred and ten yards, measured, with a single .458 slug." LaPorte tasted his coffee. "I'll never hunt another kodiak. I'll never have to." He paused again. "There's a mounted kodiak in the American Museum of Natural History, in New York, that is a record. The one in my private trophy room down in Tucson is bigger."

LaPorte adjusted his spectacles and finished his coffee. "Clyde, how about a refill, if you don't mind." While Fox poured, he turned back to Cartier. "There is a thing about hunting . . . call it intuition. I'm one of these fellows who gets a feeling in his bones as to whether a hunt is worthwhile. It's something I just kind of know. Clyde can vouch for that. Many's the time I've just let my feelings move me along, and they will take me to this place, maybe a valley or a mountain ridge—where there is not supposed to be any game at all, and where a professional guide may be laughing at me behind my back for insisting on coming to such a place—and that is the place where, as often as not, I will find the animal I've been looking for. And all my feelings now are telling me that we'll track and get this lion this weekend. I'll bet you hard cash on that, Mr. Cartier, if you're a gambling man."

TWELVE

. . . though normally evasive, the lion can in mating season exhibit behavior that is out of the ordinary. The male in rut will challenge any interloper, and not necessarily another cat. When provoked, a lion has been known to attack a fully grown bear. As often as not it is the latter who fares badly in such an encounter.

Big Game Hunting in North America

IT WAS DUSK now. The men outside the tent were gathered by the fire, and they all heard it, the sound of a vehicle grinding up the road toward the camp. Then they spotted its headlights coming toward them through the already dark-shadowed trees, and then finally it drove into the clearing, and they recognized it as Griego's truck, the *rojo* state trooper.

They stood watching as Griego parked the truck and turned off the lights and ignition. Two other people were with him in the front seat.

One of the people who got out of the cab was Virgil McCormick, the lanky Texan who raised purebred Alsatians. The other was Karen Jaramillo. At first she didn't get out.

She sat there under the pale glare of the roof light, looking pretty and blonde. Some of the men by the fire couldn't have been more astonished if the Dowager Empress of China had suddenly invited herself up here for tea. No, for a fact, they would have been less ill at ease with the old dowager. At least someone like that demanded dignity and respect. But Karen Jaramillo was something else again.

GUILLERMO APODACA WAS seated by the fire, folding a small water-soaked towel which he intended to apply to the terrible mess Lewis Bowman had made of his son's mouth. He looked over at Griego's truck, and then put it as succinctly as any of the others might have: "What in hell is *she* doing here?"

All he really meant by that was a vague but general disapproval. Guillermo had nothing against Karen Jaramillo. The thing was that women don't generally go on a hunt, any more than a man will go with his wife to a beauty shop on Saturday morning. Once in a while a girlfriend or a wife will be seen in the high country during the season, dressed in a red jacket and maybe armed with a light-caliber rifle, like a .243, but usually it is just the man and the woman themselves, a pair, and at the end of the day people like that ordinarily stay off by themselves, perhaps in a pickup with a camper rigged on the back, or maybe they will have one of those small mountaineering tents set up. Sometimes two or three couples will go out like this, but generally a woman is not counted as part of a regular hunting camp. It isn't that they bring bad luck—it's just easier without one around.

The other men by the fire were silent. Guillermo turned back to his son, Vicente, and said, loud enough for all to hear, "Well, we ain't had one single thing go right this weekend, and now we got this to put up with." With infinite tenderness he applied the compress to Vicente's mouth and said in gentler tones, "*Aiiee*, now, *pobre chiquito*, you poor thing. . . ."

She stood there beside Griego's truck. She was dressed for the weather. A thick, quilted parka, plaid wool pants, and a fur cap with turn-down flaps.

Daniel Jaramillo may have been thinking along the same lines as Guillermo. His expression was serious—almost frowning—as he strode up to where she stood.

"What are you doing here?"

"I wanted to come up," she said.

"Why?"

"I just did."

"But why?"

She did not speak. Merely stared at him. And perhaps in a way the stare she gave him was enough. There was too much now that they would never openly discuss. They knew each other well enough, these two. She said, "I was worried."

"Worried? About what?" he said, staring at her.

"They're saying in the village that there's liable to be bad trouble up here."

"Is that why Peter is here?"

"Yes."

"Vince Apodaca and a buddy got into a roughhouse with one of the Game and Fish Department men," he said.

"You and Sedgewick weren't involved?"

"Of course not," he said. "Us? That's crazy."

Her brow furrowed, giving her a look of confused anguish. Her expression—her eyes—seemed to say, Crazy? So what is going on up here? What kind of a crazy thing is this, to chase around these mountains getting into fights? I hated coming up here. Can't you see that? Do you think I'm stupid to just come up here like this? I hated it, but still I went to Peter Griego, and I said, "They say you are going up to the camp to make an arrest and to call the hunt off, so let me come with you, please," and finally he said all right, that he would take me. Because I think he knows too . . . or suspects. They all know, I think. Peter is like Father Cornelius. He knows everything. I don't like Peter. He doesn't like me. He doesn't really like anyone. All he's good for is hating, but I said to him, "Take me up there with you," and he said, "Okay, I'm leaving in an hour," and I drove home and changed and here I am, and I'll leave now, this minute, on one condition. That you come with me. Sedgewick can stay if he wants to, but you must go, otherwise I will stay. If you argue with me, I simply will not listen. I hated coming up here badly enough. It about killed me.

She said aloud, "Dan, I just had to come."

He looked at her and did not say anything.

"Will you go back down with me?" she asked.

"I'm staying."

"Then I am too," she said.

Again he stared at her, without speaking.

Between their gaze something drifted down. A snowflake. And then, another.

SOMEONE ELSE DISAPPROVED. At the big picture window of the Winnebago, George LaPorte sat staring out. On the Formica dinette table before him was a cup of coffee and his favorite rifle, a custom-built Weatherby .458, and to one side of that a plastic container of his own specially hand-loaded cartridges.

From the window he had seen Griego's pickup drive into the clearing. Seen the woman get out, and had then watched as she and the fellow who apparently was her husband—a small, trim, handsome man—talked.

No woman had ever been in a hunting camp of LaPorte's because that was the way he wanted it. But now, for the present, he watched and said nothing.

PETER GRIEGO IN a dark-blue, fur-trimmed parka and cap to match was talking to Monty Cartier, Lester Johnson, and Lewis Bowman.

He stood before them with his legs spread a little, his freckled face set in a glacial frown. The voice stony: "I'm placing him under arrest for felonious assault. If you don't like it, that's too bad."

Lewis scowled too. "Man, the fucker swung on me. What'd you expect me to do?"

Griego glanced at him and said, "Shut up."

Lewis pressed his lips into a thin, furious line, and looked down at the ground.

So that social contract between them was quickly set. It said that Griego was law, and he could, and would, if need be, draw his gun, or maybe even shoot. Maybe even without regret.

Lewis knew all about that story. Just as he knew enough to keep quiet. He knew Peter would be fast with a blackjack or wrist-twisters. He knew that any way you looked at it, it was a no-go scene.

Because if Griego didn't take him, someone else would. Some place else. If necessary, three or four sheriff's deputies in the back corridor of some cellblock, each of them wearing tanned leather work gloves or using nightsticks. So there was no argument about that. And then there would be the joint again. And that was nowhere.

But the contract also read another way.

It said that Peter Griego had better watch his style with Lewis. Who, since the contract was already written, had nothing much to lose by intractable behavior. Alongside Lewis, Peter looked like a twelve-year-old boy. He might have the uniform and the gun, and the authority, but all things considered Lewis could throw Peter halfway across the camp clearing. He'd pay for it later, of course, but there was that nice awareness that, given a chance, he could hospitalize Griego with a really interesting assortment of broken bones.

Peter knew it too. Hence the outspread legs, the straight-backed and alert pose—and the need, via the icily put "Shut up!", to put Lewis in his place. Griego did not want to be slugged by this big, moronic gorilla. Whose I.Q., though

Peter didn't know it, was about on a par with his own. If it came to that, he would slug first.

He listened now with official politeness to what Monty Cartier had to say.

"Sergeant Griego, I need this man up here quite urgently this weekend," Cartier told him. "He's one of our most valuable personnel."

"He's also a parolee," Peter said. "I ran a make on him this afternoon. At the pen he had quite a reputation. He had no business coming down on a kid as hard as he did. I'm putting it mildly."

He glanced toward the campfire where Guillermo and Vicente Apodaca and the others were sitting and watching them. He said, "I've decided it'll be better all around if I take your man down with me right now, Cartier. I don't want any more trouble up here. I ought to be out on the highway right now, because there's a storm warning in effect. Wagonmound, Mora, and Peña Blanca are already closed down. But I'm up here. I have a job to do. And the best way I see to get it done is to take this man out of here pronto, before he hurts somebody else, or before a couple of these people take a notion to teach him a lesson he'll never forget. That's my thinking. If you don't like it, you can discuss it with my supervisor."

AMONG THE LAST to return to camp in the waning light was Father Cornelius.

He was riding a borrowed horse past the opening of a small canyon several miles south of the base camp when he saw the tracks. The canyon was small, actually a steep, boxed-in ravine a few hundred yards across, with a landslide or washout filling most of the boxed-in part of it. The tracks were visible in a long patch of snow under the south wall of the ravine. Cornelius reined his horse and got down to inspect the prints. They led straight into the canyon, toward the landslide at the upper end. He mounted his horse again, regarded the canyon for a minute, and then turned his horse toward camp.

LES JOHNSON SAID angrily, "If you're taking Bowman, I'm coming along."

"Old man, I need you up here," Monty Cartier said.

"Well, all I want to know is, what in hell do you intend charging him with?" Johnson demanded.

"I told you—aggravated assault, for a start," Griego said.

"Goddamn, it was self-defense," Johnson insisted. "I was right there. I was a witness."

"I'll take your statement later," Griego said, and turned to Bowman. "Get your gear, and let's go."

Les Johnson tilted his Stetson back and shook his head in disgust. He and Cartier watched as Griego went with Lewis to the big tent, where Bowman had stored his backpack.

Griego walked a few paces behind the tall young man. Lewis's expression was sullen, angry, not exactly defeated—in fact, it was anything but that—showing the impotence he was feeling. As though he was deeply troubled and confused that something like this was always happening to him instead of others. As if he was asking himself why it always had to be him who was being taken off by an alert bull who was ready to beat him into insensibility at the wrong word, the wrong move.

It wasn't bitterness that showed in his face so much as that brooding readiness for violence, should the moment come. If it did, he would move first. As if by giving in to an adrenaline charge he could at least make some valid statement against the injustice of it all. Because this was, in essence, so grossly unfair.

But the moment did not come. Griego was a good cop. He knew some karate and judo too. Not nearly as much as Lewis, but enough—and his training on the padded work-out mats at the state police academy warned him not to get within an arm or leg's length of the big ex-con. Maybe Bowman would behave. Then again, he might not.

In the tent, Lewis began stuffing loose clothing into the backpack. He reached for his rifle, and Peter said, "Let the old man bring that down."

But if the two of them were alert, Les Johnson was in touchier shape. He was furious, and when he got this way his worse side came out.

He wanted Lewis with him this weekend. He had put in over a year teaching Bowman how to work with him. Lewis was the best assistant he'd ever had. Old man Johnson also had a considerable affection for this muscular tough. His notions on the proper way to rehabilitate a habitual felon were pretty hazy, but he figured that if Griego or some of the cops in Santa Fe went to work on Lewis, the year he and Bowman had spent in the mountains would count for nothing. It wasn't so much a matter of earning the younger man's trust—so far as Les Johnson could see, Lewis didn't really trust anything that walked on two legs, and probably never would—so much as cozying Lewis along to the point where the sullen giant could comfortably tolerate camping out on the same mountaintop with another human.

A return to what Lewis called the joint would likely place him beyond salvageable status altogether, and when he came out, if he came out at all, he would be walking trouble. Les Johnson didn't like this idea. He had a hunch that if he could somehow keep Griego from taking Lewis down—if he could stall the arrest until he and maybe Monty Cartier could somehow make a character-witness deposition in court or something—then Lewis might get off. In Johnson's mind, young Vince Apodaca's attack was by now completely uncalled for.

He thought about this while Bowman and Griego were in the tent. Monty Cartier left to get his own gear from the Winnebago. Johnson finally went to his own truck, where he had a kit box of junk under the seat. He opened the box and rummaged around inside, sorting through ancient cold patches, a broken tire-pressure gauge, a couple of boxes of .22 cartridges, and a small roll of baling wire, until he found four twelve-penny common nails, slightly rusted. Hurrying now, he walked over to Griego's Dodge pickup, glanced toward the tent, and then stooped to place one of the nails, propped at forty-five degrees, against the tread of a snow tire. Then he did the same with the other three tires.

The men seated round the campfire looked on with interest. Their feelings were mixed. Johnson was an Anglo, and an outsider. Peter Griego was Spanish, and a local, but he was a cop. Johnson had been bossing them around up here, but then, Peter bossed hell out of them down in Pecos.

All things being equal, the best course of action seemed to be to stay out of it. This is what the campfire drinkers did.

Spanish men often have a curious way of showing humor— they show nothing. These men glanced away, or at one another, with blank, disinterested expressions. No comments, no smiles. They managed to look bored.

Even so, none of them got up and left the fire. They were curious to see what would happen next.

Bowman, shouldering his pack, came out of the tent, followed by Griego. They went to the Dodge, and Lewis tossed his gear into the rear, and then returned to get into the front seat. Stopped instead. To regard Peter, standing there with the cuffs dangling in one hand. The trooper said, "Get 'em behind your back."

This last was too much for Lewis. He glared at Griego for a moment, almost—but not quite—literally grinding his teeth with frustration. Then, spiritually, he collapsed. Gave in. Muttered a disconsolate "Shit" and presented his wrists at the small of his back. The cuffs snapped, and Griego helped him into the truck. Went over to his side, got in, and started the engine. Backed the truck out of its parking space, over all four nails, and drove off, down the winding, rutted timber road.

Nobody waved a farewell. The men round the fire lit

cigarettes, drank a little, and regarded the leaping flames. Presently, from somewhere down below, they heard a couple of faint thumping noises.

About ten minutes later, Peter Griego and Bowman came into sight, walking on the road just below the camp, where it wound into the trees. Lewis was free of the cuffs and had his backpack slung over one shoulder. Apparently they had come to some kind of truce down on the trail.

They walked up to the camp clearing. Peter went over to Les Johnson's truck. The old man was sitting in the open doorway of the camper, with his feet on the back steps, drinking bourbon from a folding aluminum cup and smoking his pipe. It was a small camper with nothing more than sitting room inside, but often he and Lewis and the four dogs would pile into it, and tonight they might have Monty Cartier to boot. He looked at Griego and said, "You're back."

Griego stared at Johnson and then said, "I want to tell you, mister, that that wasn't funny." Johnson said nothing, and Peter went on. "I don't know if I can charge you with obstructing justice, but I am going to try. I sure as hell am. It looks like at least one of those tires busted its casing. I paid eighty dollars apiece for those snow treads, mister. Not only that, we skidded on ice when they went flat. Now my Dodge is jammed around sideways, rocks on one side, some trees it would take all day to chain-saw on the other. Go look for yourself—down by that first switchback curve, no more'n five hundred yards. It isn't just four flats. I don't know about obstructing justice, but you sure have obstructed the road out of here, Johnson. We'll be working half of tomorrow, trying to snake that sucker out of there."

"Son, you do what you want tomorrow," old man Johnson said mildly. "Me, I'm going hunting. And I'm taking my assistant with me." He paused and then added dryly, "And quit yelling at me about flat tires and such. A feller oughta know better than to come fooling around up here on these old gut-busting trails with inferior rubber on his wheels. Seems to me that's just asking for trouble."

Peter Griego turned and stomped off to the campfire. The men there didn't look up at him. They didn't even look at one another. They stared into the flames and puffed at cigarettes, their dark, unshaven Spanish faces thoughtful, almost doleful. Nobody had anything to say about tires.

Presently, one looked up at the darkening sky overhead and remarked to no one in particular, "By God, that damn snow, she's sure starting to come down like a double-cunted cow pissing on a flat rock, ain't she?"

It was pass-the-bourbon time.

BY SIX THAT night the snow had stopped but they all knew it would start again. The sky was a mass of gray clouds, moving steadily, not much more than a few hundred feet above their camp. The undersides of the clouds could easily be seen by stepping a few yards away from the brightness of the fire and shining a flashlight upward. It was cold now and there was no wind at all, but they understood too that if the wind came up in the night it would turn a lot colder.

Someone started a second bonfire, and Sedgewick, Virge McCormick, and Lewis Bowman went out to bring in more firewood. They worked with axes and a couple of Coleman lanterns in the trees just beyond the edge of the camp, where there was plenty of deadwood for the taking. Jaramillo and his woman joined the group of men by the first fire. The men made room for them, and someone rolled over a log for her to sit on. When Sedgewick and McCormick finished hauling wood, they joined the group too.

HE HAD NOT spoken to her when she had gotten out of Griego's pickup. Had watched instead as Daniel had gone up to her, unable to hear any of their words from across the clearing as they spoke in low tones—but he had noted Daniel's expression of aggravation at seeing her here in the camp. Nor did he have much to say now, seated there beside them, smoking his pipe and from time to time tasting a cup of watered whiskey.

Virgil McCormick, tall and angular, hunkered down with the others. Guillermo Apodaca said, "*Com' está*, Virge. How come you decided to freeze your tail off up here?"

"Want to get that big bugger, just like the rest of you," McCormick said. He looked skyward and said conversationally, "Father, it don't look like you'll be holding service tomorrow. If she really busts loose, we're liable not to get out of here by next Sunday, let alone tomorrow." He motioned toward the two dead cats strung from a tree near the trucks. "Who got 'em?"

"I got one," Vicente Apodaca said. "The Moras got the other. The one we want is still loose."

"You shoot yours, Vicente, or tangle with it personally?" McCormick asked. Vicente's mouth looked worse now than it had after the fight that morning. One entire side of his face was puffed and blue. He did not answer.

Someone else had been watching Jaramillo and his wife. Behind him, Daniel heard snow crunch under a boot, and then a voice said, "Evening."

He turned. It was George LaPorte's manager, Clyde Fox.

Fox was a big, handsome man in his middle fifties, dressed in cowboy boots, jeans, an expensive sheepskin coat, and a beige Stetson. He had a strong jaw and a bristly, sandy-colored moustache, and he spoke in a quiet drawl. He looked and sounded like something out of a cigarette advertisement, or at least like a wealthy rancher who has abandoned cattle in favor of pecans. He had a broad smile that showed white, even, teeth.

Fox said now, "Mr. LaPorte asked me come over and tell you that you and your lady are welcome in the Winnebago."

"I'd like to get her back down if I can," Daniel said.

"Road's blocked, they say," Fox said. "I walked down and

looked. No way to get a truck past. Besides, weather's coming in sure."

"Thanks anyway, but I guess we'll make do without troubling your boss," Daniel said.

"No trouble at all," Fox said. "Just me and him in that big ol' Winnebago, you know. There's a double bunk above the cab that you could use."

Jaramillo did not answer. Fox went on, lowering his voice, "No need to have her in that tent with this crowd. They been drinking quite a bit already, and tonight they'll be hitting it harder."

"Well, thanks," Jaramillo said finally. "We may take you up on that."

"I'll be keeping the Winnebago's generator going tonight," Fox added. "George likes his comfort, you know. Electric light, hot water for a wash-up. It'll be plenty warm."

"Tell your boss that's mighty nice of him," Daniel said.

"No trouble at all," Fox said again. "Mr. LaPorte's a hospitable man in his way. We was watching you out the window. He figured it'll be a rowdy bunch in that tent. I got some nice filet mignons thawing. You all just come on in and make yourselves at home when you're ready. That Winnebago's got one of those brand-new microwave broilers, the kind they claim cooks a meal in three, four minutes. We just had it installed last week, and I been dying to use it."

THIRTEEN

It is dark out now, and the snow is coming down again, in a steady fall, sometimes whipped by rising gusts of wind that send swirling clouds of white through the dark stands of Englemann Spruce. The wind is out of the northwest, where bad storms come from, and the temperature is beginning to drop, not plunging yet, the way it will later on in the night when the wind builds still more, but even so, right now, it is cold, near zero.

The big cat is laid up in its den. A shallow alcove, really, eroded into the side of a cliff—a space not much larger than its own body, which is curled into a furry ball.

Occasionally, it wakes, lifts its rounded, snakelike head in the darkness, then licks a paw and scrubs and worries at the injured eye.

In the den it is cold, but not nearly as cold as it is outside, where the wind is now rising to a clear, thin howl that comes louder and shriller in the gusts, then dies away, to rise again in the next strong gust. From time to time an eddy whips a thin swirl of snow into the den, dusting the flanks of the big cat with white.

LATELY SHE HAD been drifting more and more into the habit of thinking, or assuming, that everyone she met knew she went to Sedgewick's cabin. It seemed so clear to her. She wished she were more devious or subtle, the way some women were.

She had felt bad enough about coming up to the camp, but Daniel's coldness set her back more. After a while this feeling of being despised and out of place grew overwhelming. She felt stupid. To reveal to all these other people that she had been upset and frightened enough to come. Like holding up a printed sign for all the world to see. But there had been nothing else left for her to do. Except sit at home and wait. And she could not do that. Not any more.

What ate at her was whether they all knew, or if it was just something in her mind . . . thinking they knew. If she could only know about that for certain. It seemed to her that they had to know. It was all so clear. Yet a logical part of her argued that there was no reason to feel this way.

She argued back and forth with herself. Was left feeling dejected, miserable. Was closer to tears than the outwardly calm, almost expressionless demeanor the others saw.

Oddly, she had never looked lovelier. Seated there before the fire, her fingers interlocked across one crossed knee. Her expression pensive, inward-turned. The faint, ineffable sadness lurking in those gray eyes. Cheeks reddened by the wind and cold, and now the heat. No makeup at all. None needed.

In a while, they walked together, side by side, to the monstrous aluminum Winnebago.

Knocked. Then entered.

Inside: big Clyde Fox, building a pair of highballs.

The other man, peering at them over the tops of spectacles, seated at a Formica dinette table. The plastic veneer done to resemble oiled walnut.

This was LaPorte. He stood up, introduced himself, regarded both of them for a moment with an expression that was neither friendly nor hostile, then came straight to the point: "I don't know why in God's name you have your wife up here in this weather, sir, but it's obvious you don't know this country. Else you'd have had her stay at home. Whatever. She's here now. I understand a truck has blocked the road below. That's why I told Clyde to have the two of you in. If you want my opinion, you'll get her out of here, first thing tomorrow. Missus, would you like a drink?"

She glanced at Clyde Fox, and after a moment said in a low voice, "A rum-and-Coke, if you have it."

"There's some Ron Rico on the bottom shelf," LaPorte said to his manager.

"You?" Clyde asked Daniel.

"The name's Jaramillo. Bourbon and water would be fine," Daniel said.

"You ranch hereabouts?" LaPorte asked.

"I'm a teacher."

"I see. Hunt?"

"Not for years."

"Touchy weather right now," LaPorte said, walking over to the bar counter to get the drink Fox had mixed. "Could get some real snow before morning."

"Do you think we might get into trouble up here?" she asked.

"Trouble? Up here? Why, shucks. No way," LaPorte said. "At the worst we might get stuck for a day or two. People know where we are. Why, just a while ago I was talking to Tucson on the shortwave. No, missus. If we get snow, it'll slow the hunt, but that's all. But we're as safe as can be up here. I'd say we're a lot safer than we'd be in Chicago or New York. There's worse animals live there than you'll ever find in these mountains. If it snows for a week, all we got to do is sit tight. In this day and age, the only way anybody gets into trouble is if they're either stupid or they go out looking for it."

"That's not always true, George," Clyde Fox said. He stood

there at the counter, stirring Karen Jaramillo's rum-Coke. Glanced up at LaPorte for a second, his eyes gentle.

His casual remark, so much a generalization that it was scarcely worth paying attention to, registered with the older man, and, oddly, it seemed to register strongly.

LaPorte paused, then nodded to himself and smiled at his manager. "I guess you're right at that, Clyde. Sometimes it just comes wandering along and happens to you, doesn't it."

MONTY CARTIER WAS quietly getting drunk in Les Johnson's pickup camper. Johnson had a catalytic heater going full blast and a window cracked for ventilation. He and Cartier passed a quart of Jim Beam back and forth. Outside, the wind whistled softly, and once in a while a stronger gust rocked the entire outfit a little.

Lewis Bowman and the dogs were in the camper too. In the big wall tent across the clearing there was a strong smell of men in close quarters—wet clothing, socks and unlaced boots steaming in the heat cast by a sheepherder stove that was almost red-hot—but here in the little camper there was a powerful smell of dog.

"Lewis, when you hit that fellow, what you should have done was told everyone that old Les here did it," Cartier was saying. He drank from the bottle and chewed a handful of Fritos, and thought about the notion of Johnson attacking someone like Vicente Apodaca. "You ought to have blamed all of it on Les," he went on. "You should have said that Les couldn't tolerate the idea of anyone ruining his hunt, and so he just beat up on those two fellows. You should have said that Les has one hell of a bad temper if he doesn't get to run the show his own way. Why, I could have told them that much."

Johnson said, "This hunt ain't over yet, Monty. And if things don't improve, my temper's liable to go that route."

Lewis popped the lid on a can of Dr Pepper, and then

began stroking Cacique's head. The big Labrador lay half in his lap. Lewis said, "Les is right. Best thing I seen on this hunt is that pretty blonde who came in a while ago. Real style." Then he looked at Cartier, and said, "Guys like you can talk your way out of anything. Except when it comes to helping someone like me. You're a pretty good talker, Mr. Cartier, but I notice that that state bull wasn't doing much listening before."

"I'll be glad to talk to him again, Lewis," Cartier said. "I'll also talk to the judge, if it goes to court, and to your parole officer." He handed the bottle over to Johnson and said, "Les, what are you going to do if you find this super-lion and sedate him? A cat that big will be some job to lug through the snow."

"One thing at a time, Monty," Johnson said. "You going to make rabbit stew, first thing you do is go catch yourself a rabbit. If we find this pussycat, maybe we'll put him to sleep and then stuff him into Lew's back pocket. Why, I bet that state trooper would think twice about putting the cuffs on a man with a record-sized lion in his hip pocket, wouldn't he?"

There was a knock at the camper door. Virgil McCormick put his head in and said, "Mr. Johnson, they want you over in the tent. Father Cornelius just came in. He says he's found where that big cat's hid."

Johnson and Cartier put on their parkas and went with Mc-Cormick, 'eaving Lewis with the dogs. The tent was packed with men, lying or sitting on their sleeping bags or bedrolls. The sheepherder stove stood in the middle, with a galvanized flue that went up through a hole in the top flap, and three Coleman pressure lanterns were strung from wires fastened to the ridgepole. The Colemans hissed and threw out a hard, brilliant, blue-white light. Someone along the back wall had a transistor radio tuned to a Spanish-music station.

The men were tired, and some of them had had too much to drink, but for the first time there was a little enthusiasm in their faces as Cornelius went over the story again for Johnson and Cartier. "How big were the prints?" Johnson asked, and the Franciscan held up his hand with the fingers outspread. "Just a single set of tracks, going in?" Johnson went on.

"Just the one set."

"Of course, he might've just kept right on up through that canyon on into the mountains," Johnson reflected. "Though a lion doesn't like to cover real distance in bad weather, no more'n any other critter."

"Are you going to talk about it for half the weekend again?" Guillermo Apodaca said.

"Oh, no," Johnson said. "We'll be checking that canyon out first thing in the morning. Yessir. We might have something going for us. Father, you sure you can find this place again with the fresh snow?"

"I can find it," Cornelius said.

"Your dogs won't be much good with this new snow," Guillermo said.

"We'll bring them anyway," Johnson said.

"You going to bring that air rifle too?" Guillermo asked.

"I sure am," Johnson said. "And this time we're going to run this thing right. All you fellers want is a pickupload of dead lions to truck back to Pecos. You all want to be big-shot hunters, but what's been eating at me is why this critter ain't acting normal."

"You said it might be rabid," Guillermo pointed out.

"That's a possibility," Johnson admitted. "There's all kinds of possibilities." The whiskey he had been drinking had gotten his temper up. It was true that most of the men there did not like him. And Johnson didn't like them. "Bunch of damn-fool know-it-alls," he muttered, staring around the tent. "Why, you don't even know that this critter is wild."

"What do you mean?" Sedgewick asked.

"I seen it happen," Johnson said. "Once in a while some feller up in the hills will capture a kitten and make a pet out of it. Keep it in a cage. Feed it condensed milk out of a baby bottle, you know. They're real cute when they're kittens."

He jammed both hands into his parka pockets, and shook his head angrily. "By and by time passes. All of a sudden, this animal lover, he's got a hundred-pound alley cat on his hands. Maybe bigger . . . maybe even lots bigger. Sometimes these lions are docile and will romp around with the family dog or the children and all that, but they usually turn pretty mean after about a year or so. Unpredictable. Can't handle 'em. Too dangerous. Animal lover doesn't know what to do with a cat that wouldn't mind chewing the leg off a grown man just to keep in practice. Can't turn it over to a zoo, 'cause it's an illegal animal—it belongs to the State of New Mexico. Feller with an animal like that is breaking five or six laws right off. Can't keep it, 'cause it just goes on getting bigger and meaner. Sensible thing to do is either shoot it or turn it loose back up in the mountains. A number of these cats have been raised up this way and then released. Only thing wrong with 'em, after being raised in captivity, they don't have any hunting skills, which they'd've learned in the first year or two with their natural mammas. So they starve. Or else they go after game they can catch. A calf. Chickens. A kid, conceivably."

"If you caught this cat, is there any way you could tell whether it had been raised in captivity?" Peter Griego asked.

"Oh, sure," Johnson said. "The overall condition of the animal would tell, if it hadn't been loose too long. Caged animal is softer. The muscle tone is different. No calluses on the footpads. Best thing, though, if I got a cat like that, I'd run a cesium count on it."

The men looked at him, not understanding, and Johnson went on, "For some reason wild game in this part of the state has a higher cesium content than game elsewhere, or domestic animals. We think it's because of the work they do up at Los Alamos. Safeguards are safeguards, but they've been messing with radioactive materials for over thirty years now, and I wouldn't doubt that there has been some leakage some place. Anyway, wild game around here has a lot of this cesium isotope. The small critters get it from the natural food-chain and from drinking water in the streams. The bigger critters, like carnivores, have a high isotope count too. It stays in the system, it's absorbed. But domestic animals, like dogs and cats, they have practically no cesium in them, because they're fed on commercial pet foods that's manufactured elsewhere. So if I had this cat I'd do an isotope count on it. If it had a lot of cesium, I'd know it was wild, but if it only had a little I'd probably judge that it'd been living on pet food for a long time. And about that time I'd start looking around for the goddamned simple-minded son of a bitch that's caught that critter and tried to tame it, and then let it loose, and when I found him, by God, I'd kick his ass until he was bleeding at the eyes. Like I said, it's just a possibility. Come on, Monty. Let's get out of here. Goddamn it to hell."

FOURTEEN

There was no way for me to tell whether there was a more than usual amount of liquor present. You figure on finding quite a bit around any hunting camp. There was no rowdiness, though. Most of them were too tired.

—*Statement*, PETER M. GRIEGO,
New Mexico State Police

FELICIANO AND TOMAS Mora had brought along a gallon of cheap muscatel, charged down at the Crippled Horse, and then, later that afternoon, Tomas had swiped a full quart of bourbon out of the back of Guillermo Apodaca's truck. Guillermo had not yet found out about the missing liquor, and in time he would probably, by the process of elimination, figure out who had done such an unneighborly disservice, but by then it would be too late.

The father-and-son team had the bourbon and muscatel more or less concealed in their bedrolls down in one corner of the tent. They were drinking the whiskey, mixed with wine and thinned with water, out of coffee cups, and when they needed refills they crouched over and turned their backs on the others.

Their little corner was the only part of the tent that was kind of uncrowded. Father Cornelius had elected to bunk alongside them, taking as a kind of Christian penance the un-believable Mora odor. It was more than just unwashed clothes. There was something more powerful to it, as if, in some peculiar fashion, certain parts of Feliciano's and Tomas's bodies were in a state of advanced decomposition—feet, toes, genitalia, armpits—and the thing was that these two were so blithely unaware of it. Virgil McCormick had noticed it straight off when he first entered the tent. Spotting extra room in the Moras' corner, he had carried his bedroll over, stopping to say hello to Father Cornelius, and had then recoiled a bit, as though he'd just stepped up to the opened door of a Bes-semer furnace. Virgil, his east-Texas upbringing notwithstand-ing, was a very fastidious man. He didn't even like long hair on young people, because he figured that there was no way hair longer than two inches could be kept really clean. He stood there a moment, as if stunned or transfixed by this richness that permeated the air, trying to analyze his predica-ment. There were no other empty spaces left. He finally asked Guillermo if he could sleep in the front seat of Guil-lermo's pickup—the cramped space would be a deep freeze by morning, but that was nothing to the smells that could exist in the tent.

The Moras sat cross-legged, Indian fashion, on their bed-rolls, ignoring the others.

There was something irking old Feliciano. He scowled down at his cup, as if trying to work out some complicated thought. Some doubt, or injustice. Some wrong. Something unclarified and inarticulated as yet, that wandered vaguely among the depths of his crazy old paranoid mind.

Some gross treachery or betrayal.

A grand malfeasance.

He could not begin to imagine what this was.

He set down his coffee cup and rolled a cigarette, crimped the ends, and placed it between his bluish lips. Lit it, exhaled a cloud of smoke, and muttered aloud, in an indistinct patois, "*Hac' dano . . . no tien' razón,* goddamn, *que falso y sin razón* . . . shit 'em to hell . . .*"

Tomas turned his round, unshaven face, all rabbit-mouth and bulbous nose: "*Qué, papa?*"

Feliciano ignored this. Stared straight ahead, slumped, eyes blank, trying to sort out the tangle in his frazzled mind.

A few feet away, Sedgewick and Father Cornelius were opening a couple of cans of spaghetti for dinner. The priest also had canned sardines, and a loaf of homemade bread.

The thing that was confusing Feliciano was that he knew how to hate, but in this case he couldn't figure out what it was he should be hating, or even angry at.

This trouble in his head was too vague and obtuse. And for Feliciano, anything he couldn't confront directly was sublimely mysterious.

Still, it continued to gnaw at him, and, like a broken fingernail that has to be picked at, he turned it over in his mind.

One thing working in his favor was the liquor. It made him think more clearly. With an ordinary man, too much alcohol led to befuddlement and footling conversation, but old man Mora was not ordinary.

He would, with a kind of single-mindedness that was almost heroic, keep working at the muscatel and bourbon until the Coleman lanterns were extinguished, and then he would continue having occasional nips in the dark, through the night, dozing off to sleep, or even passing out, to waken, now and then, for another hooker, partially obsessed with the idea of keeping Tomas (who had stolen the whiskey in the first place) from getting even his fair share, and partially because this was, quite simply, the way Feliciano drank. If you had liquor, you drank it until it was gone. Then you figured out a way to get more. The result would be a crushing hangover, but in the interim there would be a most enjoyable drunk.

And in the midst of this alcohol-induced transcendentalness Feliciano knew he would find the answer to what was plaguing him.

A point would come where there would be a clarity of explanation and purpose. He would reach a solution.

It might be a solution so grandly wrong, so stupendously out of step with rational thinking—like the time he shot his neighbor out of the armchair—that no one on earth, or at least no one with a lick of common sense, could have followed Feliciano's halfwitted train of logic.

There was no kind of orchestrated celestial harmony, or music of the spheres in the heavenly clockwork, that drove the old man's raddled mentality.

Psychiatrically, he might have been evaluated as an advanced latent schizoid-paranoid, compounded by feelings of guilt and inadequacy, and with an intelligence that vacillated between that of a moron and a moderately retarded imbecile. He could, in a word, be quite dangerous.

Had he been able to verbalize his lifelong accumulation of injustices, Feliciano could have talked on and on for hours.

And so much of it would have been the truth!

For he was in fact—had been all his life—so inferior, so intellectually maimed and crippled, so emotionally and socially stultified, that the only place he really and truly belonged was in those ramshackle *jacales* above Sedgewick's cabin.

Where he could—and did—for years feebly fume and sputter and rage in a kind of wine-induced, insane euphoric-fury that *he* had never had anything, that everybody *else* had it *all*.

Yes.

All that was perfectly true.

It could have been worse for old Mora. Not that he ever realized it. In some other societies, including that of the Third Reich, he might have simply been put away for keeps. Warehoused in some mental institution for the remainder of his natural life, or even put to sleep. And, who knows, this might have been best all round. But here in this democratic society he was a free man and, in theory at least, held equal footing with a President or a Nobel laureate. In return for this, Feliciano contributed nothing, although he dutifully went down to the polls every election and sold his vote eight times over for a few gallons of wine.

He was one of society's true children. A sociological waif.

Feliciano was an *ave raro* unto himself. He had a double fidelity—not only was he unwanted, he was unneeded. He received welfare, food stamps, free medical and dental treatment (or he could have, had he not had an abject horror of any person wearing a white jacket), and got by with an unsubtle combination of lies, hypocrisy, and a variety of thick-headed stupidity so dense that it had a kind of lyrical and cunning perfection. Feliciano was a true parasite.

He finished his smoke, rolled another, drank some more from his cup. Then regarded John Sedgewick, his *patrón*, and Father Cornelius, nearby. The two of them were talking. Something to do with how much it might cost to have a few repairs done on the roof of the church.

Feliciano got up and went outside to piss. Slump-shouldered, and with his thick lips working around some interior dialogue, he made his way among the men sprawled or sitting on their bedrolls, scowling dourly as he considered the mystery of it all.

OUTSIDE IT HAD begun snowing again, and now it was coming down heavily. The big campfires had burned low, and the wind blew flurries of snow across the clearing. The horses were tethered on stake ropes, and stood with their shaggy rumps to the gusts. There was enough wind now so that the sides of the parked vehicles that faced the weather were already drifted, in some cases to the door handles. It was dark, except for the glow from the dying fires, and the lights from the Winnebago, and a glow from the big tent. The Colemans inside lighted the canvas walls, and sometimes gargantuan shadows were cast along its sloping sides as men moved about.

FELICIANO RELIEVED HIMSELF and then stared around, his shoulders hunched against the wind, collar turned up, bareheaded. Looking this way and that through the darkness of the stormy night. Faint cast of light from the tent, and a brighter spill from the windows of Les Johnson's pickup camper. And the Winnebago. From somewhere up the slope he heard a horse nicker.

Feliciano stood there a moment longer. Then, instead of returning to the tent, he approached the big motor home. The sound of its gas-driven power plant cut through the wind. The lighted picture window of the dinette area was partially obscured from time to time by snow flurries.

He went closer. What he saw in the window was perhaps nothing very unusual. Yet it held his attention.

Inside, seated at the dinette, were the Jaramillos, Clyde Fox, and George LaPorte.

The old man approached closer. Came to within ten feet of the window. Stood there in the driving snow . . . invisible to those inside. He could have stepped even closer—to within a pace or two—and still not have been seen.

The people at the table had dinner plates and drinks in front of them. The table was laid with a white cloth. There were long-stemmed wineglasses, and although there was an electric light in the background over by the kitchen counter, four tall red candles in a silver girandole illuminated the table itself and the faces of those around it.

At first this struck old Mora as odd, because it didn't seem right that anybody who was rich enough to own something as grand as the Winnebago should have to augment his lighting with cheap candles, but he finally put this down as one more small mystery, or idiosyncrasy, gringos were partial to.

The *patrón*, or boss, the one who evidently owned the Winnebago, was talking and gesticulating, and the others sat there listening. From time to time the woman broke in with a word or two.

Of the four, it was she whom the old man outside stared at hardest. He frowned every now and again, spoke to himself, unintelligibly, squinted into the driving snow, leaned closer, teetering, knee-deep in a drift, head cocked, as if by concentrating he might almost overhear what they were saying. Occasionally he glanced at the others, but not for long. It was she who interested him most.

Seen through the window—in that gentle candlelight—she looked lovelier than ever. She had washed her face, and in the yellow glow it looked fresh and clear and youthful, and even at this time of year faintly tanned. She had touched her lips with color.

She faced directly on the window, her face angled a little as she listened to LaPorte. She had brushed her hair and had it loose, over her shoulders. Her shirt was open at the collar, and her hands—large for a woman, but graceful and well cared for—rested on the edge of the table. She sat very straight in her chair, shoulders set back, head erect, listening, and at times murmuring a comment.

If she was conscious that she lent splendor and beauty to the dinner, she did not show it. Seemed unaware of her sex, oblivious to her beauty—was utterly composed. The men with her were poised too, but with the addition of a hint, a shading, an awareness of her sexuality. It showed in LaPorte's animated conversation. Clyde Fox, too . . . absorbed by her presence. Even the husband, Daniel. Sitting there. Quiet, reserved, attentive to his hosts, yet sensitive to her presence.

And, observing this tableau, so ostensibly out of place in a high hunting camp, Feliciano too was aware of her.

Standing out there in the darkness and swirling snow, he regarded her almost dreamily, raptly, yet with that curious intensity, rocking back and forth on his heels a little to maintain his balance against the thrust of the wind.

Once she looked away from the table.

Straight out the window before her, into the blackness. As if almost sensing that someone was out there.

Her eyes for a moment serious . . . alert. Then she glanced

back to her host. As though she had decided that the feeling, or intuition, or whatever it was that had urged her to look up, was unfounded. Or even foolish.

LaPorte was not drunk by far, but he had been drinking since late afternoon. It showed in the oddly intense way he had of looking at someone, almost owl-eyed, or glaring, and when he smiled—lips pressed in a thin line—there was something private, or secretive, to his expression, a certain frightening quality. The drink showed in his attitude, too. Behind the perfunctory courtliness there was an arrogance, a kind of scornful hauteur that is natural to anyone who possesses real money and power.

Sometimes he would ask Clyde to mix him a highball, but at other times he would go over to the counter and make one for himself. His guests had two light drinks apiece before sitting down to the steaks, which Fox served with a decanter of red wine, ranch-fried potatoes, and a tossed seafood salad. The talk about hunting had gotten started before they sat down, and now he kept at it, ignoring the food Clyde had set before him.

"Hunting and killing animals," she was saying. "I'm sorry. It simply doesn't make sense to me."

"Missus, there is no law that says a grown man has to make sense," LaPorte replied. "I used to hunt because it made me feel good. Fun's pretty much gone out of it for me, though I still go out occasionally." He tasted his wine, and then rotated the goblet idly. "It's a vanishing sport, you know. That's what hunting is. It's on the way out. Every time you turn around they have another species on the endangered list. Africa, Alaska, everywhere. Hunt 'em with a telephoto camera these days. Probably just as well. I'm just glad I got into all those places when there was still decent shooting."

"George has taken just about every big-game animal there is," Clyde Fox said. "Including the Tibetan snow leopard."

"Do you hunt too, Mr. Fox?" she asked.

"Oh, not really," Fox replied. "What I like best is just wandering around in the Winnebago. George and I have been everywhere. Say, why don't you try some of that salad? Don't be shy about forking out those shrimp. George has 'em flown in from Guaymas special."

"They claim men who hunt are out to prove something," she said to LaPorte.

"That's a lot of garbage, missus," LaPorte said. He smiled to himself and shook his head. "Man hunts because he enjoys it. That's all. He may prettify it with some other reason, but that's all it boils down to. Take this lion hunt. Nothing more than an execution, really. We're up here to put a varmint out of its misery. Those fools over in that tent think they're doing a service to the community because it attacked a child and killed someone, but all they're really looking for is a chance to get out and enjoy executing an animal."

"And you?" she asked.

"My weekend happened to be free," he said.

"So you came all the way from Tucson?"

"We surely did."

"Expensive," she noted.

"Money!" LaPorte said. "That's all people think about." He tasted his drink again, and then regarded her seriously, his eyes showing an almost manic intensity. "There is a time and season for every animal, missus. Including man. Why, there are criminals lots worse than this lion running loose all over this great nation of ours. I just wish something could be done about them, the same as we will do something about this lion. Maybe a time and season will come to them, too. You know, with an animal, you sometimes have to wait for years for that season. But it always comes, sooner or later. Patience is what's needed. That lion's season has come now. We'll get it."

"George, I don't reckon she's that interested in the subject," Clyde Fox said.

"Clyde, bless you, you're a hundred per cent right," LaPorte agreed. He glanced at his manager, smiling. "She wouldn't understand, would she, that sometimes getting the animal doesn't count for that much? It's the stalking, and the waiting, and the outwitting of it. It isn't just any old bear or moose or water buff. It's picking out the one—the one you especially want—and following after him, for as long as it takes. Maybe with him never even knowing it. And then, toward the end, maybe he does. And then he'll spook. And so he'll be trying this trick or that trick to get away from you, to escape, clear out, stay alive. Life is precious, and he'll be trying everything to hang on to it. I reckon that's when the real pleasure comes. When you know in your heart that you've got him, dead to rights. When he knows it too. When all your feelings tell you that no matter how hard he tries to get away, you've got him . . . that critter's as good as dead. He knows it. And you do too."

"These durned steaks are getting cold," Clyde Fox said.

CLYDE FOX THOUGHT: He is at it again. Like a badger worrying at a paw caught in a number-four trap. Worrying and chewing away at it until he's set himself free of the pain of being trapped.

He drinks too much. And then he tries to explain it, and there is no explaining of it. It can't be explained. He oughta know that.

He knows I will put up with it, all of it—and that I will try to stop him. I know what he's planning.

Because in my way I have the power over him. He knows it too. I love him and he uses me. But I have the power over him too. He will listen to me. I have always been able to talk sense to him.

He oughtn't try to explain it. I don't have to talk about it. And my loss was as great as his.

He's good at waiting. That much is true. That is something you learn with hunting, how to do that. I reckon if it takes another twenty years, old George will still be around, waiting.

And I'll be around too, to keep him from doing something that will mean the end of everything.

But there ain't no cause to go talking about it. He is driving himself crazy, for sure . . . .

That we should be together so long. Twenty-two years. And me nothing but a no-count saddlebum, drifting from ranch to ranch, drunk half the time, and the kid running helter-skelter and motherless. Growing up like a stray mongrel that nobody wants, that hangs around the back door of a kitchen waiting for scraps, and me on the likker.

And now it's me who's got the worrying and fussing with George.

They caught the man and sentenced him, and George still can't let go of it.

"We want to see 'em," he told the coroner. That's what he told him, straight out!   "You are going to let us see them, mister . . . we got that right."

And it was me who damn near fainted.

It didn't seem to faze George scarcely at all, to see them that way. Except he drank a quart that night, sitting there back at the ranch, just the two of us. He didn't talk much, just sat and drank. When the quart was all gone he said, "Clyde, be a good old boy and go fetch me another."

So I did. And by morning he had drunk that too.

He knew he owned me. He always knew that. He did so much for me and the boy. There wasn't any way in the world I could ever say no to him.

I guess we did okay. Raising those kids together, with no women around except that big old Mexican gal who never did learn to cook worth a durn. They were like brother and sister for so long, and then they weren't. They came to their growing-up time. They sure were beautiful, those two, both of them so tall and wild and yellow-headed and skinny. I used to call her Broomsticks. She never liked that, would get mad. She sure had some temper. Two horse-crazy kids, like all ranch kids are. They were something, all right.

You got to give George credit for that. He was clean-minded about them. The newspapers in Tucson made it look like two dumb college kids, stoned on marijuana, shacking up in a sleeping bag. The usual thing.

Only they had been that way together since they were fifteen. Probably even before that. Yes, I would say they very likely mighta been that way since some time before that.

George saw it coming as clear as I did. We seen it coming to them even before they did. Long before they did.

I finally said to him, "Listen, George, I am worried about this. You and I are friends. I don't want no trouble to come of this." He just looked at me for a minute and then smiled.

I give him a lot of credit for that.

We was there in the big house alone. He said, "Clyde, I sure feel like a drink."

It was only morning. I said, "I don't want a drink, George. I want to talk this thing out with you."

He said, "Clyde, we can talk it out just fine over a drink. You come along now."

Whatever George is, he ain't stupid.

So I made us a couple of whiskeys. We set down together on the couch, and he said, "Now what is there to be so damned worried about?"

I said, "I am worried about the kids, that's what."

"You figure Tim's getting into my little girl's pants?"

"Something kinda like that, George."

So then he said, "Let me tell you something, Clyde. There ain't no reason to worry about that. That is wasted worry, man. You got to learn to worry about things you can do something about. What will happen will happen. If they are that way about each other, then a team of Arkansas mules ain't going to keep 'em apart for longer than two seconds, and you know it as well as I do. You have yourself a talk with Tim, though, because I won't have her getting pregnant. I've got some fine plans for that girl, and if it turns out that Timmy is a part of her life, well, that's okay with me. He's a good boy, and he's intelligent. If it's a passing thing, it'll pass, but if they are serious about each other, they will know it, and so will we. My own feeling is that Sandy might do worse."

"She's rich. Tim is dirt poor," I said.

"Money ain't everything, Clyde," he told me. "I aim to see to it that that girl has a happy life. I want all the days of her life to be good. Why, look at you and me—just look at us! I seen you come a long way since you started working for me. You got your head together, and got yourself calmed down, and quit whoring around and drinking with both hands like it was going out of style. That boy is your piece of apple pie, just like Sandy is mine. So, here we both are—getting pretty long in the tooth. And once a month you still traipse off to Tucson for a good drunk and to stud some old gal you got hid away. And so do I. So, I'm rich, and you ain't, and we're still in the same boat. And we've got these two kids to finish raising up."

So that was the understanding, and what it all came to was us standing around in the morgue in Tucson, with George saying "We want to see 'em."

To put that many years into raising them up, and to know that they would have made it, that there was never anything mean or wrong or cheap about them. That surely was a beautiful thing to see.

And to have it end that way.

George is right. Trouble sometimes just comes looking for you.

All the bad troubles I had in my whole life were like nothing at all when I had to see them that way.

I oughta knowed there was something wrong with his mind after that night when he got drunk and said he would get that man. He said we could do it easy, and get away with it. I never doubted that. If George made up his mind to get someone like that, it would be the same as him going after a tiger or an elephant. And if I can't talk him out of it, he's liable to try it.

When we went to visit that boy, he kind of knew it too. They had him in that institution for the criminally insane. At the trial he got life. That don't mean a thing. They put him in there instead. Only relatives was supposed to visit, but George fixed that. George can fix anything when he takes a mind to.

I don't know what I was expecting to see. Maybe some kinda big old woolly-haired hippie, all crazy in his head from heroin or cocaine.

Why, hell, there just wasn't anything to him at all!

Like he'd just come straight out of a Sunday-school class. All polite and gentle and soft-eyed, kinda like a young girl, real pale he was, like he couldn't tolerate much sun, sitting there on the other side of the wirework grill and speaking through that little telephone loudspeaker, because the wire was covered with glass: "I sure am sorry for what I done, but they are going to cure me in here, they promised that, they're giving me medicines and treatment, you see, because it really wasn't my fault, I couldn't help myself."

Oh, he could sweet-talk, all right. He knew just what to say. What George's lawyers told us was that if this feller behaved himself, why, they might let him go in less than ten years, no hassle at all, and then he'd be out free as a whistle.

They oughta knowed better than to camp out up in those mountains. He had done it to three other people. The district attorney, he didn't figure he had enough evidence on those others, so he only filed charges on Tim and Sandy. But those other people had been beaten with a length of pipe the same way. They never got a chance to get out of their sleeping bag. It was like they was tied up together inside it, and he came up and did it. It must have been that way. They oughtn't to have camped out there like that. They must have seen those stories in the newspapers warning people. People was scared to even go on a picnic up in those mountains during the day. Tim would have made three of that little feller. Timmy was no runt, that's for sure. When he rodeoed summers we'd go watch him ride Brahmans. He was big and strong. If he could have gotten out of that bag, he would have put up a fight. So that feller must have been watching them out in the dark, up by their campsite, where they'd built their fire by the camper van, and cooked dinner, and then they got into that bag and zipped it shut, and he came down in the dark and did it to them. They never had any kind of chance at all.

I guess I figured the same as George, that they would marry and settle down at the ranch. Then there would have been some kids running around the old place again. Yes. Trouble sometimes just comes. No one woulda thought that when old George sent them to college that such a thing would happen.

My loss was as great as his.

That boy on the other side of the grillwork was crazy, but I don't judge he was so smart. He just laughed when George told him we'd be waiting around for him when he got out. George hates to be laughed at when he's talking serious.

The hunting now is just routine. Something to help pass the time. He didn't want to come on this hunt, but I do know how to cozy George.

That boy doesn't know George. If he did he'd stay in that place until George's mind gets straightened out. He doesn't know how George has paid money to get copies of the progress reports, and how they come in the mail every couple of months.

They say how he's a model patient, and is showing real improvement and social integration, and all that. George gets a laugh out of reading them to me. He likes hearing how well this young feller is doing, because that means they'll be reviewing his case one of these days, and then they may turn him loose. George will know about that too, and he's liable to be waiting around for him unless I can talk him out of it. He's got something planned. Sometimes he seems like his old self, and then some little thing will set him off, and then he can't leave it alone. I just wish he didn't get to talking about it so.

FIFTEEN

"El esperanto de Jesús y Dios resida en Usted," *Father Cornelius was telling Feliciano in his Cincinnati Spanish. The spirit of Jesus and God resides in you.* "En todo el mundo," *the priest added. In everyone.*

Feliciano eyed him uncomprehendingly. The stocky old Franciscan might as well have been speaking to a Barbary ape.

Cornelius had it in mind to caution the old man about drinking so much. Most of the other men in the tent were exhausted from the long day out-of-doors, and were asleep or in their down bags, smoking and talking. Sedgewick lay on his own bag, dressed in long underwear, heavy socks, and a thick sweater that buttoned up the front. Before him was a small chess board, one of those fold-up pocket sets with tiny magnetized discs. He and the priest were playing out a game under the white glare of the Colemans, drinking bourbon and smoking their pipes.

AFTER HE RETURNED to the tent Mora had made less of a secret about his and his son's drinking. The two of them flopped atop their bedrolls, the bourbon and muscatel in open sight, with a canteen of water for chasers. They spoke little. Merely sprawled in their corner of the tent, lying on their sides, turned from the sputtering light of the Colemans as much as possible, rolling cigarettes and drinking.

Like most Pecos people, Cornelius knew a little about the Moras, mostly by way of rumor. He knew that they were pariahs. None of the clan, including the monstrous Eduvigen, had ever come to his church. He didn't even know if old Feliciano was a Catholic, or for that matter if he had ever been baptized, but he assumed that somewhere in Mora's past this might have happened.

The redemption of souls was not exactly up Father Cornelius's spiritual alley, let alone a soul in such rudimentary shape as Feliciano's. He had plenty of regular work to do in his parish, holding mass and the ordained holidays, tending births and deaths, enlarging the patch of garden behind the church, and shooting and dressing out twenty to thirty deer and elk a year.

Cornelius had a hard-nosed Midwesterner's preference for souls that were willing to get out and hustle some redemption on their own behalf. He tended to forgive easier when a sinner had put in a little overtime suffering. The drunks, philanderers, and dopers of Pecos knew better than to pester him with hypocritical promises to live better lives. He had been known to get nasty in the presence of shallow lip service. It was rumored that he had once told Archbishop Montcroissier, on the subject of salvation, "I ain't no social worker, Your Excellence."

It wasn't just bluster. The toughest teen-age boys in the parish, all long hair, sulky mouths, and slouched, aggressive swagger, got abashed and spoke in nervous stammers when he turned those icy-blue Teutonic eyes upon them. Cornelius was a strong old man. If one got snippy, he grabbed an ear and twisted it until the kid yelled. Yet, for all that, he was gentle, and loved the people given into his care. Loved to joke and kid around and flirt with the womenfolk who on feast days banded together to cook bring-your-own dishes for the picnics, outings, bazaars that he organized. He also ran the weekly bingo games that were held in the church's recreation room. Cornelius was a bingo freak—but along with the rest of the town he left the Moras alone.

There was, however, the Christian side to his nature. Perhaps even a taint of mysticism—though in Cornelius's case one had to search closely for the transcendental influence. But mysticism is, after all, the basis for any religion.

It could be that, between chess moves with Sedgewick, a thought occurred to the old priest. That maybe the divine hand of Providence had guided him to bed down in that corner of the tent, alongside the Moras. These two, who were despised even among their own people.

Cornelius had as much patience with philosophy as he did with social work. All he could recall about the theosophy classes taught at the Franciscan order in Cincinnati was that God moved in mysterious ways. Perhaps this night, this hunt, this lion that had led them up into the high mountains, might have all been arranged for some specific end. God only knew what end. But he, Cornelius, might be derelict if he did not at least keep an open mind and make the most of what came his way. Hence his well-meant advice to Feliciano. He was not an intellectual churchman, and he would have been the first to admit it—perhaps defiantly. He was blunt, practical, and ideally matched to his job assignment, that of tending the spiritual needs of a boondock village in the Southwest. This did not make him less of a man of God, or a bad priest either. He was in too many ways an open and loving man. Within the Brotherhood it was said of him that if he lacked certain saintly qualities he surely made up for it with others.

The trouble was, he couldn't make a dent in Feliciano. Even sober old Mora wouldn't have paid attention to him—or understood the priest's cautionary remarks about not liquoring himself into a blind stupor.

Sedgewick moved out his bishop, while Cornelius lectured

Feliciano: "We have important work to do up here, Señor Mora. We must catch this lion that hurt the child. If you drink too much, my son, you will not be able to hunt well tomorrow."

Feliciano listened to this with a truculent expression. No real response at all. He disliked any padre, especially a gringo padre, calling him "son," although he knew that this was how padres liked to talk. Feliciano was no one's son. He couldn't remember his own father, so how could he be someone's son? He belched wetly, and began rolling another smoke. When he was done, he placed the thin cigarette between his lips, with a kind of oddly graceful and elegant movement. He struck a match to it, and when he had got it going he poured some bourbon and wine into his tin cup. Glared sulkily as Tomas reached for a refill.

"Too much vino will destroy you . . . *destruyan, malo,*" Father Cornelius labored on. "That would be a sin, Señor Mora, *porqué el esperanto de Jesús resida en Usted, sabe?*" He turned and moved out a knight to threaten the bishop, forgetting to protect his bishop. Sedgewick took it with a pawn. Cornelius said, "Heck."

About an hour later Feliciano sort of figured out what it was the priest had been trying to tell him. The Colemans were still hissing overhead. It was something about God and Destruction residing in him. He thought this was a pretty grand notion.

Someone on the other side of the tent, snoring lightly, still had a transistor tuned in to the Spanish-music station in Santa Fe, but aside from the low rock-'n'-roll beat in Latin tempo, the tent was silent.

Sedgewick had taken the first game quickly, but this time Cornelius was on guard. He played a purely defensive game for eight or nine moves, as though timidly dawdling, and then he would come on with a quick attack, plunging through Sedgewick's defenses, sacrificing an important piece of his own to get where he wanted.

He and Sedgewick had most of a fifth of bourbon beside the chessboard. They didn't offer Feliciano any. The old man had edged closer, carrying a brimming cup, not spilling a drop.

He brought his smell with him. Presently, the two men playing looked up, glanced at each other, without comment or change of expression, then glanced back at the miniature board between them. More time passed this way.

Old man Mora couldn't figure the board. Such a little thing. With discs of white and black metal stuck to it, with strange emblems on the discs.

They stared at it so intently. As if it held some kind of secret.

Sometimes one of them moved a disc. Then they both went back to staring at the strange arrangement in black-and-white. As if by looking at it long enough they would discover the secret. There was a mystery in how the discs were moved. Some went forward and back, some diagonally—others went in funny ways. There was no reason to it at all.

Yet there had to be! Or so Feliciano thought. Else why would men do such a thing? He could not fathom it. His own *patrón*.

He sensed—felt—that there were things he did not comprehend. How could all this be? How could this crazy padre believe that God was in him? How could his *patrón* be so absorbed in such a stupid thing, little squares, little discs?

There were too many things beyond his ken. He felt this deeply, and out of the awareness there came a resurgence of the ill-humor and resentment that had plagued him earlier. That anger that he had been carrying inside him. Not just this evening, or today—or for the past week—but for years . . . for a lifetime, a thousand lifetimes. For all the lifetimes of all the Felicianos of the world . . . who would never win at anything. Who were so singularly unequipped to stay alive, let alone win!

There slumbered in his mind a deep and irrevocable intuition of the injustice of it all.

He felt so sorry for himself.

Felt pathetically weak, ill-used, cheated. Was so blindly unaware of his parasitism. Was unaware, too, that the true parasite is in a certain way stronger than its host. The lamprey eel, the tropical sucker-vine, and Feliciano had much in common. By feeding off a supposedly stronger host they utilized its strength to nurture their own, surviving, more often than not, to go on to another host.

Feliciano's attention soon drifted from the game. He began staring at Sedgewick.

It gradually became clear to him, in his alcohol-fueled brain, that he was not beneath Sedgewick. Despite his own negative feelings about himself. Sedgewick wasn't so great. He himself, in fact, was as good as Sedgewick.

He was equal.

It was unfair that Sedgewick should treat him like a *cabrito* —a stupid goat. That this man—his *patrón*—should sit there, right by him, absorbed in something as stupid as a little game. That his *patrón* should give his entire attention, so calmly, so in possession of his faculties . . . to see him smile easily when he scored a small triumph on the board. As if that little toy was all that mattered in the world.

When he had seen his *patrón* in another way. In a high alpine glade, on a sunny summer day! When he had heard him cry out, as though wounded. When he had learned—seen with his own eyes!—that all men, and women too, can be reduced to the level of animals, cleaving like stricken beasts!

With some small sense of self-satisfaction, he reckoned— and very rightly so—that he was the only person in the entire world who knew how it was with his *patrón* and the *madona-bruja* . . . that incredibly beautiful and evil apparition he had been observing out in the wind-whipped snow not so long ago.

He knew!

He was not such a fool. Because he knew what others didn't.

Sedgewick struck a fresh match to his pipe and glanced up to find old Mora looking at him with a stare that bordered on the maniacal. With a grin that was manic too—the rubbery lips stretched back over infected gums and black-rotted teeth.

Sedgewick said, "*Qué pasó*, Feliciano?"

Feliciano responded. Almost cringed.

Still grinning. Moved his head, twisting his neck in a sly, serpentine side movement. The neck muscles swelling and rolling ... curiously, a graceful, sliding, snakelike dip. Abashed yet defiant. Knowingly sinuous. Eyes averted. He could not look Sedgewick in the eye.

"*Natha, patrón*," Mora whispered.

Unconsciously aping, with perfect inflection, the effeminate lisp of the Castilian Boy-King.

He drank. A sip at first. Then the cup was upended. A dribble ran down a fold of one cheek, past his chin, and into the collar of his tattered shirt. And then he hiccuped, snorted, tittered, almost silently.

A joke of his own, perhaps. Something too wildly funny, too obtuse to describe in words, but nonetheless hugely enjoyable.

Sitting there beside the two of them, he simply cracked up with suppressed glee. Wheezing and sputtering, as he had that Saturday afternoon down at Johnny Larragoite's Crippled Horse in Pecos.

Because he knew.

THE COLEMANS ARE out now and it is dark in the tent except for the sheepherder, which throws a red glare through its front grill, but even with the stove it is cold inside, and the sleeping men, despite their fatigue and the liquor they have drunk, move restlessly in their bags or blanket rolls, sometimes murmuring or speaking indistinctly out of the depths of their sleep.

Once, Guillermo Apodaca wakens and lies there in the darkness for a while, smoking a cigarette. Beside him, his son,

Vicente, his mouth numbed by aspirin and bourbon, groans restlessly.

Father Cornelius, a round lump in his mummy bag—he has on two sweaters and his parka—dreams of an elk he spotted through binoculars last fall, a fourteen-pointer at least, who rides herd on a string of cows up by Beautty's Cabin, near Horsethief Meadows.

Outside, there is no wind at all, but the snow is falling again, not hard but steadily, coming straight down.

It is dark too in Les Johnson's pickup camper, except for the glow of the catalytic, and crowded too, with the dogs.

Monty Cartier, the director of the department, is asleep on the floor between Johnson's and Bowman's plywood bunks, with Cacique, the big Labrador, sprawled half across his legs.

Cacique, in his slumber, is a heavy dreamer. In his sleep he dreams of what all dogs dream of—a chase. After the eternal rabbit. A rabbit, perhaps, to end all rabbits. As big as a calf and as swift as the wind. And in the dream Cacique pursues it through all the days of his life—never winded, never footsore, never losing sight or scent of that marvelous beast that dashes ahead of him, and never catching it either . . . perhaps aware that he could pursue his quarry through all eternity, to the end of time, and still not bring down the prize—for it is not meant to be captured. The joy is the chase itself. That is all that counts and all that has ever mattered. To be out and running forever. In his sleep he quivers and woofs. Slobbers a little. His legs pump spastically, and with a seismic gut-rumble he breaks wind.

Beneath him, Monty Cartier sleeps on. Like the men in the tent, he has had his share of liquor, and if he dreams at all it is of a wish that despite his high position and prestige he could be back again as a simple game-conservation officer, grade two, taking orders instead of giving them, free of political intrigue, free to put in his time up in the high country—young again. Monty Cartier chases something just as elusive as Cacique's eternal hare: youth.

In the Winnebago it is quiet too. Clyde Fox earlier reached a decision to shut down the gas-driven generating plant. Inside, it is warm. The snow on the long coach roof is two feet deep. In the kitchenette, a night light burns via the twelve-volt system. Through the big picture window, where Feliciano Mora watched, the dinette table is unoccupied, the plates and silver cleared away and a fresh service already laid out for breakfast. Clyde Fox is a tidy housekeeper.

SOMETIME IN THE night the snow stopped altogether, and then the temperature fell sharply, below zero, and it was silent and the air was dry and very cold, and then, before dawn, a faint breeze started again, and with that the trees began talking.

Sedgewick wakened in the darkness hearing what he at first took to be the creaking of a giant door as it opened on unoiled hinges. Such a horrendous groan that it was almost a shriek. It came from a long way off, out there, up among the higher slopes somewhere. It was joined by another groan, and then still others, some farther off, some close to the camp . . . a simply terrific rending and groaning, as if, somehow, a band of lost and godforsaken giants or ogres were crying and complaining in the night.

Sedgewick, listening, felt the hair at the nape of his neck horripilate.

He sat up on one elbow in the dark, reached for his pipe, tobacco, matches. Struck a light. To see Father Cornelius, beside him, eyes open.

Sedgewick whispered, "You hear that?"

"It's the trees," Cornelius said in a low voice.

"I've never heard anything like that in my life," Sedgewick said. "It sounds like the whole forest is being ripped apart. You must be able to hear it for miles."

"They talk like that when the conditions are right," Cornelius said. "I've heard 'em before. The air's got to be dry and real cold. Then, if a little wind comes along, it makes the deadfalls move—the big ponderosas that have died but not fallen down, you know. They fall partway, and their upper branches get tangled in the living trees around them, and they just hang there like that, until they rot. When the wind moves them, they rub against the living trees . . . bark scraping. Some nights I've heard the whole forest talking like that, miles and miles of it, just groaning and creaking. Then the wind will stop, and it'll get dead silent. Then it'll start all over, grinding and roaring."

"Does it have any significance to the Spanish people?" Sedgewick asked.

"Like what?"

"Superstition . . . ill portents, evil omens, or something?"

"None that I ever heard of," Cornelius said. "All it means is that we are in for a cold day tomorrow. Really cold." He turned on his side, squirmed, seeking warmth, and not a minute later was snoring.

Sedgewick remained awake, smoking his pipe. He thought: There is trouble all around this place. Not just small trouble but the worst kind. I ought to get away from these people. Put some distance between them and me. You can feel it. It's like the smell of doom. They are all set against each other. No good will come of it.

I thought to help myself by coming here to live. Instead it's gotten worse.

I love her, yes. But I've loved other women. And in return for the love they gave back I left them diminished . . . lessened.

What a fearsome, rotten racket it is.

I only know this: If a woman likes a man, wants him, it's over already. The wooing, the courtship, none of that amounts to anything. All that is needed is the time necessary for her to finally admit it to herself, and then it is over.

With her I wish it hadn't happened. But it did, and so that is that. She knew it would, too.

She asks me if she is the best lover I have ever been with. I lied and said yes. How can she ask a thing like that? Why do all of them always ask that sooner or later? Why can't they just accept that to be with a woman is good, and that each woman loves in her own way, differently from other women, but still good—always good. They ought to just let it go at that and not ask, but sooner or later they do, don't they?

She's a gentle girl. So emotional, but also gentle, and that is what I love most about her. When she gets wild, that's just fine, but it doesn't make me love her. I love her afterward, when we are used up. It's then that she can look at me with those slanty, sleepy eyes and strike through me. With one look she owns me.

I've got to do something about all this. I've waited too long. When this is over I'm going to leave. I'll take her with me. If she will come. We'll leave this place together.

She's ready to move. Was ready for it years ago. The life she has with him isn't enough. Maybe it once was, but not now. Not for a long time.

Her values are sound. That's what has been ripping her apart. She doesn't want ten men in her life. Or two. One is enough. I believe that about her. She's straight that way.

It's time for her to move on. That's all divorce means these days. The end of a marriage is simply the passing of time to the point where, after a while, it's time for you to move on.

I think that's where she's at. And she knows it. If we leave together, I'll take care of her. And she will know it.

I should have acted sooner. It shouldn't have gone on this long. She's tearing herself apart with all this.

The pipe he had been smoking was out. He set it down, beside the tobacco pouch, and curled up in the sleeping bag. Overhead, through the vent that held the stove flue, he saw that the sky was turning light.

It was Sunday.

SIXTEEN

Father Cornelius was an early riser. He was dressed and moving about while most of the others were still sleeping. He pumped the pressure tanks of the Coleman lanterns full and got them going, and then stoked the sheepherder with fresh billets of wood. In the lantern light the men stirred, sat up, reached for cigarettes, looking disgruntled and overtired, as if they had had too little hot food and then too much to drink the night before. The priest, though, was full of bustle. When the stove began throwing off heat he put on his gloves and pulled up the hood of his parka and left the tent.

OUTSIDE THE SKY was turning bright, but sunrise was still the better part of an hour off.

Both campfires were sodden black messes. Cornelius crouched beside one and poked at the char with a stick, uncovering, beneath the wet, a hot bed of embers. He stirred these, then stoked them with small shavings and twigs that, as soon as they had dried enough, flickered brightly in the gloomy half light, adding still more, then branches, so that in fifteen minutes he had a real blaze. The men would be needing it this morning.

He set pots of frozen ice to one side of the flames to thaw. Went over to a tree, urinated, and started back to the tent. Then stopped a moment to stare at Guillermo Apodaca's pickup. It was blanketed under several feet of snow. The windows were opaque.

He went over to it, brushed the snow from the windshield, tried to peer inside, then went to open the door. The press button of the lock was frozen, and he had to smack at it to break it loose. The rubber weatherstripping lining the edge of the door was frozen too, and some of it tore away when he was finally able to tug the door open. Inside, the surfaces of the windows were coated with a thick rime of frost. The condensed coating of ice was from Virgil McCormick's breathing. Virgil was jackknifed into the front seat, zipped into a down mummy bag.

"Virge? You okay?" Father Cornelius asked. He poked at McCormick. The body moved a little, but not much. Then McCormick groaned from inside the bag. Cornelius said, "Fire's building, Virgil. Whyn't you come on over and get warm?"

Virgil's beaky nose emerged from the head opening. Then an eye showed, then some of his face. His skin had no color in it. He said finally, "Oh, God . . ."

Cornelius had to help him out of the bag, and then out of the front seat. He was badly crippled from sleeping in one position, and he was shaking. With Cornelius holding him, he made it over to the fire, hobbling and groaning, still half bent in a jackknife position. He said, "I was in the Bulge, near Malmedy, winter of '44, when the Kraut armored divisions busted through. It was cold then but it was nothing compared to last night. My God. Father, it musta been thirty below."

"It wasn't much warmer in the tent," Cornelius said.

"I don't believe that," Virgil said. "I got no feeling in my feet, Father. I think I'm frostbit."

"You sit here by the fire. The heat'll get to you," Cornelius said. He set about making coffee in the pots of heating water. By now other men were coming out of the tent.

It was cold outside, even by the fire. The kind of dry, sub-zero chill that cuts through the warmest clothing, so cold that if a man stood directly in front of the flames the front part of him would be hot, but all the back of him would feel the cold.

A couple of men went to start up the second fire, but the rest of them stayed close to the flames, their hands jammed into pockets, hunch-shouldered against the cold. They yawned or belched, worked bourbon-furred tongues over sour gums and teeth, farted, and stared around moodily.

It was not a day to be up in the mountains, and it was no day to be hunting. Hunting was supposed to be fun, but this gray morning was a frozen hell. Virgil McCormick remembered what it had been like near Bastogne. After a few days of that kind of weather the efficiency of troops—German, American, it didn't make any difference—was halved, then quartered. It was the cold and the fatigue, and the men got by mostly on cigarettes and bottles of liberated cognac. After a week of it their reflexes were shot and they stumbled around like robots.

Father Cornelius knelt in the frozen snow and after crossing himself recited a brief service that did not last sixty seconds. Some of the other men knelt too, but most of them gathered around him, their heads bowed, hands clasped in front of them. The priest concluded with a prayer: "And, please, Dear Lord, if You see so fit within Your bountiful grace and mercy, do send a little luck our way this day, so that we may get this dangerous beast and so return in safety to the hearths and hearts of those who pray for our success, Amen!"

Across the clearing a flashlight shone in the window of Les Johnson's camper. He and Lewis Bowman and Cartier were stirring too.

Lights were on in the Winnebago. Clyde Fox was up, the percolator going on the fancy stove, canned Canadian bacon being opened, freeze-dried hash browns out and ready for the pan.

Good living in there. Of all the people in camp, only those in the Winnebago had slept in comfort. George LaPorte had done the Jaramillos a bigger favor than they would ever imagine.

The mood of the men at the fire was clear. They would have to hunt the cat today and get it, or return to Pecos. There was no wind, but the sky overhead was gray with thick banks of cumulus. They knew that this kind of weather could go on for days, and that there would be more snow. It was not dangerous weather, but it could turn that way. One storm had a way of following in the wake of another. If a real blizzard hit, even Army Reserve helicopters would have trouble getting up to them.

Storm or not, there was only so much they could get done about the lion. Even LaPorte, who had come all the way from Arizona, wouldn't argue that. So now, in the breaking dawn light, as they sat or stood about the fires, smoking and drinking coffee and talking in low voices, this possibility of failure showed on their faces. They looked bitter, the way men will get when they have been sent on a fool's errand.

The only ones who did not seem to mind this possibility of defeat were Feliciano and Tomas Mora. They had both gone to bed drunk. Had awakened groggily, and had started off the new day with a cupful each of bourbon and the last of the muscatel.

THE BACK OF Les Johnson's camper opens, and he and Bowman and Cartier and the dogs step out. The dogs, at least, are lively and full of zip. Lewis has them off the leashes, and they take off in bounding leaps through the drifts, stopping here and there to squat, or lift a hind leg. Oona, the Malamute bitch, tear-asses through the deep snow, rolls in it ecstatically, then, in a frenzy, dashes up among the horses tethered on the stake line. A big Appaloosa, startled, lets off a kick at her, and with a yelp she heads back to Lewis.

At one of the fires, over coffee, Johnson tells the men his opinion. He wants to hunt for the morning only. The weather looks too tricky. He is for returning to camp by midday, so that they can clear the blocked road below, break camp, and get out of there by midafternoon. They are to hunt on foot, walking the two miles to the little canyon where the tracks were seen. If the lion isn't there, then that's it.

Hearing that they will hunt afoot, their expressions turn grimmer. Of course, Johnson is right. They all know this. The night's snowfall has ruined any chance of getting much out of the horses. In it, their hooves would pack and slip, and the deeper drifts would exhaust them in a quarter of a mile. They have been trailered all the way up here, and now they will have to be trailered back down, to their stables and winter pastures. The men are aware of this. It is just that they don't like having Johnson tell them about it. His pronouncement makes the overcast day even more cheerless. As if all of this, somehow, is the lion hunter's fault—the unexpected storm, going afoot, the fearful cold, the lack of success.

A total lack, unless they count yesterday's trophies, the two little lionesses. The carcasses still strung from a nearby tree, heads dangling downward. Bodies frozen hard as oak planks. The cats look smaller this morning, and entirely without threat or danger. Pelts matted and torn, dusted with snow.

In the elegant Winnebago, Karen Jaramillo is insisting for the third or fourth time that she wants to come along with the party that will soon move out. "I mean, it would be just senseless for me to sit here all day," she points out.

George LaPorte and Clyde Fox exchange glances. Each senses that something is wrong. There is no reason for this woman to be up here. They feel the tension between her and her man, but ignore it. It is not their affair. There is no reason for this husband of hers—this trim, handsome, polite Spanish fellow—to be so reserved, so quiet. As if he has something on his mind.

Without speaking or looking again at each other, LaPorte and Fox take a mutually agreeable stance. They can feel out each other's mood, in the way of men who have lived together for years. They will act the part of visiting out-of-towners, here for the weekend. Which, of course, is what they are. Best stay out of it.

"Missus, you'd be a real bother out there today," LaPorte says finally. "You just stay here. You'll be nice and cozy. We've got a radio and a stereo, and a whole library of tapes, and magazines, and plenty of food in the kitchen. It's warm. You can have yourself a shower. It appears to me that we only have about a ten-to-one chance to nail this poor critter anyway. It won't be fun. You come along, you'll end up black in the toes with frostbite. No sense in it."

"I'm coming," she insists.

LaPorte shakes his head. Almost frowns, as though the concept of someone, let alone a woman, going against his common-sense judgment is something not worthy of patience. He is right, and he knows it. Why argue, then? He looks over at Daniel.

Daniel says, "He's right."

"I'll stay if you stay too," she tells him.

"I'm going," Daniel Jaramillo says. His tone is firm. As if, at last, he must take a stand about how things have gone.

On the bunk he shared last night with his wife are the things he will be taking. Jacket, hat, gloves, the .257. Earlier, she had wakened to find him seated on the edge of the bunk, cleaning the rifle with a rod borrowed from Clyde Fox, running a Hoppe's-soaked white flannel patch slowly through the bore, although the rifle, like most of the others, has been unfired this weekend.

Lying on the bed, too, is the ammunition he has brought along, three shiny, bottlenecked cartridges, soft-tipped 150-grain jobs, a sizable slug for the little .257 to throw. Two of the cartridges are spares—backups. The third is for the cat itself, should Daniel sight it. Actually, the spares are unnecessary. Daniel is a good shot. He had been taught to hunt with one cartridge at a time. He had learned this style of hunting from an uncle. One cartridge, one animal. At fourteen, he had gotten his first deer this way, with a .22, which is illegal for big game. It was then, too. That weekend his family had praised him. Over a hundred pounds of venison for a little .22 hollowpoint that had cost less than a cent.

That was judged to be pretty good hunting. But as the years passed he eased off going into the big woods for the fall hunt. It was something he knew he could do, but he knew too that at heart he lacked the spirit other men seemed able to muster—that pleasure they found in the simple and straightforward act of killing.

Yet, this weekend, it was he and not Sedgewick who had suggested they take part in the hunt.

THE MEN WERE truculent about walking, except for Cornelius, who had the reputation of being a fool of a walker, a priest such as had never been seen in these parts, whose stocky legs could carry him on a straight uphill climb for hours. He seemed almost cheerful over what lay ahead.

Peter Griego stood near him, his back to the crackling fire, shoulders squared in that parade-field stance, hands clenched at the small of his back to catch the fire's warmth. He listened to Lester Johnson with melancholy eyes. Lips drawn tight. The big Smith and Wesson revolver belted about the waist of his blue canvas parka. Fur trooper's cap. His nose was red with the cold, and the lids of his eyes were inflamed. Dark bluish cheek and jowl. No one had shaved this morning.

Virgil McCormick looked ill. He was still fiercely chilled, and shook from time to time, as though from the ague.

Vicente Apodaca's mouth and face were worse today. His lips were a swollen wreck. Guillermo, his father, stood beside him, holding a cup of coffee. The battered old Stetson with the fancy silver-and-turquoise band was tied around his head and ears with a red wool scarf.

Feliciano and Tomas looked on at the proceedings through a bourbon haze.

Jaramillo and Sedgewick stood a little distance from the others. Sedgewick looked tired. He and Daniel had scarcely greeted each other.

LaPorte, Clyde Fox, and Monty Cartier stood by, listening to what Johnson had to say. The two Arizona men seemed untroubled by the idea of tracking an animal through the snow, without horses, or even snowshoes, or gas-powered Totegoats, or trail bikes. They were, like the Moras, hunters.

OLD LES JOHNSON looked cranky as usual. It was his natural expression when he was with people he didn't care for. But there was a hint of malicious enjoyment about him as he spoke. As if he was thinking: Well, shit fire and save matches, I never *said* it would be a picnic! Hunting cats ain't fun, and there ain't that much excitement in it either, just work.

His ungloved hands were frost-nipped and blue with cold. Lewis had the dogs on chains by now. The sky was brightening. It was after seven. In deer season this would be late to be getting started. During the fall hunt they would have been up hours ago, would have eaten and left in the dark, to position themselves on ridges and bluffs to wait for the spiked bucks who would quit moving by sunrise or a little after— deer hide out during daylight, unless flushed—but now, on this morning, in this cold, they weren't doing badly to be leaving even this late.

Then something else got started. Lewis Bowman went into the tent and came out with his .30-30. Peter Griego looked at it, then at Lewis, then at Les Johnson. He said flatly, "That man can't have a weapon."

"He always carries a rifle," Johnson said.

"No way," Peter insisted.

"Officer Griego, this isn't some kind of rabbit hunt," Monty Cartier said.

Peter shook his head. "I'm confiscating it. Bowman, hand it over."

He felt someone tap him on the shoulder. Turned, to stare into George LaPorte's intent, bespectacled gaze. LaPorte said, "What's the problem, Officer?"

"This man's my prisoner. He's under arrest," Peter said.

"We need him this morning," LaPorte said.

"My God, you can't have a prisoner going around armed with a weapon," Peter argued.

"Extenuating circumstances, Officer . . . Griego, is it?" LaPorte said. "Seems perfectly clear to me."

"Extenuating or not, if a man is under arrest, you don't let him go armed," Peter told LaPorte. "I'd be begging for a thirty-day suspension if I did something as stupid as that."

That wide-eyed, fixed stare—though the voice was calm, almost gentle. LaPorte said, "Look at it this way, Officer. Suppose all of us, this morning, were going into some ghetto building to arrest a man we knew had killed someone. Suppose you were in charge of the show. You wouldn't be sending an unarmed man into a situation like that, would you?"

"Don't argue with me," Peter said.

"All right, I won't," LaPorte said. He smiled. "But I'm telling you this right now. I am holding you personally responsible for the safety of this young fellow. If we locate this animal, and if this man is injured in any way, you'll be responsible. The lieutenant-governor invited me and my manager on this hunt. He'll want to know how it turns out. In fact, we could probably raise him right now, though it's a little early to be calling on Sunday. I have a shortwave in the Winnebago that ties in with Mountain Bell. If he's home, I'd be happy to have you clear up the matter personally with him." When Peter didn't reply, LaPorte, still smiling, shook his head, almost apologetically. "After all, I'm just a visitor this weekend. I'm not a fellow who likes to stick his nose into a situation that's really none of his business."

The state trooper's face was expressionless. He knew he had lost again, as with the four flat tires. Knew that he had lost face with all these men, knew too from the expression on LaPorte's face that the Arizonan meant it when he said he would radiotelephone the lieutenant-governor. The idea of getting into an argument with that official, who was known to have a short temper, and who was probably still in the sack, held no appeal. Peter said finally, "All right, let him have the rifle. I put this Johnson fellow in charge of the hunt, and I'll stick by my word. But if anything goes wrong, if there's any kind of incident with this Bowman, I'm holding Johnson responsible." He looked at Monty Cartier. "And you too, sir." Then at LaPorte. "And that goes for you, too."

LaPorte thought this over and then nodded. "That's fair enough, Officer." He looked around at the group, and now his smile had a trace of that arrogance that had been so evident the night before. "Time's getting on, gentlemen. Let's hunt." To Les Johnson he said, "Your move, sir. How do you want to set it up?"

Johnson told them again, "We'll try to do it pretty much the way we did it yesterday. Most of you I'll put up on the ridges above that canyon where we think this cat is hid. The rest of us will come up the mouth of the canyon. Don't go shooting unless I yell for you to. You're liable to hit some of your neighbors. If we can get this animal up a tree, we can sedate him, same as we tried yesterday."

This last he knew as a waste of breath.

If they got the damned cat out into the open where it was helpless, they would shoot, every last one of them. He could sense their mood. What he had told Cartier yesterday was right. The hunt had gone wrong from the start. And with this knowledge he sensed that he had failed, too. The big air gun strapped to his shoulder seemed exactly what Guillermo Apodaca had called it: a fancy toy.

THE MEN BY the fires pour last cups of black coffee, using mittened or gloved hands to hold the hot pot handles. There is virtually no conversation now. They wait, sipping at their coffee, gazing at the burning logs, as if they may never see or experience such comfort and heat again, and so must store up in their memories this ineradicable imprint of yellow flames. A pungent, charry stench of smoke from still-wet wood. The pop and sizzle of frozen sap giving way to searing heat. At the other end of the clearing the horses stand tethered.

THE BIG PICTURE window of the Winnebago—it is made of a single sheet of safety glass—is completely fogged over with interior condensation.

Karen Jaramillo, not unlike many women when their minds are preoccupied, has absent-mindedly let a pot of water for instant coffee go unattended on the kitchenette range, thus adding to the humidity of the mobile home's warm interior.

From the outside the Winnebago looks abandoned and forlorn. Its chrome-and-enamel elegance hidden by snow or dulled in the gray morning light.

It looks like some kind of casualty of nature's indifference.

Drifted snow, angled high along one aluminum flank. A great mushroom cap of white atop the coach roof.

Inside, no lights are lit. Clyde Fox, though, has double-checked to make sure the butane heaters are going safely. It has happened before that snow can pack an exhaust vent, and that can be deadly in a tightly sealed vehicle.

It is silent inside, too. The windows are blank. Steamed over, except along their sides and at the rectangular corners. In the corners the ice has crusted into thick rime.

Outside, in the clearing, it is nine below zero, but inside the electrically controlled wall thermostat reads a comfortable seventy-five.

The picture window is like a huge, blind eye, frosted to a cataract-milky-white rectangle.

But now, almost in its exact center, a dot appears. Seeming almost a smudge against the coating of white.

It grows larger. Spreads to an oval, perhaps the size of an outstretched hand.

Visible now, from the inside, touched to the wet glass, is the extended forefinger of a woman's hand.

The tip of it leisurely tracing its ovate path, wiping the glass. The finger is removed, and in the cleared space her eyes appear, staring out. Gazing calmly, and without expression, at the men around the fire.

She watches like this for some time.

But there is no such thing as expressionless eyes. Especially those of a lovely woman.

Viewed close up—through the wetted glass—they are what? Perhaps thoughtful. Their color is lovely. That deep, clear gray. Long-lashed. The arch of the brows—unplucked, and of a lightish brown, almost unfashionably strong, in fact, rather thick for a woman—lends the expression an air of sadness, or of some ancient grief that is too hurtful to speak of even now. The bridge of the nose is thin, delicately modeled. The skin beneath the eyes and around the high cheekbones is clear, unblemished, though marked with a faint splatter of freckles. At the corners of the eyes there are the beginnings of age lines, and in the center of the brows there is a thin but permanent worry line, or frown.

They are not the eyes of a girl, or even of a young woman. Yet they have a certain youthful beauty and innocence of their own. Their gaze—imbued with that pensive sadness—is astonishingly open and direct. So steadfast, and calm, and so clearly honest. As if she, with these eyes, is utterly incapable of concealing what lies behind them. As if they are windows opening directly into the depths of her privacy. As if she, via some female magic, can gaze out through them and see what others cannot. Can plumb and fathom the souls of those who come within their scope.

It is the eyes, perhaps, that led Sedgewick to accurately define her intelligence and sensitivity. Beauty and sadness go hand in hand . . . but the eyes of an intelligent woman are a wonder.

They were, who knows, perhaps what had robbed him of whatever decent intentions he had brought with him to the village of Pecos.

There is a wearied proverb that says for a man love is one thing, but for a woman it is everything. But the hackneyed triteness of such a notion does not necessarily make it any the less so. In certain cases, anyway.

In the same vein, there may be merit in the concept that a man cannot really fathom a woman until that frightening moment when he stares directly into her eyes.

Only then can he, perhaps, get an inkling of what is on her mind. And, sometimes, on his own as well.

Or perhaps it is merely that Sedgewick is a fool for a woman with a sad expression. Daniel too, of course—since, after all, he married her.

What difference does it make, really, if she has been unfaithful to the man she swore fidelity to? Certainly no great crime in these times. Sedgewick knows this. Everyone does. If it were serious, half the population would wear the scarlet "A." A conservative estimate.

She was never even a flirt. Never was, never had to be. That steadfast gaze obviated the need for any such game. The telltale taint of the coquette or aging ingenue—and that, really, is all ingenues are good for, aging—is that they cannot look a man in the eye for more than a few seconds. They all seem absorbed in watching the flights of sky-borne orioles.

If anything, she is shy. Perhaps always has been. That a beautiful woman can also be enormously shy is not at all the contradiction it at first appears to be. As a young woman many skills had escaped her. She failed at being a good dancer. Fell short by a mile in the cuteness department. Tried flattery, but her compliments rang false. Was seldom—or never seemed to be—much impressed by any man. Perhaps it was only that honest gaze that made her seem so. Not that she was ever a wallflower. Not with her looks. If she could not simper, then it followed that things worked the other way round. The men who sought her, did. She liked many of them, smiled upon them, and, as she had once confided to Sedgewick, went to bed with a certain number. That, she figured, was her business, and it was past. By the time Daniel proposed, she was ready to settle. Had no qualms. And no regrets at all for the so-called freedom she was leaving behind. She married Daniel for the best and simplest reason of all. He was a man who she believed could make her happy. That concept is vital to a woman's thinking.

Or, at least, it is vital to a woman who still believes in the romantic image, as many women do.

Certain things contributed to this attitude. Though not tall, Daniel was, she thought, one of the handsomest men imaginable. He was decent, steady, and kind. He would not wander, and in his own quiet way he was as honest as she. Their life together had been stable. She knew he loved her, and the love she gave in return seemed to make him happy. It came naturally to her to give of herself generously, and in her quiet fashion—near to bashful at times—she could rid herself of a world of affection and tenderness. In the village they were respected. But the best they had in their marriage disappeared faster than a batch of snow in the sun when Sedgewick became their friend.

THE EYES IN the rubbed-clear space of the window are still staring out at the men as they finally rouse themselves, fling the last of their coffee into the flames, and shoulder their weapons. Leaving the clearing, headed downhill, toward the logging road. Gradually falling into single file. The old professional hunter in the lead, followed by his tall assistant and the dogs, still chained, and then the others, each showing a tendency to follow in the footsteps of the man ahead, so as to conserve walking strength. The snow is knee-deep in places, and farther on it will be deeper. It will be a long morning.

Toward the end of the file is Daniel. He stops, or rather pauses, moving slowly, to glance back at the Winnebago. She notes this. Sees from a goodly distance in the gray light the smooth, angular plane of his cheek and jaw, the thinly fleshed, beaked nose and the modeling of his face, jaw half hidden by the collar of his parka as he turns to look back, unaware that she is watching.

Then he goes on.

Following in the steps of Sedgewick, directly ahead. Sedgewick never pauses, nor does he glance around. Tall and powerful in his heavy jacket, he labors on purposefully. In his way he has a steadfastness about him too.

Looking out, she thinks:

They are fools.

LES JOHNSON THINKS: If I can get that cat alive, that is the big thing. That would mean something.

I have always been a trial to Monty. He is a friend, but he is the boss, and I have not always been easy on him. Well, I guess I would have to say that for every two things I done right for this department, I have done three things wrong.

But, for sure, if I ain't learned how to do my job as I see fit, and if I been doing it thirty-seven years, then I ain't never going to learn it, so if I can manage to rig this canyon so's I can get to that cat first, which means treeing, I will sedate him and maybe bring him in, because if he is anywhere near as huge as he looked when George Dalton and I glassed him then he has got to be a granddaddy old tom, record-size, no doubt about it.

He ain't rabid. I know that.

Nor was he ever domesticated. That was just talk. No way in the world you could cage something that big. Or keep him caged. He's one hell of a big feller.

If I got that lion, what I would do is sit and talk to him. See what's on his mind. Doctor that eye that got hurt.

If he's that big, he's old. He don't have much time left. Way past his time already.

Yessir, if we got him maybe old Lewis and I would talk to him for a while, and tell him how it is. Then maybe we'd take him some place way up in the wilderness and turn him loose, where nobody could ever get at him again.

THERE IS A kind of anger that will build in a man, such a gradual increase, so slow that it isn't even felt as anger for a long time, and then that time comes when a man's patience has been slowly and surely used up, when no matter what he has done or tried, nothing has worked, and when that happens whatever little patience that is left is shucked off, as if it is something hateful, not to be endured further, and then the anger is set, rooted. The men in file behind Les Johnson felt this, or something akin to it. It would find vent somewhere in the course of the morning ahead of them. It showed in the dogged pace they set. They labored through the snow, sometimes in waist-high drifts. Their expressions were bleak and sere in the biting cold, their necks turtled down into their coats—as if they had been withered and drained by blasts of arctic wind, though the air was unmoving. They labored on. A mere mile or two. As if this was so much.

SEDGEWICK AND DANIEL are last in the file, save two:

Feliciano and Tomas Mora.

This pair struggle on, bringing up the rear. As perhaps they should—symbolically, anyway.

Actually, Feliciano and Tomas are bringing up the rear because they are too drunk to keep up with the main group. Not falling-down drunk, but mildly drunk. Walking drunk.

For these two the hunt has become an exercise in futility. Such an endeavor, in this weather, is stupid beyond comprehension. No one but a fool would go hunting on a weekend like this.

There is a great deal that can be said against the Moras, but one thing is true: They are not fools.

Increasingly disenchanted, they lag further.

Finally, not much more than a half mile down the logging road Johnson is sticking to, they stare at each other, and then come to a stop.

Abandon the project altogether.

Back at the camp there is the tent, their bedrolls, the warmth of the fires. Common sense dictates that this is where they belong.

Not here.

Feliciano shoulders the old Savage lever-action, and they turn in their tracks, to begin the long uphill trudge back.

They are not even missed.

SHE SITS AT the dinette table. A cup of coffee before her, growing cold. Beside it, an ashtray with a burning cigarette, taken from an open carton in the liquor cabinet. The cigarette may possibly be an indication of her mood. Like Daniel, she is not a smoker. Rarely takes tobacco. Perhaps eight or ten times a year.

It is silent in the Winnebago. Silent outside, too, except, once, a nicker from one of the horses on the picket line.

She thinks: There is nothing to do now except wait. There was no reason for me to come all the way up here. No purpose has been served. I thought my coming here would somehow help. But my being here is pointless.

SO, THEN, NOW: These two.

Who are bent on sorting out their particular rhyme and reason. Who are essentially adept at justifying their own crippled existence.

Their methodology, though crazy to some, and unfathomable to all, is to them irrefutably sensible.

Feliciano. A geriatric, latter-day Merlin. The blackest of saints. Perhaps. With a mentality that is a weir of odd twists and cul-de-sacs.

The various tests run on him at the state mental hospital—this was when he had been locked away in the forensic division, after shooting down that man—indicated that he had a marginal or borderline intelligence. But what does this mean?

He could function "peripherally." This had been decided by the staffing group of psychiatrists who reviewed his case. They were correct on this point. He could, that is, with the help of welfare, minor thievery, and whatever other rackets he could think up.

Of course, this is not to say that he was in any way equipped to function in an atomic-era society.

His almost nonexistent verbal skills—simple spoken communication—was blamed on "cultural deprivation."

At fifty-eight, Feliciano had not learned to tie his shoelaces properly. He simply knotted them, and thereafter slept in his shoes. To remove them he would usually get a knife and cut the knots.

He could not really tell time. A clock, on a wrist or on the wall of the Crippled Horse, was a mysterious toy-omen that other men seemed to pay attention to. He never understood this, nor why the hands moved so slowly. He thought of them as arms. This may say something about his ability to symbolize. At nine fifteen, they were a *cruz*—a crucifix. At seven twenty, they were *cansado*—tired. At six thirty, his psychiatric workers found, he felt the clock was defecating. They did not put this down to a permanent oral-anal fixation, and this was smart. Too many areas—whole, unexplored mine fields, in fact—of Feliciano's cerebral clockworks had never gotten as far as the oral-anal stage.

In the months he was at the hospital, before his case came up and he was eventually freed (lack of evidence), they tried him with puzzle boxes—wood cutouts fashioned into stars, rectangles, circles, that had to be pushed through appropriate openings. Preschool stuff. This wasn't easy for Feliciano, who had been known to draw a box instead of an X when signing his welfare check, but with practice he got better. His glee, after fitting a star cutout into a star opening, often verged on the hysterical.

Today, in his role of sorcerer-philosopher, he has as his Igor-assistant Tomas. His only son.

Of medium height but with a tortilla-flabbed bulk, Tomas, too, in his way, has never made it.

It is Tomas's fate to be a slave to Feliciano. And old Mora is no one to be a slave to. Rimed with the same filth and encrusted funk as this man who sired him, Tomas, if anything, has reached a lesser level of sophistication than his father. Worse, he is a total prisoner of an Oedipal complex.

In his secret heart of hearts—and this thought has never registered on his conscious mind, however little of it there may be—Tomas cherishes a wonderful dream in which he successfully murders his father.

The reason why he wants his father dead is simple.

Until that happens, Tomas will cringe.

Tomas will always follow. He may or may not be aware of this in their slow meandering back to the base camp. He certainly does not know exactly how far, or to what extent, he will follow. This has never been tested. When Tomas is recalcitrant or disobedient, his father punches or slaps him in the face. The old man can also pinch fiercely enough to draw blood. Usually, this is enough.

Trudging along behind his father, his expression is docile. He has not shaved for two or three weeks prior to their coming up here. The thick, furry stubble across his lip and plump jowls is already tinged with gray and white. At thirty-four. It also horribly italicizes the inexpert repair job on his lip.

Tomas does, indeed, look like a wide-eyed, whiskery rabbit.

He also has a bad cold, and this adds to the impression. His thick, reddened nose is mucusy, and when he isn't wiping at it with the back of one ungloved hand he wrinkles and twitches it, sniffing noisily. The delicately parted delta-cleft is chapped and scabbed. A gentle and miserable two-hundred-pound rabbit.

The sorcerer-seer, and his apprentice.

Homeward bound.

STERN-FACED PETER GRIEGO has a secret, like most people. The secret is this: He sometimes feels that he is losing his sanity.

It is not easy to be a model of propriety when everybody hates you. If you are disliked as much as Peter is, the need to be loved can have an awful urgency.

And so there have been evenings—quiet nights, when nothing much is going on in the area—when Peter, driven by a wretched loneliness and despair, drives out of the village, to park atop a hill not far from the old monastery, off the road a way, there to contemplate in his brooding and melancholy way this entire business of what is right and what is wrong.

Is he doing right, or is he in error?

THE MISTRESS HE has in the village loves him. Her house is some distance from the neat mobile home he and his family own. Peter visits this young woman from time to time, and uses her in certain ways.

Like many others, she is on welfare. Has three children, who conveniently are in bed when he drops by.

One of these children, in fact, is Teresa Apodaca, the little girl who was so terribly mauled by the lion.

The young woman's name is Roberta, and the fetus she has been carrying for several months is Peter's. She is not especially disturbed by this situation, nor is he. She has told him, and her welfare worker, that she hopes to have a kid every few years until her tubes give out. Fertility in these parts augments the income.

She loves him not because he is all-powerful in this area but because of what he and she do together in the privacy of her small, ratty bedroom. It is a room without taste or femininity, furnished with a simple bed, junky plywood furniture, and lit by a single, naked bulb overhead. It is a room made for punishment or love. And for finding a kind of sanity.

What they do in there is their business. And Cornelius's, who listens weekly to her confession. Cornelius hands out a mild penance. He knows that in a week or two he will be listening to the same old thing all over again.

But to sin takes nerve.

That is why Peter, in his fearful loneliness, often parks his Dodge truck on a hill before going on to his surrogate home.

There to sit quietly. And smoke at leisure a small toke of marijuana, which, some time ago, he adeptly pocketed in a house search of a hippie couple he subsequently ran out of town.

This is good stuff. Not garbage out of the Nogales slot. In comparison the best Acapulco gold is Twinkies. This brand is black and tarry. A small pinch is all that is needed in the little clay pipe.

He keeps it and the clay pipe, along with some peyote buttons, rolled in a plastic pouch under the front seat of his pickup, with a tagged and dated slip fastened to it, so that if he is ever caught with it he can at least plead forgetfulness— can claim that he meant to turn it in but forgot about it in the press of other duties.

An atrociously lame excuse, of course, and not one that his supervisors would ever believe—but, all things considered, it is an excuse that will never be tested.

Because nobody in Pecos is likely to fool around with Peter's rolling stock. His vehicles are sacrosanct. No, no one would ordinarily ever lay a hand on that pickup truck.

So Peter has been free to use this small method of relaxation. With its help he has been able to achieve the only degree of freedom—sexual or otherwise—he has ever felt. The young woman he visits later on during these evenings does not know of this indulgence. All she knows is that she has on her hands a Griego who is wonderfully different than the man the rest of the village fears and respects. The loving, weeping man she holds in her arms, and through whom she herself again achieves youth, is hers alone. She is satisfied with this. The other Griego, the one that everybody else knows, is off some- where else—like a dream figure, a parade-field ghost, perhaps calmly observing what takes place, standing straight-backed in a corner of the shabby bedroom, beside the chair on which has been tossed the uniform, black boots, the cap, gunbelt, and cuffs.

But that big blue four-wheel-drive Dodge, sitting now with four flat tires down the road from the camp, is not totally inviolate.

At least not this weekend.

No Pecos high-school kid would dare go near it, but Lester Johnson did, leaving his mark with four twelve-penny common nails. And now someone else.

Feliciano and Tomas.

On their way back to the warmth of the tent. Trudging along in the snow.

They stop for a look-see. Peter has locked the door on his side, but the other one—the door used by Lewis yesterday—well, the locking stud on that door is in the raised position. Peter can perhaps be forgiven for this oversight. It isn't easy to be a model of efficiency when you are skidding around on four flats. So the truck is open.

And with the directness of a homing pigeon, Feliciano gets the stash. In mere seconds. You always look under the driver's seat first. That is where whiskey or loose cans of beer are most likely to turn up.

Feliciano has some concept of what grass is. Peyote he knows too. You chew the dried buttons. A Santa Clara Indian had shown him how. The buttons made you vomit. But afterward, you felt good. Drunk, only different. "*De lo alto*," the Indian had claimed—"It comes from heaven." Now he holds up the little plastic sack and shakes it back and forth before Tomas's vaguely interested gaze.

Feliciano figures if Peter has no liquor this will have to do. What he doesn't understand is that this is a shade better than the finest twelve-year-old bourbon.

In fact, considerably better.

In the deserted tent he and Tomas proceeded to stoke up the clay pipe.

They lit it, and kept it going, passing it back and forth. Along with a little bourbon. Neither of them really had any idea of how to hold a puff properly. Just as well. Else the tops of their heads might have been blown clean off. Presently, Feliciano munched a few buttons. He gave some to Tomas. The bourbon was almost gone now. Too bad.

Still, the effect was appropriately salubrious. Invigorating. Even heady.

Tomas smiled, then presently laughed. He didn't know what the joke was, but whatever it was it was killingly funny.

He sat there on the bedroll, opposite his father, and laughed. And the more he laughed, the funnier it all got. He laughed till the tears rolled down his fat cheeks. Stopped a bit, got hold of himself, then had to give in to it again—and started all over.

Staring at him, Feliciano began laughing too. He had never seen an unshaven rabbit laugh. Tomas's disfigured mouth in repose was comical enough—but when it laughed, well, it was simply too much!

The pipe was done now. Feliciano stoked up another load. Then, with blithe aplomb, his son suddenly leaned forward and wretched, over his crossed knees and onto the bedroll they were sharing—a thin, sour flux, mostly fluid. The old man watched as Tomas got to his feet and wandered about the tent, dancing on bedrolls, in a kind of cockeyed strut, slapping at the slanted sides of the tent. For just a moment Feliciano felt something akin to paternalistic affection. How often does a father see his son relax?

SEVENTEEN

There are many concepts that Feliciano cannot shape or articulate in his mind. Even intuitively. Yet they are there.

And, curiously, the mind, liquor-and-drug fueled, is now in certain ways, working with amazing clarity.

It still cannot grasp a certain attitude—a certain chain or sequence of information—that lies buried in that mass of febrile brainy matter. But something is there, working. It exists, no doubt about that. Feliciano feels it in him. Something.

He may have to grope for it. But sooner or later it will come clear to him.

And that, of course, is one of the most exquisite moments given to any man to experience.

That moment when . . . it all . . . becomes . . . clear.

THERE IS A vision. A dream.

A halcyon fantasy, somewhere in Feliciano's mind, that is rich and lovely.

There is a time, a moment, that brief instant when, no matter what her age, a woman becomes a girl.

That is the moment when she casts her spell, her magic. When all her power swells and enfolds the man she is with.

That is when the shucking off of clothing is a mere symbol. For it is not her body that she is baring. It is her self.

And the giving of herself is like a gift.

That is her power—the ability to give. Any man who has ever felt that with a woman cannot reject it. There is no richer blessing. That is the true beauty of woman.

In that isolate glade. Grassy and sun-dappled in the summer heat.

When she turned silently, without so much as a brief, murmured word, to stare up at her companion. Then so naturally, like a child, stepped forth from her clothes . . . the shirt, the faded cotton jeans so easily shed they seemed to melt from her, and more quickly the brief undergarment. Stooping momentarily as the elastic caught at a foot, standing one-legged and hopping a little, good-humored as she bent to free and rid herself of this wisp of nylon fabric. Stood erect, finally, and turned with that open smile.

Faint crenelated imprint of elastic banding that slender, supple waist.

Curve of thigh so lovely in the blinding light. No shame or modesty to her casual stance. Brushes a strand of hair from one shoulder with a toss of head and upraised arm. So unconscious a gesture . . . and so quintessentially feminine. Swell of breast and dusky tan of pointed nipple. The stomach smoothly fleshed and flat. Below, a patch of darker fleece, and inward curve of thigh. Warm and secret now. That wet welcome man never tires of. Homage to the goddess. Her companion kneels. With such a tenderness and sweet simplicity, despite his strength and massive bulk. This she tolerates. Standing calmly. Gazing down. A hand hanging limply, uselessly, at her side. The other stroking the back of his head and neck. Hips arched slightly forward. Such a patient giving on her part. As with her hand she helps her friend to find his way.

She gazes down in dreamy silence—a smile graces her lips

—she is so serene and gladly caught. And, in her eyes, that giving. As if she alone of all women knows the secret: In the utter giving of it there is the ultimate receiving.

Beauty. In the sunny glade.

This gentle tableau is too much for Feliciano, the drunken voyeur. Sprawled against a pine, not fifteen yards off.

All this he cannot understand. It is beyond him.

There is that curious twist to the old man. For all his awful history of rape, murder, incest, he has that weird prudishness. Those dark and evil feelings about anything lascivious.

He has known but three women. His wife, Eduvigen, who on a lifelong diet of carbohydrates and sugared soda pop, and with an endocrine system gone haywire, is certainly no candidate for Queen of the May. Also, she is not clean. It is a long time between oases for Eduvigen in her Sahara of personal hygiene. Let Jungians find in her unwashed bulk the prerequisites of some earth-mother symbol . . . the fact remains: Eduvigen is a foul, fat slob. A fitting mate to Feliciano's scrawny insanity. The second was the daughter, who effectively crossed the bar with taloned fingers, in some back ward at the mental hospital. The third was the slut who infected him.

Small wonder, then, that Feliciano does not harbor in his male psyche some romantic notions about sex. How unlikely it is for him to perceive that woman is beauty, when he has been surrounded by such stunning companionship.

And so, to see Venus, a pre-Raphaelite nude, in that glade. So unabashed, yet with that sweet shyness. That awful beauty. She seemed so frail beside the tanned and ruddy bulk of her friend. Such a sweet and fulsome passion. This unholy rite. If all the world would grind to a stop they would still go at it—finish out their obscene business—and find a spastic consummation in some mutual epiphany—performed in the splendor of God's given day.

Yet he is morbidly attracted, finds himself incredibly aroused. Feels half in a trance. His breathing suddenly shot.

Lungs pumping for air, and, though unaware of it, he has a tendency to drool. This spectacle before him cannot be viewed. Yet for the very life of him he cannot look away. He dares not move.

It may not be too great an exaggeration to say that on that summer afternoon a fuse, so to speak, blew in his mental computer. After that day he was never quite the same—would never again conceive of men and women in exactly the same way.

The sheer visual and aural input of what he took in produced a kind of electrical overload. As if a conventional human had suddenly looked upon heaven—or hell!—and had been left dumbfounded and crippled. As if the Olympian view, accessible only to gods and devils, was too much for mere man, but nonetheless was comprehensible enough to leave him with the feeling that there was something in this life, as we know it, that was missing. Something he would always miss, be robbed of.

And from that day to this dismal wintry morning Feliciano had never been able to piece it all together. Not all of it. Something was missing.

That he should be one way, and that others should be so immeasurably different. That there could be such beauty.

It had something to do with right and wrong. Or at least with his crazy old notion of fairness.

But there is one thing to be said of him. Given time, Feliciano will piece it together. He will make the puzzle complete. And interlocked within it, all will be well.

There is a rightness and a wrongness. There is no denying that.

THERE ARE VARIETIES of hatred. The worst is founded on need ... the urge to possess, and, in possessing, punish and destroy. What better way? In punishing, there is a vindication of one's self. Thus, a double purpose is served. To make the wrong-doer kneel, and in that act sublimely elevate and justify one's own existence!

To master a situation. And in that mastering achieve a kingly status. If only momentarily.

To be just. Perhaps punitively so, but, still—just! To mete out the proper apportionment of what is right and wrong.

To reign supreme over the fallen one.

What an awful glory!

And now a match is struck. To the third small pipeful. A mere thick pinch. But it is enough.

In the smoking bowl is clarity. Reason. And a singular purpose. It is by no means entirely clear yet. Either to Feliciano or to Tomas.

But it is taking shape.

THE PURSUITS OF man will take him far afield. The hunting party is gone now, for the morning.

She will, she knows, be alone. And since nothing is to be done about this, she accepts it. A part of her may be worried to distraction, yet another part tells her that all the worrying in the world will not change anything. In this mood she sets her attention to other tasks.

She uses the bathroom in the Winnebago for a lazy shower. Outside, it is still below zero, but in the mobile home it is warm. The water: scalding hot.

When done, she dons the same underwear she has been wearing since yesterday. There is nothing to be done about this. She had, with luck, expected to return yesterday evening. Still damp from the shower, she takes the liberty of checking a closet. Finds a blue terrycloth bathrobe belonging to her host, sizes too large, and slips into it, tying the belt about her waist. The effect of this large garment is not without a charm of its own.

She pours another coffee. Sits at the dinette table, and with the cup and still another cigarette before her, attends to the long, lank, still-wet blond hair. Brush and comb she did bring.

Seated there, she bends a little, head obliquely tilted. Applies the brush to snarl and tangle.

A lazily paced stroking. Her expression dreamy, as if she is almost unaware of this leisurely task . . . yet, at the same time, she uses the brush with a total, inner absorption.

The Degas view again. Graceful sweep and curve of inclined neck. The slender nape laid bare. A paler, golden down, almost a dusting of delicate fuzz, along the naked nape.

Musing idly, she strokes the stiff bristles through the long hair. Her movements—upraised arm, the wrist bending— would be erotic except that they are so unconscious. That inward-turned self-possession. A private serenity.

As if to perform this one task right—the brushing of her hair—was the total all. No man alive could look upon such a pose and view and not be moved. To the core of his soul. That is when the breath will catch in his throat, and he will feel his heart swell.

To see tranquil beauty.

In fixed repose.

IN THE GRAY morning light the cat watches. Looking out from its shadowy alcove of broken rock.

Last night there had been the fall of snow. Everywhere it is white and clean, and there are no tracks—the cat has stayed put—except for the little hen-marks of starlings and jays, and once in a while the one-two-hop imprint of a rabbit.

The lion is hungry. It is a big animal, and it needs meat to keep it going. But it stayed in the den all last night in the storm. That would have been no kind of hunting at all, because in a storm no game moves about.

And now, of course, it can't move either, because the men are down there.

THERE IS SOMETHING in the hunt itself that exceeds the prize. It has always been this way. The thing is in the search, never the getting. Then there is the excitement that afterward turns sour and leaves a flattened taste in the mouth. Once grasped, the silk becomes slime and grit.

Thus, to seek the beast:

A straggling file of men, spread an eighth of a mile, toiling into the small canyon where they think, or feel, or hope, the lion is bedded. More on the bluffs overhead. If this is the one they are after, the injured one, perhaps it will be too far gone to run, and thereby make them run too.

But that kind of thinking amounts to fooling yourelf. Les Johnson knows this. Though often scrawny, a lion is tough, and at times unbelievably difficult to kill.

He remembers one cat down Lordsburg way, years ago, when there were still lions in that area. A small tom. Johnson himself took it. Just one shot, but he knew it was a good one. Yet that tom took off.

Johnson was never a man to leave a wounded animal. He tracked it three days. Across rimrock and broken arroyos. Hot out there in the desert around Lordsburg, especially in summer. He had a short-legged mixed hound along, part basset, part mutt. Dog's name was Glenn. So Glenn and Johnson tracked this cat for three days. Finally cornered it up in a sun-baked arroyo where it had dragged itself. Johnson shot it again, and then inspected the carcass. The first .32 slug had taken out a fist-sized piece of stomach and guts. Damned near shot the little cat in half. Yet it had gone on like that for three days, no food or water. Still had a little fight in it, though not much, when Les finally walked up and placed the second shot, at a distance of thirty-five yards. He was glad it was over. He had a feeling that maybe the young tom did, too. The basset-mix certainly did. It didn't even charge the body to wool it, the way most dogs will. Merely limped over to the shade of a runty juniper and flopped under it. Its footpads had given out two days ago, from ranging back and forth across the rocky ground, and they were a bloody mess.

Old man Johnson was like that, though. Any dog or man with him he would work as brutally hard as himself, and that was going some.

THEY ARE CLOSER now, small, dark figures moving along the floor of the canyon, and they have dogs with them. The dogs are useless in the fresh snow, or will be until the cat moves. Or until the wind comes up enough to carry a scent.

The air is cold and unmoving, thin at this altitude, and it is unnaturally quiet, such a heavy silence. No cry of bird, or even the faint sigh of a breeze drifting through the tall pines. Almost a pure silence. Except for the men. The sounds of their movements carry a surprising distance in the silence. Small sounds, and once the whine of a leashed dog.

In the snow the men are clumsy. Seem almost crippled and pathetic as they struggle up the slope. Out of place in this natural setting. Unfit even to survive, let alone hunt. Yet they have something no animal has: persistence. They will keep at it until they have done what they came to do.

There is a break in the cloud cover overhead. The sun is visible for the first time that morning. The snowy slopes beneath the den light up in a dazzling whiteness—a blinding swath of brilliance that spreads and moves, to catch, finally, the men, still moving slowly, scanning the heights above them. Not far from one of them a rabbit breaks from a patch of scrub oak, soaring above the drifts and then sending up small geysers of white spume each time it belly-flops in the snow. The cottontail finally makes it to safety in a copse of pine.

Presently, the cat gazes round. Sighting with its one good eye the choices available to it.

The ridge above the bluff is the way to go, but the cat

seems to sense that men are already up there on the heights.

On a level with the den and some eighty yards off is a stand of heavy timber. But all that lies between is open.

The den is situated badly. From it, the cat can see everything around it, but can likewise be seen, and easily, too, against the snow. There is too little cover. The rubble of the bluff itself—great scattered heaps of boulders and broken slab, wearing white caps of snow—this is where the den itself is located. There is no way, really, that the cat can keep out of sight of the men below.

In that glaring, yellow eye scanning the view there is a murderous calm. As if the lion is somehow indifferent to all this. Almost as though none of this concerns itself. As if, perhaps, it is looking down, observing from some Parnassian height, some other lion, some other men, with an immense detachment for what has passed and for what will come.

It lies sprawled on one flank in the rear of the alcove. The tail twitches wickedly from time to time, a quick, nervous jerk of the tip, but this is the only thing that shows the lion's uneasiness. All the rest of the cat seems focused on the men.

And in the calm detachment of the eye there is something else. A realization.

It has waited too long.

It should have left this place. Should have been off and moving. Before they came into view. Even earlier than that. Too late now.

The game is already lost. It has waited too long.

The thing is this: Had it been left to itself, it would have kept to the den. Perhaps killed a deer nearby, in another day or two. Would have gorged itself with fifteen or twenty pounds of venison, then hidden the carcass, to return to the den, stomach-heavy, to rest and sleep and heal itself. Would have stayed in the area for a week or more, returning to the remains of the deer to feed, waiting out a change in the weather, and then, later, when its strength was back, it would have moved on, deeper into the mountains probably, where, with luck, it might have attached itself to a herd of elk or deer, staying with them through the rest of the winter and pulling down one every so often, always the slowest and weakest in the herd, thus practicing its own rudimentary form of game management.

But too late for that now. That time will never come. Nor other times.

Never again to experience whatever pleasures it is that lions cherish. The excitement of the stalk—so different from the clumsy way those below are going about it—when every muscle in the feline body is attuned and in harmony with killing, so silent, such a total focusing of what it is *for*, a flawless and deadly apparatus, with all that great strength coiled within the body, which, when unleashed, can break the neck of a horse or a fully grown cow, or leap atop an elk, all claws dug in as it rides the plunging beast—hanging on to life itself as the monstrous jaws lock on the spine at the back of the neck. Nor will it lie stretched out basking in a hot July sun, atop a rock slab, half asleep, washing itself lazily, purring in the heat. Never again the awful feline amorousness of the seasonal rut, when in the night it calls out in a wrenching scream that sounds, they say, like the wail of a woman in labor—a sound that can be heard for a mile or more along the high forested slopes. Then, no animal stirs, large or small. That drawn-out shriek tells the entire forest that a lion has gone mad with love, and that it will battle anything it comes upon.

The calm yellow eye blinks, once, twice. The tip of the long tail twitches again.

Then, finally, as though rousing itself to a task it has no interest in, the big cat slowly rises. Looks round once more, and with a low snarl—a deep, bass rumble—it moves out.

VIRGIL MCCORMICK saw it first. Stopped in his tracks and yelled to the others. The men looked up. Saw nothing. Looked to Virge. He stood knee-deep in the snow, pointing. To the base of the bluff, above them, among the heaped and broken boulders.

Then, it was there, the briefest blur of tawny yellow. Moving fast. Snaking in and out among the snow-covered rocks.

Les Johnson, some distance ahead, turned to face the others, his arms upraised. He was shouting something. The men couldn't hear what it was.

The cat disappeared briefly. Then showed again.

Just as Vince Apodaca began letting off rounds from his .44 Magnum, one after the other, firing way too fast. Vince was a good shot, but at a hundred yards the range was too far for a pistol, even using a two-handed grip. Some of the .44 slugs geysered into snowdrifts. The nearest round exploded a chip off a boulder a good ten feet from the lion.

Up until this time it had been running easily, in long, loping strides. Now, with the sharp whine of the slug that ricocheted off the boulder, the lion took off. In marvelously long leaps. Trying to get to that stand of timber.

Others were shooting. They stood or knelt in the snow and aimed and fired, ejected spent shells and chambered fresh rounds, fired again, quickly and excitedly.

Lewis Bowman had loosed the pack. The dogs spotted the lion and began plunging through the snow toward it.

Some men held their fire. Sedgewick and Les Johnson, for two. They stood and watched. Saw the quick spurts of snow shot up by bullets hitting all round the running cat. It was really moving now. They heard the different sounds of the guns—the heavy crack of .30-30s, the solid, thumping reports of Vince's .44, and the occasional blast of a .30-06.

Vince claimed later that he had hit the lion first—with his initial round. Those who watched knew better. No one had hit it yet. It was no easy target, and no easy shot. Uphill shooting is deceptive. Most of the men were out of breath, or at least breathing hard, and their aim was not steady. And this lion was moving through the snow faster than any lion had a right to.

Along the ridges that boxed the little canyon, the men Les Johnson had posted looked on. Except for one, Guillermo Apodaca. He began descending the steep slope—actually, he was quite close to the lion—skidding on his bottom in snowy places, almost somersaulting at times, as if caught up by a frenzy to get at the cat face to face, disregarding old Johnson's orders to stay put . . . either not realizing, or forgetting, or ignoring, that he was putting himself directly into the line of fire coming from the men below.

By now some of the others, besides Johnson, were yelling, warning the shooters to stop, but still they kept on.

The lion would have made it to the thick timber except for a snowdrift. It hit that, actually plunged out of sight for a moment, as though it had gone underwater and had to swim back up to the surface. Then it reappeared, or at least its head and shoulders did, and they watched as it struggled to where there was firm footing again. It seemed to pause there for a moment, as though confused, and then was tumbled, knocked flat, as a bullet struck it. It rolled in the snow, biting at the wound. Let out a fearsome squall that sounded across the slopes. Then rose, and once again started toward the big pines. Got another few yards and was struck down again. Still struggling, hurt badly, perhaps mortally, but still a long way from dead. The two rounds that had struck had sounded different from the slugs that went into the snow—each made a solid thump. Downslope, Vince Apodaca was frantically trying to reload the Magnum revolver, fumbling with a handful of loose cartridges, most of which fell into the snow at his feet. Some of the other men were reloading too.

The huge cat was running again. On a different tack, suddenly abandoning the stand of timber, heading instead for the rimrock that surrounded the canyon, even though other men were up there. All its cunning gone now.

One creature stood—or sat—between it and the crest of the rimrock. Guillermo Apodaca. Who looked on, horrified, as this creature bounded up the slope toward him—it was out of the deep snow now and had found footing, and even with its wounds it was moving in fifteen- and twenty-foot leaps.

Guillermo screamed once as the lion closed on him. Dropped his rifle, tried to scrabble out of the way. No way. Suddenly, he and the lion were one. Guillermo, face down in the snow, arms covering his head. He felt a terrible weight descend on him, felt his down parka rend. Then it was over. The lion, quite simply, ran over Guillermo—later, at the Crippled Horse, they would say *el rano* had been steamrollered by this *gato*, this cat—which then continued on, following the same path Guillermo had made in his excited descent . . . up to the crest of the rimrock, away from the men and dogs below.

Incredible, that it could have that strength and beauty, hurt as it was. From below, they watched it snaking its way up the steep slope of rocky cliff, almost vertical now, for the last few yards—here, at the last, it wasn't running but was actually climbing, the big forepaws clawing at anything they could hold on to.

And, actually, it made it, to the lip of the rimrock. The men below watched. The lion's movements were weaker now, slower. It was almost gone. Still, it struggled. Reached the top of the rimrock, and, with still another squalling snarl, began to pull itself over the edge of the crest, mouth dripping slather, the one good eye glaring.

Ten feet back from the crest, Daniel waited. For one brief moment, the lion and he regarded each other. Each transfixed. Each, in a way, caught by the other. Neither, in that same curious way, angered, or frustrated, that it had come to this. The hunted, who hated men; and the hunter, who despised hunting.

Daniel fired once, from the hip. He was that good. The round blew off half the lion's head. Without a sound, its grip on the rimrock relaxed, and it slid backward, to disappear, tumbling and flopping, to come to rest, at last, not very far from where Guillermo Apodaca now stood. Guillermo fired another round into the bloody carcass, to make sure that the lion was dead. Then, for the first time that weekend, he untied the long red wool scarf that he had wound around his old Stetson, rolled the brim, and adjusted the hat's angle, tilted a bit, over one ear, the way he liked it.

IT WAS INDEED a record tom. A shade over ten feet, from tip of tail to nose. Old, though. Coat worn, urine-stained in places. One upper canine broken off at its base, the other teeth badly aged and heavily stained with tartar.

A big old cat, in poor condition. Still, it was one of the biggest lions taken in the state in years. Even with one eye it was a lot of cat.

Another fight almost got started. Vince Apodaca, claiming first hit, wanted the pelt. By then Les Johnson had put on plastic gloves and was down on his knees in the snow beside the body of the lion, working with a tape measure. Lewis Bowman copied the statistics into a notebook: Overall length, width of footpads, breadth of the skull, probable age and weight. Johnson looked up at Vince and said, "No one's skinning this animal. I'm declaring it confiscated state property."

"You mean to just leave it up here?" Vince demanded.

"That's right," Johnson said. "I ain't even going to cremate it, which is what I'd do after taking a sample, if I thought it might be rabid. This cat ain't rabid. I'd bet money on that. It's just an old-timer. Far as that goes, we'll never know for sure if it was the one went after that kid or killed that sheep-herder. You can tell from that eye that this was the feller that tore up those Alsatian shepherds, but we'll never know for sure about the rest of it. Probably it was him. If more attacks come in the next week, we'll know we killed the wrong one today. But I doubt anything like that'll happen. My own guess is that this is the one we were after. No proof, but that's my feeling."

He took out a plastic sack from his parka pocket and unfolded it in the snow. Then he paused and looked up at the men who were gathered round. He said, "So I hope you're all satisfied. The hunt's over. Damn it to hell. Damn all of you."

"Why don't we take the whole carcass back?" Vicente Apodaca insisted.

"I just need what's left of the head," Les Johnson said, and set about accomplishing his task.

EIGHTEEN

There are ways by which even the most humble can practice salus populi suprema lex esto ... *"Let the welfare of the people be the supreme law!"*

PASSING SLOWLY FROM west to east the same sunny break in the cloud cover that had lit the canyon where the lion was denned drifted over Walford Flats to a high ridge known as Puente del Oso—Bear Point—thence across the cleft of Bull Creek Canyon, and finally up Singer Canyon to the base camp itself. Not much over a mile, direct line, but more like two for the men, who had walked.

The camp, lit to a glaring white by the morning sun, appeared deserted. The big pyramidal tent, at one end of the clearing. The fires, burned down now. The stream, hardfrozen, except where the men had chopped holes to scoop out cooking and drinking water. Down under these holes the water circulated, and in the deeper pools a few native trout lurked in somnambulistic stupor—they might or might not make it through the winterkill.

Up at the far end of the clearing is the string of horses, heavy in their winter shag, useless here.

Footprints, tracks, pathways, are stamped in the snow. The fires smolder in hot black scars. Pots and pans, their bottoms sooted, set to one side on rocks or rotting logs. A grill, still across a bed of gray, smoking coals. A drift of smoke, rising from the fires to spread in a thin layer of haze, blurring at treetop height in the brilliantly lit, unmoving morning air, to create a film, or screen, so that despite the sunshine there is a faintly dimmed, almost optically altered, perspective to the camp and the view. Faint smell of wet char and pungent, half-burned pinewood.

There is no movement. Not even among the horses, who stand quietly, appreciating this first faint heat of the day. The Winnebago looks deserted, its coach roof heaped with last night's fall. Within the old Army tent, there is life.

Of a sort.

Feliciano and his simpering son. But they are hidden for now. Just as well. They are busy with their own affairs.

IN THE WINNEBAGO it was perhaps conceivable that she might have heard the sounds of the rifles. Except for the stereo tape deck that had been turned on. Not that it would have made any difference. One mile or ten, it didn't matter . . . it was far enough. All the sound of the shooting would have told her was that they had come upon the cat. As if that mattered any more.

Hair now dry at last. A brown-gold mane. Almost to the small of her back. A few streaks of gray, at the temples and nape of her neck. No rinse needed yet, but, well, in a few years it might be worth considering. Still in the borrowed blue terrycloth robe. Belt cinched tight about the slender waist. Barefoot. The toenails neatly square-clipped, unmarked by color. Narrow-footed, the middle toe longer than the others, in the style of Michelangelo. Slim ankles rising to gracefully modeled calves. A faint, dusty tan, the last souvenir of summer. The smooth calves unblemished. Her face today is still clear of makeup, save for that touch of lipstick. The skin still moist and smooth from the shower, faintly flushed with pink.

A fourth cup of coffee is on the table, and, in the tray, a third cigarette.

The music plays from a built-in alcove beside the bathroom. The tape deck, fed off batteries. George LaPorte, it would seem, has excellent taste for a man supposedly absorbed in pecans.

The cassettes, beside popular music, include Berlioz, Wagner, Liszt, Schubert, Brahms, Mendelssohn, Saint-Saëns, Mahler. A born romantic, LaPorte. Despite the deadly business eye.

She has on one of the *Brandenburg Concerti*. The stately music fills the Winnebago. She walks to the tape deck, splayed toes sinking into the shag rug, and idly chooses several more cassettes—it is one of those automatic things, where the cassettes can be stacked—inserts them into the mechanism, and turns.

Then turns back, to raise the volume quite loud.

For this has meaning.

Sedgewick has played the Brandenburg series for her. And the Lizst preludes. The divertimenti. The *Goldberg Variations*. The same way. Loudly. Last summer the windows of the mountain cabin would vibrate. It was his way of teaching her. About music, and what it was, and what it meant.

And she had understood.

He would explain. Stop his own stereo to point out a passage, assess a player's endeavor.

She had listened attentively. Whatever he was, lover, fool, or demon, Sedgewick was a born teacher. That was the thing about him. There was all that burned-out deadness in him, yet when his excitement came, he was different. Talking about music still did it. Then he filled the room, got larger than life. He seemed filled with vitality. It carried over to her. She could feel it inside. She had never gotten that kind of excitement from any other man. That was too much. She couldn't fight that. So she had lost. To her own tumultuousness, as well as his. And now it didn't matter.

The purest beauty of all. Music. So Sedgewick once claimed. With music you couldn't counterfeit, slough off, fool around. It was either good or bad. No middle ground. It was right there. All you had to do was listen. So he said.

For an expensive gadget, the tape deck's programming mechanism is erratic. There is a click . . . the *Brandenburg* is gone. A moment later, Mendelssohn is heard. The *Overture to a Midsummer Night's Dream*. Halfway through. Perhaps the tape was not rewound properly.

The lyric music swells and builds in volume. A quickening allegretto.

String section, and then the woodwinds . . . passing the voice back and forth.

Full symphony orchestra.

Monteux conducting.

AND NOW, AT last, a knock. At the Winnebago's door.

She pads over, barefoot, to answer this summons.

Thinks nothing much of it. Her mind elsewhere, only casually wondering who it might be. Daniel and the others can't be back yet. They can't be.

Opens it.

To the blinding, snow-bright, wintry view. The morning out there.

And an avenging angel.

Feliciano. Eyes like volcanic pits. Standing on the aluminum fold-down steps.

Looking up at her.

With relentless calm. And a gaze as implacable as a clenched fist.

Behind him:

The hulking rabbit. All split-lipped smile and moist, round eyes. Unshaven, filthy, a blue knit wool cap pulled down around his ears . . . but, still, the resemblance is uncanny.

Br'er rabbit. TOMAS.

And *Reynaud.*Teetering on the aluminum steps. Bloodshot, foxy eyes. Hunch-shouldered. That one direct look was too much. *Reynaud* cannot hold it, looks away. All of him evasive.

Yet now not to be repulsed or in any way put off.

Both of them.

Come to visit.

WITH SIGN AND gesture and mumbled incoherent word—that sly obsequiousness—he steps up past her. The Rabbit a pace behind.

Into the elegant splendor of the Winnebago. All polished chrome and glistening Formica. Sheen of plastic. Dacron drapes. Aroma of coffee.

And an atmosphere that, compared to the freezing cold outside, is literally tropical.

Such a luxuriousness of warmth. A wealth of humid comfort.

No myrrh or frankincense needed here. No mead, or silken tapestries shot through with spun gold. No lyre or lute, or serendipitously lilted flute . . . no fair maid's silvery voice.

For this is not the Arabian Nights.

No legend, myth, or saga here. No epic *chanson* of fanciful deeds bigger than life.

This is no fabled fairy tale.
For this princess they have come to visit is all too real.

WHAT CAN SHE do?
She stands aside. Not in invitation, but with an automatic recoiling, involuntarily, with a visible shrinking. An inner coiling together of her own self . . . aghast. Too stunned to even speak.

They take her silence and the involuntary step backward as a kind of tacit permission. Feel themselves welcomed.

Fingers loosely grasping at the open collar of the robe. Head back. Her expression startled—yet, oddly unperturbed, a shocked blank. Eyes wide—yet strangely drained of emotion.

They step past her. Simpering and grimacing, twisting their shoulders oddly.

Even now she could banish them. One word, a single gesture. That might have been enough. But that word or gesture she does not have. She has been robbed of that.

Stands regally erect. Straight-backed, the shoulders squared. Fingers distractedly moving and touching at the collar of the terrycloth robe. Wordless. In appalled muteness. Beyond even despair. Immobilized. In body and mind.

A rigid, waiting stasis.

AND SO THEY enter.
Feliciano and Tomas.
Into the kingdom of heaven.
Like innocent, wide-eyed children.
Turned loose in a gingerbread house.

WHAT STARTED IT is not known.

Very possibly it had to do with the Winnebago itself.

The only civilized home Feliciano had ever entered was Sedgewick's mountain cabin. In that place, while carrying out various simple tasks for his *patrón*, so that he might earn tobacco money, he had marveled at the opulence. The Steinway grand. Rugs on the sanded and oiled floors, books lining the walls, pictures. In that cabin most things were wooden. Were the place Feliciano's most of the furniture would have been broken up long ago for firewood.

But the Winnebago is something else!

No matter that its like could be as well, or better, mimed by any Holiday or Ramada Inn.

All this Formica and plastic. So easily wiped clean. In imitation marble or richly browned polymer walnut. Plastic walls, and a deep rug of acrylic.

There is nothing that came from a living tree or animal. Everything is steel or aluminum or plastic, or textured fiberglass. Even the cup that holds her cooling coffee is of high-impact Melmac.

Nothing can break or be soiled much.

That is why cross-country travelers are so partial to the style. It is as clinically aseptic as the inside of a test tube, and just as devoid of human warmth or personality. This motel-milieu is the same in California or Maine. In effect, these travelers are literally nowhere—they come and go in a plastic wasteland, and this splendid sameness breeds a certain sense of comfort and familiarity.

The large aluminum motor homes seen on highways are modeled along the same same sterile motif. They may repulse some. But not Feliciano.

In here he has never seen the like for sheer luxury and comfort.

To him wood is common, but plastic is rare. So smooth and glossy and sleekly clean. What a wondrous thing.

And the warmth here—what a warmth!
And in here, too, a rather special person:
The goddess contained!

THE MUSIC LOUDLY plays. Again, a malfunction and the cassette is switched. Orff's *Carmina Burana*. An expressionistic medieval liturgy. Latin chants, both sacred and profane.

A mixed chorus and timpanic percussion fill the air, but go unnoticed. Because the air is filled with something else— the various and stunning odors of the Fox and the Rabbit.

THESE TWO. So out of place. Sly, smiling gargoyles. They belong in a Bosch painting or atop the fretted battlements of some thirteenth-century Gothic cathedral, where sculpted demons were faced outward into the four winds to ward off satanic spirits.

The acrylic rug in inoffensive gold-brown. Its shagged pile so thick their frozen boots spring and sink.

Wet imprints, but easy to clean.

Nothing here can be soiled for long. Smudge of hand or muddied heel . . . neither spilled drink nor untended cigarette can stain or char the mahogany counter top. The air conditioner, though not on, will quickly cleanse the air of any odor. Few homes are as spic-and-span.

Feliciano is simply incapable of absorbing it all. Tomas too. Like simple children, they stand and gape about. Afraid to even reach out and touch anything. As if in the touching they will soil or break or in some fashion ruin anything they fondle.

WHAT BROUGHT THEM is a mystery. Some vague impulse, or urge, that perhaps overcame their natural insularity. The liquor, the peyote, marijuana—*quién sabe?*

They knew she was in there. They had knocked. Standing on the aluminum steps. Knocked and waited for the door to open.

That took audacity.

THEY HAVE ABOUT them a certain air of easygoing good-naturedness, even joviality. And that shifty obsequiousness.

At their sober best neither is verbal. Even with each other the spoken word is seldom used. Why trouble to form and shape a word when a gesture or even an expressive look is enough? Of course, if they have to, they can talk. They are, after all, civilized. However, it doesn't come easily. Among provincial mountain people there is that natural wariness about loquacity. Talk makes trouble. So far as that goes, Feliciano and Tomas do not even show much sign of listening to what anyone says to them. In the area of communication, these two present a kind of blank wall.

Feliciano especially. When addressed, he has a way of blanking out whatever is going on behind those simian eyes—small, black, bright-buttoned, glittering marbles, sunk in wrinkled sockets beneath a furrowed, receding forehead and massively boned browridges—there is about him more than a passing resemblance to a hunch-shouldered, skinny ape dressed in tattered clothing. The eyes look this way and that, darting swiftly, but rarely at the speaker. Oh yes, Feliciano knows how to cope with these fancy, educated types! They soon give up in exasperation. Abandon him, without ever knowing if he has really heard or understood a single thing they have been trying to put across to him.

And now, too. Amidst all this. Glancing about, but never really speaking. Their glances meet, then look away, then meet again. Over and over. While the music soars in a fullness of profane ecstasy.

Once Tomas pointed—to the soft blue glare of the kitchenette fluorescent light. Another time Feliciano nodded—toward the bar, on which stood bottles of liquor, glasses, soft drinks.

Finally she spoke. She knew who they were. Had seen them in town, heard of them from Daniel and Sedgewick. Still standing there, in static pose.

She said, "Can I help you? Is anything wrong? What is it you want?"

How COULD FELICIANO have replied to this? If he'd had the words?

Slave to instincts he was not even aware of. Beset by an insane logic he could not recognize, let alone define. That crazy old brain, by now a humming dynamo of drug-induced energy. Brain cells detonating throughout that spirochete-scarred gray mass, like small, fissionable infernal devices, split-tracers, chain-reacting. A cloud chamber of the mind.

An eerie tintinnabulation in those dirt-encrusted ears. The entire visual apparatus oddly detuned. Or enhanced.

Never had colors been so vivid. As though, for the first time in his life, he had removed heavily shaded sunglasses and could see clearly. The aural too. Feliciano could not differentiate between a mariachi and a madrigal, yet he was sure of one thing. He had never heard such a sound of music as this . . . now.

THE SOUND OF her words strike through the music and do something to him. In some way they impinge upon his hot consciousness. Not their meaning necessarily, but merely their presence. They tell him she is here.

And now, finally, it all grows clear.

Why he has come. Why they are there. What it is about. There is a reason and a purpose to this methodology.

In response to her "What is it you want?" Feliciano smiles. Still abashed.

Bows his head—stares down at the rug—at his snow-soaked boots.

Unconsciously mimicking a pose astonishingly similar to that mock-humble bow of the conductor of a symphony orchestra when he turns to face his audience's accolades. The massed ensemble behind him—obediently waiting for the tapped-baton signal that will permit them to rise and share the acclaim. Humbly aware that the musical dictator on the podium above them has played not only the music, but them as well.

BUT THE PLAN that is taking shape in Feliciano's mind could not have been without premeditation. Its germ was planted earlier.

Else what could have led him to leave the old canvas tent in the first place? To cross the clearing. The Rabbit at his heels. To knock at the door, and wait. Knowing she was in there. The liquor and drugs might arm him for that much of the task.

But the origins of the deed that must be done go back much further:

To that grassy summer glade when she had stepped forth from her simple costume—that singular day. So caught by need. So perfect in that bright and dappled light.

A smiling Eve. So beautifully unashamed. All of her revealed. Her breathing deep and measured, arc of ribs rising to ridge the smooth skin. Stepping forward now, to accept the renewal of life.

Such a devout and endless interplay. That tender, friendly playfulness. What diverse ecstasies . . . such a happy commingling of flesh and spirit. Until with tender signs and voiced endearments, they became one. Sank down in a glad tangle of arms and legs to find their confirmation in a measured leisure —an indolent pace—drifting together, no hurry here, hours seemed to pass and still they moved, testing and exploring, playing at it like children, mouth to mouth, his folded arm a pillow for her head—and once they stopped altogether, for a long and tender moment, to solemnly regard each other, and then they smiled and began all over again, until their needs, at last, became too great and they were caught up in a splendid frenzy, and then that was the end of both of them; he, Feliciano, could see that, could hear it, too—the weak cries of anguish that were, somehow, without anguish.

Before that afternoon he had never comprehended that such a love could be. That a man and woman could want each other so badly. In daylight.

Most certainly he had never comprehended female beauty. Until that day.

And now.

THEY SENSED HER fear. It lay behind the poised and haughty stance.

All the outwardness of her was show. A thin pretense. Beneath the surface she was numb.

The erect and queenly pose, they clearly knew, masked a baser fault. She was, quite simply, too horrified to move. To flee the Winnebago was unthinkable.

She could not walk let alone run, could not even take a single step. Could not move at all.

Incongruous, though. She was no timorous girl, but a woman. She knew men well enough, and how to cope with them. She was as attuned to their sexuality as they were eternally aware of hers.

Why, then, is she now stricken dumb? Those expressive eyes opened wide now, unblinking in their direct regard of these two confronting her.

What goes on that she cannot muster a flare of feminine spirit—turn aloof, glacially cold, authoritatively order them out? She is certainly capable of a hot and nervous temper. Daniel Jaramillo can testify to that. At times, when provoked, there is a stubborn and dangerous defiance to her expression, indicative that she will have her way, else there will be hell to pay.

What, then? She seems at such a loss.

All competence gone from her. And though erect and poised, there is something pathetically limp in the curve of her hand and wrist up at the collar of her robe. All of her is somehow drained of strength.

As if in that fear—horror—that drains her, there is a special knowledge. A certain insight.

There would have to be. So simple, when finally intuited, that even old Feliciano would appreciate the rare humor of it.

THERE WAS A nuance in Feliciano's last sly look, before he bowed his head, that caused her to make a certain connection.

For of all the many things the old wretch is, he is one thing more.

Neighbor to Sedgewick.

The Mora spread is just over the ridge from the cabin.

And the grassy, sunlit glade is on the forested slope separating the two properties.

As man and woman they had practiced caution. Until, of course, in the nature of things, caution had become unbearable.

That glade had been used more than once last summer.

Had Feliciano known this he might very well have set up permanent quarters nearby. Would have turned into an arboreal naturalist without peer. As a matter of fact he had frequented the glade. It was only bad luck—a coincidence of poor timing—that when he was there they were not.

There was—now—something so lewd and foul to his manner. As if he was party to some private knowledge.

Shared until this very moment—or so she had reckoned—

by no other human on earth except her and her companion of those stolen, carefree afternoons.

If there was truth in this—if this ghastly old wreck had shared their happiness—then the limp wrist, the wilt of the hand, is understandable. The paralysis of mind and body, the open staring eyes behind which, if anything is discernible, is a mad horror.

There is another lovely aspect of woman—sometimes aggravating, but at times imbued with charm—and it is the inner containment of her private self, her most secret feelings.

And now this. Old Mora!

If it is so, it is appalling beyond belief.

Now HE LOOKS up. Foxy Feliciano. Monkey-eyes blinking knowingly.

He does what is for him a rare thing. Manages to look her in the eye a second time. No evasive shiftiness now.

Still smiling crazily. And now the wellspring of his inner humor overflows. Sends up a frothy bubble of silent mirth. And, quite beside himself, he shifts and turns away, the rubbery lips working and funneling of their own volition. As if he is desperately trying to keep from sniggering. Gripped by a suppressed glee.

Turns again. His back half to her. Looks over his shoulder. To bare in her direction a blue-lipped grin or grimace. Rotted and broken teeth set in ulcerated gums.

He punches at the shoulder of his docile Rabbit-son. Tomas, not seeing the joke but ready to go along, grins widely, his face split by a happy smile, the lip, too. Tilts back his head, set on saurian neck, a thick trunk of fatted muscle springing from the massive shoulders.

Shoulders twitching—he *knows* she knows—Feliciano steps across the room. To the counter. Upon which sits a nearly full quart of Cutty Sark.

SHE DOES NOT speak again. Stands now, with her back against a wall, arms folded across her breasts, waiting.

The bottle passes back and forth between the two. Old Mora regards his son. Tomas stares intently into his father's eyes.

No word is uttered. As if Tomas is listening with his eyes. And understanding. Their minds slowly blending. As if they are feeling out each other's thoughts, and are evolving, without discussion, a technique of action.

Tomas senses, perhaps, that this creature with them is evil.

His father's eyes tell him so. Senses that she is wrong, and they are right.

There is a rightness and a wrongness. And rightness will triumph. It cannot be otherwise. Evil will be punished, and the sinner put down—if necessary by fire and sword.

He feels his father's thinking. Knows that something is about to be done. Doesn't know what it is, not truly, but senses that it is important.

And, never an initiator, always the cringing follower, he stands there at the marbled Formica bar, tilting the whiskey bottle to his mouth, and then smiling, regarding Feliciano.

Who knows what it's all about, and who finally steps forward.

To confront her. Face to face, close enough to reach out and touch. Which he does. As her eyes now mercifully glaze with shock and roll up over half-closed lids.

The three of them. And the crash of cymbal and kettle-drums. The music, rising in a voiced chorale.

ONCE SHE TWISTED to escape that hand. With that he struck a blow. It knocked her to her knees.

And, as if suddenly infuriated beyond endurance—as if

pushed beyond the limits of reasonable patience because she had insulted *him*—Feliciano!—he momentarily abandoned her.

Stalked off, hunch-shouldered, in a swelling, berserk rage.

PICKED UP A bar stool and battered the kitchenette area with it. The fluorescent light went. The paneled cabinet doors collapsed. And, wild now, he clawed at the cabinets' interiors, flinging about cups, plates, saucers, which bounced off the walls.

Tomas, cowering over by the bar in ecstatic terror.

Feliciano, maddened now because this Melmac stuff would not shatter. The dinette table was ripped loose, cushions flew. Tomas set down the whiskey bottle to lend a hand. Shelves of books were emptied, closets kicked in, their contents—clothing, camping gear, the shortwave radio—strewn about. Drawers, cupboards, everything yanked out, emptied, upended, kicked in, torn or ripped, broken. Bottles of ketchup, Worcestershire, and Tabasco sailed through the air. Mayonnaise. A ten-pound sack of flour disintegrated in a snowy cloud. An extra rifle, a thousand-dollar custom Weatherby engraved with LaPorte's name and the trademark of his ranch, was smashed across the bar. The Circassian walnut stock—at least that wasn't plastic!—splintered, the telescopic sight shattered. The barrel actually bent—who would have thought the old man had that kind of strength?

Slouching, he turned back to her. Reached down, to haul her to her feet by her hair. She screamed then—heard clearly over the music—and opened her eyes, the shock at last gone. Shaking her head in negation. Crouched back against the wall, hands raised in protest. The robe torn loose. Old Mora reached. Took her single-handedly by the throat and put her against the wall. While with the other he got the robe off, and the undergarment—curious, what a wild strength there was in those skinny talons: Nylon is tough, yet it tore like tissue in that angry grasp.

So, naked now, she stood before them. No longer really sane. Nor were they. Feliciano got a wrist and with a single violent twist put her down on her knees. Motioned to Tomas, who took command, all cheerful smile, taking both wrists to hold her so, As his father wished.

For the meek shall inherit the earth, and everything she did that sunlit day she will do again, now.

WITH THAT SHE fought. They beat her and she screamed again.

She would not acquiesce, knowing full well that they would kill her if she did not. Her nose bloodied, one eye already puffed shut. Again she screamed, and lost two teeth for her trouble. Was knocked to the wreckage-strewn floor, weeping at last. They stood back a pace, the better to survey her sprawled humility.

FELICIANO TRULY INSANE now.

Caught by a double irony that brings to the surface his worst capacities.

That glade that afternoon—the beauty—all that which he witnessed. To have it here and now. To be the master in this palace of ruined luxury. To visit vengeance and have his way at last. All this is too much. Far more than his primitive mind was ever equipped to deal with. Something in him has gone dead, or burned out.

He is bursting with adrenaline-fueled power.

But the core of him is limp and impotent.

As if, somehow, in this hateful life nothing will ever go quite right for him. What a bitter knowledge. Before his gaping son he feels no embarrassment or humiliation, but a raging disappointment.

To have it all at last. And then to have nothing. The intrinsic unfairness of it is too unbearable.

This ignominious wilt. As if, somehow, in all evilness, she has worked a dreadful spell upon him. This *bruja*-sorceress.

But if not one, then another. The grinning Rabbit. Tomas, goofy now, almost gibbering, jigging up and down, all split lip and bulbous, twitching nose. From which is heard a steady sound—not grunts, certainly—but a kind of happy baritone honking.

With arrogant, patriarchal dignity, Feliciano gives the nod.

Tomas is at her, not to be denied. Unlike his father, is neither inept nor unequipped. Despite her struggles, the rape is quickly done, no more than a minute, for Tomas is rabbitlike in more ways than one, and, finished now, he withdraws, leaves, crouches, stands erect, laughing as he hops across the room to the whiskey bottle again, clutching his britches at knee level, displaying dirty, hairy buttocks and a pendulous swing of genitalia. He drinks, hands the bottle over to his father, who drinks too, then tries again to accomplish entry. Fails. Despite her total lack of resistance.

Rises again in epileptic stance, drooling. The bluish lips drawn back in chimpanzee rictus. The insane eyes no longer human. Nor for that matter, animal either. Mirroring all that is in him—a devilish pain and anguish, all the horror of a demon on the loose.

Too far now. He is beyond recall.

Lurches this way and that, glaring down at her. Slaps his hands against his skinny shanks, almost drumming them. He throws his head back, tilts the scrawny gobbler's neck, chin angled ceilingward, eyes squinched shut, the crusted lids aglisten with real tears, and lets out a feral howl. A bestial wail that keens above the full chorus on the tape deck. The two sounds so disparate in the savaged Winnebago. That lupine howl cutting through a Latin chant.

Looks about for some method of vengeance. One way or another, Feliciano will have his way, is not to be denied. Not today, not anymore. Not ever again!

Spies amid the mess and clutter on the shag rug the contents of one of the kitchenette drawers . . . can openers, chrome spatulas, soup spoons, a French whisk for omelettes, bottle-openers, serving forks, and several knives, one, long-bladed, stag-antlered, its serrated edge quite sharp, polished, of fine surgical steel.

Seizes this. And motions once again to the Rabbit. Who understands and follows his father's sign-language instructions. Takes her by the ankles and throws them wide. While Feliciano sits atop her waist, his back to her head, to stare down for the briefest moment at her foul abomination. Then begins. Grabs with one hand. Strikes—slashes—once, with the other. The keen blade quickly cutting.

She shrieked then—an incredible scream to match and surpass his own wail. Roused to consciousness by the blade. Displayed, then, a fearful strength. Her taloned fingers reached out to rake at his neck and back. Opened deep furrows at the nape, ripped the collar of the worn mackinaw clean off, went right into the thick wool, tearing the cloth. The nail of one finger came off, caught in a seam. And then she rose in a frenzy. Shrieked again, bucked, her entire body an arched bow, clear of the rug. Threw Feliciano right off, got one ankle free and kicked wildly, and, with accidental accuracy, got the astonished Tomas squarely in the nose with one naked heel, flattening the snout with a crunch of gristle and bone. He howled, went over backward.

She rose to her feet, staggering, cried out again, a banshee wail of despair, looked about, eyes gone madder than theirs. Saw Feliciano, rising too from the corner where she had flung him, to come at her again, still clutching the serving knife, and in his other hand a scrap, or tatter, of something else. She turned then, and ran as best she could. To the door. And with a single twist of the handle, flung it open.

To the freezing, wintry morning. And a blinding sunlight that lit up the snow out there. A dazzling whiteness, so that the interior of the Winnebago seemed a darkened cave. The lair of underworld beings.

At the foot of the fold-down steps she fell . . . then rose to stagger off, crying out loudly, like a maimed bird. Leaving a trail of red, and the prints of naked feet. Her wails of anguish, almost furious, rose above the snowy slopes. Unheard by any, save the string of horses and the forest animals.

And these two. Who emerged from the shadowed doorway opening.

In cruel and casual pursuit.

SHE LIVED. THEY found her. The hunters, home from the chase.

Themselves frustrated and sour, even in their success. Cold and tired, retracing their trail up the logging road that led to the camp.

Saw soon enough as they entered the clearing that something terrible had happened. Automatically connected it to Feliciano and Tomas, whom someone in the group had discovered missing. Saw the blood the moment they entered the camp area.

Guillermo Apodaca said, "They finally went at each other. Those two always hated each other's guts."

But even as Guillermo spoke he and the others made the mental jump to the woman that had been left behind. They grew quiet—paused—then moved across the deserted clearing at a quickened pace. Saw more blood.

Peter Griego, unsnapping the holster that held the heavy Smith and Wesson.

The door of the Winnebago, gaping wide. They knew then.

Cornelius crossed himself. Peter, gun drawn now, raised a hand to halt the others. He said, "You all stay put. Let me check."

They obeyed. He went to the open door, mounted the steps. Hammer drawn back on the revolver now.

Peter, all deadly business. Ready to fire at the least movement.

Inside, it was still. The tape deck automatically shut down. Feliciano and Tomas, both asleep, passed out, gently snoring, sprawled together on the floor amid a crush and welter of stuff, broken bottles, ripped curtains. The interior a total ruin.

The two, father and son, curled up like contented children. The woman nowhere to be seen. Drops of blood across the shaggy rug; on the metal steps; in the snow.

He approached them, the muzzle of the revolver swinging from one to the other. With calm deliberation, Peter kicked the old man in the ribs as hard as he could. In fact, fractured a rib. A grunt, but that was as close as Mora got to consciousness. Tomas, the same.

Peter, at the door again. Staring down at the others. "She isn't here," he said. "Some of you follow the trail she left."

The others turned. The prints were clear enough. Three sets of tracks, going up the slope and into the trees. Two returning. They follow.

Expecting to find a body, but finally spy her, kneeling in the snow, in a clear place up in the pines. They break into a run, and so come to her. She kneels there, sitting back on her haunches, hands folded in her lap. Almost as if in prayer. But her eyes are blank, empty of expression.

They see blood, but not the cause, and conclude: rape. Cornelius already with his parka off, covering her shoulders, the others following suit, outer garments quickly shucked to cover her, bundle her, protect her nakedness. They do not want to look at any of this. The man in each of them recoils. There is something about this they can't stomach. She had been terribly battered. Scratched, kicked, pummeled. Badgered and harassed.

Until, perhaps, her tormentors grew too tired to strike any more.

Or lost interest.

The mental reconstruction of what they reckon took place

is not difficult. Their anger mounts. It is already clear to them that this is why Peter is staying down at the Winnebago with those two. To protect them.

There is a common outrage, and it grows. That protectiveness that at the core virtually all men have for women.

They can't figure why the Moras brought her up here. Perhaps to finish it for good.

For several yards round the place where they found her the snow is stamped flat, roiled. Flung about.

As if some wildly choreographed ritual dance or ceremony had been acted out. And then she had been abandoned . . . still alive, but fearfully used.

THEY RETRACE THEIR path. Father Cornelius, with all his burly German strength, carries her as though she were a child. Only her feet and head showing. The rest of her cocoonlike, wrapped in layers of jackets. She is in shock, breathing raggedly, head sunk forward on her chest, the split and battered lips parted.

AT THE CAMP they set her down in the big tent and let her be.

They spotted the folded plastic sack and clay pipe then. Lying on the Mora bedrolls in a dreadful smear of sour, watery slime. They brought the sack to Peter, confronting him.

Even stocky Guillermo, never one to turn against his own people, declared, "Something ought to be done about those two. Now is as good a time as any."

Peter maintained firm command. Whatever his faults, on the job he is cool. He said, "They're my prisoners."

Among his virtues, too, is that magnificently expressionless face, and the quick turn of mind. Whatever terrific shock he felt when Guillermo handed over the pipe and tobacco pouch was hidden. He waited, listening, as Guillermo explained, "This dope they had was laying right out there in plain sight, atop their bedrolls. They must have had it with them all along, Peter."

Griego inferred, then, that he might be safe. That Feliciano and Tomas had thrown away the tag he had intentionally tied to the sack, dated and signed in his own hand, attesting that he had confiscated the stuff nearly a year ago. That shallow story he had fabricated. Some place out there, perhaps hopefully already sodden with snow, perhaps near his truck, was the tag. With luck, gone forever.

He took personal charge of this evidence. As he had already garnered certain other evidence, which his eye, trained to search out evidence, had spotted amid the mess scattered about the floor of the Winnebago. He himself had lost all the color of his ruddy complexion in the recognizing of it, had actually felt nauseous for a moment before he forced himself to pick it up, using a folded paper towel, dropping it, paper towel and all, into a plastic sandwich bag. Looked round at the two sleeping men, now manacled wrist to wrist, and felt a dangerous revulsion, felt his gorge rise, and so had his own moment of temptation, then and there, to end it easily with the Magnum pistol. It wouldn't be the first time an "incorrigible" had been shot while "resisting arrest." And so be done with this. But Peter controlled himself. They were not his prisoners, but the state's. He was doubly thankful to have kept the others outside. They were happy enough now just to have her alive. So they could not have seen. Must have bundled her up real quick. Without a look. If they had, they might as easily have wished her dead.

The Moras, Peter figured, had ruined her good. They had gotten something her stupid husband could not control. They had gotten to her all right.

Standing in the doorway of the Winnebago, Peter tossed Virgil McCormick the key ring to his pickup. He ordered Virge and the others to get it off the timber road, get it out of the way fast, clear a way right now, even if they had to wreck the truck to do it, so that she could be gotten down to Santa Fe. Sent them along, the ones with jeeps and four-wheel-drives, telling them to get out chains, jacks, come-alongs, anything, so long as they got her to the hospital quickly. They obeyed, figuring he wanted her there pronto for a medical exam that would hold up in court.

Leaving the two Moras inside, he went to the tent and stepped under the door flap. Father Cornelius was with her. He and the priest could hear the men at work on the road below, transmissions grinding, faint shouts.

Peter asked, "Is she conscious?" Cornelius looked up and nodded. "Father, please step outside. I have to talk to her. For just a minute."

Cornelius left. Peter squatted beside her, leaned his face close to hers. Her eyes were open. He said, almost in a whisper, "Can you hear me, Mrs. Jaramillo?"

She looked at him.

"Has the bleeding stopped?"

There was no response. He sat back on his heels, glanced down at her body, now wrapped in blankets as well as the jackets—somebody in the group had had sense enough to keep the warmth in her, so the shock would not worsen.

He began again. "I know what happened, Mrs. Jaramillo. I don't think any of the others do. Has the bleeding stopped? Can you tell? We're getting you down to the hospital as quick as we can, but you have to tell me . . . has it stopped?"

She spoke then. In a low voice. Nodded weakly, acknowledging his concern. "I think so."

"We're getting you to the hospital as quick as we can," Peter said again. "You just rest easy. Don't try to move. You just lie as still as you can."

She nodded.

He rose. Stood above her, staring down, and said finally, "I'm real sorry."

Then he bent over her again, and asked, still in a soft voice,

"Did they mention anything about narcotics? We have some evidence that they may have been using drugs."

"No," she said.

"They didn't say anything to you at all?"

"No."

He turned, and went to the Moras' bedrolls. Searched their stinking interiors quickly and efficiently, shaking them out, and, finding no slip of incriminating paper, walked out of the tent with a clear conscience.

NINETEEN

"*They ever let that old man out of jail, there is liable to be some real trouble.*"

"*Somebody might do for him?*"

"*There are ways.*"

"*I suppose so.*"

"*The son—Tomas—he never knew nothing. But Feliciano—he knew, all right. He knew right from wrong. He ain't nowheres near as dumb as he makes out. He just likes to act estúpido—but he knows. You can bet on that.*"

—*Conversations in the Crippled Horse*

THE CASE NEVER came to trial.

Less than a month later, in closed court, Judge Harvey Burrell, a thin, bald, elderly man of immense dignity and old-fashioned formality, remanded Feliciano and Tomas over to the state mental hospital for psychiatric evaluation.

All it took was one look at the two of them. Somewhat cleaner and shorn of hair, in the gray cotton shirts and trousers provided by the county jail, they looked improved. It was obvious, though, that they were incompetent.

They had been brought before the court earlier. Judge Burrell wanted to look them over. As if to be convinced that such a pair actually existed.

And there, before the bench, for the first time in a long time, Feliciano spoke. That cringing stance again, the foxy smile and twisting lips. He knew the proper face to put on before supreme authority. He'd been in court before. Knew what it was all about.

He tried to explain to this august presence his—Feliciano's —version of the charges. He had, after all, been taken from his family. They needed him, or more exactly needed his share of the welfare check, which, now that he was a ward of the county, had been suspended. He had done nothing so wrong. Too much to drink, and some marijuana. But he hadn't killed anyone, had he? If you went and put people in jail for such simple weaknesses, why, he could argue that half the county would be locked behind bars.

A cogent argument, but unfortunately beyond his verbal skills.

And in another triggering of frustration, he lost control of it all, his voice rising in a croaking bellow—with eyes that stared wildly into those of the appalled black-robed man seated above him. Hammering his flattened hand on the polished bench top, Feliciano made his point: *"Yo soy inocente! Los otros tienen las culpas!"*

I am innocent! The others! They are guilty!

With the grinning rabbit-face of Tomas bobbing in enthusiastic agreement.

Tomas went peaceably, but it took two bailiffs to haul Feliciano out of there.

The whole thing had taken less than ten minutes.

Later, in his private chambers, over coffee, Judge Burrell talked with the district attorney and the defense counsels, who had been appointed by legal aid.

"The state hospital, I think, will concur with the preliminary psychiatric evaluations we've been able to put together," he told his younger colleagues. "The real question, as I see it, is how to keep this pair put away."

"You mean for life?" one of the defense counsels asked. His name was Franklin Rudiger.

"Not necessarily," Burrell said. He rubbed a hand over his bald pate. "But at least until there is a change . . . by that I mean a real improvement in the competency of them both. Frankly, I don't see much of a possibility for that."

"That's taking a rather hard line with them, isn't it?" Rudiger argued.

Judge Burrell stared at Rudiger a moment. He said finally, "See here, Frank. Don't think that you have any sort of real case to argue here, just because the woman has disappeared. Arguing, perhaps, from the circumstantial. You can't pull that with me. If this had happened in the middle of Santa Fe, you might have a ghost of an argument. Just barely, though. It wouldn't hold water with me—not after hearing that madman out there—although an appeals court might entertain it. But, personally, I'd never tolerate the argument that somebody else had committed these offenses and that this pair might have innocently and coincidentally stumbled upon the scene in time to be accused. Not in my court, sir. Besides . . . up there in the mountains. That part of the wilderness isn't exactly crawling with tourists at the pitch of the summer season, let alone the dead of winter. Every other man who was up there at the time has been accounted for."

"I didn't mean to imply that I was rejecting your opinion," Rudiger said.

"I'm glad, then, that you agree," Judge Burrell said. "Because without the testimony of that woman, there is only the existing evidence. The utter carnage they made of that Arizona fellow's mobile home. I understand it's still up there. The peyote."

Judge Burrell mused on. "The question, gentlemen . . .

that is, what I am trying to comprehend . . . is precisely *why* something like this could take place. That's what I'm after."

"The evidence pretty much speaks for itself," the second defense counsel pointed out.

"Not to me it doesn't," Judge Burrell said. "Eyewitness statements. Medical and psychiatric reports. The change of venue. Oh, we have the legal superstructure, properly prepared and properly presented. Except for a few blank spots, we have a clear enough picture of the events that led up to the assault. Even so, I still ask, why? The motive is what I'm after."

"For the rape?" the district attorney said.

"Alleged," Frank Rudiger corrected.

"No need to bicker. We're not before a jury," the judge said. "I mean all of it. The mutilation."

"Liquor. Drugs."

"That doesn't satisfy me."

"The two of them are insane."

"A little better. But still insufficient. At least to my mind," Burrell argued.

"I understand she was quite lovely," Frank Rudiger remarked.

"She wasn't when I talked to her in the hospital," the district attorney said.

"Nothing at all to do with it," Judge Burrell countered. He paused, reached for a cigarette, lit it. Against his doctor's orders. Went on. "This case is a precedent for me. Not the rape aspect. That's everyday stuff. But the abuse they visited on her. I read the medical report. She may have to wear an indwelling catheter and carry a bag for the rest of her life." He paused again, inhaled, sighed, and said, "Necrophilia is bad enough. I had such a case years ago. But this. We speak of the rights of the co-defendants—but what of the rights of this woman? What she underwent I refuse to gloss over with an inadequate term like 'indignity,' or 'invasion of her human rights.' Nor does felonious assault satisfy me. Atrocity is the only word that comes to mind, and even that is pallid as far as I am concerned. What of the injustice that has been done *her?*"

Frank Rudiger stared down at his coffee and then observed, "Perhaps she asked for it, sir."

"Oh, I wouldn't mind buying that—or at least a part of it —if this were mere sexual violation," Judge Burrell said. "Rape, gentlemen, is something we're all familiar with. Aside from the difficulty of establishing incontestable proof, there are often, as we know, mitigating or extenuating factors. But this. Look at the case record. A woman in her middle thirties, by all accounts attractive, intelligent. Married six years. No children. Settled in a small mountain community. Both she and her husband were well regarded, it seems. He teaches at the high school. He's a local fellow, Spanish-American. Outwardly, they seemed happy and adjusted."

"She was having an affair," Rudiger said. "I'm speaking informally, of course."

"What if she was?"

"I'm merely pointing out the precariousness of the outraged-virtue line of argument."

The judge shook his head and lit another cigarette. "All right, Frank . . . I've asked a few questions on my own, too. We'll let the inference stand. It doesn't follow, though, that there is a link between her indiscretion and this assault—it still doesn't excuse the criminal acts that were committed against her."

"It was a flagrant affair," Rudiger insisted.

"Indiscretions of that nature usually are."

"Apparently, this summer it was the talk of the village."

"People will talk."

"All I'm pointing out is that her reputation could have attracted a certain type of attention from men," Rudiger said.

"As far as I can see, all you are pointing out is that she was human, and perhaps had certain human weaknesses," the judge observed.

"I'm merely interested in keeping things in objective focus, sir."

"So am I," Judge Burrell said. "What troubles me is that I am afraid this entire business can dwindle into felonious assault—or even a misdemeanor—especially since we have no principal witness. Suppose things like liquor, drugs, mental incompetence, and infidelity *did* enter into it? What interests me is the unforgivable behavior that took place. What I ask is, if such things happened, then what made them happen, and what are we to do about it? We can go to trial, and struggle through the whole business, and it can end up nowhere." He snorted irritably. "Certain things happened. I don't intend to let them be casually dismissed."

"Pretty hard line," Rudiger said.

"Perhaps," Judge Burrell replied. "But it's liberal compared to what that woman went through. Let me put it to you another way. If these two are, in fact, guilty—this Mora and his dreadful son—would you concur that, in essence, they represent a menace to society?"

"Well, yes," Rudiger said.

"I'm not talking about social misfits, or criminal mentalities," Burrell said. "Nor will I debate with you the Moras's legal and human rights as citizens of this country, because if you pull that line with me I will counter with the legal and human rights of that poor woman. Actually, I'm not arguing at all. I am merely pointing out that certain acts took place. If you agree to this, then I think it behooves us to address ourselves to the problem of preventing a reoccurrence."

"How?" Rudiger demanded.

"We will see," Judge Burrell said. "Gentlemen, we can't make the world right. But we can start with these two. I am going to talk to a few people, here in our medical community, and at the mental hospital. The complete psychiatric evaluation on these two men may take quite a while. Quite a long time, in fact."

"You mean you're going to warehouse them?" Rudiger asked.

"Frank, our courts come in for a lot of criticism, and much of it is deserved," Burrell said. "Even so, the operating characteristics of the American judicial system are designed so that there are more ways than one to skin a cat."

Neither Rudiger nor his colleague responded to this. Nor did the district attorney. The cold, wintry light lit the judge's broad desk, and the faces of the men who sat across from him.

Judge Burrell puffed at his cigarette again, exhaled. His expression once more became introspective. He said, "You know, in my reading I have heard of various unsophisticated —usually warlike—peoples who, as part of their culture, have a tendency to collect grisly souvenirs. Cossack cavalrymen, Afghanistanian nomads . . . the breasts of women, fashioned into tobacco pouches, that sort of thing. A kind of intentional corruption of all that is admirable and fine in the human spirit." He drew again at the cigarette. "There is, I understand, a primitive tribe somewhere in the Amazon. The matron ladies of that tribe are known to practice clitorectomy upon certain young women who are too free with their charms. But, of course, that has to do with female insatiability, and the proprietary attitude women feel toward men, and toward something they feel they alone ought to have access to—all that is comprehensible. Barbarous but understandable. This business, though . . . these Moras. We know the type. Forgive me. I am interested in objectivity, but I am also human. You might think that people of this sort, with such insurmountable handicaps, would go to any length to avoid attention. Yet—even in the most insane moment—to utterly defy everything! I simply can't understand it." He looked at the men with him. "Well—we will do what we can do, gentlemen."

IN SENDING THEM to the state mental hospital for an indeterminate period, Judge Burrell was acting in what he felt to be the best public interest—after seeing and listening to Feliciano's wild tirade, the thought had occurred to him, as it had to the district attorney and the defense counsels, that old Mora was a walking case of dynamite. Turned loose, he might commit a similar atrocity, or something even worse —there was not a reason in the world to doubt such a possibility.

But if Mora could be successfully warehoused for even a couple of years, well, there was some hope in that concept. Among the various reports in Feliciano's case folder was a medical prognosis on the condition of his tabes dorsalis— the venereal eating away of his skull. In time—less than five years, the report indicated—debilitation and collapse would take place. The condition had already progressed into the advanced stage. Judge Burrell understood that by depriving the old man of his freedom he was doing him a disservice, even though society very likely might benefit by not having Mora roaming the streets.

On the other hand, in a very real sense, the court, by putting Feliciano away, may have provided the old man with a sort of protection that was not without value. Locked up, Mora could not get at society—but, then, neither could society, or what passed for it in Pecos, get at him. In that part of the world, men had been shot for lesser crimes. Lynching was out of the question—the Spanish-American mind does not lend itself to organized group violence—but a spur-of-the-moment ambuscade or bushwhacking was not an impossibility. It had happened before. A rifle or shotgun poked out of the window of a pickup or sedan. Daniel Jaramillo had reason enough. Sedgewick, too. Even Peter Griego, who had his own notions of right and wrong, had had his own moment of temptation there in the wrecked Winnebago that sunny Sunday morning.

So perhaps it was just as well that old Mora and Tomas were sent off. If, in time, they should ever be released, the affair would have died down. Memory is short. The rage felt by the men in the hunting party that morning up in the high alpine camp would diminish, be forgotten. Perhaps. For the present, and with luck for a long time, the Mora men were out of sight.

THE HILLSIDE CABIN is vacant now. Months later. Summer again. Fields of mountain flowers score the alpine landscape.

Door ajar, windows gone, curtains rent and flapping in the breeze.

Bands of roving teen-age youngsters from the valley have found it.

Books, shelves, furniture. All gone, or smashed. The Steinway a ruin.

Field mice, rats, squirrels, and a king snake are among the permanent residents. A barn owl hides in the unused chimney.

In one corner of the living room a small mound of dried excrement, where some person, in delight or defiance, voided. Childish graffiti, paint-sprayed on the plastered walls, along with crayoned and penciled symbols, designs, scribbles, initials, obscenities, and profane hosannahs:

"*You are what you eat.*"

And, in another script, beneath it:

"*I'm a pussy!*"

HE WALKED AWAY FROM IT. Two suitcases, and no forwarding address.

There was a rumor that she went with him. It is known that he spent the better part of three days in the waiting room on the second floor of St. Vincent's, and that a nursing sister finally admitted him to her room. There they talked.

The battered jeep he used on the rough road to the cabin was found at the bus depot downtown, abandoned. The bank he used reported that he had withdrawn all his savings and closed his checking account. Left town. No good-byes to anyone. The jeep, eventually confiscated by Santa Fe police, was later auctioned.

By then, she had gone, too. But here the trail is easily followed.

Daniel, at last spurred into action by the bitter sting of jealousy, was convinced that she had left with his friend.

And a lesser friend, in fact a second cousin, sworn to secrecy, assisted. A minor executive in social security. An official tracer was sent out. If she was using her real number, if she was anywhere in the country working for a salary, she would turn up.

Months later, the tracer paid off. She was in Carmel, California, under her unmarried name. Working in a combination cocktail lounge and steakhouse as a hostess.

Daniel does not go out there. There is no need to. No purpose would be served.

Why see her now? A tall and stately girl, still quite beautiful. No longer young, but there is style to her. A regal calm —aloof, polite, even with the younger waitresses who work the tables. At closing time, she leaves with the man who shares an apartment with her. Right on the beach. Where they sit together, drinking a little, and watching the incoming fog. And the surf, pounding away at the coast. Hour after hour. A peaceful rush of breaking waves, black-silvered clouds against the night sky, lit by stars, and, sometimes, a moon, gibbous, then full, then quartering again, an endless cycle. A brief respite. Perhaps the only one she—or they—will ever know.

This man who shares her life also works at the same cocktail lounge. That is how the rumor about their being together got started. A Santa Fe couple, man and wife, vacationing in California, saw—or thought they saw—him, or somebody who looked sort of like him, or a man named Sedgewick, who they had once met at a party. The man in the Carmel steakhouse was at the piano, half drunk, playing. It was the piano music that made them think of John Sedgewick. This man really played quite well. But when they went up to him and asked, he said his name was not Sedgewick and he had never been in New Mexico. Said he couldn't stand the desert. When they explained, with a friendliness induced by several margaritas, that Santa Fe was up in the mountains, the piano player shook his head and smiled and told them, "I didn't known there were mountains in New Mexico. I thought it was all desert." So it couldn't have been Sedgewick after all. Probably someone who just looked a little like him, and who really knew his way around on the piano.

MONTY CARTIER CAUGHT forty kinds of hell for the hunt.

Rumors of the weekend got around the state-capital complex. Cartier squelched them, but that Tuesday one of the governor's aides phoned to ask him about the murders up in the Pecos Wilderness. The governor had heard that someone had been killed on a Game and Fish Department deer hunt that weekend. Monty explained that no one had been killed, and that they had gotten the lion. "What lion?" the aide asked. "We heard it was a deer hunt."

"You don't hunt deer in December," Cartier said. He did some more talking and got the aide calmed down, but he knew he was not done with it.

Word got around, all right. Later that week his board of directors got a quorum together and met with him.

Bud Hunnicut was the member who didn't like Lester Johnson. He was also hung up on maintaining a good departmental image. He said, "Monty, what in God's name is all this talk I been hearing about shooting and rape and plunder and murderous ex-convicts in G-and-F uniforms going around wrecking homes and beating up on folks?"

So Monty told them what had happened. Hunnicut said, "Les Johnson ran the hunt? You were up there yourself, and you let Johnson run it?"

"It was his hunt," Cartier said.

"Well, that just beats me," Hunnicut said. "What about this convict who's working for us? They say he attacked some local residents."

"It was more like self-defense, Bud," Cartier said. "Actually, two people were hurt."

"And he has a record?"

"He does that," Cartier admitted. "In fact, I guess I'd have to admit that he's got one about as long as your arm."

Bud Hunnicut said, "I'll be damned." He thought about this and then looked at the other members of the quorum. "Well, I guess the first thing we better do is dump this convict fellow."

"I'm arranging it," Cartier said.

"I'd say get rid of him *muy pronto*," Hunnicut said.

"It's already been done, Bud. He's under arrest. Parole violation. He was on parole."

"Monty, what in the goddamned hell are we doing with people like that on the staff?" Bud Hunnicut wanted to know.

"He wasn't so bad," Cartier said. "Les Johnson gave him a straight superior rating on his semiannual evaluation."

"Don't talk to me about Johnson," Hunnicut said. "I could as well ask what in hell we're doing with someone like Johnson on the staff. He should've retired years ago."

"He's got almost forty years in the field," Monty argued. "That adds up to a lot of know-how, any way you look at it, Bud."

"You sure couldn't prove it by me," Hunnicut said. "Not from the way he ran this hunt."

So Monty Cartier knew then that he would have to throw two bones to the dogs, not one. He had been hoping to satisfy them by just getting rid of Bowman, but Bud Hunnicut wanted Johnson too.

Cartier thought this over. He was a good director. He knew that a department where the director and the board members were at odds was as good as three quarters crippled. He said finally, "Well, maybe you're right, Bud."

THE HEAD OF the cat was clean. As Les Johnson had insisted. The lab analysis found no trace of rabid organisms. Abscessed teeth, though.

A big record-size hungry old lion, getting too old to bring down game. That's all it was. Maybe it went after that child, and maybe it was some other cat. No knowing now. Still, too bad this one had to go.

Lester Johnson owns a small house up on Camino de la Luz. He and his late wife bought it in the fifties, and he spends a lot of time in it now that he is retired.

Johnson has no skill at letter writing. But he writes one anyway. To his friend, Lewis Bowman, back out at the pen, his parole suspended for antisocial behavior. Lew really wanted to know about the cat, and about that poor woman, and the Moras, and all the rest of that awful weekend. Toward the end of the letter the old man adds:

> . . . *well, Lew, I had to get rid of the dogs, as they were too much of a hassel to have all the time here in town. Cacique was run over a couple of weeks ago right in the street out in front of the house, a couple of pachucos in a pickup, they weren't watching where they were going, drinking beer, he was hit pretty bad, all caved in on one side, I about broke down when I saw him like that, he was a good dog, only dumb, never would stop chasing cars. Anyway I hope you are okay out there and getting along alrite, and I will try to get you those books you wrote asking for. Anyhow you take care of yourself and as I said you always have a place to stay here, it's not such a bad little place and nobody would bother you much. Your friend,*

>   *—Les*

Out at the joint, Lewis reads the letter and readies himself for that day when they must turn him loose again. Goes back to his project.

He is into another neurotic, self-imposed program. Can now press, vertically, with ease, a two-hundred-and-thirty-pound barbell ten times.

No easy task. He runs ten miles a day in the big yard. Can do three hundred pushups, and works to earn his keep in the penitentiary kitchen, where he pilfers forty to fifty eggs a day, a pure-protein diet, so that the muscle on him bulges in thick, supple slabs. A two-hundred-and-forty-pound man with a thirty-inch waist.

It's one way to keep sane.

VIRGIL MCCORMICK WENT into the hospital with pleural pneumonia. Claimed it was just bronchitis, and kept trying to work around the farm and kennels until he collapsed—for most of the first week he was listed in critical condition. Virgil had hospitalization, so his not going in earlier wasn't a matter of money . . . the truth is that he was scared to death of hospitals, and his wife knew that nobody in the world was going to get him into one so long as he was on his feet.

When he had recovered enough to talk again and have visitors, he blamed it all on the Moras.

Lying there in his white hospital gown, showered and shaved, his graying hair—at the longest it couldn't have been over an inch—anointed with Wildroot and severely parted and brushed flat, encapsulating his narrow, bony skull, he told Mrs. McCormick, "It just goes to prove I was right. Mexicans is Mexicans, and whites is whites, and every damned time the two races get together there is trouble! Not that I'm blaming those Moras *personally*, any more than you can blame a nigrah for the way he is, or a polecat for smelling the way he does. But still, there is one thing I know for sure . . .

if they hadn't of been up there, I sure wouldn't be *here*. That's all there is to it!"

But there was a little more to it than that.

It was Virgil who had caught the ring of car keys tossed by Peter Griego that morning by the Winnebago. It was he who had gotten into Peter's Dodge and started the engine, while the other men were busy hooking up chains leading from the Dodge to their own four-wheel-drives, so that they could snake it out of the way.

It was Virge who found the abandoned dope tag. Lying right there on the floor of the Dodge, by the brake pedal. He picked it up, read it, and, when he understood, knew, for the first time since he'd been in Pecos, real fear.

A standard New Mexico State Police I.D. tag, made of cardboard, with a little string, still knotted, attached to it. Neat printing, in ballpoint:

CONTENTS—ONE PIPE, CLAY. ONE BOOK PAPER MATCHES. ONE SMALL POUCH, PLASTIC, CONTAINING UNKWN. MATERIAL, POSS. NARC.

—PETER M. GRIEGO
N.M.S.P.

Virgil had slipped the tag into his pocket, and revved the cold engine. He did a lot of thinking while it slowly warmed.

He considered what Peter might do if he ever found out he had the tag. One way or another, Peter very likely would do something about that. Virge, sitting there in the cab of the truck, chilled to the core, as he had not been since he was a youngster facing death in the Bastogne breakthrough, considered all the philosophical, moral, and ethical possibilities involved.

He had spent years building an acceptable life in this valley. And while he was perhaps not the easiest man to get along with, he was at least tolerated. Virgil liked Pecos. He figured on spending the rest of his life there.

Peter was really too scary. That tag just might ruin Peter's career forever. Then again, it mightn't. If Peter got off with a reprimand, or a suspension, that wouldn't be so good. He might just come around, one of these days, looking for Virgil.

Virgil thought about that tag a lot while he was in the hospital. It was in the pocket of his parka in the closet. He decided that the reason he had made such a success of settling in the valley was because he had minded his business, and had not meddled in folks' affairs.

He concluded, finally, that this was a piece of information that he would have to live with. There was no way to share it. When he was discharged from the hospital, his wife drove him home. There, later that day, in his bedroom fireplace, he burned the tag.

ONE GOOD THING came out of the hunt. George LaPorte had a breakdown.

Clyde Fox had seen it coming. A man who's willing to wait around for years to put a bullet into someone just can't be right in the head.

Clyde got him into an expensive Tucson sanitorium. This was some time after they had returned to Arizona.

LaPorte had the idea that evil had taken possession of the world, that a satanic conspiracy existed, ramrodded by Watergate cossacks, a Kissinger who spoke in the tones of a German butcher, a Kiplingesque England that had lost everything, including Churchill's war, and now, finally, these splintered, emerging Asian and African so-called nations who made their point by bombings, assassination, and universal discord. Kennedy, King gone. Goldwater, the last defender. The good people of the world were being killed off one by one, or defeated in some way by the forces of darkness. That was the only way he could explain the nightmare of what had happened in the Winnebago.

They gave him ECT—electroshock—and enough tranquilizers to immobilize the Green Bay Packers, as well as ten hours a week with a psychotherapist. The treatment had a salubrious effect.

Clyde Fox visited him every day. The place was only thirty miles from the ranch. Sat and chatted easily. And watched LaPorte, his boss and best friend, come back to sanity.

So, that boy in the facility for the criminally insane was saved. Maybe it was just as well.

"Clyde, I want to use my knowledge of the wilds—our knowledge—constructively," LaPorte told Fox one day. Still with that weirdly intense stare. "Why, Lord Almighty, Clyde, there aren't two men in the world know half as much about hunting as us. We must have fifteen, twenty thousand Kodachromes to prove it. We got to preserve all that for our children and their children's children."

Forgetting in his excitement—the first excitement Clyde had seen in years—that their children no longer existed.

Within a year after his discharge, LaPorte was a regional director of the Sierra Club. A dollar-a-year-man. He put tens of thousands of his own money into the lobbying effort. Hell, it was as good a way as any to keep from being eaten alive by the I.R.S.

Classes of Tucson schoolkids came out to the ranch for barbecue lunches and a tour of the vast hunting gallery that took up one wing of the main house. Viewed the mounted heads, the racks of antlers and horns, saw stuffed bear, ibex, a mountain gorilla, and a two-horned rhinoceros. Marveled at the gun room, with its endless cabinets of rifles, shotguns, pistols. A one-man armory.

He gave talks to groups about the need to preserve wildlife. Badly at first, with halting unease. Then got better.

Brought in Clyde as participating aide-de-camp. Big old burly Clyde, with that easygoing drawl. Clyde helped run the slide shows and sixteen-millimeter color movies. He was shy. Later on, though, George got him to help with the lecture part. Clyde was pretty good up there on the speaker's platform. He just naturally looked and sounded like all those safaris and expeditions George talked about.

Clyde had a way of turning the edge of LaPorte's deadpan seriousness, easing it somehow, for a chuckle at least, if not a downright laugh. Clyde had a gentle sense of humor, and didn't mind having a little fun at his own expense.

They got to be a kind of Mutt-and-Jeff team. At high schools, and then, later, at regional and even national conferences in Washington. They worked well together on the podium. Appeared on television talk-shows. The incongruity of the two. Clyde's story of the time he ran through the shore reeds beside Lake Victoria holding a copper pan of crêpes suzettes, with a charging African water buff at his heels, cracked up audiences. His big, weathered cowboy hands had a way of moving expressively.

Countered against LaPorte's urgent delivery. George sometimes tended to lose control of himself, and his audience too.

Thus, often, at the end of a lecture—LaPorte, face sheened with sweat, his diatribe winding down, breathless, but still searching for words.

The topper:

Gentle Clyde. Thick wrists dangling down from the sleeves of a three-hundred-dollar suede hunting jacket. The easy-going country boy. Equally at home over a chuck-wagon campfire or at Paris's George VI. The broad, toothy, moustachioed grin, a little lopsided, as he gazes at his boss, nodding.

The lazy Arizona drawl:

"Sure 'nuff, George. You go on an' tell 'em!"

Always good for a laugh.

PETER GRIEGO RECEIVED a letter of commendation that went into his personnel folder at state police headquarters for his efficient handling of the incident. He is still the Pecos *rojo*, still tough, brooks no defiance or challenge to his authority, and does his daily round, staring out at the world through cold, blue, hating eyes.

DANIEL JARAMILLO TRANSFERRED to the Albuquerque school system the following spring. The entire life he had built—the home, her, his career—was gone, or ignored now. He sold the house. Packed and left.

Very little of the scandal followed him. Only that there had been some dreadful tragedy in his personal life.

He taught his field successfully: physics, chemistry, biology, general science.

Showed southside Spanish kids how to make a Leyden jar, which in turn could be used to make an amputated frog's leg kick spastically.

Showed them how caloric heat loss could be scientifically measured in a tall, graduated chemist's flask filled with boiling water that was monitored by a simple Centigrade thermometer.

Taught dye-stain techniques, so that blood samples and tissue samples showed up brilliantly under the microscope.

Helped make, with a couple of advanced students, a small astronomical telescope, using a hand-ground reflecting mirror polished to Foucault's exact parabola.

Was a success with hydroponic gardening. The south windows of his classroom a veritable jungle of zucchini, tomato, and bean plants, set in shallow gravel, which their roots could grip while bathed in scientifically prepared fluids.

Made a solar-heat cell.

Showed, on the blackboard, how you could prove the speed of light and the theory of relativity with two jet planes flying east and west respectively, at the equator, and containing accurate clocks.

Made a barometer out of a tube filled with mercury. A

thermocouple out of two strips of scrap metal: copper and steel.

Constructed a miniature arc-welder out of a transformer and two carbon rods, salvaged from old flashlight batteries.

Proved Newton's laws with steel balls attached to string. Demonstrated Planck's constant.

Made a Faraday coil. A Wheatstone bridge.

Illustrated to his classes that nothing short of nuclear fission can really destroy matter, only transform it, using a piece of ice in a sealed container that he heated, until there was water, then steam. The vapor-filled container weighed as much as it had when there was only a piece of ice in it.

His work was good, and he was admired, as he had been in Pecos, by both students and his colleagues.

That fall, three of his students took prizes at the Albuquerque School Science Fair, and two weeks later, sitting in an armchair in the living room of his small apartment up in the north valley near Dietz Farms, he fired a bullet from a 9-millimeter Luger Parabellum through the roof of his mouth.

SOME ODD THINGS happened to Feliciano Mora.

The medical staff at the state hospital discovered that he was too unpredictable to be assigned to a regular ward. This was after he had attacked and knocked down a nurse and a ward orderly who—to his mind—had treated him unfairly.

That meant permanent assignment to a seclusion room, which is what the maximum isolation cells are called. There were not many of these.

They also feared that he might do a walkaway. There are walls and gates and locked doors at the state hospital, but it is not a maximum-security facility. Its patients can, and do, wander off at times.

Tomas, his son, was no problem. He was happy there. Was fed three good meals a day, had a warm place to sleep, television to watch, and could earn Coca-Cola money. He rarely saw his father, and this suited him, because Feliciano always abused him.

When it was apparent that Feliciano was not responding in any way to chemotherapy, behavioral modification, or other forms of treatment—his prognosis had always been negative— the hospital asked for and got permission to transfer him to the state penitentiary, which had maximum security. This occasionally was done with forensic or dangerous patients.

The penitentiary didn't want him either, for good reasons.

One was that, after glancing over his record, the assistant warden knew that Feliciano was trouble. With his sort there was always the chance that he would, sooner or later, kill someone, or be killed. In accepting responsibility for such a prisoner, the penitentiary, in theory anyway, accepted the responsibility of protecting him as well.

There is a caste system among the prison census. Lewis Bowman, in a division Feliciano had never seen, ranked high. He was young, big, dangerously hostile, and tough. The crimes he had committed were "clean" offenses.

But among the lowest members of the prison population was another slice of humanity—the deviates, perverts, rapists, child molesters—those guilty of what used to be called inhuman crimes. They are despised by guards and inmates alike, and are often harassed, humiliated, sometimes even murdered. It is best to keep them segregated.

So it turned out that Feliciano was assigned to solitary confinement.

For his own good.

A SINGLE SMALL cement cell. Iron-doored, and lit by a grilled overhead electric light. A trap in the door, through which is passed water, coffee, and three trays of food daily.

Cot, blanket, chair, toilet—no wooden seat or lid—nothing

else. The light burns twenty-four hours a day. In here there is no day, no night. No passage of seasons.

Time suspended.

Men are supposed to suffer in solitary, but it does not bother Feliciano that much. He does not flourish, but at least he doesn't get any crazier than he already is.

That there is absolutely nothing to do does not trouble him.

He had often, up in that mountain *jacal*, sat for weeks doing literally nothing, staring straight ahead. His mind simply turned off.

There was no trick to it at all.

He could do it for the rest of his life if he had to.

His only break from the cell—a once-weekly shower, under supervision—annoys him more than anything else, because he hates the business of getting his scrawny body wet with water.

He sits on the fold-down cot. Back crouched against the wall.

Knees drawn up under his chin. Arms and hands flopped loosely at his side. The hands resting on the blanket, palms up. In the attitude of a decrepit old ape.

Comes down off the cot slowly at the thrice-daily sound of the steam serving-table being trundled down the corridor outside.

The meal done, he climbs back up on the cot.

Some of the guards stare in at him through the peephole from time to time, marveling. Days, weeks, months have passed. And all he does is sit there.

Never speaks. Stares straight ahead. As though lost in a reverie. Dreaming:

I was right!
It was wrong.
So I did it.
It was the right thing to do.
It was their fault.
What else could I do?
They'll be sorry.

I show them!
Now they know.
I show them!
Now they are sorry.
Yes.
I am happy.
Because I was right.
I am always right.
I show them.
Yes.
Someday.
I will . . .

AFTER SIX MONTHS, one of the prison psychologists tried to interview Feliciano.

Not out of any hope of rehabilitation. He merely had a clinical interest in what made the old demon tick.

Like others before him, he failed to break through.

Except at the very last. Then he got a reaction from old Mora. He had not the slightest idea of what the reaction meant, or what had triggered it, but he noted it down in Feliciano's case-record anyway.

The old man had been sitting before him in the interview room for over half an hour, exhibiting his customary un-responsiveness. The face and eyes blank, fixed ahead. So that his tormentor could not even guess if he understood the questions. The expression impassive, dead. That simian mask.

"Can you tell me anything about your childhood?

"Do you remember where you were born? When, What year?

"Do you have any bad feelings?

"Do you remember anything at all about that weekend?

"That weekend, in the mountains?"

At this the slack lips twitch, but that is all.
He remembers.
Oh, yes. He remembers all right!
He is not estúpido.
What do they think he is? Some kind of estúpido fool?
He remembers all right.
Yes.

The questions continue. Without success. The whole interview a waste of time.

Until the last. The psychologist closes his notepad, looks up.

The interviewer-interviewee relationship has never really been established. Now he gives up trying—and in doing so reverts, unprofessionally, to a sympathetic person. It can happen to anyone.

He says, staring at Feliciano, "Mr. Mora, you must have had a very sad life. Never to have known happiness . . ."

At this, Feliciano's gaze fixes upon him. The black, beady eyes. So oddly intense. A dreamy, burning stare.

And then he grins!

Deep-furrowed smile-wrinkles crease his cheeks. A broad and open smile.

Then, as quickly, he shuts it off. As if to hide a self-betrayal.

The psychologist's curiosity is aroused. But to no avail.

Try as he may, he can get no further response from the old man. He can't imagine what made Mora grin like that.

For all he can tell, it could have been a simple gastric pain. The way a sleeping infant will sometimes grimace.

Never to have *known happiness . . .*
How wrong he is!
Oh, life, she hasn't been easy. There have been many bad

times. It isn't easy to find some pleasures in life, when nothing goes right.

You do the best you can.

Life is hard. It isn't easy to get through her when they look down on you, spit on you, when they hate you. When they do the evil. When they have so much and you have less than nothing.

To be truly poor is never easy. But someone, he has to do it.

To be hated, no, that is not so easy. When even a dog has lived a better and more easy life than you.

When it has gone on like that for a whole lifetime, well, that is not easy.

That is hard. To know you are right—have tried to be right for all your life, oh, yes!

A whole life of it!

It is not easy. When you know that God He has given you nada . . . nothing.

He gives so much to others, but nada to you.

Why is that? Por qué?

God He sends good luck to those who never know how lucky they are. And God He gives you nada.

Yes. It would be too much . . . except for this:

To know . . . to really know . . . claro! . . . that you have had happiness. One single day of it. That is not too much to ask, not out of one lifetime.

If you have that, yes, that is a great deal. You have everything. Nothing can ever hurt you again, not if you have that.

They don't have to know it. But you yourself you know this.

Then the lowest man he is like a king. All men, they must make way for him.

That weekend, yes, but, oh, not forgotten . . . nunca! nunca! . . . not in a thousand year. That you never forget.

That morning with the snow so beautiful, and the sun.

When all you did was right. When you yourself could do no wrong.

So beautiful.

One day. One day so beautiful. If a man he knows he has just got that damn' one day, that is enough, that is all he really need. He can get by.

He can be happy. Creo! *That's all he need. Then he can say, "Oh, sure! That was one fine day, all right, that was the best day I ever know in my whole life!"*

THE PARANOIA OF the Spanish-American, like that of any insulated minority group, is about as variable as the effect of gravity, and as easily cured.

And, like peristalsis, it is happiest when it has something to act upon.

Vicente Apodaca, the pistol-packing young leader of the Pecos chapter of the *la Raza* berets, in time heard that Feliciano—the old man was a distant uncle—had gone to the pen.

Vince, now wearing a partial bridge to cover the damage of that weekend, mentioned this one evening at an Albuquerque meeting of the organization.

The group's Chicano lawyer, Paco Rodriguez, picked up on it. Paco was intelligent and feisty, and he knew how to rattle the bones of discontent. He investigated the case.

And so uncovered the entire ignominious scandal.

Learned first and foremost that no formal charges really existed against the old man. That he was in isolation at the pen instead of the state hospital, where the courts were supposed to have remanded him.

What a travesty. Here was an uneducated, simple old fellow who had not even been charged let alone tried—*God damn!*— he hadn't even been convicted, let alone sentenced—in solitary confinement at the state penitentiary. For the better part of a year! A man with a name dating back to the conquistadors who had come up from old Mexico.

Paco Rodriguez walked into the Santa Fe district attorney's

office and started talking. He went next to the state attorney general's office, and did the same thing.

They knew him in both places. He had visited them before. And they knew that he meant it when he informed them that he would, in forty-eight hours, have over two hundred bereted Chicanos parading around the governor's offices, waving placards. Just as they knew that he was, legally, one hundred per cent in the right.

Judge Harvey Burrell was on extended vacation with his wife, in Australia and New Zealand. He had had a second coronary, a mild one, and on medical advice had stepped down from the bench. And, anyway, the disposition on Mora's case could not really have been blamed on him. The case had simply been lost in the shuffle—pigeonholed, mislaid—forgotten in the endless bureaucratic processings that take place daily on the judicial-penal-mental hospital playing-field.

All that could have kept Feliciano in the state pen—and even this is doubtful—was a totally negative psychiatric evaluation, backed by a judicial decision to commit for life. Very difficult. Doubly difficult when Paco Rodriguez had enough demonstrators on hand to mess up the lawns of the state hospital, the penitentiary, and any judge or doctor who wanted to stick his gringo nose into the affair.

The people will be heard.

A fundamental tenet of the American way of life.

THE CELL DOOR swings open. The old fellow is beckoned out.

He comes down off his hard cot and shuffles toward the waiting guard outside. Perhaps wondering if the time has again come for that awful shower-bath.

But no.

Through endless, high-ceilinged corridors. Locked gates, manned by guards who slide grilled doors open to let him and the corrections officers accompanying him pass through.

In an office he is told to make his mark—a crude and quavery X—on many printed sheets.

He is taken to another office, where people talk to him. The *estúpido* psychologist who said that he, Feliciano, was not happy. Other *estúpido* gringos are there, too. The psychologist tells him that he will be released.

"Do you understand, Feliciano? You will leave here. You will be free. *Comprende?*"

Feliciano scarcely listens. Appears bored. Stands there, waiting.

"In three or four days," the psychologist adds. "We have to wait for some more papers. *Más papeles* from Santa Fe. Then you can leave."

No sign from the old man.

"Until you can go, we are putting you in a better place. More comfortable. You will like it better," the psychologist concludes.

With that Feliciano is led away.

To a dormitory, with locked doors at each end, but otherwise not so different from a military barracks. Neatly made-up cots, wall lockers, night tables, ashtrays, transistor radios, a communal TV. Comfortable chairs, magazines, books. Not bad. Two inmates are washing windows spaced along the long room. The guard with Feliciano says to them, "Keep an eye on him. He doesn't know his way around. No work details. He's due for release in a couple of days."

The guard leaves, and the two convicts assign a bed to the old man. They give him a cigarette, and he sits on the edge of his cot, smoking and thinking. It slowly dawns on him.

He is to be freed.

Savors this concept.

And finds in it a growing pleasure.

He was right, after all.

Right is right!

All of them were wrong, and he was right. That is why he is to be freed. The wheel has come full circle.

He sits there, smoking. The small, black eyes calm, the wrinkled face impassive . . . stony. But in his heart, a serene realization. He was right, after all, about that old saying: there just ain't no way you ever gonna keep a good hombre in jail ver' long!

EVENING MEAL. THE penitentiary cafeteria, a huge brightly lit room, is filled with hundreds of men. At one side, the corrections officers have their own tables—in this facility, guards and prisoners eat the same food.

The two inmates from the dormitory escort Feliciano through the chow line. He doesn't know what to do . . . is used to having his meals served to him. One of his companions has to hand him a plastic tray, utensils; the other has to actually take him by the elbow and guide him to the line of waiting men. These two are amused by the old man's simplicity, and they exchange a wink and a grin as the line slowly moves forward. Feliciano shuffles along with the others, getting the idea: He holds his tray out to the food servers behind the counter, and it grows heavier as portions are ladled into each compartmentalized section.

On this evening there is meat loaf; carrots and peas; potatoes; bread, butter; gravy; a plastic mug of steaming coffee; and, lastly, dessert—lime jello, laced with fruit salad—spooned onto the tray by big Lewis Bowman. The two of them pause a moment, separated by the food counter, each looking different in the gray cotton prison clothes than they did when they last saw each other, but even so there is the shock of recognition. No word is exchanged. Feliciano's eyes blink once, that is all. But he knows that Lewis knows. He turns away, bearing his tray, and follows the other men to a vacant table. Sits, and begins eating, holding his fork in a clenched fist. The other men at the table talk and gossip as they eat, indulging in a low murmur of laughter and profanity, but Feliciano is silent. For the most part the others ignore him, eating quickly despite their easy conversation: Only so much time is allowed for the consumption of a meal. Finished, they leave, taking trays and eating equipment with them, and Feliciano follows.

BY MIDMORNING THE following day, Lewis has learned enough of the story: that the old man is to be released before the end of the week, that no charges exist against Mora, that the Spanish ethnic thing is involved, and maybe some politics, too, that orders have come down from the assistant warden's office to give the old geezer VIP treatment until they can get rid of him. Learns that Feliciano is being temporarily quartered in one wing of D-building, where his own dormitory is located. True, Mora is in another dorm, on the second floor.

Lewis acquires this information without much trouble. A minute's conversation with one or two clerical staff inmates who work in the offices. Small, casual exchanges for which Lewis is ready to give something in return: The job in the kitchen is good for other things besides the dozens of fresh eggs he pilfers daily for his own weird diet, and there is always a demand for a few cans of tuna fish or evaporated milk. From time to time Lewis has even laid a few choice items on some of the corrections officers. With the latter he has finally reached a kind of truce. He is so big and so dangerous that he doesn't even have to carry a sharpened spoon or razor blade, as so many of the other prisoners do . . . his strength and his bare hands are protection enough. The turnkeys and guards know this, and they know better than to mess with him. The unwritten contract he has with them is simple: "Don't hassle me, and don't lean on me, and I'll behave, do the work, put up with all this shit and do my time, only, baby, never put a hand on me." In the penal system such a contract is good for inmate and guard both. Lewis's behavior since his return had been superior. Among his fellow prisoners he belonged to the power elite—his size, strength, and the kitchen assignment

guaranteed this. With the security officers, he got respect and
was left alone. Without wanting to, some of the guards even
liked Lewis. After all, he was a model prisoner who did what
he was told. He could have been otherwise, and they knew it.

At seven that morning, and again at noon, Feliciano and
Lewis saw each other across the serving counter in the cafeteria, and again, on each occasion, no words were exchanged.
At two-thirty that afternoon, Lewis carried out one of his
daily assignments, that of trundling a small nickel-plated cart
bearing hot coffee and sweet rolls to the administration building . . . midafternoon coffee break, and a break for him, too,
from the kitchen routine. To get himself and the cart from the
cafeteria to the various offices, Lewis passed through six
locked gates. Despite improvements, that is one aspect of
prison life that has never changed: A penitentiary is like a
huge locked box. Inside it, are other locked boxes, and inside
there are smaller locked boxes, down to the smallest locked
box of all, the individual cell. Yet even with these precautions,
there is a degree of freedom. Trusted inmates, on various work
assignments, come and go. That is how Lewis got into D-
building, on his way back to the cafeteria. Leaving the cart
at the entrance to the dormitory building, he told the guard
on duty at the door that he wanted to get a candy bar from his
locker. The guard, of course, knew Lewis. A dozen other
inmates were in the building, carrying out various cleaning
assignments. The guard pressed a button, and the grilled door
slid open on electrically driven roller bearings. "Make it
snappy, Lew," the guard said.

Lewis walked past him and said, "I'll only be a minute."

FELICIANO WAS USING one of the toilets in the latrine at the
far end of his dorm on the second floor. He had been having
a touch of diarrhea. The bowl he sat on, like all the others
in this facility, was lidless. The roll of paper on the wall of

the booth was mounted on a plastic bracket . . . all metal was precious because it could be made into weapons. The lights in the latrine were turned off, in accordance with the latest federal directives on conserving energy. The place was dark and shadowy and cool. The only light came from an open door at the far end of the latrine, and from a small window over by the shower stalls. It was quiet. There were no doors on the toilet booths. Suddenly, Feliciano had an impression—an intuition, really—of something emerging from the shadowed darkness, silently and quickly, to loom over him. He looked up.

Later, the medical report indicated that death was caused by a broken neck and a crushed skull. Neck muscles and tendons had been literally torn loose, the windpipe and larynx crushed, in some kind of fearsome grip, which had then lifted the old man clear of the seat and the floor and slammed him against the back wall of the cubicle. The entire rear of the skull was gone. There was a hole, or indentation, some seven or eight inches across, in the rear wall to show where the head had punched through . . . fragmented porcelain tiles, and behind these plasterboard, all of it crushed inward. The body was not discovered until that evening, when the men of D-building returned from dinner. The menu that night had been a good one: enchiladas, *refritos*, or refried beans, tacos, and salad. Most of the prison census was Spanish-American, and they had petitioned the warden to permit regional fare once or twice a week, and he had acceded. Lewis Bowman had never much cared for that kind of chow. Later that evening, after he and the rest of the kitchen crew had cleaned up, he cooked up a solitary meal—one of his favorite snacks: fourteen eggs scrambled in butter, washed down with a half gallon of low-fat milk.